About the Author

C. Cole currently resides in Louisiana with her partner of over twenty years. She has five children.

Mortal

Christy Cole

Mortal

Olympia Publishers
London

www.olympiapublishers.com
OLYMPIA PAPERBACK EDITION

A CIP catalogue record for this title is
available from the British Library.

ISBN: 978-1-80074-965-8

This is a work of fiction.
Names, characters, places and incidents originate from the writer's imagination.
Any resemblance to actual persons, living or dead, is purely coincidental.

First Published in 2023

Olympia Publishers
Tallis House
2 Tallis Street
London
EC4Y 0AB

Printed in Great Britain

Dedication

I would like to dedicate this book to my mother, Betty Katherine, who always believed in me. I love you. Always.

Chapter 1

January 11, 9:48 p.m.

The woman eyed the church warily from the darkness. She wondered if it could be a trap.

The face of the cathedral undulated with the shadows that bumped and swayed in the dim light. Tiny snowflakes had just started a lazy descent from the night sky. The building looked quiet as the woman surveyed it, but her brow furrowed deeply.

A chorus of men, from inside the church, sang chants in Latin and the sound drifted, muted, yet comforting in the still air. For a moment she closed her eyes and listened to the song as it rolled down the empty street. She knew the blood on her coat could no longer be seen in the darkness, and the blood under her coat was oozing into a sticky mass inside her silk dress shirt. Trying to keep the fat drops of blood inside her clothes, she stood one handed against the cold brick wall, holding her wound with the other, struggling to think clearly

She had to leave the cover of the alley and cross to the church one block up, but she wasn't sure if she had the strength. Even if it was a trap, she had no choice. She would not fail. She must not fail

The thought of the boy propelled the woman away from the wall; using one bloody hand to push off, she almost buckled and fell.

Pain and dizziness made her unsteady but determined. She forced herself to stay upright. With one hand inside her coat, holding her wound together, she staggered into the street; seemingly pulled by the chants echoing softly down the empty avenue. She tried to walk upright as much as possible so as not to draw attention if anyone was watching. She scanned the church for any movement.

Instead of walking up to the front of the building, she prayed that the side door would still be there. So many years had gone by and the building was changed; but the little gate to the side path was still there. Seeing it gave her hope, but the sadness she felt threatened to make her cry.

"No," she said aloud, blinking back the tears.

The gate was a delicate wrought iron and as she tugged on it a familiar fever hit her. She had expected it. The burning always started in her thighs and crept upward.

She grasped the gate and pushed, as her knees buckled with the effort, and the unnatural heat flushed upward through her. The wound inside her shirt seemed to electrify her skin and she gasped in pain. As she fell onto her knees, she clutched the gate harder, trying to stay upright. Her shoulders and neck were suddenly on fire, blistering. The skin on her face tingled and burned as her scalp drew up into a million jagged pinpricks. Her eyes rolled back and closed; not even the cold winter air could cool her. Trying to pull herself up, she knew she didn't have the strength. She knew she couldn't hold on much longer.

As suddenly as it came, the fever broke. The iron gate swung inward, and the woman toppled, face forward, onto the flagstone path.

Shivering in the cold night air, she lay there listening to the voices of the choir, and she contemplated bleeding to death where she had fallen. Her wound no longer hurt, but she could feel it, deep inside, taking her life. It was just a matter of time now.

It would be so easy, she thought, to just let go. Her thoughts were starting to swirl, and the boy's face suddenly broke the fog.

She instinctively pushed herself up with both hands and crawled a few feet into the garden. Knowing that she was on holy ground pushed her further, giving her some strength, until finally she was able to stand again.

To the left of the small garden was the priest's house. She looked that way, but she decided to go right, towards the cathedral. There was always someone in the house and she couldn't set off any alarms. The church was her best bet, so she stumbled farther into the courtyard. She followed the path as it split between the two structures, the right path going directly to the little door that led into the back of the church.

She almost laughed when she saw it was still there, unlit and unnoticed by almost everyone. She knew the priest would still be there, too. The small smile on her lips turned bitter. The only reason he was ever there was because of her.

At the door, she looked around the garden to make sure she was alone.

Memories again pushed at her focus but fresh blood dripping from under her coat pushed reality back to mind.

Was it a trap? She was alone as far as she could see.

The door was just as she remembered it. Low and simple, it was made of old planks and though narrow, it was extremely heavy. She held the ancient handle and shoved, sending a shock through her body as the wound tore from the inside. She saved herself from falling by grabbing the wall; as a fresh gush of blood poured from her. She didn't feel the pain but she did feel the impact of her wound tearing.

From the pitch black, narrow stone hallway beyond the door, the choir's hymns echoed through her now; and the sound made her think of both a cry of salvation and a death toll. She was paralyzed by the fear of discovery. As one fear gave way to another, she huddled against the wall. Tears of pain, sadness, and frustration made her remember her own weaknesses; remembering made her angry.

She knew she could no longer defend herself and she panicked, thinking it may already be too late. What if he had already found the priest? What if it was a trap? Her weakness made her doubt. What the hell was she walking into?

Trying to scan through the darkness of the hallway, she knew she had no choice. She closed her eyes, trying to focus on the singing that echoed through her. It was calming. Taking a deliberate deep breath, she wondered how many more breaths she would get. Not able to pull the heavy door shut, she didn't even try. Her only thought as she pushed away from the door frame was the hope that she still had enough time.

The woman knew that the choir would be on the third level of the structure, in the balcony above the nave. Because of the late hour, she also knew the second floor should be mostly empty. Here on the first floor, it was completely deserted and still. Past dark offices and classrooms, she squinted through the darkness, trying not to imagine the shadows moving crazily. She lurched closer to the singing by hugging the walls of the narrow hall. At the end of the corridor, stair steps suddenly ascended into a large space above her. Muted light spilled down the stairs.

As she had years before, she thought of the description of being born. The light at the end of the tunnel; she shook her head as she realized it was also the description of death. The thought sobered her, and she stumbled up the stairs, thinking of the boy.

She stopped for a moment at the first step, resting and listening. Looking up, she could see most of the pews to the right and the altar, barely visible to the upper left. She heard only the choir. Nothing moved. She had to keep going. Every second counted now.

She started climbing again, as best she could. One hand in her coat, one hand on the wall, she furtively looked around the altar. She let her eyes quickly sweep the pews. The entire sanctuary was lit by candlelight and the soft glow sent ill-defined shadows gently swaying against glittering, gilded sacraments. In the far row of pews, a very tattered, dirty man lay prone, completely relaxed and unmoving. Above the singing, she could hear the bum's snoring; even, and natural. Pulling to the last step, she watched him a moment more but saw no one else moving about. She stepped into the openness of the room, staggering, but determined, trying to hold her blood into her clothes but dripping on the carpet anyway.

Walking down the length of the front pew, she turned right, between the two lines of pews, in the direction of the magnificent front door of the cathedral. Immediately behind the rows of pews and to the right was the confessional; beyond that, a marble reception area with huge racks of slow burning candles. Near the confessional was a large stone urn on a huge pedestal, filled with fresh water that was blessed daily.

Keeping a weary eye on the sleeping homeless man, she looked longingly at the urn. Her throat burned with thirst. Grasping a pew here and there to help her stand, she knew that her thirst was unimportant. She was almost out of strength by the time she came near the confessional. The parishioner's door of the carved wood structure was ajar and the small booth was empty. The clergy's side door was closed and the light was off, indicating that it, too, was empty.

Slowly, clumsily, she gripped the open door to the sinner's side and pulled it shut behind with a quiet click as she sagged onto the little upholstered bench.

Closing her eyes, she started to drift towards unconsciousness, wondering what the flames of Hell felt like. The light rustling noise seemed to come from a distance. Drifting further away, she tried to swallow but her parched throat was not working right. Too late, she thought, realizing there was someone in the other chamber. Before the fear could register, a soft warm voice spoke through the tight lattice work connecting the sinner to salvation.

"I'm sorry, child, I'm no longer taking confession tonight, it is getting very late."

The voice was comforting, bringing her back softly to reality. Her fear of a trap receded somewhat.

"Where is Father Joseph?" Her voice cracked.

"I'm sorry again. Father Joseph will not be taking confession until sunrise. I'm afraid he's sleeping."

Swallowing hard, she tried to control her voice, but she could not hide the bitterness.

"Go and wake him, priest. Tell him, and only him, that Sara Katherine is here, and go now."

She heard more rustling from behind the screen, and the voice now seemed tired and sharp.

"Father Joseph needs his rest, child, as I do. Now, whatever business you...."

"Go get Joseph, priest, his life is in danger. And don't ever call me child again!"

She was so tired. Weakness flooded through her, the momentary flash of anger costing her dearly.

"Go get him, priest. I may have put you all in danger...Tell only Joseph, and go now, I don't know if I can hold on much longer."

The choir voices faded as darkness overcame her.

"Lady?"

Only silence answered.

The priest, Father Matthew, sat listening to the silence a moment. "Lady?" he called again.

Nothing... He stood, feeling a dread he could not identify.

Pushing his large frame from the small chamber, Father Matthew looked at the other door with alarm. There was blood smeared on it. Trembling, he reached for the handle.

Close to panic, the young priest wrenched open the door and saw a woman slumped on the bench. Her head was hanging down and all he could see was long auburn hair streaked with silver, pulled into a wild tangle at the nape of her neck.

Her neck and shoulders were slim and the long black coat the woman wore was pulled down past both shoulders and gaped open to reveal the white shirt underneath. Well, not exactly white, Matthew thought, she was

13

covered in blood, as was the confessional. Putting his fingers to her thin throat, Matthew felt a faint pulse, but the contact with her skin shook him. He moved quickly out of the booth and closed the door. His own pulse was now out of control.

Glancing around quickly, he determined that Samuel, the homeless man, was the only other person on the floor and he appeared to be still sound asleep. Still wearing his robes, the young priest nearly ran to the stairs, caution slowing him slightly. Going down the stairs in a run, he could still see blood smeared on the wall of the stairwell. Once on the deserted first floor, he ran full out as panic engulfed him.

Coming to the door at the end of the hall, Matthew saw it was standing open, moonlight lighting the frame. There was a large puddle of blood here and he paused for a moment, realizing the woman had come this way.

There was blood all over the door, the walls, everywhere. So much blood it was almost unbelievable! What the crap was happening here? He left the doorway at a slower pace.

The woman had said the old priest was in danger and Matthew knew he was in the middle of something he totally did not understand. Until that moment he had never truly been afraid, or paranoid before.

When Matthew crossed the garden, he saw that Joseph's window was dark. The housekeeper, Gail, was also apparently sleeping, as the house was totally silent. Quietly, he opened the front door, listening; for what, he wasn't sure. Going into the dark house, Matthew relied on memory to pass through the living area to the narrow staircase. He tried to walk lightly, but he was a very big man and the stairs groaned under his weight. At the top of the stairs, he turned left into the hall leading to Father Joseph's room. He tried the knob and, finding it locked, he knocked lightly on the old man's door. Impatient, knocking a little more forcefully, he called through the door.

"Father Joseph?"

Matthew heard a slight movement, then Joseph's sleepy voice ,

"Who's there?"

"Father, it's me, Matthew. I need to see you!"

"Matthew?"

The voice suddenly seemed concerned and the young priest heard more rustling just as the door swung inward.

The younger priest dwarfed his elder, but what Joseph lacked in mass

14

he made up for in presence. The old man's eyes swept Matthew; he looked disheveled, but alert.

"There's a woman in the church. She's bleeding," Matthew blurted.

Joseph's brows drew up as if puzzled.

"My goodness, did you call for an ambulance?"

"No, sir, she said to tell only you. She said your life is in danger!"

As he said it, a strange look crossed the old priest's face. Now babbling quickly, Matthew continued. ,

"She said we may all be in danger. She's bleeding bad, hurt bad! You must come quickly!"

Joseph seemed frozen.

For a moment, the old man did nothing. He stared at Matthew like he was dazed. When he finally spoke, his voice was shaking,

"Did she say her name?"

It came out as a fearful whisper.

"Sara. Sara Katherine." Matthew said slowly.

The name made Joseph jerk as if he had been slapped. Suddenly flushed and animated, he grabbed the robes covering Matthew's chest, pulling him closer to his face.

"Where is she?'

He hissed the words as Matthew looked down into his elder's face in amazement and was caught off guard at the snarl.

"Does anyone else know she's here?" Joseph demanded.

"No," Matthew said, recovering only slightly. "No... no... only us. She's in the confessional."

Joseph seemed to toss the bigger man aside. He ran down the hall, careening wildly into the stairwell. Matthew's astonishment at watching the old man rush past him was only momentary before he, too, ran for the stairs. He caught up with the old priest at the front door, where Joseph had stopped to scan the yard through the window in the door.

Matthew realized Joseph was looking for something, but what?

The unfamiliar fear was giving Matthew a headache. As he approached, Joseph, seemingly satisfied, opened the door, and passed into the cold night without a backward look. Matthew was only a step behind.

The moon was out in full now and Matthew knew it was a little past ten p.m. The cold garden was quiet, with the new snow barely sticking to the evergreen shrubs. The choir had fallen silent , having finished their practice for the evening.

The two men could hear each other breathing as they shuffled across to the church. By the moon's light, they were both aware of the streaks of blood on the path and smears on the door. There was a blood pool just inside.

Pausing only a moment, Matthew felt a suffocating dread and then quickly, quietly, made his way into the dark hall. They could hear voices, speaking casually, drifting down from the main floor.

Stopping in the dark shadow close to the stairs, Matthew whispered to Joseph.

"Stay here! I'll get rid of them."

They both knew that the choir members would be surprised to see Joseph that late, especially in his nightshirt. Joseph could hear two or three voices and both men prayed that the woman would not be discovered in the confessional.

Matthew ascended hastily while the old priest stood in an office doorway, trembling. After all these years, he thought. Had it been so long? God, he was getting old.

The choir members greeted Matthew warmly. Joseph heard the young priest say something about a terrible headache and a bitter sadness made him flush. He could see the blood on the floor as well as a bloody handprint streaking up the wall of the stair well.

Joseph begged angels to get the choir away from here quickly. He listened as Matthew casually lied to them, all the while moving them towards the front door, directly past the confessional. Joseph prayed harder.

"Yes," Matthew said to some unseen listener, "as soon as I snuff these candles I am going to lay down; I just feel awful."

Footsteps sounded further away, closer to the door.

From that direction, a distant voice said goodbye.

"Night, Matt, I hope you feel better, so when I beat you tomorrow at some hoops, you got no excuse!"

Laughter that sounded far away, some shuffling, and finally Joseph heard the bumping creak of the massive wooden doors and the *thunk* of the bolt being struck.

Joseph jumped to the stairs, taking them two at a time. He skidded into a dangerous turn right into the aisle between the pews. Matthew was running straight towards him and they almost reached the confessional at the same time. Matthew got there first and wrenched the door so hard he felt the hinges give. Matthew froze.

Joseph crashed his slighter body into the dazed man, pushing him back. He pawed at the door frame and got past Matthew. Matthew stared over Joseph's shoulder, understanding nothing.

The woman was awake.

She had pulled her legs onto the small bench. Her long skirt was split to mid-thigh, revealing long, well-tanned legs, streaked with blood. Holding a hand inside her shirt, she had managed to discard the coat, although one hand was still caught in the sleeve. Facing upwards, she was looking straight at Joseph.

She was the most beautiful woman Matthew had ever seen. She was also gushing fresh blood from somewhere under her shirt. Seeing Joseph's face, she smiled.

From somewhere low in his throat, Joseph let out a low guttural moan. Matthew didn't think to catch the old man as his knees buckled and he began to sob loudly. Surprised, Matthew looked down at his teacher and back to the woman. Her breathing was hard and gasping but the smile was still there. As the old priest moaned, her face hardened, and she raised her eyes to Matthew.

The candlelight softened her face and Matthew felt like a candle that was too close to a flame, melting into hazel eyes. She took his breath away.

In a voice that sounded more like a croak, she grimaced and spoke as clearly as she could. ,

"No crying, Joseph. You always knew it could be this way."

The older priest sobbed louder.

"Stop it, Joseph. I'm dying. You have to get me out of God's house."

Her voice was sharp now, demanding. She closed her eyes.

"He'll be coming for us soon." She whispered.

She seemed to sink into herself.

Getting to his feet, leaning in close, Joseph asked her softly.

"How much time do we have?"

Without opening her eyes, she whispered "Not long…"

Her body went slack and Joseph lunged forward to catch her as she started sliding off the bench. Holding her against his chest, he could feel her intense body heat, so feverish it seemed to burn his skin. He felt his nightshirt getting wet with sticky blood. Her head lolled back as she moaned

17

his name but did not wake up. Joseph looked deeply into her face like a thirsty man sees water. It was as if not a day had passed since the last time he saw her. He knew his heart was breaking.

All these years, Joseph thought, and now here was the face that had haunted him most of his life. That face he thought of everyday was only a breath away from his own. At that moment, he had no regrets, no doubts.

Clutching the unconscious woman to him, Joseph struggled to stand with her. He turned and rushed past a still dumbfounded Matthew. Not knowing what else to do, the young priest hurried to follow.

Back down the stairs, down the hallway, they came to the wood door at a full run. The old priest never seemed to look up from the woman's face. Stopping at the door, he told Matthew to go ahead of them and make sure no one was out there. The young man, not understanding why he was trembling, braced himself for any attack as soon as he left the doorway, but the garden was completely still.

The soft snow had stopped falling for now and Matthew turned a full 360 degrees, listening, trying to look into the shadows. He could hear Joseph talking to the unconscious woman.

"You remembered the garden, didn't you, Sara? I kept it the same all this time. I knew you would come back. I knew you would…"

Matthew stepped back to the door and signaled for Joseph to come outside. Fresh blood dripped down the older man and onto the stone walk, looking like big, black blobs of oil. Dim moonlight made the night feel shrouded, heavy with secrets.

Following Matthew across the garden, staggering with his burden, Joseph felt himself getting choked up by the on-rush of memories, somehow crisper in the cold air.

The young priest held the rectory door open for his teacher and quickly closed it behind them. Matthew ran to the window overlooking the garden and watched for any sign of movement. All was still, and yet he had the overwhelming urge to lock and barricade the door.

He had an unsettled feeling of being watched, as if the night were staring back at him. What in God's name was happening? Matthew thought to himself.

Suddenly, feeling ridiculous, he turned and once again climbed the stairs to Father Joseph's bedroom. Hearing shuffling from that direction, he also thought he heard crying. Coming to the door, he realized it was crying and it was coming from the old priest.

Matthew had never seen Joseph cry in all these years, and he had known him most of his life. Stopping at the half-closed door, Matthew wondered what this woman's presence meant. The uncertainty added to his fear, making him swallow hard. Fifteen minutes ago, Matthew would have said that he had never known true fear. Sorrow, yes. Rage. Yes. Regret, definitely. But never fear.

The woman's presence terrified Matthew and he had no idea why.

There were blood droplets all over the floor that Matthew tried to step over as he pushed the bedroom door open. A giant four poster bed stood across from the doorway, now occupied by the woman. Even in the circumstances, it was shocking to Matthew to see a half-naked woman lying in Father Joseph's bed. The old priest, holding her limp hand in his, was kneeling on the right side of the bed, his face buried in the mattress. He seemed to be both praying and sobbing into the sheets, the words an indistinguishable, mournful babble.

Forcing modesty aside, Matthew made himself look at the woman.

She lay as still as an effigy in her unnatural slumber, and her beautiful face looked smooth, almost angelic to the young man. A straight nose and full lips dominated a strong face, and wavy auburn hair haloed her head. Her olive complexion looked unnaturally pale under the dark tangle of curls. Her throat was long and thin, and Matthew again forced himself to look at her chest. Her breasts, though not large, were unlined, with a youthful plumpness; but before he could let himself flush, he focused on the wound below her left breast. The big gaping hole in her chest tore away any thought of modesty, or hope.

The old priest sobbed painfully, mournfully.

To Matthew, it sure looked like a knife wound, but it had to have been one big knife to make a hole like that.

Though her shirt had been stripped away, she was still wearing the long black skirt, and she seemed very tal on the large bed. Fresh blood seeped from the wound, making dark red splotches on the white sheets.

Seeing her bleed jolted Matthew and stepping through the door, he started pulling off his clergy robes. He crossed the room hurriedly, going to the other side of the bed from where Joseph was hunched in misery. As he sat beside her, Matthew bunched up his robe, trying to hold most of the cloth directly to her wound. He could see her breasts rising and falling raggedly and her breathing was very shallow. Joseph, still holding her hand, still had his face buried in the mattress. He was quieter now but his whole body was shaking. They were all shaking.

Reaching across the woman, Matthew pressed the robe tightly to her side. He was trying to stay calm, but his heart was beating like a trip hammer.

"Joseph?" he said softly.

The old man didn't move.

"Father Joseph!" Matthew said it forcefully, and the old priest turned his head out of the mattress, looking at the woman, but he didn't raise his head.

Matthew's head hurt.

Joseph's eyes gazed upwards to her wonderful face and the muscles in his own started twitching. After a long moment, he finally sat up, resting upright on his knees. His eyes were glazed but he never let go of her hand as he stared at her.

Keeping his own eyes on the woman, Matthew spoke slowly to Joseph, aware that the man was in a state of despair. Matthew knew he could not comfort his teacher.

"Joseph, she is going to die. We have to go get help!" Matthew snapped.

The old man just stared at the woman as if he were memorizing her face.

"Joseph?"

Matthew tried hard to keep the fear from his voice.

"Joseph? She said your life is in danger. Who is after her? If we don't do something, she'll die!" Matthew blurted.

The truth was that it probably wouldn't matter whether they got help or not. She only had a few minutes at best, but Matthew was panicking and he needed some answers.

"Who's after her, Joseph? What is happening here?"

The old man's eyes cleared somewhat but they never left her face. He reponded to Matthew in an oddly flat voice.

"She'll die anyway. The wound is too large, pierced her heart."

Tears started again and Joseph finally closed his eyes against the sadness.

Now confused and frustrated to the breaking point, Matthew snapped at him.

"Joseph! You cannot let this woman die! Not here! What in the hell is going on? Who did this to her? Why is she here? Why are you now in danger? Damn it, Joseph, say something!"

His voice was getting shrill. Matthew wasn't afraid of anything that he could see, but this was a whole new ball game. The robe in his hand was getting soaked; he could feel the heat of her blood through it.

"Who did this to her?" Matthew demanded to know.

Suddenly, Joseph's eyes opened, and he stared solidly at the younger priest. . He was studying him intensely; the blood felt so hot in Matthew's hands as they stared at each other.. .

"Matthew…" Joseph rasped, his voice jagged.

"I know you're a man of faith, but you have to understand that what you believe is not as important as how you believe it."

The young man squinted at him, not understanding.

"You are in danger too now, Matthew, and if you have true faith then all that is coming will not be hard for you. All that you know will seem to change, but it really only seems that way."

Joseph returned his eyes to her face. He knew Matthew was looking at him as if he had gone mad, but it didn't matter now. He could no longer comfort him or protect him.

How could he explain that the destiny of all of them had come upon them this night? He had trained the young man well, but he never told him what the purpose was, never told him the training was all for this night; for tomorrow and the next day, if they survived tonight.

"Who is after her, Joseph?"

"The same one who's after us all, son." Joseph retorted.

The woman suddenly turned her head, coughing slightly. Her arms flailed weakly for a moment and then one of her small hands covered Matthew's huge one, the one holding the robe to her wound.

She clutched at his fingers , the skin-to-skin contact searing the young man. She must be feverish, he thought. Rotating her head, she started moaning low, painfully. Her breathing, already ragged, quickened as her eyelids fluttered.

Joseph put a hand to her face, cupping it longingly, lovingly.

"Sara…" he whispered. "I'm here, Sara. I've always been here, wake up, Sara…"

Her eyes opened a moment then closed again. Her face fell in a grimace as she seemed to try to form words but it only came out as a moan. Both priests leaned in closer to her.

"Sara...wake up. Tell us why you've come back...?"

She moaned again, breathing hard. Her struggle caused Matthew's hand to thrust up and down with her attempts to breathe.

"Sara..." Joseph tried again. "Wake up, Sara."

Her eyes snapped open. She blinked wildly, rapidly. Gasping, she looked towards Matthew, her body involuntarily jerking on the bed. Matthew struggled to keep the robe pressed to her. When her eyes found Joseph beside her; she stopped flailing, relaxed into the pillows, and she smiled. She knew now she had not failed.

The way her smile lit up her face made her seem ethereal to Matthew; he drew in his breath sharply, surprised at his own reaction.

Joseph, too, was smiling; no, grinning from ear to ear was more like it. Matthew was sure he was caught in a bizarre dream as he watched Joseph start to cry again with a huge smile on his lips. Looking directly into her face, drawing closer to her, Joseph said,

"Hello, Sara. I've missed you so much. I thank God you came here!"

At his words, she started crying too. Her smile broke and an infinite sadness crossed her face. Matthew could feel the agony of it. These were not tears of pain but of sorrow. Matthew knew sorrow well and he had to look away because he felt he would cry too. Watching her beautiful face twist into sadness filled him with a hopelessness he didn't know how to bear.

He knew she was mortally wounded, but he knew not by whom, or how, nor even why. After a long moment of muted sobbing, she seemed to calm herself as Joseph brushed her tears away with his fingers, pulling on the sheet, trying to wash away her tears completely.

"I'm dying, Joseph, I have to tell you..."

Her voice faded in a harsh whisper and her eyes rolled, coming to rest on Matthew. She looked at him a moment and her eyes cleared as she snapped at the young priest

"Who the hell are you?"

She had a distant fleeting memory of the confessional, but she was fading fast and knew it. She was confused and angry. She was afraid, too, but only of failing. Was this huge young man trustworthy?

Before Matthew could recover and respond, Joseph leaned in again, speaking quickly.

"It's ok, Sara, he's here to help."

Help what? Matthew wondered. He looked at Joseph.

"He's the warrior I've prepared to take up this sword. Sara, I've prepared him well." Joseph purred to her.

What in the crap was the old man talking about?

"Prepared me for what?" Matthew blurted.

Joseph ignored him.

Sara nodded weakly even as her voice became sharp.

"Josh! You have to run! You have to go now!" she glanced at Matthew. "You both must go…run!" She insisted.

Neither man moved.

"What has happened, Sara?" Joseph asked quickly.

For a moment she looked at him, blinking hard as she tried to remember. To Matthew, she seemed to begin to glow with an inner light; her voice was strong and even.

"The prophet has come, Joseph. He was born five days ago!"

Joseph froze. Matthew's entire body jerked and twitched suddenly, though he had no idea why.

The woman's blood was scalding Matthew's hand as the hair on his scalp and entire body stood on end. Feeling both confused and foolish, he felt a panic rise in him. Sara's beautiful smile grew even bigger and she giggled; it was a silly giggle. Her eyes glazed and the sound became a laugh, a rolling heartfelt laugh that shook Matthew's hand as he tried to stem her wound.

The sound overtook the room and the young priest thought of sun dappled waves, rolling. The pitch of it crested and the laughter became a sob that broke over all of them. The mournful sound seemed to snap Joseph out of his stunned trance; he leaned closer to her, laying his cheek on hers.

"It's ok, baby. I'm here." He whispered. "I love you, Sara; I have always loved you."

The old priest kissed her ear, her eyelid, her forehead, and she relaxed into him, eyes closed. Matthew was shocked that he could still be shocked. Did Joseph just say…?

Matthew actually pulled his hand away from the robe and examined it to see if he was burned. Only blood. Her blood. Matthew's head was going to explode, he was sure of it.

"Sara…" Joseph said the name deliberately, letting it fill his mouth, his mind, his heart.

She responded surprisingly even.

"I have always loved you too, Joseph, I have loved you every day since the first day I saw you and I'm so sorry…"

She was whispering directly into his ear.

"I'm trying to save you, Joseph. You have to leave now, baby." She sighed, eyes tightly closed.

"Where is he, Sara? Who is his mother? "

Though soft, Joseph's voice seemed urgent. Sara smiled slightly, eyes still closed.

"It is Morgan. Do you remember our beautiful Morgan, Joe?"

She weakly rubbed her cheek against his. Matthew's hand was scalding.

"I left them in Boston, Joseph. You know where. He needs you, she needs you. I'm sure I drew them here but they'll figure it out before too long; you have to run Joseph! Both of you, leave now!"

She opened her eyes again, looking directly at Matthew. She begged him.

"Please, make him leave me! Save him!"

Matthew was stunned into silence. He sat, transfixed. Looking into her eyes, he realized they were not green-brown, but a green-gold, almost catlike. He had stopped breathing, looking at her stupidly, not knowing what to say.

She pressed her face back to Joseph's. Never taking her eyes from Matthew, she asked softly,

"Is he ready, Joseph?"

Matthew's head hurt badly.

Joseph shifted away slightly and pulled up on one elbow. He sat looking at her closely. That face, he thought.

Joseph was rolling and stroking locks of her hair with his fingers and she returned his gaze straight on, forgetting the young priest.

They gazed at each other silently. Their roles in life were completely understandable, yet fate itself had made them a mystery to each other. The devastation hit Joseph like a freight train.. Looking into the face he had loved most of his life, he was pleasantly surprised to see slight crow's feet around her eyes and the beginning of laughter lines around her full, beautiful lips. It was the first time he had seen a sign of the years passing; but that beauty would never age or mature now. His sorrow consumed him. He knew sorrow would turn later, but for a moment he didn't struggle against the pain of his heart breaking and his soul dying. The loneliness of his life overwhelmed him.

Still looking at Joseph, her eyes glazed unnaturally. In a tiny voice she called out softly. ,

"Where did Ana go?" the sound seemed distant,

"Ana! …?"

Closing her eyes, she repeated the name and Joseph bowed his head, knowing the end had come.

Matthew's hand was on fire. Looking down, he honestly expected to see smoke rising up from his flesh, from the robe. His headache was turning into a brain eating monster.

Joseph started to lay his cheek on hers but stopped short, feeling her heat. Suddenly remembering, he looked quickly at Matthew.

"Go Matthew! You must pour water on the blood in the confessional. Oh God, do it now!"

The young man, startled, looked at him blankly. Joseph screamed at him,

"Go now and pour water on her blood!"

The old man was animated, now half standing. He shouted at Matthew,

"Pour water on the blood that's on anything wooden or flammable!"

Matthew let go of the bloody robe and stood beside the bed, his entire body shaking. Joseph hissed at him, trying to get through.

"Go pour water on the confessional, dilute the blood! After you wet the wood and the carpet, pour water on the stone where she bled! Move your ass! Now! Matthew!"

Without understanding, Matthew turned and ran to do as he was told.

Running from the room, he almost crashed into Gail, the longtime housekeeper, who jumped back against the wall to let him pass in a rush.

Her even features were drawn up into an expression of surprise. Matthew passed her without stopping to explain. Seeing her made him even more frantic; he bounded down the remaining stairs and turned sharply left into the kitchen. He figured that, since Gail was awake now and about to discover a dying, bloody woman half-naked on Joseph's bed, there was

25

really no reason to be quiet. Slapping on the light as he entered the kitchen, Matthew was momentarily blinded by the bright lights flooding the room. Hanging from hooks on a large square rack above a cooking island were huge gleaming cook pots. He grabbed the largest one and went to the sink. He heard voices from upstairs, but over the rush of the faucet he couldn't make out what they were saying.

After what seemed like forever, Matthew turned off the water and pulled the large pot with him to the front door, struggled with the weight of it. He could hear Joseph giving the same orders to Gail as he stumbled into the cold garden, not even bothering to shut the door.

The outdoor space was foggy and at first Matthew paid no attention, but as he approached the small wooden door on the back of the church, he realized it was not snow or mist, but smoke coming from the stone path where blood drops had fallen. A large spot in front of the gate that led to the sidewalk was virtually billowing. The smoke, caught between the two buildings, hung in the still, cold air. Matthew was too numb from the cold and confusion to wonder about it, he simply did as he had been told and approached the little door rapidly.

The blood streaks on the planks were smoking too, turning black.

Matthew started splashing water against the old door ; not sure how much he needed, he splashed more and then ran into the stone hallway.

Not pausing for the smoldering streaks on the floors or walls here, he could smell smoke and knew the charring could not be coming from the stone. Matthew ran as quickly as he could to the stairs, the water in the pot swishing wildly. In the stairwell, he mentally noted a perfect small handprint on the wall halfway up. Coming level with the top step, he was aware that Samuel was now awake, sitting quietly on the front pew.

The homeless man watched, startled, as the huge young priest topped the stairs; running straight at him for a moment before turning recklessly into the aisle between the pews. Matthew ran, full out, towards the front door holding a huge silver and copper pot in his hands. Samuel turned his body to watch as Matthew reached the confessional.

At the confessional, Matthew could see that the blood on it was already starting to smoke heavily. He heaved the pot, splashing water into the chamber; as the water hit the sticky, blackening blood, it popped and hissed. He soaked the bench, the walls, and then started cupping it to splash the now smoldering door. He was very aware of the smell of charring. From somewhere behind him, he heard Samuel speak.

"Ummmm…Father Matthew?"

Turning his head slightly, Matthew saw the flames on the floor.

The aisle between the pews and around to the top of the stairs was covered in rugs and carpets. The floor was on fire. So were some of the pews. Not a wall of flames but drops of it; the ends of two pews had small flames licking up the back rest.

Matthew panicked. He didn't have enough water. Jerking around, facing away from the confessional, Matthew lunged for the giant urn of holy water, sinking the big pot into it. It was a tight fit and as he tried to pull it out, he had to wrench it from the urn, breaking the big stone vessel as the pot freed. The rush of water across the floor put out two of the drops and spurts of flames in front of the confessional. Father Joseph had blessed it that morning and Matthew thanked God it was there as he ran back into the aisle, splashing water as he went. The two pews were now flaming up, the fire going upward along a drip pattern down the backs of the pews.

Rushing to them, Matthew mentally noted the six or seven flame spots left. He doused the pews and the old wood along the back of one of them cracked in half with a sound as loud and crackling as lightning. The back of the pew split the entire length of it. Momentarily stunned, Matthew looked at it, wide eyed, then, rushing back towards the altar, he took out most of the remaining patches of flames.

As Matthew got to the front pew, to the last two burns, he turned left and stopped short, staring past the flames on the carpet into the stairwell. A man was standing on the steps.

Standing erect, the stranger was softly silhouetted by the flames and candle light. Wearing a dress jacket and dress shirt under it, his collar was casually opened.

Matthew, looking down on him, estimated him to be about six feet tall, certainly shorter than Matthew's large stature, and thin, too. He was lean without being gaunt and he was smiling. He was looking intensely at the wall of the stairwell. He was studying the bloody handprint.

Well, not exactly bloody, Matthew thought, seeing it was sizzling and smoking itself into the stone, charring its image with little hisses of smoke. His presence made Matthew's blood run cold.

Suddenly remembering the fire, the young priest looked at the floor where the flames were getting bigger. Moving automatically, he walked to the first spot, pouring and stomping at the same time. Keeping one eye on the stranger, he moved to the last spot, coming about eight feet from the top of the stairs. The man stared at the handprint, smiling. He had to be aware of the priest's presence but he showed no indication. Matthew stood silently, uncertain. His thin t-shirt was soaked with sweat and holy water and the cathedral seemed to be freezing; he knew he was trembling but couldn't help it.

Samuel had also noticed the man's presence. When Father Matthew had passed him to put out the flames, he had seen the man and instinctively started backing away, putting the priest between himself and the stranger. The alcoholic fog gone now, Samuel was sure that the crack that tweaker had given him earlier was freaking him out. The flames had been cool, he wasn't worried about them; he just called for Matthew. This man was different, his presence made the old bum sober instantly. He didn't like it at all. Samuel was shaking hard as he backed towards the wall flanking the unburnt side of pews. He wasn't aware that he was backing himself into a corner.

While Samuel backed away noisily, Matthew was surprised when the fair-haired stranger suddenly turned away from the handprint to look at him. Locking eyes with the young priest, the man deliberately climbed the stairs with swift catlike grace. As the man came to the top step, Matthew's eyes widened in surprise at his height. The man understood that Matthew had miscalculated. This man was actually taller than Matthew's impressive 6'3". An enigmatic smile played on the man's face as he paused, just one step out of the stairwell.

For the first time in his life, Matthew was afraid of another human being. From the confusion came a fear, so great that Matthew actually took a step back. The smile unnerved him.

"Do they no longer have a fire extinguisher in the altar?" the man asked, his eyes sweeping past Matthew, towards the altar behind him.

The stranger spotted Samuel hugging himself against the far wall, trying to disappear under the pews. His smile widened as the old bum visibly started flailing and jerking.

Seeing movement behind the man, Matthew craned his head to see Father Joseph appear suddenly from the darkness at the bottom of the stairs. His hurried momentum actually carried him up two or three steps before he became aware of the stranger. Joseph was wearing a sweatsuit, holding his shoes in one hand. The clothes were dry, but Matthew could see that Joseph's hair and skin were dripping wet, slowly soaking his clothes.

The stranger turned halfway round and, seeing Joseph, he jerked in surprise. He smiled, without the least pretense of humor.

Matthew suddenly thought of a leering wolf. Father Joseph stood poised, frozen three stairs up. After a long moment, the man laughed. It was an amused laugh but devastatingly menacing. Matthew stared at the remaining holy water in the pot he was still holding.

Positively gleeful now, the man spoke with a singsong voice, "Soooo good to see you, Joseph! I'm so happy you're not dead!"

Joseph smirked at him.

"You always did think too highly of yourself, Alex," Joseph hissed.

The man, Alex, chuckled back at him.

"It's ok that you're not dead Joseph, don't be bitter! I'll simply get the pleasure of killing you twice!"

The stranger smiled sweetly at the old priest.

Now Joseph was smiling too.

"You couldn't do it once, what makes you think you could do it twice?"

His tone was mocking and Alex's smile hardened. Before Matthew could blink, the man was lunging at him.

In less than a second, the bigger man was on him; Matthew saw the attack too late.

The gold blade in the man's right hand flashed in the light as it arched upwards from his hip; it was aimed at Matthew's left rib cage. Matthew instinctively rolled the pot he still held to shield the spot, deflecting the blade into his upper right ribs instead. As the it sank into him, he could feel the man try to roll the blade up into his collar bone, going for his throat.

Grabbing the stranger's hands, Matthew was able to stop the forward motion of the stab; but he didn't stop the twist of it and he screamed oddly as it deflated his right lung. Prying the man's hands away from the hilt, Matthew turned and staggered backwards; the seat of the front pew caught his legs from behind and he sat down, hard.

The pot, finally freed from his grasp, clattered across the floor. Matthew stared in amazement at the large dagger protruding from his chest. The woman's wound flashed through his mind and understanding dawned in a distant way.

Samuel was screaming, terrified, trapped against the back wall.

29

The man did an exaggerated swirling dance past Matthew, who was going into shock on the front pew. He pirouetted obscenely, bounding and leaping towards the altar in a dance of celebration. Matthew pulled at the dagger weakly, trying not to breathe. Gasping, his vision blurring, he looked at the big fat ruby embedded into the hilt, surrounded by a strange pattern of emeralds. Father Joseph appeared in front of him. He looked at Joseph blankly. Joseph felt sick as he put his hands on the handle and pulled.

The stranger kicked over the heavily carved altar, still in a buoyant ballet. Matthew screamed as the blade tore out of his chest; gasping, he tried standing up, but passed out before he could even move. Only the pew caught the young priest as he fell back onto it. Samuel sobbed loudly against the far wall while trying to disappear into it.

Alex had reached over and pulled a fire extinguisher from the overturned altar. He was holding it jubilantly over his head as Joseph turned to him, slowly, the bloody knife in his hand.

"I will kill you as many times as it takes, Joe-Joe! After all, I got Sara once enough, didn't I?" Alex exclaimed.

He swept his arms in an exaggerated gesture towards the obvious burns on the floor. Holding the extinguisher in an offer to the old priest he asked flatly.

"Do you think she could use this?"

The tall stranger snorted with laughter.

Somewhere inside Joseph, the dam burst. He lunged at Alex.

As he did, the big man turned, jumped past the altar, and ran straight at Samuel, who started screaming and trying to claw his way under the pew. He was trapped. Joseph was still a good six feet behind as Alex snatched Samuel up in a smooth motion, turning back toward an on-rushing Joseph. He dangled the struggling, homeless man in front of Joseph, forcing him to stop.

Joseph still had the blade in his hand that he had pulled from Matthew's chest . Samuel was completely suspended, shrieking. Alex shook him a few times, letting him dangle like a rag doll.

"I'll snap his neck, Father," he drew out the title mockingly.

"Drop it; you know I will."

He squeezed Samuel's neck in demonstration and the old bum screamed in pain. Joseph hesitated, and then let it go. The dagger bounced off the carpet with a thud and clattered onto the bare marble under the pew.

30

The sound echoed through the cathedral. The two men stared at each other, with a squirming Samuel as a barricade between them.

After an eternity, Joseph finally spoke, his hands feeling very empty.

"If it's me you want, Alex, then do it. He's an innocent."

Alex burst with laughter and shook Samuel easily,

"Only you would dare say this old drunk was an innocent!"

Thrusting the helpless man forward, he hissed at Joseph.

"Where's the boy? Tell me now, or I'll kill this piece of trash!"

Calmly, the old priest looked at Samuel squarely . His poor old friend's eyes were bulging, his body twitching from being suspended on his toes. He was looking wildly at Father Joseph. He had only one chance. If it didn't work, he knew he would watch Samuel die. Looking directly at the old bum, the priest tried to calm him. Samuel watched Joseph intently.

Joseph told Samuel the truth as calmly as he could.

"Sam, he's going to kill you anyway."

The bum's eyes widened and instantly he turned on his toes, striking out, catching Alex full in the face twice before twisting from the stunned man's grasp. Joseph immediately lunged toward the pew, throwing himself to the spot where the dagger had disappeared. He remembered his boxing days, when a young Samuel had won the match in a move almost identical to the one he had just pulled on Alex. Though not hurt, Alex was obviously surprised by the move and as the man twisted from his hand, he shoved him, sending the homeless drunk flying. Joseph was scrambling under the pew stretching, searching.

Joseph managed to get his hand on the dagger's hilt and tried to come up off his knees; but Alex was faster.

Joseph was slammed backwards, the bigger man's body weight forcing his head to smack the floor, the hard-won dagger once again clicking across the floor out of his reach.

Alex, using the mass of his body to pin the priest, put his hands around the smaller man's throat, squirming up him to straddle him. Joseph was able to push him off slightly, his strength born of panic. Alex was crushing his throat. Rolling and bucking under him, the priest was able to gain some ground, but he could not throw the big man off him.

Desperately, Joseph pried one huge hand off his neck, but the other was still crushing his windpipe. Alex, his face contorted by hate and effort, used the hand Joseph had pulled away to reach inside his jacket as he squeezed

31

his left hand harder around the priest's neck. Joseph was suffocating, blacking out and all he could do was scratch at the man's hand. From his jacket, Alex pulled a dagger; a duplicate of the other, except in size. This one was shorter, narrower. With his right hand he thrust the dagger between them, missing the ribs and piercing Joseph's heart in one smooth motion.

Joseph, his eyes bulging, felt the pressure ease on his throat just as the blade sank into him. He felt the damage. There was, oddly, no pain, and just as he wondered about pain, he saw Matthew over Alex's' shoulder.

White as a ghost and trembling, Joseph could see the bloody young priest was clutching the larger dagger. Alex pushed the smaller blade into Joseph as hard as he could, all the while smiling triumphantly.

Not able to draw a breath, Joseph looked Alex directly in his eyes as Matthew swooped on him from behind. He arched the blade directly into the middle of Alex's back. Looking down at Joseph, the smile on Alex's face froze. For a moment, his eyes squinted in confusion and he let go of his knife. Still sitting on Joseph's chest, Alex placed one hand above each of the old priest's shoulders. On his hands and knees, suspended above a dying Joseph; his look of surprise slowly turned into understanding, as Matthew wrenched the dagger free. Without hesitating, Matthew swung the blade again; this time leaning forward and across, he hit Alex so hard that Joseph heard the ribs breaking.

In spite of it all, the old priest smiled, proud of himself and his protégé.

Too weak to stop his own momentum, Matthew crashed forward near the altar. The jolt made him scream out in pain. As the blackness overcame him again, he saw Alex stumble to his feet, heaving himself off Joseph. With the dagger still protruding from his ribs, the big man staggered to the pews. He reached around to his back, pawing at the daggers handle, and tried to pull it out. Matthew knew the man was mortally wounded, and as he blacked out, he was mildly surprised to realize that he didn't feel guilty about it in the slightest.

Joseph watched Alex as he bumped into the pews. Still impaled with the dagger, he stumbled into the aisle between the rows and out of Joseph's sight.

Trying to breathe, Joseph produced just a desperate gasp instead. He was glad he hadn't told Sara about Matthew; she wouldn't have come to him if she had known.

Darkness started overtaking Joseph just as Gail's face appeared above his . She was crying. He shook his head at her. Trying to speak around his damaged throat, he barely could form the words at all.

"Is Matthew…alive?"

Crawling quickly to the young priest, trying not to let sadness overwhelm her, Gail saw that he was rolling his arms, trying to come to. Turning around, going back to Joseph, she whispered loudly.

"Yes, he's alive!"

Weakly, Joseph looked at his old friend as she tried to cradle him. He slid away from her and gasped.

"Go…Get him out of here…" His strength faded.

He felt his eyes glaze as he mouthed, "Tell him."

Using his last movements, Joseph smiled at Gail warmly. An interesting darkness came over him and he thought of Sara.

Chapter 2

January 12, 2:19 a.m.

Doug Daniels caught the car just as it started sliding. The fresh new snow was not sticking yet, but the plummeting temperature was making the damp street freeze in a few places.

The black ice was making his middle-of-the night trip to the church hazardous, as well as tedious. Cursing himself, Doug slowed the sedan even more, as he swished across another frozen patch, making his progress little more than a crawl.

The fat white flakes hit the windshield like a million points of tiny star light; and Doug had to make himself blink rapidly so as not to be mesmerized. Checking the clock on the dash, he again felt unsettled, wondering what the hell had happened at Joseph's church.

A phone ringing in the middle of the night was never good news, but the biggest surprise was who the caller turned out to be, and what they said.

Wanting to speed up, Doug braked instead. His turn was right ahead and he tried to give himself extra room for stopping. He squinted through the dark, looking at the unlit, well-kept houses and small shops along the street. He smiled sarcastically, thinking that if he did crash, no one would know it until morning.

As Doug eased to a stop, to the right he could see colored strobe lights flashing their warning about two blocks up the street. Pausing a minute, he took in the scene in front of the church.

Police cars, ambulances, fire trucks, and television news vans clustered the street for a block before and a block past the cathedral. Dammit! The press had beaten him there. Doug cursed the snow, and pulling right into his turn, he prayed that what he was going to find wasn't as bad as he imagined. He was pretty sure though it was going to be bad news for him.

Through the dense snow, Doug saw maybe four or five reporters corralled with police tape, about a block back from the church. Some of them turned as his headlights came into view, but for the most part, the little crowd stood silently looking towards the lights. Overly bundled, they looked comical to Doug ; but, he thought, they look that way to him anyway most of the time, even without looking like the "Stay-Puff Marshmallow Men."

The flashing red lights were like bloody red-blue pulses, making the snowflakes momentarily freeze into a strange, hot pink tie-dye.

Doug had already passed some very neat little shops, tightly spaced when an alley cleaved the block to his right, giving residents and customer's easy access and extra parking space behind the buildings.

The two shops immediately flanking the alley were dark, quiet, but Doug's attention snapped to the figure in the alley. He instinctively slowed to a roll, suddenly aware of the crispness of the air.

The man was turned away from him, studying the wall of the building and Doug could see he wasn't wearing a coat, or even a jacket. He also seemed abnormally tall. As Doug tapped his breaks again, the man turned toward the sound of the approaching car. His fair hair and features were momentarily washed out by the lights of the slow-rolling car.

Now almost even with him, the man smiled and gave a curt wave, then turned to look towards the flashing lights. Doug dropped his foot from the brake, letting the car inch past the alley and gain a little speed.

Doug shook himself. Nerves, he thought.

It wasn't abnormal to be tall, when he thought about it. And if that reporter wanted to freeze his tall ass off out there, who was he to stop the poor bastard?

Unsettled and grumpy, Doug turned his focus back to the church.

The captain's personal car, a minivan really, was parked behind a fire truck about half a block away from the church. Doug made a zigzag past the intersection that was clogged with emergency vehicles. Almost taking out an ambulance, he lurched to a stop behind the minivan. He turned off the engine and a strange silence descended over the scene. The pit of Doug's stomach started trembling. He tried hard not to think of Matthew, thinking of the phone call instead.

The captain's voice had been terse, edgy, jerking him from a dead sleep with no apparent sympathy.

"Are you awake?"

Doug didn't recognize the voice at first, and, suspecting his brother of trying to trick him, he had responded rudely.,

"Hell no! I always talk in my sleep. What do you want?"

The answer snapped him awake instantly.

"This is Cappy, you little fuck! Are you listening?"

Doug started stammering, awake, but still slow. He started trying to apologize,

"Oh! Oh God! Cappy! I thought you were…"

The interruption stopped him cold.

"You need to get to Saint Mary's'…Now…"

Doug blinked himself awake. Without thinking, he asked, "Matthew?"

The captain seemed to expect the question.

"No. Not him. But you need to come. The FBI guys are already here."

The weight of the words froze everything for an eternity of a second. Doug felt relieved and sick at the same time.

"I'm on my way now," he gasped with a terrible dread in his throat.

Now, here in the eerie silence outside the church twenty minutes later, Doug again felt choked, like the air was too thick to breath.

Gripping the wheel, he told himself it was ok, but as he looked around, the oddness seemed to touch everything. At most crime scenes, movement, and noise were unavoidable. But here, in his car, Doug could see only one person outside the large structure. One lone patrolman, bundled in his duty coat, stood guard at the giant front doors. He was a lonely figure but incredibly vigilant, his head turning back and forth slowly, carefully measuring the misty night around thee cathedral.

The cold has him on his toes, Doug thought to himself, and then he started noticing that in the ambulances and fire trucks around him, the workers sat in darkened, warmed interiors, also watching the church, and watching him.

Doug got out of the car, trying not to vomit with fear.

He saw that the patrol cars also had officers in them, some doing paperwork, some watching. It must be bad, he knew, simply by the sheer number of vehicles.

The cold wind, tearing at him, actually helped to push down the queasiness a bit. Glancing back down the block, Doug saw the obviously inconspicuous Fed-mobile. He started up the front walk, thinking about Matthew, trusting the captain when he had said 'Not him'.

What the hell had happened here? Doug deliberately didn't try to answer himself. The scene would tell him what he needed to know.

Approaching the front doors, he saw that the patrolman was an old friend of his named Jason. The patrolman was bundled from head to toe against the cold.

Speaking across the distance to him, Doug asked, "How's it goin', Jay?"

The beat cop, watching Doug close the distance, did not respond.

The patrolman's hesitation was almost palpable, and, interpreting his reticence to whatever was inside, Doug started trembling again.

Just as he got to where Jason was standing above him on the steps, Captain Edwards thrust his head through the door behind the cop. He seemed about to say something to Jason, but seeing Doug, Edwards stopped, stood up straight and stepped halfway out the door.

Looking Doug in the eye, Edwards spoke softly across the distance between them.,

"Douglas! There you are. Come on, son. I've been waiting for you." His tone seemed soft, almost Zen-like. Doug looked at Jason who momentarily looked away.

Doug waited by the door a second longer, until Jason turned to look at him. Doug mounted the steps to pass him when Jason caught his arm and spoke rapidly under his breath. ,

"Remember Doug… whatever you need, I got your back. You know where I'll be."

For a second, Dougg was touched by the gesture of friendship without understanding it, but deep in Jason's eyes he saw the tremble of terror that was barely held at bay.

Now angry at being caught off guard, Doug ground out, "Thank you, Jason."

Pulling his arm away, he tried not to look at the captain as he climbed up the last few steps. Something was terribly wrong, Doug thought stupidly.

What in God's name had happened? Doug would talk to Matthew, he thought, and it made him feel better; but as he came level with the captain, he saw the old man was trying to avoid his gaze.

Doug was shaking like a willow tree in a stiff wind. The captain deliberately bridged the gap between them, putting one hand on his shoulder; he held the door close to himself with the other. A burst of bright light spilled from the crack in the door.

"He's not letting me see something." Doug brain duly noted.

Captain Edwards cleared his throat lightly and then addressedhe younger man in a sober tone.

"Douglas, before you come in here you need to understand two things…"

He shook Doug's shoulder slightly, as if that would cause enlightenment.

"First of all, the rest of those Feds will be here soon, so we don't have much time. They'll have warrants by then, so we have to be quick."

Edwards let out a deep breath that floated on the stillness like a misty plume.

"Second of all, and listen to me Douglas , no matter what you hear, or see right now, know that everything that can be done, is being done… Do you understand me?"

Doug blinked, not really understanding at all.. He nodded anyway.

"Where's Matt?" Doug asked.

The captain's brow knotted with tension.

"He's not here." He said it casually.

Doug thought he understood. There were witness reports, lineups to do; he would see Matthew in a bit. He was sure of it.

The captain let go of his shoulder, repeating the odd forewarning. ,

"Everything that can be done, is being done." Edwards sighed.

He let the door swing out.

As the door opened, Doug smelled it, a split second before he saw it.

Burned flesh.

Just inside the immense doors was a small marbled reception area. Highly decorated with plaster and paint, it seemed obscene in the bright glare from the flood lights that were sitting on the floor illuminating murals of salvation on the walls, and a body spat from the fires of Hell onto the floor.

Flanking each side of the large space were two elaborate wrought iron racks that held candles; they were big and heavy, a place for parishioners to light a sacrament candle and leave it burning throughout the day.

The rack to Doug's left stood undisturbed, the half-burned candles on it were extinguished, cold. The rack to the right, however, was pulled over, spilling candles all over the floor.

It looked as if it had been pulled from the front and had toppled forward onto the poor bastard who lay under it, charred like a crispy critter.

Looking closer, walking into the chamber, the captain shut the door behind them with a heavy thump.

Stepping carefully, Doug crossed to the overturned rack, peered at the body under it.

Shit, Doug thought to himself, the fire under the rack must have been intense. He had never seen a dead body like it.

Almost all of the flesh was not just burned, but in ashes.

The skull and skeleton's limbs were mostly intact, but brittle by the look of them. All of the spine was missing, giving the charred body the impression of being cut in two, as the lower half rested on the floor, while the ribs were caught in the support bars of the rack, some twelve inches above the rest.

The position indicated that the person curled up underneath it had apparently wrapped their arms around one of the bars of the rack after it fell. Even in death it appeared half of the skeleton was trying to escape this unnatural cage.

Doug's face pulled into a scowl. The huge rack above the body still had candles stuck to it, maybe a few dozen of them.

Doug figured the dripping wax must have caused the intense heat. He looked at the marble floor, not comprehending the scorch marks that only showed immediately around the skeleton.

Standing upright, Doug looked at the captain, bewildered Dreading the question, he asked it anyways. ,

"Who is that under there?"

The captain seemed to fidget, and his answer was surprising.

"I don't know." Edwards said with a shrug.

They both looked back at the body, sensing the strangeness of whatever had happened in this room.

"Douglas, there are three bodies." Edwards said softly.

The younger man jerked around in shock. He saw the captain's expression and his guts twisted.

Losing control, Doug jumped at the officer, grabbing him up by his lapels, he almost screamed in the older man's face. ,

"Where in the hell is Matthew?"

The captain, expecting it, put his smaller hands around two huge fists.

"Calm down!" he snapped at Douglas..

"The Feds are in there; they'll toss us both! Shut the fuck up and let go of me!" He hissed it in the bigger man's face.

Realizing who it was that he was shaking like a rat, Doug let the man go. Suddenly, he swayed, unsteady a moment, before the captain grabbed his arms tightly.

"Listen to me!" said Edwards, as he glanced around, looking for the Feds.

He quickly turned back to Doug. The young man's eyes were wide, wild.

"Doug, I said Matthew's not here. The truth is we don't know where he is; Gail either."

Doug breathed hard through his mouth to regain some composure as a terrible realization dawned on him.

"Where's Father Joseph...?" Doug asked flatly.

The captain looked away, not wanting to say what was obvious anyway. A sob rose in Doug's throat, and he choked it out, trying not to hear his own cry.

"Oh god, where's Matthew?" he asked in a ragged whisper.

He repeated it. "OHHH God, where is Matthew? What do you mean missing?"

Edwards pulled Doug closer, pushing up on him at the same time and forcing him to stand erect again.

"Everything that can be done is being done, Douglas, I promise you! Even the Feds are looking right now; their lab rats and federal warrants are on their way here now to close us down...can you do this?"

Edwards forced the younger man to look at him.

Not sure what else to say, Doug merely nodded. The captain frowned.

"Yes," Doug said, this time with more focus, calmer.

The captain relented and let him go They simultaneously turned and walked into the nave.

Just inside the arched door going into the sanctuary, the confessional stood to the left. They could see the charring on the wooden structure, but Doug saw no sensible pattern to it.

Three scene techs Doug knew were milling around it, inspecting this, plucking up that. All of them turned to him, acknowledging his presence with nods, looking away quickly.

Doug severely wanted to scream.

He walked numbly on, glancing right; he paused and noted the urn, cracked in two. The sight confused him more.

At the front of the church several people, including the coroner, were moving about, silently, all seeming to be focused on one area. A man in a suit, the Fed, Doug assumed correctly, was taking pictures of something on the floor.

Every few seconds he changed positions and continued to shoot the photos. Doug knew there was another body up there. He didn't want to know who it was.

Another scene tech was in the aisle, about three fourths of the way up. He was inspecting a pew that was broken in a horizontal line along the backrest, all the way across. The oddness was no longer a shock.

"Watch your step..." the captain reminded him, and Doug automatically looked down to see burned spots in a crazy blot pattern going up the aisle.

Doug's thoughts swirled around Matthew.

The craziness was steadily pushing at Doug's nerves , and he cursed Matthew, silently, at the same time praying he would be found soon.

Following the captain up the long aisle, trying to walk delicately, Douglas remembered Matthew as a youngster. So arrogant and ego driven. The little bastard, he thought, instantly regretting it.

Doug thought of the accident that had changed Matthew forever, made him find his path. The accident that had made him a murderer.

"No." Doug said aloud to the thought, and, hearing it, the captain stopped and turned to him.

"It'll be OK, Douglas, whatever happened, has happened, and Father Joseph would want your eyes here..." he said, misinterpreting his involuntary blurt.

Doug nodded, and the older man, turned again and started walking towards the alter. About halfway up the aisle, he could see the top of the altar platform and the body that lay on it.

It was Father Joseph.

It took every ounce of control Doug had ever learned not to vomit. he walked on in a daze, no longer caring where he stepped. Walking past the damaged pew, he puzzled at the burn marks on it and the one in front of it.

What had burned it? The old, beautifully crafted pew was in ruins. What the hell was this? Doug's head was pounding. The confusion was only

41

deepening.

As they passed the front row of pews and came close to the group of people there, Doug glanced to the front left pew beside him. It was covered in blood and a huge silver and copper cook pot lay on the floor in front of it, grossly out of place here and smeared with blood.

Doug stared at the bloody pot with a frown, trying hard to understand it as he avoided looking at the body laid at the alter.

A powerful floodlight stood at the far end of the pew, shining into the stairwell going down to the first floor, where the classrooms and offices were.

Doug turned back around and forced himself to look at Father Joseph.

He was aware that the Federal agent had stopped his photography and was looking at Douglas blankly.

Father Joseph's struggles marked his broken body. The deep purple black marks around the throat covered him, from his chin to where the shoulders disappeared under the cloth of a tattered old green jogging suit.

In death, the damaged tissue had obscenely swollen, pushing into the flesh of the chin. Doug felt the sting of tears threatening the back of his eyes as he studied the evidence of murderous brutality left on his old friend's neck.

The stab wound into the priest's heart was a direct shot.

Doug's guts twisted as he realized Joseph had been stabbed after being strangled. A huge puddle of blood had formed around him from the wound.

Perhaps he was already unconscious when he was stabbed? Doug hoped that had been the case. He noticed the old man's shoes were gone.

Joseph's swollen neck had caused his head to tilt back, but Doug could see that Joseph had a slight smile on his lips, on his death mask.

Doug let out a long breath, saying under it, "My God…"

Suddenly looking back towards the burned body in the front, Doug's eyes swept the aisle, the pews, and the confessional. Remembering something, he asked the group.

"What time did all of this go down?"

For a moment there was complete silence. Doug looked away from the confessional to the captain.

"Cappy?"

"Near as we can tell, between ten and eleven." Edwards said casually.

"What do you think you are doing, exactly?" This came from the Fed, in the bad suit.

Looking at the captain, the agent demanded answers. ,

"Now, who the hell is this guy? What is this, Edwards?"

The coroner standing beside the body snapped her head up. She shook her head at the question's tone and kept writing on her clipboard.

She was an extraordinary looking woman, obviously of Latino descent; she definitely stood out in a crowd even if she was barely five foot tall. She gave Doug one of her wonderful smiles, as the captain's eyes narrowed dangerously.

"Just take your pictures, asshole. Until I'm handed a warrant this is my jurisdiction!"

"Do you doubt that it's coming?" The agent asked, amazed that the captain was not over-awed at the power of the federal machine.

Edward's barley contained a sneer that went on for an uncomfortable eternity in just a few seconds.

"Are you federal boys having trouble getting Justice Thomas to come to the door?" the captain retorted snidely.

They all started grinning at the now flustered Fed; it was common knowledge that the presiding federal judge was a total drunk.

His habits were infamous with the local cops, who had to deal with him and his wife. She even one-upped the judge by adding a pill addiction to her repertoire. Even though they were wild, they were, after all, elderly; and the local cops knew that if they had not been called by eleven p.m., then the judge and the lovely Mrs. Thomas would be passed out, or maybe have killed each other.

Either way, the captain figured if their luck held, the warrant wouldn't be signed until the good judge woke up at his usual six fifteen a.m.

Several of them must have come to the same conclusion, because all of them started looking at their watches, the Fed scowling at his. The others still were grinning, except for Doug. He didn't care about Judge Thomas; he was still looking at Joseph.

He had known Father Joseph most of his life and a slow anger burned into Doug. .

The pitiful, broken body laying on the altar platform deserved better, he thought. No one deserved such a violent end.

"What was he stabbed with?" Doug blurted. .

The scowl and grins suddenly forgotten by the group, they turned their

43

attention back to different things.

The Fed, looking back down at his camera finally answered. ,

"We don't know. We have not found any weapons."

Turning to the captain, Doug gestured to Joseph.

"You said three bodies. If Gail is missing, too, then who is the other body?"

The silence was palpable. No one responded.

Doug looked back to the captain, who nonchalantly said, "A woman."

Captain Edwards put his hands in his pockets and diverted his eyes. He looked towards the stairwell, maybe twenty-five, or thirty feet to Doug's direct left. The young man's eyes followed without seeing.

"What woman?" Doug blurted, surprised.

Silence again that echoed between them all was only reluctantly broken.

"We don't know," said the captain.

"But not Gail?" Doug insisted.

Silence.

"No, not Gail," the coroner, Maria, told him, not looking up from her clip board.

"Where is she?" Doug asked, his eyes automatically going to the stairwell again.

A tech was there, photographing something on the wall above the steps.

The Fed got flustered again. "What is this crap? Who is this guy, Edwards?"

"Shut up!" the captain told him, and the agent turned to complain to the coroner.

Maria met his gaze, full on, and, mimicking the captains voice perfectly, she calmly responded, ,

"Just take your pictures , asshole ; until I get a warrant, these bodies belong to me!"

Her mocking smile pushed at the Fed and he cursed explosively then turned to stomp away. He disappeared into a wall behind the altar that concealed a beautiful marble staircase that went to the balcony seating and choir area.

They all watched him go in a huff. Maria stuck her tongue out at his retreating back.

"Come on," the captain said in a tired voice.

He gently pulled the big younger man towards the stairwell. Maria walked silently behind them.

"What are you doing to find Matthew? What happened here?" Doug asked, keeping his eyes straight ahead.

The captain sighed hard before answering.

"Everything. Hell, right now the press has the APB for Joseph's car, so even the press helicopters are looking for them. Feds are already assembling a full task force to do a grid search as soon as daylight breaks. Every trooper in a three-state area is looking. They are supposed to inspect all the interstates and rest areas. We'll find them."

The last part sounded hollow.

As they descended the stairwell, the tech working there stayed focused. He was kneeling, face almost to the wall, tweezers in one hand, a magnifying glass in the other. He was examining the several large, charred spots in the aged marble.

Frowning again, Doug glanced up and jerked to a stop. Three large uneven burn marks ran up the wall like black ribbons, hangingut it was the handprint that made him stop.

Almost halfway up the wall, a small, perfect handprint was burned into the stone.

There were other tiny spots that appeared to be burns made in the polished stone around it; but the handprint sat there, scorched into it, obviously human.

Impossible, Doug thought. The captain had stopped a few steps lower. Maria was close behind Doug with the tech virtually at her feet. They all watched his reaction.

Taking three or four steps, Doug thrust his face close to the burn while blinking hard. Bracing his hands on the wall, he didn't care that he might be contaminating the scene as he came face to face with the impossible.

The tech knew Doug and as he pushed himself to the wall, the tech just looked up at his boss, Maria, who shook her head at him.

Soon all this would belong to the feds anyway; let them figure out the traffic evidence. She smiled, thinking about challenging all of Langley's boys at FBI headquarters.

In her years as a coroner, Maria knew that if this case were ever solved, at all, it would probably be covered up in some way. Probably as a sex scandal, she thought bitterly. The evidence they did have would help them prove that easily, even if it were not true.

She suspected it was not true. She had met Joseph; he did many good things in her childhood neighborhood a few blocks away.

As a coroner she knew that some people were secretly, horribly twisted. But never once, even after breaking from the church after her divorce, did she ever sense or hear of anything wicked here. She had grown up with Matthew and Douglas and she was as frightened for Matthew as she used to be afraid of him.

Father Matthew had once been the sidewalk bully, long before he had ever found his calling as a priest.

There was no sense to what Douglas was seeing.

The handprint was small and slender. The surface of the stone was burned into a recess in the shape of a hand; like acid had been thrown on it. The entire thing was etched so clearly into the stone that everyone had no doubt a human hand had made it.

What kind of human hand could burn into stone? Doug could not even process that it existed, much less what it must mean.

His head was swimming; weirdness flooded around him. There were questions everywhere and no answers in sight. He wished he could vomit. Now truly confused, Doug pushed back from the wall suddenly wanting away from the human mark of carnage..

The floodlights hurt his eyes and his head. If he could get hold of Matt right now, he'd shake the story out of him. Doug realized that the captain had only half-answered his question.

"I asked a second ago, I'll ask once more…" He looked the captain squarely in his eye.

"What in the hell happened here!"

The captain looked at the handprint that was silently screaming a story from the wall.

"I wish to God I knew, Douglas. I wish to God I knew." He said it heavily, hopelessly.

They followed the trail of floodlights as they continued into the main hall of the first floor. Doug pushed past the captain, edgy in a foul way. He made his way past the lights on the floor, taking care to step around the spots and dots of burns on the bare stone floor. The walls were sanded stone on this level, but here, too, streaks of charring and burn basically spanned the entire length of the corridor, first on one side, then the other.

At the small door at the end of the long hall, two techs were examining the door itself.

A very large burn spot, just inside the door, had burned maybe a full foot into the foundation below. The spot was almost as large as the width of the hall, stopping just short of the left wall.

The door was burned from the bottom up, and more than half of it was gone. Only one charred hinge, in the upper door frame, kept it in place. The rest of it was nothing more than ashes, mixed into a grey-black mixture with the new snow. The guy on the ground kept swatting away the flakes falling through the empty space into his very interesting hole in the ground. It wasn't working very well.

Getting past the techs as best they could, trying not to muck things up more, the captain informed Doug of what they knew so far. ,

"These guys pulled five distinct footprints from this hall. One we are sure is Matt's, so we know he came this way at least twice. Bruce here thinks he was running into the church, at least once."

The tech at the door absently nodded his head. The captain continued,

"There's also a large bare foot track; we are assuming they're Joseph's, but…" he drifted off.

"But, what?" Doug pushed him to explain.

"At least two of his footprints, coming back this way toward the garden, are burned into the stone…" the captain paused taking a deep breath

"There are no burns on his feet; and his hand is too large to have made the handprint; we measured it."

They looked at Maria who looked at the floor.

Doug swept his eyes across the burn marks, coming to rest on a spot where he could definitely see was a footprint, toes and all. What had burned?

The huge black hole in the floor seemed to mock him. Doug could almost feel it staring back at him.

"You said five," he reminded the captain, who was also staring into the hole.

The tech at the door casually gestured towards the hall floor saying, "One set is definitely a woman's, coming and going; but the other set…."

He looked at Doug, as excited as a kid with a new bike. He pointed to a certain spot on the floor.

"Those big marks with the spot charred behind it…if you look, you can see it's a high heel shoe, a small one, has to be female. Those prints are pointed inward, but not out. She went up the stairs as far as the confessional, but then no more…"

Doug jerked upwards. "What?"

The tech looked at him, not understanding his question.

"Well, she went into the church but didn't walk out," he said, trying to explain. "Her every step is burned into the floor!"

"No! The confessional. Were either of the priests in it?" Doug interrupted.

The tech looked around, uncomfortable.

"I only tracked the footprints, the guys up there on it could tell ya…" He looked around again, unsure.

Doug ground his next words out to no one in particular.

"Matthew was to be taking confession until ten…"

He let the thought hang in the air.

"I know," the captain said, playing whatever cards he held very close to his chest.

Doug nodded at the helpful tech and stepped around the burned door into the now frozen courtyard. The cold air felt good, instantly clearing his mind but making his nose run.

Because of all the evergreen plantings, the courtyard was always moist with humidity, wicked hot in the summer. But it was a great spring and fall garden. All of the evergreen bushes, shrubs, and trees made it a nice winter garden, too. Not on this winter night though.

Doug was surprised to see five or six uniformed cops, bundled tightly, quietly standing at various places around the perimeter of the courtyard.

One cop leaned against the wall where the burnt door was hanging, but he snapped to attention when the captain and coroner stepped out. They all knew Doug, too, his presence there completely understandable to them.

The threesome turned quietly onto the path that angled right into the center of the courtyard. The left side was exactly the same, so a perfect 'y' shaped path sliced the garden into sections.

At the center intersection of the stone path, a tech was looking at more burn spots on the sidewalk. They turned right toward the front porch of the two-story house.

The cop standing duty on the front porch looked around nervously. As the captain approached, the patrolman took a few steps towards them to address Edwards.

"Cappy... that Fed ordered me not to let anyone in but his Fed-buddies. Can he do that yet?"

The captain drew in a heavy breath, rolled his eyes and responded in a tired voice. ,

"Not until they get a warrant, son. Until then, I'm your commander. Don't you need a smoke?"

The young cop looked at him, then glanced at Doug, and walked off the porch silently, following back along the path they had just walked.Doug and Edwards looked at each other a long moment.

Why they were going into the house, Doug wondered.

If there was a dead woman in there, why was she in there? Before Doug could ask, the captain and Maria opened the door and entered.

They heard one side of a very loud conversation as they stepped into the dimly lit home.

"Don't bother me with this shit, again! You have been there for two hours already!"

A pronounced pause, some thumping around from upstairs, and it continued.

"I don't give a crap! Break the damn door in! Crawl through a window...!"

They realized they were listening to one end of a phone conversation. The someone who was speaking started down the upstairs hall and moved into the stairwell right in front of the door.

A very well-dressed, clean cut federal agent appeared at the top of the stairs, saying, "Just do what I tell you..." into the cell phone that was stuck up to his left ear.

Seeing them below, he stopped short, surprised into sudden silence. He looked down on them for a good ten seconds. Finally, remembering his conversation, he snapped into the phone.

"Get back to me when it's done, and that better be soon!" Without saying goodbye, he snapped the phone shut.

The captain asked, "Drinking problems?"

They all chuckled, and the Fed stood even more erect, hands on hips like a grumpy grandma.

"Edwards, this is bullshit! You know he shouldn't be here!"

He gestured toward Doug, as if anyone was unsure who he was talking

49

about. The young federal agent knew exactly whom Douglas was.

The captain feigned surprise.

"Wooow…" he said mockingly.

"You're a smart FBI guy! You can actually tell me what I already know. Now that is talent; you should consider a career in…"

"Whatever! Dumbass, suit yourself. It'll be here soon," the Fed answered, showing some spunk.

Doug, the captain and Maria started climbing the stairs. The captain couldn't resist baiting the agent.

"You know, if you Feds had time between paperwork adventures, you could actually try picking a lock, instead of breaking in Judge Thomas's door. That is illegal!" He chuckled at his own wisecracks.

The Fed allowed them to pass, saying, "Try not to touch anything."

Doug was agitated at the guy's manner, but Maria grabbed his arm from behind.

"It's not worth it," she whispered.

The agent stomped past them on the stairs, refusing to engage in this argument any further until he had clear jurisdiction to kick them all out of his crime scene..

Turning left at the top of the stairs, they went down a short hall. Outside the open bedroom door, another floodlight sat on the floor, shining into the room. This was Joseph's bedroom.

Doug suddenly did not want to know, sick at the uneasy questions. Maria slipped quietly through the door, followed by Captain Edwards. He hesitated a second, and stepped into the room.

The bed was directly in front of the door, spotlighted by the powerful light in the hall. Doug thought he'd seen the worst of it. He hadn't.

A small, smooth skull was lying on the head of the bed. Most of the shoulders, arm, and ribcage were intact, but the spinal column was completely destroyed.

The hip bones and pelvic bones thrust upward from the bed like a strange tangle of wasted humanity. The leg bones were scorched heavily, but intact.

The flesh, once covering the bones, was nearly all ashes.

The only place the bedding had burned was directly around the body. The size of the skull was definitely feminine, and Doug's trained eye went to the hips, looking at the end of the pelvic bone. Maria was right. It was definitely female.

Standing just inside the door, Doug put his hand over his mouth and rubbed at new stubble. He realized that the only way to find Matthew was to figure this out, but absolutely nothing made any sense.

Trusting Maria's professionalism, he asked her for answers.

"What's your official opinion of this?"

She had leaned over the bed, looking into the skull, when he asked. She let out a deep sigh, stood erect, and looked down at the poor woman's remains. .

"The closest I can come to any reasonable explanation is spontaneous human combustion," she said, never looking away.

Silence seemed the only acceptable response.

Doug felt a little like he had the night he'd been trapped into sitting through a Fellini film. There were no markers here to relate to; everything was pretty surreal.

Maria continued.

"The body inside the front door, I'm certain is a man. He's burned the same way this one is; not one bit of soft tissue left."

Surprised, Doug thought about the body just inside the front door of the church as his face pulled into a deep scowl.

The captains jacket rang, making all of them jump.

"Excuse me," he said, going towards the door of the room.

He was pawing at his many layers trying to find his cell phone in the thick jacket he wore as he walked out past Doug and left him alone with Maria.

Douglas rebuked her in a soft tone.

"Bullshit, Maria. You don't believe in spontaneous human combustion," he said, scoffing at her.

She turned her head and smiled at the man who had caused her divorce. They had been together ever since, though not many people were aware of the relationship. Her mother, her ex, Father Joseph, and Matthew; they had all kept the secret of Maria and Doug's affair for political reasons.

Doug's guts clenched as she insisted.

"It doesn't matter what I believe. Here it is, but it's not like the other cases I've read about. It had to have happened rapidly; maybe fifteen minutes, at the most."

Even as she said it, they both knew that it was impossible. Doug's jaw dropped slightly.

He asked incredulously. "Fifteen minutes?"

"Yes, from death to ashes in maybe fifteen minutes…"

She let the impossible hang there, not able to help it. She thought of Matthew: wondering where he was, and in what condition. It made her sick.

The captain walked back in, tiny cell phone in hand, and took charge of the conversation immediately.

"That was the sheriff. He was able to keep that damn Fed from breaking and entering, but he couldn't stop him from throwing rocks at the judge's bedroom window. Thank God, Judge Thomas is a cat person, or he would have been awake hours ago!"

Edwards wagged the tiny phone at them.

"That damn FeeBee is in with the judge right now! We have two minutes, tops."

Maria started some intense looking around. So did the captain; the old man literally went to hands and knees, rooting around under the bed. While they were busy, Doug stared at the woman's remains on the bed.

Whoever she was, whatever she was doing in Joseph's bed, he felt sorry for this woman. Whoever, or whatever, had done this to her, she surely couldn't have deserved something so grotesque.

Suddenly, feeling stupid that he had missed it, Doug blurted out to the room. ,

"How do you know this is not Gail?"

The thought made Doug panic; he looked at them.

His muscles jerking, he asked, "How do you know the other body isn't Matt?"

Doug's knees started shaking and losing strength.

He wanted to scream until he died. He paused motionless as a phone rang out in the dead silence from the courtyard.

"Dammit!" the captain whispered.

He went into the connecting bathroom that had a window overlooking the courtyard. Doug and Maria looked at each other, helpless.

"That's it!" Edwards called from the tiny room.

"The jig is up! That little prick is coming in."

The captain took four steps back into the room. Going directly to Doug, he grabbed the big man's jacket sleeves.

In a loud whisper, he hissed at the younger man.

"I swear to you, Matthew was last seen alive…no, shut up and listen!"

Heavy footsteps were coming quickly up the walk.

"Listen and say nothing. When he gets in here, say nothing, understand?"

Doug nodded wildly.

"We have a witness…, they don't know about." Edwards said.

His head thrust towards the steps coming up from the small porch. His whisper dropped to just a sliver of sound.

"He saw Matthew leave with Gail. He was hurt, but he walked, well, mostly…and got into Joseph's car. They chose to be missing! …They are on the run from something! …these dumbasses don't realize that yet."

The front door was flung open. There were lots of footsteps headed their way now.

"What are they running from?" Doug asked quietly in disbelief.

The captain let go of him. The pair of Feds hit the bottom stairs together, like it was a race.

The captain, staring at the bed, answered his question.

"They are running from whatever did this," Edwards said softly, sweeping his hand towards the unknown woman.

The Feds beat each other into the room, huge jackal-like grins on their faces.

The captain grinned, too. Turning to the agents, holding up his right hand, he challenged them.

"Arm wrestle ya for it…?" Edwards told the well dressed agent.

Doug turned from the grinning skull on the bed and pushed aside a federal agent on his way out.

On the way to his car, Doug stopped in the open air of the garden and tried to breathe deeply to calm himself. He knew that no matter what it took, he was going to bring Matthew home.

He prayed that his little brother was safe.

Chapter 3

January 12, 10:23 a.m.

Staring at his cousin silently, Michael knew that he would have to kill him. Apparently, the same thought had crossed his cousin's mind, too.

Sitting as though he were made of stone, Michael watched his young kinsman, Adam, fidget on the leather sofa.

His eyes looking at anything but his cousin, Adam was manfully trying not to squirm. Taking a deep breath, he quickly glanced at Michael. Pausing noticeably, Adam tried to comfort his older cousin.

"I know you're upset, Michael, but don't jump to conclusions. I was ordered by your father to stay where I was. We could have taken Sara , before she ever got to the church, if he had come back to tell me she was there."

It seemed that even Michael's breathing stilled. His eyes narrowed and he slowly started to rise from his chair.

"So, then it IS my father's fault that he's dead?" He said it slowly, hissing.

Adam showed genuine frustration. With a snort, he sat over his knees, elbows perched on them, and he dropped his head and exhaled loudly. He tried to speak; looking back up at Michael, he implored him to reason.

"Listen…"

Michael suddenly bolted over the small, narrow table. He picked Adam up by the front of his shirt and shouted into his face.

"No! You listen, you little bastard! My father is a fucking french-fry because you're too much of a pussy to kill a woman!"

Flecks of spittle hit Adam in the face, as Michael literally hauled him to his feet. They were the same size physically; though Adam was much younger, and all his attempts to push his cousin away only made Michael grip him harder.

Before Adam could say anything more, Jerold spoke from behind the desk.

"Michael. Put my son down."

It was spoken softly, but firmly.

"I can assure you that he is no bastard."

Michael immediately let go of Adam, pushing him back into the sofa. Adam sat down, hard.Standing there a moment more, nostrils flaring, Michael turned and went to his uncle's desk.

He felt reckless, but he wasn't stupid. He forced a veneer of calm on himself; looking at Jerold made it easy to stay focused. Putting his hands on the desk, he leaned in close to Jerold, bowing his head as he did. Jerold watched him approach without flinching.

"I'm going to Salem," he said, softly, to his uncle.

"You need to find out what happened here, before more of us die!"

Before Jerold could respond, Michael stood up and abruptly turned to his right. He marched to the door and out of the office, slamming it closed behind him.

Jerold looked at a deflated Adam. This was beyond horrible.

It was almost inconceivable that his brother Alexander was dead. The full impact had not hit Jerold yet, he knew. This mess had to be cleaned up first; then, he would grieve.

"Why did Alex put you on Abdullah?" he asked his son, slowly.

Adam sat back into the sofa, sighing.

"I don't know, Daddy. He said that he wanted to re-check the market."

Adam stared straight ahead; the last thing he wanted was to anger his father.

"After two hours, Alex didn't come back, so I went back there myself. The old woman said that she had seen him come back, but he then left with a very tall woman. That's when I knew there was going to be trouble...I started looking for him..."

His father already knew how the story ended, in the church.

"Where did Abdullah go?" Jerold asked Adam.

Jerold already knew the answer to that, as well..

"I don't know..." Adam sighed. "I lost him when I went back to the market to find Alex."

Jerold wanted to throttle his son. The hunt had been a disaster. If they had been able to kill the boy before he was born, then none of them would be exposed. But now the child was not only born, but missing.

"Did you see Morgan in Charleston, at all?" Jarold asked his oldest son.

"No; not in Boston, either." Adam sat forward slightly before continuing.

"The nest in Salem was pretty easy to find, but as you know it was already too lateI'm sorry Daddy. I wish I had gotten there sooner."

The women had moved as soon as the boy was born. They had all simply vanished. Jerold felt sick.

Jerold stared at Adam as he thought about the scientist.

He knew someone had betrayed the family; someone close. Even had the boy not been suddenly found to exist among them, they already faced an external threat from the scientist that only Jarold knew could expose their entire family in a way that none would survive.

"Adam..." Jerold hesitated, slightly.

Adam looked at him carefully.

"Yes, Father...?"

Jerold played with the thin folder of papers before hm, wavng it slightly before dropping the file back onto the large desk.

"Do you understand, son, if this betrayal is yours, or your brother's, I'll have no choice but to kill you...?"

He looked solidly at his child, putting one finger on the file in a downward point Adam's eyes followed the finger and flinched, not at the threat, but from the exposure that the file threatened.

"Yes...I do understand..." Adam returned the stare, unflinching.

"I swear to you, daddy, it's not mine. I never even met that scientist! If James' did...I'll kill him for you."

He actually needed no excuse to kill James, his ignorant little brother. Adam would have done it for kicks alone.

Seemingly satisfied, Jerold looked at his desk while trying to ignore the file, and then slumped back into his seat.

"Go to bed, Adam, get some sleep...I'll need you to go to Salem tonight, with Michael. I don't trust your cousin right now. ' His fathers' death will only make him more reckless."

"I'll be ready by six." The younger man said as he got up to leave.

"Make it four!" Jerold snapped.

Adam paused at the tone, and then nodded.

Walking directly to the door Adam tried to comfort his father with words that sounded hollow even to himself. ,

"I'm sorry, Daddy, about Uncle Alex."

Adam walked out the door and was gone before Jerold could chide him for lying. Adam had hated Alexander for most of his life. As had Jerold.

Now alone, Jerold lowered his head and thought about the boy Alex had been. He absently played with the harmless looking file as so many memories burst forth, sweeping away any other vision with the sheer scope of time spent between them.

Jerold finally wept bitterly for his older brother.

***

January 12, 1:56 p.m.

Gail drove silently. She knew going in this circular route would take a few hours longer but it should be safer. Looking into the rear-view mirror, she saw Matthew shivering in his unnatural sleep, lying scrunched up across the back seat of the car.

Her sore eyes returned to the road. She had wept for Joseph for the last two hundred miles.

Staying on busy highways, Gail had gone to a bigger city; about one hundred and eighty miles out of Boston. She caught the fast-food joint during rush hour and no one seemed to notice her as she bought them some food. She had stopped only one other time, to trade cars.

Thinking of Joseph again, her ancient heart broke.

The old priest had prepared well; the old car was well provisioned, well maintained. The old Chevy had been picked up years before, had been parked at a storage garage all that time, waiting to be needed.

She missed her old friend, terribly. Josephs loss still did not feel real to her.

Looking in the mirror again, she became alarmed at Matthew's chills. He was in shock, she knew. Gail also knew that if the shock didn't kill him, he would live. ''She had to get him settled. She was afraid the movement was causing him to worsen.

Joseph had prepared Matthew, as well. The old priest had trained him to fight, just in case this day came. But for all the fencing and boxing lessons learned, Matthew had never known it was more than just exercise and games. Had Joseph told him it was more serious, the young priest may have reacted differently when confronted by Alexander.

The image of Joseh dying at the alter in her arms turned her face to stone as she drove on. Gail ignored Matthew, knowing his wounds could only be properly attended once they were safe.

The national park was coming up on her, as civilization started thinning considerably on the snow-covered road. Gail knew this area well, as she and Joseph had prepared many different plans over the years.

Joseph had never doubted that Sara would come back to him.

Gail scowled at the thought. He had been right all along, and death came with her. The loneliness of it all threatened to overwhelm her.

Before Gail could start crying again, the little road appeared on her left. Careful of the snow, she turned onto the wide dirt road. It had been plowed recently, and for that, she was thankful.

Gail was driving through forests covered in their winter blanket as the bright afternoon seemed to dim under the canopy of trees. Signs pointing to the recreation areas were scattered and she drove deeper into the woods, trying not to think of her destination.

Her mind was reeling, swirling through years, in just the space of a thought. Gail thought of Sara again, this time with no scowl. She thought of the woman's flesh, charring. The thought made her sick.

The camping area came up on the right quickly as a clearing appeared. Gail moved the old car up cautiously to the one structure there, the Quonset style bathrooms. Putting on the parking brake, she lowered the heater and stepped out into the cold air. The late snows had kept away campers and they were alone in the camp; Gail was sure of it.

As she went around to the trunk of the car, she looked at Matthew through the window as she passed by. The sleeping bag covering him was shaking.

"Oh God…" she said under her breath, "Please don't let him die."

Popping the trunk, she looked at the duffle bags inside. The space was stuffed with supplies. First aid kits, canned food, there was a tent too, but she knew they wouldn't be using it in this cold. Moving a sleeping bag out of her way, Gail picked up a bag and wrestled it out as she shut the trunk lid. She prayed that the park rangers still left the bathrooms open and unlocked 24/7.

Going directly to the women's bathroom she found it was indeed open, and Gail quickly locked the door behind herself. The smell was horrible, musty and foul. The bare bulb hung over a rusted mirror. It didn't throw off much light, giving the room a jaundiced feel.

Half dragging the big duffle to the sink, Gail took the pistol from her thin sweater pocket and laid it on the counter. Quickly, she opened the bag.

The room was freezing but she paid no attention to it at all.

Looking into the unzipped duffle, she saw many different garments, all wrapped in plastic and rolled tight. Finding some men's undergarments, she laid those on the counter and continued her search. Deep into the bag, she found the suit that she knew was there.

Trying not to think of the cold, Gail started stripping out of the house dress she had worn since the tragedy at the church. She had used the sweater to cover the blood on it, not sure if it was Joseph's or Matthew's blood.

She knew whose blood it wasn't. Sara had not bled on her, neither had Alexander.

Gail's mind flashed on Alex. Unbelievable!

Throwing the dress to the side, she unwrapped the suit. Joseph had packed them with dryer sheets, so, even though the clothes were deeply wrinkled and creased, they smelled fresh. Clothesline fresh, she thought, wryly.

As she repacked, Gail came across a bundled jogging suit that was marked xx-large. Placing it with the men's underclothes, she put her bloody dress on the top of the bag and shut it. It was best not to leave it behind, she thought.

Standing upright again, she looked into the old mirror; into her old face.

Her wavy fly-away hair was flying higher than usual, and she immediately started trying to smooth it. The mostly grey hair wanted no part of it and finally she decided just to wet it, comb it, and forget it. .

Her old face did not seem as old as before and Gail smiled dumbly at herself, showing perfect teeth that almost appeared to be dentures in their precision.

If people only knew... she grinned at herself for a second longer.

Joseph had known; her grin disappeared. Pulling on the suit, she was amazed that it fit so well.

The suit had been put in the trunk almost seven years before. A simple black suit, conservative and comfortable; she slipped it on. Considering her age, she figured she could still stop a clock in the suit.

Well, if not for the habit.

The nun's habit was light grey wool with a black headband. As soon as she doffed it, Gail was surprised at the sudden transformation from elderly housekeeper to middle aged nun.

She looked much younger, slimmer, and unquestionably holy.

Smiling again, Gail applied some eyeliner she found in the side pocket of the duffle bag, along with false beards, mustaches, glue, and full theater makeup kits.

Looking at herself, she decided that a little more couldn't hurt and so she removed a small fleshy lump from one of the boxes, gluing the small, fake mole to her jawline, just above her chin. Perfect, she thought.

For the first time in years, Gail remembered how much fun it was to play dress up. Except this was no game; the smile disappeared. Putting on some pinkish lip gloss, she completed her transformation.

Looking down at her long, knitted sweater, she decided it showed no blood stains, so she put it back on and slipped the pistol back into the pocket.

Outside, over the sound of the old Chevy's motor, she heard a diesel engine coming towards them.

For a moment, Gail froze, listening. Snatching up the bag and the bundles from the counter, she burst out the door, looking around. With one hand in her pocket, she waited a second longer to see a game warden's truck pulling into view. She took a deep gulp of air to calm herself, and she walked back to the car trying to seem caual.

Gail glanced in at Matthew, as she passed the window on her way to the rear of the car. At just a glance he seemed only to be a sleeping passenger.

The game warden was surprised that someone was here at this time of year. The nun stepped out of the bathroom with a duffle bag, and nodded a greeting. He noticed the out-of-state plates on the car. She had the trunk lid up and seeing the baggage in it , the warden figured that she was a traveler; probably just needed a restroom break.

Gail pushed the bag into the space, slammed the lid and got into the car.

As the truck passed the restrooms, slowly, the warden could see that she had put the car in reverse, leaving the campground.

Yep, just a potty break, he thought, driving on into the forest. In all these years, he had seen many things in these woods; although, he was sure that this was the first nun he had ever seen in the forest. In his mirror, he could see the car behind him, going the other way, back towards the highway.

Looking back at him through her own mirror, Gail breathed a sigh of relief. Matthew was still shaking behind her under his blanket.

Time to find a hole and crawl in it, Gail thought; she hoped it would be a deep hole.

***

January 12, 2.12 p.m.

Michael sat in Diana's living room. She knew he was angry, but he was always angry lately, even before his father died.

She gave him the bottle he asked for, knowing it wasn't a good idea. He was staring at her belly again. His dark eyes were little more than agitated slits as he stared at her expanding center, and she shivered inside.

Michael swigged the whiskey, straight from the bottle. Until the moment he walked through the door, his uncle Jerold had been calling on his cell phone incessantly.

Michael had been in a foul mood ever since he sat down; stomping the cell phone into oblivion first had not helped.

His only conversation with Diana had been a bombshell.

"My father's dead. I have to go to Massachusetts this afternoon. Go get me the Jack Daniels."

She had paused long enough to make him look up at her. Seeing her pause, he rolled his eyes slowly and sneered,

"Pleeeeaassse…?" He asked in mock politeness.

She brought him the whiskey.

Diana had known Alex, but did not like him. He was tall, handsome, wickedly rich, but still… Diana had loathed her lovers father.

It was the way he looked at me, Diana thought to herself.

That cold, dissecting stare from Alex , like she, and all women, were just so much meat had been withering to withstand. The memory of his eyes on her made her squirm inside her own skin.

Predatory; that was it. Funny she had never thought of that word until now. It fit him perfectly. Not like a wolf's passionate, volatile nature, but

61

more like a shark: a stone-cold killer.

Until Diana had met his father, Michael's dark underlying nature was somewhat charming. After that first meeting withs Alexander , she had noticed that Michael had some pretty scary ways, himself.

Michael had always been the perfect gentleman; even when upset he could still be charming and graceful. Even though he was moody, he had never been rude to her. Well, never, until…

Diana cupped her fast-growing belly, feeling exposed.

Michael stared at her new expansion, rather distractedly. Feeling terribly uncomfortable, Diana got up from her chair and walked to the huge marble fireplace.

Even turned away from him, she could still feel his eyes, looking at her belly with an emotion she could not pinpoint or describe.

Wiping off some imaginary dust from the immaculate slab of mantle, she tried to get him talking.

"Would you like to eat something before you leave?" She said it softly.

In the gilded mirror above the fireplace, she raised her eyes, and met his. Michael seemed to soften, or harden. It was difficult for her to tell which sometimes.

"No," he said rejecting the offer of food, his speech slurred already.

Diana was once again amazed that someone so large could not handle his whiskey. Within only two drinks, Michael's eyes had already began to get puffy and red as he continued to trace her belly under her long dress.

This was only the second time she had ever seen him drink. The first time had been when Diana told him about the baby. He had looked stricken, sick.

She had felt just awful about it, though she knew it wasn't about money. Michael had plenty of money, but if not, her father certainly did.

His reaction to impending fatherhood still confused and upset her.

Miccharel had broken down on the news, even crying, telling her for the first time that he loved her. She had loved him back, not understanding why he acted like it was a bad thing. She had reassured him everything would be fine as he sobbed like a baby.

He then got drunk off his first two drinks; Diana was still amazed at how little it took to get him slurring. This time was the same, as she watched him take a third drink, knowing it was too many.

Michael stood and walked over to her.

Diana turned to face him, unsure of what was coming. Putting his hands on her upper arms, Michael looked her in the eyes. He looked down on her, making her feel petite.

He was a full six feet, five inches tall. He was drunk and he couldn't seem to stand over her without swaying.

"Everything will be ok," he lied smoothly.

"I have to go with Jerold tonight to make arrangements for my father, and the firm."

Sometimes the lies actually tired Michael, but he continued, unable to say anything else but what would calm her. .

"When I get back, perhaps we can go away for a while, take one last trip before the baby is born."

She smiled up at him. He thought she looked stupid.

"I'd like that, Michael." She said it softly, hugging him.

"Well we have to figure out some way to spend my meager inheritance," he teased her.

Her smile got bigger, and his stomach fell into his belly with a thud

Diana gave him a sad smile, pulling him down so she could kiss him on the forehead.

Sincerely, she said, "I'm so sorry about your father, Michael. Will the funeral be in Massachusetts?"

He gripped her arms tighter, suddenly stiffening. Standing abruptly, he let go of her arms and grabbed her hands.

"I don't know," he said tersely.

He pulled her along with him towards the bedroom, suddenly wanting to explore her now pronounced belly.

"I have to leave in two hours; I don't want to think about it." He said.

She let him lead her, feeling better about his mood. While they made love, Michael tried hard not to think about the fact that she would be dead soon.

***

January 12, 2:34 p.m.

Abdullah watched Morgan from the shadows of the large open room.
A small smile of satisfaction played on his lips as she swirled around the

chamber, oblivious to everything but the music that echoed through the space at high volume..

Trying to stay hidden, Abdullah watched as she measured a step, a thrust, and then bounded around, swinging the slim sword expertly in a sharp parry, slicing through the air in a deadly ballet.

Morgan's face was pinched in concentration, her tall body lean and flexible as she bounded around, striking down invisible foes. A light sweat had formed on her skin, making the revealed flesh of her neck and shoulders gleam with a healthy glow.

She still took his breath away. Abdullah grimaced. If he wasn't careful, her real enemies would take his breath too; literally. He watched on, feeling not at all guilty about spying on her.

The rapier in Morgan's hand dipped, twirled, and sliced.

The loud sound of Prince blared from the small stereo she had set on the floor. Her timing was perfect; the dance took her in a wide sweeping pattern to the front of the structure, then back slightly, and to the front again.

He knew she was aware of his presence, but he hid anyway.

Morgan threw the sword to the floor. Now empty handed, the dance continued as she ducked, pivoted, and punched hard. Swooping down and around, her tight tank top was developing wet patches between her breasts and under her arms. The sweatpants she wore were rolled up at the ankles.

Abdullah thought she looked like a teenage cheerleader. He smiled again, catching the irony of that perception.

Morgan may look like a teen, he thought, but watching her jump and kick with a natural grace, he suddenly realized how old he was.God! How utterly depressing.

Abbdullah looked down at the sleeping baby in his arms.

Morgan left him breathless, stunned, and confused. Her baby had a totally different effect on the old cleric..

Just knowing about this child's existence was truly inspiring, but holding him, looking at his tiny mouth working in his sleep, Abdullah was in total awe. His old heart twisted, feeling the danger.

Trying to comfort himself, he smiled down at the baby. Under the music, he whispered to the tiny soul snuggled safely into the crook of his elbow.

"It'll be OK, little one. I love you both so much." Abby said softly.

He kissed the baby on his little cheek, almost wishing he would wake up just so Abdullah could explore his awe of the child.

Almost was right, he thought. After last night, he was glad the six day old baby slept peacefully. Abdullah turned his eyes back to the boy's mother.

Morgan was still in the midst of a concentration so intense it was surreal. Abdullah could feel the fierceness of her dance as she also tried to throw off the raw nerves of the disastrous day before.

When he had left with Sara, Morgan had finally been hopeful. When he came back alone, early this morning, he had seen the devastation hit her. After telling her that Sara was dead, Morgan had become upset, and then angry. If Morgan was angry, it could only mean one thing. He shuddered as he watched her maniacal workout.

Morgan had left the building at daybreak, though Abby had begged her not to. Using some of his housekeeper's traditional Muslim clothing , she had left the house, fully veiled, and trying to stoop so that her height seemed more average.

He had watched her go because he really had no choice but to stay with the boy until she returned.

The baby didn't seem to realize that his mother dreaded his very existence. For all the hope that the baby's existence signaled, Morgan knew that his birth would bring death to those she loved, maybe even to herself.

At this point, Abby knew Morgan felt that she could not protect the baby. That's why she had called Anna.

Abdullah shuddered again. He knew even now Anna would be making her way to them.

Before last night, he was sure he could protect Morgan and her child ; but now he was sure he couldn't. He looked at the baby to calm himself.

They were both helpless, he thought sadly.

The loud music faded away with the final shriek from the artist. In the quiet, Abby stared at the baby, begging for a sign, a way. He received neither. After a long moment, he realized that the music was finally finished, and after two hours of howling, Abdullah was grateful.

He glanced slowly toward Morgan.

She was squatted on the ground, holding the sword, wiping her forehead with a towel she had retrieved from the floor by the stereo. She sat that way for a long time. After drying her face, she wiped the swords handle lovingly. Concentrating her efforts around the hand protector, she rubbed the slender, silver steel design until it gleamed.

Gingerly, she wiped imaginary blood from the long blade. She shined it, examining it closely, then polishing it again. Abdullah felt helpless and angry as he watched her. She finally addressed him without looking back.

"You can quit hiding over there; I knew you were there as soon as you walked in."

She said it firmly, never taking her eyes from the sword.

Abdullah smiled.

"I was trying not to interrupt your practice," he replied.

"Did you see the news?" She asked, never looking up from the sword.

He sighed audibly and walked into the large, empty space with her.

"Yes. I saw the news."

He sat down at the front of the room holding the baby to him. Trying not to watch her, he studied the Moorish design on the ceiling above him instead.

"Have they found them yet?" she asked bluntly.

Getting up from her stooped position, Morgan walked to the stereo and laid the towel on top of it while palming the sword.

"No. They haven't found them. They found Joseph's car, though."

He tried to say it nonchalantly,

"There was blood in it. They think Matthew is hurt, but no one is saying how bad it might be…"

Morgan snapped her head around, looking at him finally. She seemed to be contemplating the situation in her analytical mind.

"Well, at least he's not dead yet, that we know of…" She let the thought stand, unfinished.

Turning abruptly, Morgan walked directly to Abby , still clutching the sword. Stopping over him silently, she stared at her new son for a long, thoughtful minute. He watched a thousand strange emotions touch her brow all at once as she stared at her tiny baby.

She dreaded asking Abdullah what she desperately needed to know. Looking at her child, she saw his father in him and she shuddered. She asked anyway.

"Are you absolutely sure that it was Alexander?"

Abby looked up at her lovingly; she ignored the emotion in his eyes.

"Yes, Morgan, I am sure. It was him. It's been many years…but he hadn't changed much. I saw him clearly at the market. " he sighed hard.

Abby remembered his own shock at seeing Alexander himself, after all this time.

"He saw me, too, but Sara had already gone toward the church. I thought I could lead him away… At least one of them did follow me for a while. I think it was James."

Now Abby was looking at the floor, trying to be sure. She kept her voice neutral, knowing he was hurting.

"Do you think Alex knew that Joseph was still alive?"

Abby shook his head slightly, hesitated, and then shrugged, still looking down at the baby.

Morgan touched Abby's temple lightly, her touch unnaturally warm on his skin. He looked up at her helplessly.

She tried to smile reassuringly, but only managed a grimace. They both felt helpless.

"I'm going to make something to eat, are you hungry?" she asked him softly, trying to calm him.

He shook his head; how could she possibly eat at a time like this? The thought almost made him chuckle.

"No, go ahead. I just want to sit here with him." He answered.

Abby looked at the tiny baby's face. Morgan's eyes followed his and she, too, watched her son, all the while feeling emotions she didn't like.

As she walked out of the open space into the rear of the structure, Abdullah called back to her.

"By the way, Morgan…does this boy have a name yet?"

Coming back to the doorway, she threw back her response

"How about…Boy?"

As Abby started laughing at her, she slammed the door between them and was gone. The cleric looked around his hushed, quiet mosque. He rocked the baby, knowing that when Anna arrived, Hell was going to follow.

***

January 12, 3:03 p.m.

Samuel was becoming ill again. He was already sick to his stomach and sitting in this little airless room with these nerds didn't make it any better. It was more than he could take.

67

The agents watched him. Frustrated.

The well-dressed one, Napoleon, or some crap like that, smiled at Samuel tightly. He was trying not to leap over the table at the bum and choke the life out of him.

Samuel could see his thoughts plainly and he decided he was going to puke on him first. He smiled at the agent, showing his rotted teeth. His guts were twisting, needing a fix. The thought of Joseph, his only friend, made his insides twist impossibly hard. He hugged himself, moaning, shaking.

The agents looked at each other. The one with a bad suit and mealy skin, Agent Webster, rolled his eyes at his partner. He was tired of this old drunk, and his even more disgusting attitude.

The younger agent in the nice suit , Napoliss, tried bribing him again.

"Would you like a cheeseburger, Samuel? A pizza, maybe?"

The old bum looked at him hatefully.

"No, I would not like a cheeseburger, a pizza, or anything else your dumb asses could come up with…unless it involves a joint and a bottle…?"

He looked back and forth between them as they refused to respond.

"I am a U.S. citizen, you can't keep me here! I have rights ya know! I didn't do anything!" Sam spat at them.

Napoliss leaned forward, trying to close his nose to the smell.

"We are all U.S. citizens here, Samuel. As a citizen, you have a duty to tell us what happened at Joseph's church." He sounded very matter-of-fact.

Samuel cried out in true frustration.

"That's not right! I already told you what happened. It's not my fault you don't believe me! Just 'cause I'm a drunk, don't mean I'm a liar!"

He had been in here for hours and hours already and Samuel was seriously getting sick. He had to leave. He was getting frantic now.

Napoliss again addressed the bum firmly,

"Now, Samuel, you admitted you were smoking crack right before this all happened."

He held up his hand as the bum started to object.

"Do you think maybe the crack made you see things differently, Samuel?" He tried to ask it lightly.

The answer surprised Napoliss , chilling him deeply

Samuel looked at the table, defeated. He said it slowly, clearly.

"Even on crack…I know the Devil when I see him."

The man hugged himself tighter, suddenly shivering again. The agents looked at each other, frowning hard.

Agent Webster got to his feet. Leaning down into Napoliss' ear, he whispered, and they both looked at Samuel. Napoliss decided it was their only chance.

"OK. Samuel, you win."

Napoliss also stood.

"Come on let's go…" He said it with an exaggerated sigh.

Looking at the agent suspiciously, Samuel asked him bluntly.

"Where are we going?"

'

"Let's go get a joint and a bottle. We're buying…" Napoliss began.

Samuel jumped up. Walking to the door quickly, he turned and said under his breath, 'Bout damn time!"

The two agents scrambled to catch up to him.

Chapter 4

January 12, 3:21 p.m.

Doug looked at the man across from himself in total disbelief.

Maria, sitting beside Doug in the captain's living room, showed no emotion either way, but she kept looking at her lover with a frown. . She knew how his mind worked. The captain sat with his wife at their dining table. They were also giving each other long, sideways glances, watching and listening to the man sitting in their recliner.

Doug wanted to sleep forever, wake up and forget what a nightmare life had suddenly become. He looked at the man, who was slumped in the chair. He had to be lying. And yet, Doug's gut told him there was no reason for this man to lie to them, so he asked the question he couldn't avoid.

"How badly was Matthew hurt when you put him in the car?"

The man started shaking his head, absently. He had been a medic in the Gulf war. Having assessed Matt very quickly, he, too, was worried about the young priest. Before the police had arrived, he had sat with Joseph until the old priest took one last painful, ragged breath. The memory of his friend dying in his arms sent a shudder through him.

Sitting up, he tried not to alarm Doug too much.

"He was in bad shape…Wound in his right chest punctured his lung. He lost a lot of blood… But, if she takes care of him, then he might be OK"

He hated using maybes and mights, but he couldn't avoid it. The stranger looked at Doug, who was looking hard at the floor. He knew he should have skipped choir practice. He sighed hard and continued.

"I can't tell you about the burn on his hand. Gail poured water on it, but, the flesh of his hand was literally burning."

The hand he had used to stab Alex.

Doug, elbows on knees, closed his eyes and rubbed his temples. As he spoke, he formed his words carefully; he didn't want to call the guy a flat-out liar.

"You do realize, what you have told us, flies not only against reason, but in the face of science itself?" Doug asked softly.

Maria looked at the choir director. She knew this man named Danny, and like Doug, she was a person of science, but Danny's story was seamless, and disturbing. It fit every piece of evidence she had seen at the church, although she dreaded the thought any of it was true.

Danny looked at Douglas almost pitifully. The choir director didn't really know this man, but he was close to Matthew. He looked to the captain.

The old cop was holding his wife's hand and staring through the window at some focal point that was beyond the bright afternoon. Looking back to Maria and Doug, Danny held his hands out in a gesture of confusion.

"I'm sorry," Danny said, as if it was personally his fault.

"I don't know what else to tell you except what I saw." He sighed heavily.

"When I first heard them run back into the church, I looked over the balcony. I only needed those glasses for reading; I'm getting old, I think."

Here, he looked at Doug straight on.

"I didn't know what I was seeing when they took the woman out of the confessional..." He stopped; confused again, he looked back at the floor.

"I'm sure Joseph knew her..." Danny said it pitifully.

They had all seen the news reports. It was all there; a sex scandal, a murdered woman in a priest's bed, a murdered priest, and last, but not least, a mysteriously burned unknown man. The networks didn't yet know the woman had burned, too.

Young, handsome priest, missing, possibly also murdered. Then there was the housekeeper, Gail, the only active witness, also missing with no presumptions on her fate.

Doug again thought of the comical reporters. The odd man in the alley suddenly flashed through his mind. Doug stood from his chair and started pacing. He asked again about the unknown dead man.

"Are you absolutely sure that the dead man was burning before he got to the sacrament candles?"

Doug paused his nervous walking, looking at the choir director.

"Yes." Danny swallowed hard, his throat suddenly constricted.

"His clothes were..."

He breathed out; exasperated and tired.

"His clothes were…charring…before he got to the confessional. Just before I lost sight of him, I definitely saw a flame, going up the back of his jacket. Right after that I heard the rack fall. He was in flames a full thirty feet before he got to the candles…"

Danny looked at Maria. She sat silently, staring at the coffee table. The room seemed too small to all of them.

The captain now asked, "Do you know if Gail also recognized this man?"

Danny looked at him a moment, his brow knitted. He considered it for another second, finally shaking his head.,

"I don't know. I'm just not sure."

The captain again, "But you're sure Joseph knew him?"

Danny started nodding his head.

"Joseph called him by name. He said that the man had already tried to kill him before…Alex…That's what he called him. Alex."

They all became quiet again, trying to think what this meant.

Doug asked, "Did Matt know this Alex, or the woman?"

Danny thought about that, too, before answering.

"I can't say…Matt seemed kind of confused. When he saw the guy…he just stopped. I couldn't see his face, but…" He let the thought drift off.

"But what?" Now, Maria pressed him.

"I saw the man's face very well. I think he knew I was there." Danny responded softly.

Again, silence filled the room.

"Why do you say that, that he knew you were there?" Maria asked him, pressing him gently.

Danny's forehead scrunched up as he thought about it.

"I don't know; I just had this…feeling…That he knew I was watching him from above."

They could all see the man shiver. Danny's entire body seemed to jerk in the chair.

The captain asked him, "What did this Alex look like?"

Finally, a question Danny could answer.

"He was huge, wearing a suit."

The captain's wife, June, quiet up till now, interrupted.

"Big how? As in fat or…"

"No." Danny shook his head. "He was tall, extremely tall, much taller than even Matthew. Skinny, but still very big…Blonde hair, blue eyes."

Doug's heart slammed into his ribcage. He stopped dead in his tracks.

"Oh my God!" Doug said to no one.

He held onto the wall, suddenly unsteady. Maria jumped off the sofa, going to him quickly. Danny and the captain looked at each other.

Putting a hand on Doug's s shoulder, Maria tried to reassure him.

"It's OK, we'll find Matt."

He shook away from her quickly.

"In the alley, as I drove up to the church, there was a man standing there. He was odd. You just described him perfectly! He was very tall, blonde, he just stood out. At the time, I didn't know, I just figured he was a reporter…"

Now Doug was pacing frantically.

They just looked at him, blankly. Doug became agitated. The captain looked back to Danny and ignored Doug's strange outburst.

"The woman in the confessional…have you seen her before…ever?" the captain asked Danny.

He was trying to find something, anything, that would put them on the right path.

Danny looked miserable.

"No…" He said it in a defeated tone.

Doug had stopped to listen to the answer. June got up from the table, disappearing quietly into the den.

The captain watched her go, and then said to Danny,

"What did the woman look like when they took her from the church?"

Danny sighed in relief at a question he could answer.

"I saw her too, pretty clearly, she was beautiful. She was covered in blood."

Maria and the captain raised their brows in unison at the description. Danny caught himself trying to explain.

"Her face…She was just stunning. She was definitely passed out…there was blood everywhere…I was shocked; I thought that I must be seeing things."

"Did this homeless man…" The captain looked at Danny. "He definitely saw you? I mean…he knew you were there?"

They all had a sinking feeling as Danny answered.

73

"Yes…Samuel saw me. At first, he seemed to be asleep, but as they ran by him with the woman, he sat up. After they had run out, Sam started looking around, and he looked right at me. He saw me looking at him from the balcony…After I helped Gail put Matt in the car, I looked for the woman, but then just went back to Joseph…I never thought to look in his bedroom…"

They all left that thought unfinished.

"Did Matt ever say anything about this man named Alex…" Doug ground out the words, "The one he…killed?"

Danny looked at him oddly and paused before answering.

"After Matt stabbed him the second time, he passed out…When we were putting him in the car, he started mumbling…"

Danny's tone shifted, became a whisper.

"Matthew was saying…'I killed them, I killed them!', but I don't think he was talking about last night…I think it had something to do with his parents. With your parents."

Doug knew instantly what Danny meant. His guts twisted, hard. The hatred towards his little brother exploded into…nothingness. God damn Matthew! God damn him to Hell, Doug thought for the one millionth time

The captain, unaware of Doug's reaction, asked Danny quietly searching. ,

"Why do you think he was talking about his parents?"

Danny, totally aware of Doug's reaction, said very softly,

"He was… um…telling his mother he was sorry…" Danny said evenly.

Doug moaned, low and mournful.

The silence settled into the room like an uninvited guest. Doug sat down on the closest chair, a recliner matching the other that Danny sat in. Doug put his hands over his face; he was sure the pain would kill him. After a moment, he hoped it would.

The captain crossed the room to him, kneeling in front of Doug and put one hand on each of the young man's shoulders.

"Douglas, look at me." His tone was compelling but comforting.

Without wanting to Doug looked Captain Edwards in the eye.

"You are my nephew, and I love you as a son. What happened to my brother and your mother almost killed me. The anger was too much…"

The captain's voice cracked, and Douglas locked eyes with him now, refusing to look away. The older man's face contorted, eyes watering, but

74

he held Doug's gaze, steeling himself.

"But you have to understand something , Douglas. Matthew died that day, too. It was only luck that we didn't lose him, too. He did what is rarely done with second chances; he turned his life around. He is as humble as he can be and not die of guilt. You have to remember, Matt lost them too."

Douglas turned his head away, unable to look at his uncle. Grinding his teeth, he blurted out a response.

"He lost them because he killed them!"

Silence hammered the room.

The captain, bowing his head, breathed deeply in sorrow. Standing, he stood silently above Douglas for a long moment.

"We all lost them, son."

He took a step back from his nephew.

June appeared in the doorway of the livingroom. Her kind, aging face twisted into a grimace.

"I think y'all should come and watch this."

Her voice was abnormally gloomy. They all stood, filing into the den in a group.

The artificial-looking woman on the news was talking about Father Joseph. As they came into the room, the scene switched to the local precinct, where, obviously, Agents Webster and Napoliss had been interviewing their star witness.

On the screen a, Napoliss smiled handsomely for the camera; his perfect suit was perfectly pressed. He sauntered to the microphones.

"In response to your questions," he paused for effect.

"Yes,wearenowconsideringone Father...Matthew...Miles...Daniels...As a suspect in the slayings that occurred in St. Mary's Cathedral last evening. He is considered armed and dangerous."

The captain blurted, "Bloody hell!" as their jaws collectively dropped.

The news continued.

"We are now also considering Gail Strappling as a person of interest whom we need to speak with. She may be a hostage, but we are not certain at this time."

Someone beat on the front door, in a burst of sound that startled them all. The captain, already standing, turned his head to inconspicuously check out the new presence on his porch.

"Oh shit!"

He twisted around and in a loud whisper he said, "It's the Feds!"

Danny looked around, feeling trapped.

The captain, used to snapping orders, started ushering them towards the kitchen.

"June, go answer it…Make them wait at the front door till you come get me! Just stall them!"

June, used to giving orders herself, nodded and turned back to the front door, chest out, eager to harass the ignorant Federal Agents she only knew from TV.

The rest of the group wound through the kitchen and down into the basement. Giving her husband the time to get everyone in place, June opened the door. She lost no time in taking the initiative by asking to see their IDs.

Downstairs, the captain herded them into the playroom. "Stay here," he commanded, as if they had anywhere else to go.

Running back up the stairs, Captain Edwards opened the basement door to hear his wife chastising the agents.

"Young man, are you honestly saying you're more worried about my nephew than I? You're the half-wits calling him a murderer and telling the world he's some kind of menace…"

The captain slowed his pace, smiling slightly at his beautiful, fiery wife. He had never regretted marrying a redhead. As he was coming through the den, he heard one of the half-wits try to respond.

"Ma'am, I just need to speak with your husband, please…I know you're both upset, but…"

He let the thought pass as the captain walked into the entry hall. June half turned, smiling lovingly at the husband she was so proud of.

"These nitwits were just asking for you, dear. Should I just slam the door in their faces, instead?"

The agents , now humbled, looked at each other, then at the captain.

The captain smiled a slow smile. Looking at his wife, he gently said, "Wait on that just a second; when I'm done with them, you can slam it as hard as you want to, baby."

The Feds looked at him, scowling, no longer humble.

Napoliss, tactfully kept his frustration in check, and asked, "May we come in? We need to talk…"

Looking at June, her husband asked her, "Darling, would you like for federal agents to come into the home I built for you?

Staring directly at Napoliss, she replied firmly.

"No, I just fumigated for pests, so the interior of my home may kill them, in a horrible, chemical way."

She smiled at the younger men , sweetly.

"Well, boys, there's your answer. Now, what in the hell are you harassing my wife about?"

Agent Webster, finding his voice, replied in pure frustration

"Enough of this bullshit, Edwards, where is the choir director?"

As a look of homicide crossed June's face, her husband stepped in front of her. Through clenched teeth, the captain started hissing.

"First off, I don't know any choir directors! Second of all, you are on MY front porch making demands. Third! ...and most important of all, if you continue to use words like that in front of my wife, I'll choke the breath out of you right here..."

The two men stared at each other, eye to eye, no more than three feet apart.

Napoliss, trying to diffuse the confrontation, kept his tone soft.
"Edwards...we have a witness who saw Matthew kill."
The captain shifted his deadly look to the perfectly manicured agent. Napoliss continued, his tone even softer.
"Your nephew's blood was in Joseph's car; we think he's been hurt...very badly."

The captain looked back to June, only she saw the fear in his eyes. She pushed her husband aside very gently, placing herself between him and the Feds. In a cutting voice, she addressed the well-dressed agent.

"Exactly how credible is this witness? From what I've been told, he's a crackhead."

The two agents looked guiltily at each other, both thinking about the liquor and weed they had pumped into the old bum. Putting up his hands in a gesture of surrender, Napoliss responded gently. ,

"That's why we must find this man, Danny Ulrich. He's the choir director, he was there..."

June snapped, "How can you be sure of that?"

Webster, now less confrontational, answered her.

"All of his things, including his glasses were in the balcony. We also

77

know that he touched Matthew after he was already bleeding… We believe that this man, Danny, was probably in the church the entire time…"

The couple stood for a long moment, looking at the Feds. June, suddenly becoming agitated, asked in a desperate voice. ,

"What makes you think we know where Matthew is?"

Napoliss, now agitated himself, responded without thinking.

"You helped Matthew before; we need to know where he is…"

At this, the captain pulled his wife aside, less than gently, almost jumping at Napoliss.

"Are you trying to accuse us of something?"

Before anyone could move, Captain Edwards started shouting into the man's face.

"If my nephew was hurt, possibly dying. Do you honestly think I would just bring him home and let him die on my couch?"

Napoliss stepped back, surprised by the man's sudden viciousness. Webster, too, retreated one step.

Webster told him in a sneering tone, "We just need to see this man, Danny; we're not accusing you of anything!"

He sounded like he was pouting.

"And I suppose when you find him, you'll be saying he's a murderer, too?" This from June, looking over her husband's shoulder.

"Truth is, you have no better idea of what happened last night than we do."

Now stepping back in front of her excited husband, she told them both. "For all we know, you already have Matthew in custody, and are here looking for a way to convict him!"

Now in a pitch, Webster addressed her directly.

"This man, the choir director, could lead us to Matthew and the housekeeper; but perhaps they don't want to be found because they have something to hide!"

The slap echoed though the cold bright afternoon. June used all of her tiny frame as leverage to strike the federal agent. She hit him so hard that his head snapped around, taking his upper body with it. Catching himself, he wobbled slightly; holding his face, he glared menacingly at the woman. In an instant, her husband stepped between them.

"The next time you come to my property, you better have a warrant!"

Pointing at Webster, he lowered his tone into a growl.

"If you ever approach my wife again, I'll make sure you both regret every day you have left!"

With that, he stepped back into the threshold of the doorway, pulling June with him back into the safety of the house.

The captain looked at his wife and he said, "OK, baby…now!"

Without further hesitation, June slammed the door so hard and fast she almost took off the hand of Napoliss, who was trying to reach outward. The windows embedded into the door rattled in the frame so hard the captain was sure he would have to replace some of them.

Still looking at the stunned Feds outside the door, the captain lowered his voice to a whisper. His wife waited for him to speak.

"Listen, baby! Shit! You just struck a federal agent…no, no…just listen…They may be desperate enough to arrest you, but they'll be trying to get info on Matt."

He glanced at the Feds, who were speaking softly to each other outside the door.

"Just remember what I taught you, and don't worry, they won't have you for long! I promise you…"

June nodded in response.

The Feds, watching them through the door, hesitated then knocked again lightly.

"Just remember…Danny, who?" Edwards sad.

June nodded again, smiling at him lovingly.

Opening the door once more , June thrust both arms out, holding them steady, waiting to be cuffed.

Napoliss seemed flustered and unsure while Webster, still holding his face, glared first at June and then her husband.

Napoliss, trying not to stutter, told the woman, "We don't have to cuff you, but you will have to come with us…"

June, her husband at her back, smiled at him brilliantly.

"Of course I will…"

Webster's pride was stinging as badly as his cheek as he turned around and stomped off the porch to the Fed-mobile parked at the curb. Napoliss, walking in front of June , opened the back door to the car in as cordial a manner as he could, considering the Captain was with her at every step.

As they approached the car, Captain Edwards, holding his wife's arm, stiffened as he saw the man standing on the corner of the block, about five houses down.

The captain immediately noticed that he was abnormally tall, thin and blonde. And, he thought, the man was staring straight at them.

June, feeling her husband's grip tighten, stopped just short of the door. She automatically turned and also saw the man, who was standing by the big tree on the corner. Before she could say anything, Napoliss also turned and followed their gaze.

"Who is that?" The agent asked offhandedly.

Napoliss saw the captain grimace before tearing his eyes away, turning them back to his wife.

Looking at June, Edwards told the agent casually, "Just one of my neighbors watching you arrest my wife."

Her eyes crinkled as he cupped her face and kissed her lightly on the forehead.

"I'll be there in just a bit, honey. Let me find Doug and we will both be there shortly." She smiled up at him then slipped quietly into the backseat.

As she did, he looked into the young agents face and sneered.

"I'm holding you personally responsible for this."

The agent stared back and slammed the car door in a fit of bravado.

"You think that just because Doug is a county judge, that somehow federal jurisdiction don't exist suddenly?" Napoliss smiled at him proudly.

"You're rolling with the big dogs now, Edwards!"

The captain smiled back at him sweetly.

"Arresting old ladies…you look more like 'bitch' dogs than big dogs." Edwards retorted.

Napoliss glared at him then turned into the passenger's side. Webster had already started the car.

Pulling away into the street, the captain kept his body turned towards the car, but looked at the man on the corner they were about to pass. As the car came to a stop at that corner, the blonde stranger waved casually at the captain, then he stepped into the street in front of the oncoming car. He walked to the opposite corner, seemingly at ease while Edwards studied him intenttly. As the car turned right, the man disappeared behind the corner house to the left.

From inside the car, June shuddered, as the man stepped ahead of them, and passed directly in front of the car. She didn't know what the hell was happening, but she knew that this man was not her neighbor. She wanted to panic; instead, she mouthed a silent prayer for her family and started loudly singing her very own rendition of "The Star Spangled Banner."

It was best not to speculate, she told herself, making sure to hit all the wrong notes.

After the car passed from sight, the captain started walking towards the corner. Coming to the big tree, he stood where the stranger had stood. He looked across the street, seeing only a few people down the long avenue, none of them tall. He turned, and suddenly headed back to his house in a dead run. Crashing into the doorway of his home, Edwards stopped short, listening.

Only silence. The hairs on the old cop's head were standing on end. He felt sick yet could not explain why. The house only responded to his abrupt return with an eerie quiet.

Opening the basement door, Edwards called down to his nephew. Doug, Maria, and Danny all appeared from the playroom and looked up at him silently. He motioned for them to stay quiet, and waved them up the stairs.

Doug looked around the kitchen while his uncle was making an intense search out through the kitchen windows. Doug felt totally paranoid in an instant and all of them started looking around, at each other, then around again, none of them certain what they were looking for.

"Where's Aunt June?" Doug whispered it, instinctively

Still looking out the back window, his uncle also whispered.

"She's been arrested for assaulting a federal agent."

Startled, Danny and Maria looked at each other. Doug snorted a muted chuckle while trying to see what his uncle was looking at.

Still whispering, Doug asked, "What are we looking for?"

His own eyes took in the detail of the empty back yard.

"And why are we whispering?"

Without looking at him, the captain said quietly, "Your tall blonde friend was just on the corner, watching us…"

Doug looked at him, now truly confused.

The old man broke away, going back towards the front of the house, peeping out of his windows.

The remaining three looked at each other, not sure what to do. Now in a total state of paranoia, they all started moving into the front of the house and peeping out windows as they went. The captain met them coming into the entry hall and started giving orders.

"Danny, go get in my car; lay down in the back. There's a bunch of blankets and stuff...Here, Maria." He handed her the keys. "Get it started. C'mon Doug, quit dawdling...!"

They all three turned back into the house. The garage door was on the wall opposite the basement door in the kitchen and the confused threesome immediately followed their orders..

Captain Edwards went to the front hall closet and took down a locked box. He had good instincts and they had served him well for over thirty years as a cop. He contemplated the end of his career. Once the Feds knew they had Danny, it was all going to hit the fan.

But, he thought, smiling, first they would have to hear June's rendition of 'Silent Night.' He giggled to himself even as he looked at the guns.

The box held four pistols. He grabbed up two of the 9mm and some ammo, shoving them down into his sweater jacket. On second thought, he also took his .38 service revolver. He looked longingly at the twelve gauge pump shotgun, leaning against the wall of the closet, and decided against it.

Good Lord, Edwards said to himself, hastily shutting the door.

He had no clue where he was going exactly, but wherever it was, he was not going to be caught unaware, as Matthew and Joseph must have been. The .38 had a roll cylinder, an old fashioned six shooter; he was loading it as he stepped into the garage.

When Maria, who was sitting in the driver's seat with the engine running, saw Captain Edwards come into the garage with the pistol, she automatically hit the device on the visor above her head to open the garage door behind her. She was mildly surprised that the sight of the gun made her feel better.

As the garage door started to climb, the captain put another bullet in the cylinder and walked quickly to the minivan. Feeling a little foolish, he jumped up into the passenger's seat, still fumbling with the gun.

Maria was backing out, even as he slammed the door.

Doug, sitting immediately behind Maria asked them about Danny, .

"Where are we going to stash him?"

Just as he spoke, the minivan slipped from the now lit garage and Doug instinctively glanced left.The blonde man, gun ready, stood at the corner of the house.

Doug jerked backwards just as the window beside him exploded.

Thousands of tiny shards of glass exploded between Doug and Maria; the left side of Doug's face stung like hell as the little chunks of safety glass cut into him from the shattered window.

Maria, too, had seen the man, just as he fired. A split second after the shot, she slammed on the gas pedal hard. The minivan shot backwards like a drunken sprinter, driveway unnoticed, and jumped the curb. Danny was screaming in the back under a pile of old blankets.

The captain had not seen it coming; he had snapped shut the cylinder of the .38 just as the window exploded and blew glass all over him, too. Instinctively ducking, Edwards looked around frantically as they bumped through his yard and out onto the pavement. Doug was holding his face and crouched low in the backseat.

The captain screamed at Maria, "Go! Go!"

Once he realized that he was not hit, Edwards pulled himself past Maria, stooping over his nephew; he thrust the gun out of the window and started firing at the man who was now crouched at the corner of his house.

The cold, still air of the afternoon was suddenly shattered by the squealing tires and gunshots. Another of the man's shots hit the roof of the van right above Maria, as he targeted her. Not thinking about it, suddenly sure there was a God, Maria jetted backwards up the street, trying to pull out of range.

The captain was now hanging halfway out the missing window, firing on his own home. At the street corner, Maria picked a direction; she turned left. She could see the man had left his crouch and was running across the yard, trying to keep them in range and duck the returning shots.

He went down hard on one knee in a jerk and rolled away from the captain's wild volley as the group pulled even further away from this deadly stranger.

Halfway down the next block, seemingly without stopping at all, Maria turned the van violently in the middle of the street. Danny was quiet under the blankets. Now going forward, the woman pushed the van for all it had, running stop signs until she was about six blocks away from the house.

The captain was pulling Doug back up onto the seat behind Maria; pulling at his hands, the old man breathed a sigh of relief, as he saw there were only cuts and scratches but no bullet holes.

"Danny?" The captain screamed in panic , letting go of Doug and crawling over the rear seat, hopelessly entangling his grandkid's hockey equipment.

Pulling back the musty blankets, the captain saw that the choir director was unharmed, but wide-eyed with shock. Relieved, Edwards looked back at Maria, just as she screeched to the right into a strip mall parking lot.

Before going to the captain's house, they all had met June here, leaving their three cars in the otherwise abandoned parking lot.

Pulling up by her own little Nissan, Maria slammed the van into the next parking space and cut off the engine as she put it in park. She virtually jumped over the seat to Doug, who was cupping the left side of his face. She tried to pull his hand away, but he pushed her instead towards the slide door on the side of the van. She saw the captain pulling Danny from his blankets and out through the back door.

Fishing her keys from her jeans pocket, Doug waited impatiently as Maria unlocked the driver's door of her car.

All of the locks popped together, and the shocked foursome piled into the little car. Two of them were bleeding. Maria glanced at Edwards. His eyelid was cut rather badly above the left eye. She pulled out into the quiet street and tried to still her heartbeat, trying to keep calm, but her heart was about to explode.

Danny asked what they were all thinking.

"What in the fuck was that about!"

He was shouting; he gulped a few times, hard, trying not to panic, but looking around in all directions as Maria drove further north. Danny tried speaking again with more calm than he felt.

"Who, in God's name, was shooting at us?"

The other three stayed silent again, thinking.

Danny started pulling at Captain Edwards head, exclaiming, "Oh, Jesus! Your eye…"

The old man pushed him away.

Maria, with a calm she did not feel, gave Danny instructions. ,

"My bag is on the floor, under you; there's bandages and gauze."

Danny automatically reached down, suddenly back on the battlefield, familiar with the medical bag. Even though he had been in war before, that had been the first time he had ever been directly fired on, and he didn't even know who was shooting.

The captain also leaned forward, holding on to Doug's shoulder.

He asked his nephew , "Was that your friend from the alley?"

Edwards eye was swelling fast. Danny pulled at him again; this time he tried not to resist as the man started cleaning the cut to his eyelid.

From the front, Doug answered from behind his own hands.

"Never seen that bastard before, but…"

"But WHAT?" Maria almost screamed it, trying to control her voice and drive.

Doug hesitated,

"Well…he uhh…he wasn't the one in the alley, but…ummm…He looked almost identical. Ugh…different, but the same. Not the same guy, but, like his twin."

The odd answer made them all widen their eyes just to make sure they were hearing properly.

They all became silent, until Danny caused a burst of cursing from the captain by pulling a shard of glass from his cheekbone.

Maria glanced at Doug to see if there was any major damage from the broken glass, but except for a couple of cuts on his cheek, most of it was scratches. She deliberately breathed deeply, calming herself.

She was switching streets every three blocks, staying on a steady north and west direction. Seeing an open fast food place, Maria pulled into the parking lot and drove to the far corner. She parked in the last spot at the back, behind the restaurant. Leaving the engine running, they all sat in sudden stillness, the captain holding a gauze pad to his left eye.

Turning in her seat, she looked at Edwards and asked him with real dread.

"What now?"

Before the older man could answer, Doug responded, instead.

"Go to St. Mary's. Go back to the church."

They all looked at Douglas , startled at that suggestion. After a long second, the captain started absently nodding his head.

Maria thought they had both lost their minds.

"WHY?" she snapped.

"Because we can't go anywhere else…And besides…we still don't know who is shooting at us…" Doug said flatly.

Danny was now fussing over Dougs face, using sterile water to wipe the blood off his cheek and chin.

Maria sat very still for a moment, thinking about their options. She decided he was right; at this point, there was nowhere else they could go.

The church would be swarming with armed federal agents, and she was surprised she found comfort in the idea. Whomever was shooting at them surely could not attack them there.

Pulling the car back out of the space, Maria silently navigated back onto the street and started driving back to the south, to St. Marys.

Doug stayed silent. The unexpected violence felt very surreal and seemed to drift further away from reality by the minute. He was physically and mentally exhausted. He held the gauze to his face as he watched the houses and businesses go by in a blur.

Doug thought of Matthew. My God, he wondered, what was all this about? The familiar anger he usually felt towards his brother was forgotten; he knew Matthew was in serious trouble. This time, it didn't seem to be of Matthew's own making. He couldn't see how Joseph could have brought such horror on to them, either. With a start, Doug blurted at Danny.

"You said you were sure Joseph knew that woman…What makes you so sure?"

Danny, who had also been silently staring out the window, did not move as he responded.

"Well…While he was carrying her from the church, I could see he was crying…It was kind of weird."

They all smiled as one, thinking about the definition of weird. If you looked it up in the dictionary, it would probably have a picture of today beside it.

"I'm pretty sure that when he first pulled her out of the confessional, she said his name. Not 'Father'…just 'Joseph'…"

The captain spoke up, confused.

"I thought you said she was passed out?"

"She was passed out, mostly, when they ran back out, but, I'd bet my life that she was speaking to them while she was still in the confessional."

Danny thought a moment, frowning at the passing view..

"No…" he corrected himself.

"I'm pretty sure she was talking to Joseph…Matthew was standing back, kinda in shock. But I know she was speaking to them in the confessional, Joseph was speaking to her.…"

Maria, her eyes on the road, absently remarked what they were all thinking.

"That musta been one hell of a confession."

They all looked at her quickly; no one responded.

Nearer to St. Mary's, Maria drove in a circular route, approaching like a predator, closing in slowly. About three blocks away, Doug suddenly pointed to a small alley and said, "Turn there."

Following the alley, she drove along it another two blocks before stopping in a parking lot behind some small, neighborhood shops.

Doug pointed to where the alley squeezed between two brick buildings and ended, suddenly, at the street in front of them.

"He was standing right there." Doug said.

He pointed to the building on the right, and they all followed his direction. Maria and the captain both saw the marks at the same time. In a horizontal direction, about five foot up, small streaks, and then larger ones were charred into the brick of the building.

Danny, leaning up, could see the small handprint at the front corner of the building, close to the street. He blinked at it, not understanding.

Small burned patches on the pavement, below the streaks, could have been mistaken for common potholes. But they had seen this particular pattern before; inside the church.

Maria put the car in drive again, and pulled slowly in-between the buildings. They all looked at the streaks, and as the alley opened up into the street, she stopped the car completely.

They all looked in silent amazement at the handprint. A human hand, burned into the brick and mortar of the wall so perfectly, only a human hand could have made it.

Doug's mind told him that it was, impossibly, undoubtedly made from a human hand even as he knew it could not be. The small handprint that was burned into a wall held them all enthralled. The each tried to imagine the struggle that could have resulted in such an impossibility.

Maria, thinking about what was left of the woman on Joseph's bed, felt a tremendous sense of sadness. She was certain the print was a woman's, and for a moment considered that the unknown female must have approached the church from this very spot.

Unexpectedly, from the back seat, Danny exclaimed, "Holy crap!"

They all turned to him in unison, thinking the shock of the burned handprint had rattled the man. Danny, however, was not looking at the print but at the sidewalk in front of the car.

They all followed his gaze.

A woman stood casually against the front of the left building, seemingly oblivious to them. She was breathtakingly beautiful.

Her long black hair was loose in the frozen breeze. Her olive complexion was ruddy from the cold wind that had kissed her cheeks and left a pink glow. Standing in the afternoon sun less than 15 feet from the handprint, her long coat seemed too thin for the temperature.

She was calmly staring down the street to the church, which was clearly visible to their right.

The woman was also every bit of six foot tall, and as lean as a greyhound. Even though she was not looking at them, they all had the distinct impression that she knew they were there. They could feel her presence sense them, even as she stared past them.

Feeling their stares, the stranger finally looked directly at the car and acknowledged their existence. Her blue-black hair fell in breezy wisps around her face.

"That's her!" Danny shouted, excited.

"No!" He caught himself.

"She looks just like the woman at the church!"

They all registered it with renewed scrutiny of this gorgeous woman in a coat so thin that it could not possibly be keeping her warm. None of them knew what to do with the odd accusation.

The woman looked into the car for a moment, then abruptly turned and walked back to the left out of their sight.

Maria, hesitating only a moment, pulled out to the very end of the alley. The woman was walking away from them now at a fast pace, already almost to the stop sign at the next corner.

When the car slid out of the alley and out onto the street, they all instinctively looked to the right, back to the church. It was literally swarming with reporters and official vehicles.

Maria drove away from the church, following the woman; keeping her eyes glued to her every move. The woman kept walking and turned left; so did Maria.

The dark haired stranger knew they were following her; she glanced back at the slow rolling car occasionally, with no sign of fear. Maria paced her, for an entire block. At the next corner the woman turned left again. Maria followed her, thinking to herself that they were going around in circles.Halfway through the block, the woman turned left, yet again, back into the alley they had all just left.

Maria also turned into the privacy of the alley and sped up to pull slightly past her. She slammed onto the brakes and threw the car into park. Before the car was stopped, Doug and the captain were opening their doors and moving to block the woman's path. She stopped walking, but she did not speak, only looked at them with a curious smile. Danny watched from the back seat and made no attempt to get out.

Doug took a couple of steps toward her but stopped as her expression changed and became menacing. She deliberately, and slowly, took two steps backward, her eyes never leaving Doug's face. The captain, now virtually shoulder to shoulder with his nephew, watched her expression shift, and immediately tried diplomacy.

"Can we speak to you a moment, please?" Edwards asked her.

The woman, hands deep in her pockets, smiled again but didn't move or speak.

Doug blurted, "Do you know the woman who was killed here last night?"

The woman's smile froze, and a mask of hatred creased her beautiful face. Her black hair fell across her nose and pink cheeks on the persistent breeze.

She said nothing. She looked at all of them, taking her time. Measuring us, Doug thought.

Maria, from over the car roof, asked her, "Do you know Matthew?"

The woman's attention snapped back to Maria as she finally spoke.

"I've known several Matthews..." Her voice was warm and low pitched.

Doug became agitated, taking one more step towards her, he stopped as she matched his step, going backwards. He stopped and blinked hard at her measured retreat.

Now angry, he almost growled at her.

"Matthew is the priest who's missing from that church; he's also my brother, lady. If you know where he is, you had better—"

"Better what?" She said it viciously, surprising them again.

Her slender body seemed to tense oddly.

"I had better what?" she repeated her question, showing perfect white teeth.

The captain, laying his hand on Doug's shoulder, pulled him back. His

89

eye was almost swollen shut but he could see well enough that Doug was only continuing to make the stranger defensive.

With his one good eye, Captain Edwards locked gazes with the stranger, asking her bluntly.

"What happened to Joseph? If you know, please…we need help. Matthew has been hurt badly!"

The woman's face became thoughtful, almost serene with sadness as the kaleidoscope of her emotions played out once again across her even features.

She looked back to Doug and asked flatly , "He's your brother?"

Doug knew in his gut that she already knew it to be true. Without waiting for confirmation, she questioned him further.

"Do you trust your brother?"

Doug looked at her for a long moment, confused, unsure of his own feelings. Turning his eyes away from her, he looked at the ground, not certain how to respond. ,

"I do love him. I just need to find him, he's been hurt…" He sounded like he was pleading.

She smiled at Douglas, the way a mother smiles at a confounded child.

"That's not what I asked you…" She scoffed lightly, amused.

They all looked to her, unable to say anything, or even look away. The woman nodded towards Danny in the backseat, staring at her, mesmerized.

"Who is he?"

The captain, holding his one good eye steady, responded.

"He's someone who saw something he doesn't understand."

At that, she burst into a short, loud laugh. Captain Edwards tried to get to the point.

"He says you look like a woman he saw at the church last night…A woman who is dead now…"

Her face changed again suddenly to something beyond emotion.

She looked back at Danny through the window, and started walking toward the car. Going around the captain and Doug, she went to the open back door of the car, stooped, and looked inside at a squirming Danny.

Doug was totally aware that she still watched him, too, every second.

"You saw a woman who looked like me?" She asked it softly, calming Danny with her voice. .

"Well…" Danny started, unsure of himself.

She smiled, slowly dipping her head to show that she was listening.

"Yes…Not exactly, but close. You look the same."

He looked at the Captain and Doug for help. They looked at him blankly.

"How do you mean, 'Not exactly'..?" She asked Danny, needing confirmation of it.

Her voice pulled at him, her face stunning, mesmerized them all..

"Her hair was different than yours…a different color…like a reddish brown…She was older than you, I think…But other than that…" He let the thought drift.

"Other than that…? We could have been twins?" She asked.

Her brow furrowed, waiting.

"Yes! Exactly!" Danny sighed his relief, not knowing how to explain what he could not understand himself.

Her smile returned, but it was a sad, thoughtful smile.

In a very soft tone, she asked, "Where was she when you saw her last?"

Hesitating, Danny said, "The priest, Father Joseph, was carrying her from the church."

Her brows knitted.

"Do you know if she, the woman that looked like me, she spoke to Joseph? Or to Gail?"

Her question surprised them all. She held her gaze on Danny. He looked around, unsure again. They all thought of the old housekeeper Gail, wondering how she could factor into any of this.

Doug spoke from behind her, "Look, lady, who are you?"

She turned on her heel, looking up at him from her crouched position. Finally, she stood, able to look Doug in the eye.

"Since you don't already know, is the only reason I will tell you. "

Her eyes narrowed at Doug again, and she spoke to him through clenched teeth,

"I also have family missing right now…and that woman that died in the church last night …she was my mother."

All of them stood in confused silence, not wanting to know, yet not able to keep the knowledge from changing them. .

Offhandedly, the stranger asked the captain, "What happened to your face?"

Coming around the front of the car, Maria answered her sharply.

"Someone is following us! He just tried to kill us less than an hour ago!"

Now the stranger's face showed surprise. She looked at Maria, knowing these people were already in deep trouble.

Finally, she looked at Doug again. She reexamined the cuts on his face as she spoke. .

"You are all in terrible danger…" She said it slowly, clearly.

"No shit, lady! Haven't you got a clue?" Doug could not contain his frustration now.

Her eyes narrowed to slits, but, just as she opened her mouth to respond to him, a pained look came across her face that seemed to take even her by surprise.

A burning sensation hit her thighs unexpectedly, making her knees lock. Her eyes, once clear and steady, suddenly clouded and rolled back into her head. The fever flushed upwards through her, and she swayed, unsteady, as a searing heat pushed up her thighs, searinginto her belly.

Doug, standing face to face with her, stepped back at first. He wasn't sure what was happening, but he grabbed to hold her up when she started to give way.

The contact sent a ripple of electricity up his arms and into his shoulders the moment he touched her. Through the thin coat, he could feel an immense heat rolling off of her. As she started falling, she grasped at him, trying to hold herself up.

She gasped and shook violently as he gripped her hard.

"Go, get out of here!" she hissed at him.

She let go completely and Doug literally fell with her, into the backseat of the car.

Maria started running to the driver's door as soon as she heard the words. The woman's statement carried such conviction that she didn't even think about it, she just acted.

From inside the car, Danny tried to help Douglas pull the woman further in, as the captain was trying to push them from behind. Edwards was trying frantically to get the door shut behind them. Finally, with the three bunched in a strange heap in the back seat, he slammed the door and jumped into the front seat. Maria already had the car rolling as the captain encouraged her to go faster.

Doug and Danny had tried to untangle themselves from the woman.

Her eyes were closed, and her breathing was labored. The interior of the car had been cold, but it was heating up rapidly as waves of mist literally formed above her skin and rolled across it in wisps.

The familiar fever hit the woman like a hammer. The sensation traveled up her ribcage, then her breasts, pulling painfully at her nipples. The intense heat inside her body seemed to close off her throat; and she actually quit breathing for a long moment.

Maria, almost in a panic, kept the car steady, looking around in a state of paranoia. What the hell? She could feel her own backside warming quickly as the woman's legs slumped against the drivers seat.

In the back seat, the woman suddenly started breathing again in a heaving gasp. The windows of the car started fogging, as strange, humid warmth filled the interior.

Seemingly breathing easier, the woman opened her eyes.

Breathlessly, she very clearly said, "Oh shit!" and started forcing herself from her slumped position. As they got to the rear of the store building, where the handprint had confounded them earlier, Maria sped up, just as the woman behind her gasped.

"WRONG WAY!"

Too late.

The shooter from the house stepped into the middle of the alley, blocking their passage.

They were already between the two buildings before Maria saw him step out some 75 feet in front of them. He was staggering badly, holding himself up with the wall. He placed his hand almost directly over the charred handprint just as Maria slammed into reverse.

With his free hand, the big man held up a pistol just as they squealed backwards. Maria skidded away from him and turned left backwards into the small parking area behind the building, just as a shot rang out.

Slamming forward now, knowing they still were not safe, Maria drove into the alley, trying to pull away from the armed stranger before he could recover from his odd stagger

As she pulled past the building and into the ally, another shot rang out. Maria could hear the *pop* of the window behind her as the bullet pierced it, but did not shatter it.

Not bothering to look back, Maria floored it. Roaring recklessly down the alley, she skidded into the street. She took the first right, then left, then right again into another access alley.

She fought the wheel, while Captain Edwards climbed toward the backseat. Leaning over them , he was trying to pull Danny's hands from his throat. Maria slammed on the brakes, put it in park, and turned to help.

Doug had his back against the door and he looked almost catatonic as Maria and Captain Edwards reach for them all from the front seats. They both stopped short, their eyes following his.. He was staring at the woman; at Danny.

The woman had pushed away the captain's hands and placed her own hand over Danny's, the one holding his thoat.

Danny was looking into the woman's eyes, and she was smiling at him, that sad, terrible smile. Holding the left side of his neck and throat, Danny seemed to smile back at her as his body slumped over and against his own door.

His eyes clouded and his hands slid from beneath hers. The bullet wound to his neck suddenly released a torrent of blood directly into her hands.

The woman, her face twisted in horror and regret, held the wound tightly, trying to reverse the flow with sheer will. She let Danny's shoulders slump against her and she held him as his body shuddered, one last time.

Doug had been in CSI before his parents died. He had met Maria there, a fresh intern who preferred dead patients to live ones. The captain had been a cop all of his adult life, he had started on the streets. All of them knew that there was nothing they could do to save Danny. The woman stared straight ahead. Holding Danny tightly, she seemed to be cradling him by the throat. Oblivious to the blood, she swallowed hard, blinking rapidly at the tears that filled her eyes.

Maria turned back around, looking blankly through the windshield. Edwards also turned and sat hard back into his own seat.

From behind her, the woman said softly, "His heart has stopped…It's over…"

All of them looked straight ahead, not wanting to look at the carnage. They heard sirens blaring in the distance, but coming closer. Maria put the car back into drive and left the alley, moving steadily away from the church and the oncoming sirens.

They drove in complete silence for a long time. No one dared to speak. As they neared the interstate, the woman finally spoke and told Maria to take the onramp headed south.

Angry, confused and horrified beyond belief, Maria demanded answers instead. ,

"Why? Why would I do that? What in the fuck is going on? Who in the hell was that? And who in the hell are you?" Maria spat at her in the rearview mirror.

Sounding tired, the woman only continued instruction.

"We have to go to Boston…"

All of them started shaking their heads, but before anyone could say anything else, Maria yelled at her, locking eyes with her in the mirror.

"What? Boston? Are you crazy? We have to find Matthew!"

Turning her eyes back to the road, Maria's voice became a growl.

"Lady. Why don't I just pull this car over instead and beat the shit out of you?"

Doug looked back and forth between the two women and saw the stranger smile at the threat, slightly.

She was still cradling Danny's lifeless body as she responded in a soft voice.

"Because trying to beat my ass would be the death of you all…And if my mother was able to get to Joseph…or Gail, in time, we should find them in Boston."

The silence in the car was deafening.

Doug studied the woman and she paid him no attention. She seemed to be staring at something in the passing view that he couldn't see. Finally, she looked down at the dead man in her lap. Doug saw the quivering of her full lips. With a deep sigh, she looked at Douglas across the back seat and answered the question before he could speak it.

" Quit calling me 'Lady'…My name is Anna."

Coming to the interstate on-ramp, Maria took the south turn without hesitation.

Chapter 5

January 12, 10:21 p.m.

In the dream, Matthew was drunk again, but he really didn't care. His mother, sitting beside him, was tense. Fidgeting in her seat, she asked him once more to let her have control. ,

"Please, son, let me drive?"

Like all drunks, Matt knew he was past his limit; so, he became agitated with her.

"Why can't you just enjoy the ride, mom?"

Damn it! She was killing his buzz.

"Just once, can't you enjoy being with me?" he asked petulantly.

Matthew took the turn at a reckless rate of speed, almost enjoying her terror.

"I just wanted to have a good time and not hear this crap from you!" Matthew spat at her.

From the backseat of the shiny new car, his father mumbled drunkenly, incoherently. His mom gripped the armrest tightly, clenching her teeth at the thought of the next turn. Matthew had wanted his new car to make an impression; and that, it surely was doing.

She felt sick as Matthew accelerated. She knew her seventeen year old son had been selling drugs to his friends. Young Matthew was 'Mr. Money' now, and he figured the sports car would bridge the gap between them. She was a Christian woman, and she had indulged him for a long time, but this was getting stupid.

"Son, please! Slow down just a bit!"

Matthew only growled drunkenly in response as he rolled his already unsteady eyes.

Dinner had been a disaster; both her husband and son had taken one more opportunity to get wasted.

Matthew was getting totally annoyed now. He looked at his mother out of the corner of his eye. He had just bought the car that afternoon, paid in cash, and the old gal just had to take all the fun out of it; she took the fun out of everything else. Matthew was so angry at her in that moment.

Just once, you would think, she'd let up on the responsibility crap. Well, he was taking care of himself pretty well now, and if she didn't like the way he was doing it, she could kiss his ass.

"Stop it, Ma! I'm driving this car! Why can't you just relax?" he hissed.

The turn was coming fast but he wasn't worried. His pretty new toy handled beautifully.

In a dream state, he saw the lights coming, but didn't panic. He was turning left. The oncoming car appeared to be far off.

The slow motion of his turn seemed odd to his impaired mind; his mother's scream was in unison with the squealing tires. In his drunken euphoria, the sounds merged into one and the impact was inevitable; he knew it now…Too late…

The full-size van hit the new little auto dead square in the passenger's door at 65 mph. Matthew felt himself pushed hard against his door. He was barely aware that the car was tipping and rolling. The sound of tearing metal pierced the fog, as he felt the slam of the roll. Then another. He lost consciousness after the third roll.

The screaming had stopped long ago, strangled off by ripping metal, and leaving only the sound of the crash.

From the bed where he was lying, Matthew tried to scream himself awake, but it came out as a terrible moan.

Gail's face floated above him, pinched with worry. The rough texture of the wet washcloth on his face almost brought him to the surface. He was vaguely aware that he was in an unfamiliar room, and he felt the awful pain in his chest.

Matthew heard himself say "Mama!" as he drifted back into his nightmare.

The face above his, now, was Jason's. The young rookie cop was trying to hold Matthew up. He was confused, not sure how he had gotten to his feet. The police lights were making a bizarre strobe effect in the warm night, making him dizzy. What was Jason saying? He tried to focus. Both of his arms hurt like they had been torn off.

"Matthew…come on, man…sit down." Jason had told him.

The smaller man tried to hold Matt down but was unsuccessful. "The ambulance will be here soon, Matt ...sit down. It's ok..." Jason pleaded with him.

Gail watched as Matthew screamed in horror, unable to pull himself from the dream. She flinched hard at the sound, knowing exactly what haunted him.

Matthew fought against Jason, now even more confused. The terrible truth came to him, slowly.

He literally pushed the young cop on his rear end, both arms seeming to squish oddly as he did. He looked at his new car. Matt didn't realize he was screaming. Still drunk, and now in shock, he tried to stagger towards it. Jason came up off the pavement. The young cop saw more police lights in the distance and decided there was only one thing he could do.

Lifting himself from where Matt had shoved him, Jason tackled the huge young wounded man, finally bringing him to the pavement.

Matthew never stopped screaming.

Trying hard to hold him down, Jason was hoping the approaching cruiser would hurry up. Both of Matt's arms had been shattered, but he was still more than a match for the smaller man, especially now that he was in a panic.

"STOP IT!" Jason shouted as Matt grappled with him while desperately trying to crawl to the ruined car.

"Mama!..."

The shrieking scream broke into a sob. All of Matthew's strength left him.

"Jay! Let me go! ...I have to...I have to...Oh, my God!"

Virtually sitting on Matthew's back, Jason gripped his shoulders, telling him softly as possible.

"Matthew, stop! There's no one alive in that car... I'm so sorry."

Matthew collapsed, scraping his face against the grit of the pavement. His screams seemed hollow to him, but he could not stop the sound.

Another officer ran to them, helping Jason, trying to keep the broken man from floundering like a landed fish. Matthew started beating his head against the pavement. They held him. He screamed. He sobbed. He cursed God.

Finally, mercifully, a fast blow to the pavement with his face and everything went dark.

Matthew opened his eyes and tried to push himself off the bed. His sudden movement startled Gail, whom was sitting in a chair beside him with her hands over her ears. He was gasping; his old regret and newly punctured lung felt the same. Searing pain from the stab wound and tortured memories making him cry out, weakly, he tried to sit up.

Gail pushed him back into the mattress without much resistance.

"Matthew? Are you awake now? …" she asked quietly.

She was wiping his face again. He nodded awkwardly while trying to open his eyes properly.

"Shhhh now, its ok…just stay still…" Gail cooed at hm.

She looked on as the man's face contorted into a mask of horror, pain, and sadness.

" Matt? Can you hear me?"

He moaned loudly, nodded his head in a jerking motion. He was thirsty; his throat felt like it was on fire.

As Gail passed the wet cloth close to his mouth, he instinctively tried to pull at it with his lips, needing the moisture. She let him have it, a little at a time, and then pulled the cloth back. She held it to his dried, cracked lips. He tried to suckle at it again, but she pulled it away.

After a few moments, she pushed a straw between his teeth. He drank at the apple juice clumsily, biting at the straw. His body was limp, useless.

Gail pulled the straw away from his mouth, wiping his cheek again with the washcloth. She looked different to him, as Matt tried to focus, blinking hard at her almost familiar face.

His voice cracked as he asked, "Where's Joseph?"

Since Matthew had walked up on Alex from behind, he had not seen the dagger that the man had pushed into Father Joseph. .

Gail bit her trembling lip, blinking back the tears. She forced a tiny blue pill into his mouth. As soon as it hit his tongue, he could feel it dissolve quickly, the taste terribly bitter. She pushed the straw back between his lips; he pulled at it desperately, greedy for the liquid. In less than a minute, his eyes were rolled back again, his mouth going slack, but still trying to work.

His breathing became easier, and so did hers when his rattling decreased.

Gail had no idea where Joseph had gotten the little blue morphine pills that she had found in the rather well-stocked first aid kit. She had known the book on battlefield triage and surgical tactics was there, but she had still been surprised when she found the little manila envelope, clearly marked, full of the little blue tablets.

She smiled, sadly, thinking of Joseph's resourcefulness. Probably traded them with some crackhead who needed money and couldn't read that they were morphine. She thought that it was just like Joseph, always thinking ahead, bartering with some junkie for them. He was a sweet, good man, she thought, but wickedly cunning. Both she and Sara had loved him for it.

Gail prayed for mercy. She thought of all the fencing and boxing lessons Joseph had goaded Matthew into, in the name of exercise. It had never seriously occurred to either Joseph or Gail, that Matthew would ever be chosen, much less wounded so badly he had no chance of utilizing such skills.

She watched as Matthew fell deeper into his drugged sleep.

Gail had come to love him, too, through the years. . She had been in Matthew's life for almost the entire length of it. When he was younger, she was sure that he would wind up dead in a gutter.

Well, she thought, that was before… The image of her dear friend, Matthew's mother, flashed through her mind. She suddenly felt very old. The years at St. Mary's had definitely broken her heart many times, and her soul.

It was obvious to her now, that Joseph and Sara had been in contact this entire time. That Sara knew where to seek Joseph out in her final moments could only mean that.

Gail started grinding her teeth at the thought. Not able to avoid it, the old questions came rushing back, as did the familiar rage that went with it.

Sitting back from the bed where she had knelt beside Matt, Gail wrapped her arms around her knees, drawing up into a tight ball. It was almost as if she was trying to physically hold in her soul.

The day's losses crushed her spirit, and Gail suddenly felt very alone for the first time in almost 70 years.

Sara Katherine, Gail's own mother, had given her life to protect the boy. It seemed so unbelievable to her.

That Gail was now an orphan, was only slowly sinking into her numbed flesh.

Gail put her head down on her knees and allowed the pain to come to the surface. She melted with hot, bitter tears and grieved for her mother. She wanted to scream. She wanted to, but didn't, knowing it was futile.

How many times had she already screamed at God? It never really worked. Gail could not remember God being in the room where she had found her mother, bursting into flames.

Clenching her fists, digging her knuckles into her temples, Gail forced herself to not cry. However the energy of the silent scream could not be stopped, and she fell sideways; catching herself on one elbow. She fully collapsed into the horror of this day.

She balled her fist and started to punch the floor, needing to release the rage and fear. Striking hard and fast, Gail pounded against the uncaring floor, until a sharp pain ran up her hand as she dislocated the knuckle on her ring finger.

The pain forced her to jump straight back, curled up and cupping her wounded hand, and sobbing now with little gasps of agony.

'Ohh, God!' she thought. 'Why don't you just let me die?'

Even as she thought it, she knew she would always choose life.

Forcing herself to focus, trying to control her breathing, she swallowed hard, getting up the courage to look at her self- inflicted damage. Her eyes, now swollen and gritty, still leaked huge tears as she forced herself to look at her hand. Seeing the displaced, throbbing-like-hellfire lump, she drew in a sharp breath.

Yep, it was definitely dislocated. She watched it swelling, not able to breathe out.

A strange burst of blue lights wiggled under the skin of her hand, dancing around the knuckle.

She finally released it in a soft outburst of "Ow… Ow… Ow… Ow… Damnation, ow!"

Cradling her left hand, she mentally shook herself, and got to her feet, unsteady but upright.

Holding her hand to her chest, she went to the bathroom of the cheap motel room, put her back against the wall and slid upwards, clicking on the light with her shoulder. She saw herself instantly in the mirror above the stained, ancient sink. Her almost totally grey hair was matted and dull, hanging around her face. Her red, swollen eyes glared back at her image, angry and narrowed with pain.

She told the mirror Gail, "Bite me…"

Her back still to the wall, she examined her hand in the light.

Now, there's a good way to stop yourself from crying, she thought ruefully, looking at the obscenely swollen knuckle. Great…

The small blue lights under the skin gathered around the finger above the knuckle, until the entire digit glowed almost like a magic wand.

Gail watched the lights with no surprise, and wiggled the finger, knowing she needed to intervene and force it back into place, or else she would heal too slowly.

It throbbed like fire with every pulse beat. Feeling weak, and sick, she staggered to the toilet, sat down on it, wondered how to fix the damaged hand in her lap without hurting it further.

She had gone to the ice machine earlier, getting enough to fill the small cooler bucket that was sitting on the counter, between the sink and the toilet. Half of it had melted, and after pulling out two small bottles of apple juice, she thrust her whole fist into it. Instant relief! The power of the throbbing would not be deterred. The shock of the ice water made her suck in the air again. It was hard to breathe around the pain.

Just great, she chided herself. You damned old fool! That was just stupid. She frowned again, biting her lip, trying to think if repairing dislocated knuckles was in that first aid book.

Wrapping her good hand around the bucket, she pressed it to her stomach and carried it to the other twin bed.

Matthew was snoring, still as an effigy, and she hoped he wouldn't wake up any time soon. She sat cross legged on the bed, holding the bucket of ice water in her lap as she pulled open the book. Her eyes were almost past using and the lamplight wasn't very conducive to medical procedures.

She looked through the index, squinting at the tiny letters. Yep, Dislocated/Broken Knuckles, page fourteen. Gail started flipping through the book with her good hand. Oh man! she thought, frowning at the graphic illustrations.

Out loud, she said, "Holy crap!" and started pulling her now frozen hand out of the water.

She grimaced, looking at it, and she still didn't like what she saw. The blue lights were not working fast enough. She looked over at Matt, once more biting her trembling lip.

The open tackle box-style medical kit lay on the floor, between the beds. There was an ACE bandage that she would need, so she bent far down to grab it. Her eyes came to rest on the little manila envelopes that crowded one of the compartments. Suddenly inspired, she bent back down and grabbed the one with the morphine. Her dread retreated somewhat as she contemplated the other envelopes. There were other narcotics in there, some very powerful antibiotics, and some cyanide.

She looked at the morphine. The other painkillers were not strong enough. She had some knowledge of the potency and decided it would have to be the little blue pills. She looked at Matthew; he would be out for a while, she knew, but then again so would she.

His breathing seemed pretty normal, and she shuddered at the memory of having to cut into his flesh. She manipulated a small pill out of the bag.

Watching Matthew breathe for a few more minutes, letting her knuckle freeze again, Gail talked herself into some courage. Just one little snap, she told herself, no big deal. She bit her lip. Slipping the pill into her mouth, she felt it dissolve almost instantly, the bitterness making her taste buds draw up. She wanted to gag; instead, she took a deep breath and pulled her hand out of the water slowly.

The entire hand glowed as the blue lights wiggled together at the base of her ring finger, pushing internally against the dislocated lump.

Gail felt her head go wobbly. She thought she was rocking forward, and then realized that it was the drug working. Trying not to hesitate, she moved her good hand quickly and snapped her damaged knuckle back into its original position.

She wasn't sure if she screamed out or not, but the trauma of it threw her involuntarily upward; her head snapped back. She slammed the fist immediately back into the ice water as the blue lights broke apart in a shattering effect, and then reformed to crowd the flesh around the newly replaced knuckle.

Her neck and facial muscles strained so hard they started to cramp. The cold was working; she gasped once, then forced herself the let her breath out slowly.

She knew the blue lights were working it as well. She breathed out hard in relief, knowing she would be completely healed by morning.

The pain overwhelmed the drugs, but not for long. She leaned over drunkenly, caught herself at the edge of the bed, and set the bucket in the floor, with her hand still in it. Letting the cold do its job, she looked at Matt and smiled woozily. Before her hand could thaw out, she sat up and began to wrap the elastic bandage around it as the blue lights again made the injured area glow from within the skin.

Gail's mind started to play tricks on her as the walls started waving slightly, seeming to breathe.

What a day! She numbly thought of Sara Katherine. Gail could not believe her mother was dead. That she had lost Joseph, as well, did not even seem possible.

She knew she was rocking, but she tried to keep her eyes on Matt as she wrapped the hand.

He would be ok; everything was ok. Gail smiled stupidly, digging in the little metal clip to tie off the bandage. No longer able to sit up, she lay back, melting into the bed. Just before she passed out, she thought of the mother. Poor Sara. The thought of Joseph caused her to absently clench her fist, and before the pain could hit her, Gail passed into a blessed sleep to heal.

***

January 12, 11:18 p.m.

Morgan lay in the big bed, watching the darkness surrounding her.
The baby lay at her naked breast, now asleep again, but still suckling. His tiny head rested only skin deep away from his mother's steady heartbeat.
The white walls gleamed in the moonlight, giving the darkness a faint silvery glow. Morgan thought of her family, without tears.
She was worried but could no longer sustain the tension of it as she held the baby to her body. The mosque was quiet, the entire building seemingly asleep. Abdullah lay at her back, spooning her. His breathing was even and deep; Morgan relaxed into him.

It seemed that he was trying to protect them, even in his sleep. She thought of the young man he had been, all those years ago. She smiled in the darkness. He had been such a tease: clever, always making her re-think him.

They had met in his home country of Iraq, at university.

Morgan's life in the shadows had seemed intolerable when compared to his happy family. Abby's sisters, she had loved them all. His father had also been a terrible tease. He had brought up his brood as a widower who was still in love with the ghost of his wife. Then came the revolution.

The political throes of violence reaching far and wide through the country, tearing families apart, at first had not affected them. It had seemed far away from their life of privilege. She had stayed with Abby's family for years, she and Abdullah so in love that they barely noticed the upheavals around them.

She knew she had been so stupid, so blind, thinking it could last. She instinctively pulled the baby closer as the memories came flooding back.

When the soldiers had come that first day and then left without incident, she had assumed it would all just work itself out.

They had respectfully questioned Abdullah's father, knowing the cleric was too respected to try to use overt force. They had questioned him about Morgan, and he had told them, truthfully, that she was from Egypt. She was here getting an education. In those days, Iraq was a great learning capital, a modern world leader. The new president, Hussein, was promising that it would always be so.

When the soldiers had returned the next day, she realized the cost of being naïve and stupid. They used her presence as the pretext to get rid of a troublesome cleric whom questioned the new president's policies.

Lying here with Abby so many years later , she still shuddered at what happened next. Her eyes stayed dry as she examined the memory, though the heartbreak was still fresh, even after all these years.

They had already intercepted Abdullah in the fields, as they stormed the house. They pulled him into the family home, where his seven little sisters had been herded into the main hall of the huge house. Morgan , too, had been forced there along with the others. As they brought in her lover, she knew that it was too late.

What a fool she had been! Blinded by her love for Abby, forgetting the nature of men Morgan had let herself and all she loved be trapped in a political situation she should have seen coming.

As Morgan and his sisters screamed in horror, the soldiers had beaten Abby badly . They shot him in the legs as he lay on his father's floor.

The oldest sister had started fighting with her captors; she cursed them, she spat on them. Two more of the sisters had jumped at the soldiers, hitting, scratching, and being beaten and stomped in return.

Their anger led to a viciousness that was uncalled for and deadly.

Morgan had tried to crawl to Abby. His broken body lay twisted on the cool tile floor. One of the soldiers started shooting.

He shot Morgan in the back, as she crawled, shattering her spine.

Lying flat, helpless, Morgan watched as they held the second sister by her throat and put the gun into her teeth as they pulled the trigger. The screams of the children stuck like burrs in her mind, as she lay helpless on the floor.

Morgan passed out. When she came to, she was on the hard marble floor, lying in a pool of her own blood.

The soldiers had moved to another room, somewhere behind her head. She recognized the screams coming from the nine-year-old girl and the laughter from the men that chilled the blood.

There was nothing here, she thought, but death and insanity.

Abby was gone; they had moved him from the house. Alive or dead, she didn't know.

Morgan had tried to roll over, almost succeeded, and felt someone shoot her again. The bullet entered her shoulder and lodged into her left chest, and she smiled, slightly, thinking it would all be over now.

Morgan had been so sure that bullet had pierced her heart she had silently prayed for the first time in centuries.

Finally, lying on the bed decades later, tears spilled from her. Morgan used the pillow to absorb them, trying not to let the droplets of sorrow taint the precious head of her new son.

Even now, she could still feel the weight of the bodies on top of her that night, crushing her.

The floor of the truck bed under her was thickly coated in blood. There was more dripping from the bodies above her, mingling with it.

Morgan could hear the terrible buzz of the huge black flies that were following the vehicle as it moved, stopped, and then moved again. More bodies would be added at each stop. After a while, she realized that the truck was following the soldiers, going from homestead to homestead, steadily increasing its horrific load.

She could feel the wounds in her body slowly stitching together. The blue lights under her skin burst into the open wounds with a white flash of spark as it came into contact with the still desert air.

Lying there, under the bodies, Morgan wished she were dead. She knew the itching of the lights under her skin meant that her heart was indeed still intact.

Drifting, in and out. At one point, she remembered feeling the torrential rain that had started to fall. The water made the pool of blood even more

106

slick and ghastly. Morgan realized that it was dark outside, and they were still stopping and starting. There were no sounds or movement from any of the bodies that were piled above her.

During one of the stops, she had weakly pushed a mutilated body away from her, trying to listen.

From a house to the right of the truck, Morgan could hear women screaming out in Aramaic, the language of Christ himself. An odd rushing sound permeated her fog, and as she listened, she realized could hear the sound of running water. She knew that they were close to a river. By leveraging her feet against other bodies, she pushed herself near the tailgate of the truck. She saw that there was a whole convoy of trucks behind and ahead of the one that she was in.

Screams from inside the house suddenly erupted into the open field. Scuffling, shouting, and gunfire followed the screaming.

Morgan weakly crawled across the bodies, on top of them now, trying not to put her hands into the unthinkable wounds they had suffered. She caught herself looking at the dead, trying to find Abby, but seeing mostly women and children instead.

A body that appeared to be a naked teenaged boy lay at the back, near the tailgate. His head was missing.

Morgan didn't see anyone moving around the trucks. She was unable to move quickly, so she slid over the boy's body and half-jumped, half-fell, to the hard desert sand.

The rain caused the blood that saturated her hair to run down her face in rivulets, blinding her. Her clothes were still on, but blood soaked. She pulled herself along the ground on her belly, to the canal about a hundred feet to the left of the truck. The wet sand got in her eyes, her mouth, and coated her hair. The blessed rain could not wash it away.

Morgan begged God to let her die, even as she scrambled weakly for the water, trying to save herself.

The screams had stopped, except for one man, who was also begging God for mercy...And vengeance. He screamed at the soldiers, and they laughed back at him. She heard the tramp of boots against wet sand, then dragging sounds, coming from the truck behind the one she had been in. Morgan crawled faster, coming to the reeds that grew along a small, swift waterway. Sounds of fists striking flesh came through the night. The man's screams for revenge turned into broken, garbled phrases. More laughter, then someone screamed back, mocking him.

A burst of gunfire brought the man all the mercy he could expect from the animals in charge. Morgan blindly grabbed some reeds and rolled her body into the water.

The swift current tore her hands from the grass ; and she felt herself pulled downstream. She floated and bobbed with the movement of the water.

She knew that she would be safe in the water; she could not drown. However, she could be shot, she thought weakly. As she passed out, she hoped she wouldn't wash up under the soldiers' feet.

The rain was just fat random teardrops crying from the sky, when Morgan woke up. She was sprawled face up onto a sand bar, her legs still gently floating in the water.

Her wounds had healed completely, not even a scar remained. In the 18 hours since she had been shot, her shattered spine had repaired itself, as had the bullet wounds.

The full moon looked down on her, mocking her wide-eyed stare. Water is life, she smiled, grateful for life, even as she started crying there in the moonlight.

On the bed, the baby finally let go of her breast, and she moved a hand to wipe the tears away.

From behind her, Abby whispered softly, "Shhh now…shhhhhh…it's ok."

He ran his hands through her hair, petting her.

Morgan had saved Abby from that prison, had saved him from the horrible torture, so long ago. He had known, when she boldly burst through the door of his cell, that he would be cursed to love her forever.

They lay in the moonlight, not speaking, no words needed. He moved his hand from her hair and cradled the baby, too, pulling them both to him.

Abby had always known how she had found him in that hellhole. He had gotten her drunk, on a thimble full of wine, and had gently coaxed the story from her.

After pulling herself from the waters, Morgan had befriended and seduced a high-ranking official in the new Iraqi government. The head of Abby's father had been displayed in the city square, but she knew that her lover had not been killed.

At knifepoint, lying in the bed of that befuddled fool, Morgan had made him write her out a pass. Abby had been in that place for nearly four months before she had been able to devise a plan to get him out. The pass would get her through the prison gates. She had used the man's driver too, not needing to seduce him, as he, too, had watched his family members die.

After the official signed her pass, Morgan savagely cut his throat.

Leaving his naked body on the bed, she had dressed quickly, and went directly to the car waiting for her in the front of the house.

The single guard would have been surprised by any movement at this late hour; however, he was already in the trunk, dead at the driver's hands.

They had immediately gone to the prison, passing easily through the checkpoints with her coerced documentation. Like storm troopers, they swept across the desert to try to beat the sunrise and the inevitable discovery that would come with it.

They had made it. They were both horrified to realize that the prison was actually an elementary school.

Between Morgan and the driver , they had quietly dispatched every one of the prison guards who had been scattered throughout the complex. The torturers hadn't believed that anyone would dare bring the fight to them and most of them went to Allah from their sleep.

As the sun rose just above the horizon, she found Abby's cell.

Wrestling with unfamiliar rings of keys, Morgan finally found the right one. She shoved open the door and stood there like an avenging Fury, bathed in the blood of murderers. She nearly lost her mind to see the man she loved suspended from the ceiling by arms too many times broken.

Abby had been expecting the guards, but seeing Morgan walk up to him instead , he had smiled so big at her, in spite of the pain.

Morgan and the driver had half-carried, half-dragged Abby to the car, unlocking what cells they could along the way. Without looking back, they headed east, toward Iran. They came to the border just as the sun reached midday.

The Iraqi border guards were looking for them, having been alerted to the slaughter at the prison some hours away. The Iranian border guards had inadvertently helped them cross the border. When they saw a car running the checkpoint, the Iranians had opened fire on the Iraqis from their rear flank. The Iraqis, watching the car speeding toward them never got off a shot before they were attacked from behind.

The car made it through completely unscathed. The Iranians knew who

Abby was, who his father had been, and gave him immediate medical attention and asylum.

Some years later, Morgan and Abby had flown to Turkey, and romanced their way through ancient Istanbul, once in her lifetime, also known as Constantinople. She showed him all the old streets and houses like a tourist guide, telling tales of centuries past.

They refused to let go of one another for years. As the time passed, Morgan had pushed back the truth. On the night he found out about his prison break, he also learned everything else about her.

Her secrets devastated him.

Even now, holding her and the baby to him in his bed a lifetime later, he was overcome by the tragedy of it. They both cried softly, trying not to wake the baby.

**

January 13, 1:45 a.m.

Jerold sat in the dark car; in his darkest hour.

His nephew, Michael, stood leaning back against the car, near the driver's door. He stood silently, arms crossed, watching the shadows in the trees being torn back and forth by the frantic winds. He was perfectly comfortable in the freezing gusts.

Jerold's oldest son, Adam, was slowly pacing, about fifty feet away.

All of them watched the road. The wind whipped up to a frenzy and Michael, putting his face to it, wished he could see the beauty it created among the canopy of forest. The bursts of cold air made him feel reckless, and painfully dangerous.

He thought of her. . He hated himself for it. In an odd way, Michael also missed his father.

Headlights illuminated the road beyond them, faint at first, but getting steadily brighter. Adam stopped pacing. He watched the lights of a car get brighter as it got nearer. Eventually, the lights turned into the drive beyond where they were parked. An expensive sedan gleamed a silver-black in the moonlight. The newly arrived car pulled alongside the one where Jerold was waiting. The night went dark and silent as the engine noise disappeared.

The wind battered the earth, demanding to be noticed.

110

Adam waited for the auto to stop, and then walking quickly from behind, he went directly to the passenger's door. Without hesitating, he pulled open the door, simultaneously snatching his little brother, James, out of his seat by his throat.

James came out swinging.

Michael watched the two men go to blows, never leaving his position, still leaned casually against the wind. His uncle's door never opened.

Jerold quietly watched his only two living sons battle fist to fist. After a few moments, not able to take anymore, he opened the car door forcefully.

As their father stood from his seat, the brothers let go of each other, both heaving from the exertion.

James's lip was busted badly, a large scratch marred Adams left cheek, from cheekbone to chin. James looked at Jerold with wide-eyed surprise.

"Father…What are you doing here?"

James was holding his torn lip; his sudden outburst a surprise only to himself. Tiny faint blue lights began to appear around the wound.

"Better question…" Michael told his young cousin. "WHY would we have to come here?"

Adam looked at his father, his own cheek almost healed already as the blue lights easily stitched the scratch back together.

The animosity toward his brother spent, Adam swallowed hard, as James stood silently, looking his older cousin in the eye. James was afraid to look at his father, knowing he screwed up badly.

Michael stared at James, watching as his lip began to repair itself..

James could feel the heat fill his mouth , stitching the tear in his upper lip. Along the wound, it burned like hell, but James stood quietly, considering Michael's question.

An electric charge was pulsating through his face, slowly working on the deep cut.

Knowing he had failed, James turned to his father. He looked into eyes identical to his own, searching for any hope of fatherly compassion.

"Why are you here, Daddy?" James asked.

The fierce wind almost swept his words away. They all already knew the answer.

Jerold considered his favored son for a moment. He had always liked the boy's frankness, his honesty. Unfortunately, his older brother Adam had adjusted better to life on the edge of mankind.

With regret, Jerold thought about the fact that James had done well, despite always having had time against him, from the very beginning.

Jerold would never get over this night.

"Come talk to me, James."

His father said it plainly over the wind, turning around and getting back into the backseat of the car he had arrived in.

James swallowed hard, watching his father get into the car; he quickly followed. Michael looked at the ground as James passed by. Once inside, he slammed the car door, leaving them alone in the sudden still air.

Both James and Jerold sat silently, staring straight ahead. Even when Jerold finally spoke, he looked only at the seat in front of him.

Very softly, he said, "Son…what the hell were you thinking?"

His annoyance was evident to James and fear pulled at him like a magnet. He tried to keep his breathing even as he answered his father.

"I don't know, Daddy…" James lowered his eyes, feeling his failure

"I was just trying to do what Adam told me. He said that Gail and that priest, Matthew…must be found. He told me to stay on the priest's family. That they would know how to find him. "

James looked up quickly, and saw Michael walk away from the car, to where Adam was talking to the driver of the silver car.

He looked quickly back to his father.

"I swear! I didn't even know Anna was still alive…"

At that, Jerold snapped his head around, literally hissing at his son.

"You should have known she was alive!…You're a damned fool, boy…"

Jerold looked away from him, clenching his jaw.

"You walked right up on her! You did not even have a clue until the fever locked your fucking knees! "

Jerold fingered the crease on his pants with annoyance.

"I can see her now…sitting there with a smile; she probably knew you were coming a mile away!"

Turning back to James , spitefully, he started screaming at his son; unable to mask his fear now.

"You opened fire on a police captain and a fucking judge! Not to mention the god-damned coroner, too! … My God, son. …Do you have any idea what you've done? To all of us?"

Looking into his own eyes, Jerold wanted to be anywhere but here.

James, looking his father eye to eye, trembled but did not blink.

Jerold loved his son more than he could ever say, and he wished he could kill himself, instead. How many times had Jerold wished for that?

It would be too easy, he thought, because he would damn sure finish it, even if God wouldn't.

Knowing his son would die tonight, Jerold did not know what to say to him.

The needs of their family required absolute secrecy.. They were forced to live that way, because the humans around them would only allow them to exist, if their presence was not known.

Many of their kin had already been lost to panicked human mobs that could not fathom the nature what they killed.

Jerold looked away from his son before he started crying.

"What's going on out there, Daddy...?" James asked bluntly.

He was focused on Adam and Michael, who were gathered around the open driver's door of the car that James had been pulled from. They seemed to be talking, looking casually toward the other car now and then.

James had a terrible feeling in his stomach.

"I suppose they are trying to figure this out..." Jerold sighed.

They both knew he was lying. Jerold continued, trying to keep his voice casual.

"We could have blown off this thing at the church, kept the baby's existence from being known. .... But when you try to kill the police, judges, or coroners, they're going to come after you...after us!"

Jerold shook his head heavily, slowly.

"You know how clever humans can be." He reminded his son.

James was watching the men outside; he was suddenly nervous.

"I know, Daddy. ... I exposed us, and I am sorry for it." James admitted softly.

He looked at the floor, straining to hear the conversation outside. A violent gust of wind rocked the car; just as James knew he was dead.

"After all this time, I'm grateful, Daddy, for this life...and this death. I'm glad it is over."

Even as he said it, panic forced James to jump for the door.

He was irrational and that did not help at all, but he knew, for certain, that he was about to die at the hands of his own family. He jerked the door open and spilled his enormous body out onto the ground. Before he could touch the grass, he was off and running for his life.

Startled, Michael and Adam scrambled to their feet. Before Jerold could react, Michael was running after James, with Adam hot on his heels.

James tried to pull away from his brother and cousin, his long frame stretching ahead. The silver car was pulling around, flanking him; his only hope was to make it to the woods. He heard shots from behind and the sting of a bullet tearing into his right thigh made him stumble. In desperation, James pulled back up, still trying to run, aware that the car had just outflanked him.

James tried to change directions so he wouldn't be cut off. His legs went out from under him; James hit the ground hard, shoulder first.

Adam and Michael were on him in a second, as the car pulled in front, blocking any hope of escape.

The driver of the car stepped out, pistol in hand. Watching the three men grappling, he saw that James was losing, so he leaned against the car and watched, as Jerold approached from behind.

Adam and Michael managed to pull a still struggling James to his knees, facing his father, who was approaching calmly. As Jerold came closer, all of the men could see that he was crying. Adam held his brother firmly, but seeing his father's tears made him look at his feet. The only ones not crying were Michael and the driver of the car behind him.

James covered his face with his hands, sobbing loudly.

Instead of holding him down, Michael and Adam were now holding him up as he tried to curl up in the fetal position, racked with terrified sobs.

Jerold stood before them. He forced himself to look at his son. The swollen, split lip had healed, but still appeared irritated as Adam let go of his brother's arm and headed back to the silver car. When Adam saw the driver standing by the car he veered off into the woods instead. Michael also let go of his young cousin, but he did not step away from him.

James had always been a favored child, and even Michael had enjoyed his playful company. The mournful sobs coming from the younger man were ripped from his lips by the wind and thrown amongst them like the cries of a wounded animal.

Jerold watched his son curl up and his tears could not be stopped. He knew he could not kill his son. He stood for a long time, unwilling to let the others know that he could not protect them from his own child.

The driver of the silver car watched too, sensing the struggle within Jerold's heart and mind. From the ground, a sobbing James pleaded with his father.

"Please...Please! Daddy, I don't want to die!"

The words were broken into gasping phrases by desperation.

"Pleeeeaassee?…I'm sorry! I'm sooo sorry…Please…Please…"

Jerold watched a retreating Adam. All of them had failed. He could no longer look at his son, curled up at Michael's feet.

Not able to bear anymore, Michael swiftly grabbed James by his armpits and pulled him up quickly, allowing him to regain his balance. James looked up into Michael's face and froze. The older cousin pinched his brow in concentration; before James could look away, or even blink, Michael pushed his will into the young man's mind.

James stood up straight, no longer trembling as his eyes bulged and then rolled lightly as Michael took control of him from inside James own mind.

Michael's hands went to either side of his face, as he forced James to look into his eyes. Standing there, both of them swayed slightly in the wind. The silence of the night was broken only by the savage gusts pounding at them. The two cousins, eyes locked, seemed to be telling each other something; both of their lips were moving, but no sound could be heard above the wind.

Jerold bowed his head and wept.

From the silver car, the driver watched Adam disappear into the woods. Barely able to discern his shape among the dark trees, he saw Adam hold onto a sapling as he vomited.

Looking back to Jerold and Michael, he saw that James was being held captive in Michael's will. Jerold was crying silently, and he knew that Jerold was not able to finish it. Hesitating for only a second more, the driver pushed away from the car and walked quickly toward Michael and the now mesmerized James.

He walked up to within an arm's length from them, but they never acknowledged his presence. He held the pistol to James's left ribcage, leveled it at his heart, and pulled the trigger twice in a rapid burst.

As the man pulled the trigger, Michael was inside his cousin's mind. He, too, felt the shock of the blast and saw the rapidly approaching wave of darkness.

James dropped to his knees, Michael's hands still cupping his face. As the younger man's eyes started to cloud, Michael screamed, trying desperately to pull back, seeing death as it came swiftly to James.

As his lifeless body fell against Michael, he screamed again, unaware of the heat coming from James's body. Michael could not feel Jerold pulling at his hands, trying to push him back. Seemingly locked to James's body, Michael screamed in agony, unable to let go of his dead cousin.

The driver and Jerold tried to unclench his hands from James's head. The body was starting to smoke heavily in the cold night.

Jerold tried to not look at it. His son's handsome face was turning into a blackened mask, his hair turning to ash. The flesh on Michael's hands was also starting to burn, but he could not pull away from James.

From somewhere deep inside him, Michael was able to choke off the next scream by will alone. Coming back into himself, he slowly focused, the smell of burned hair and flesh making him gag. Adam had returned to the group; he also was trying to pull James away from Michael.

Flames started licking at James's back from the wounds in his chest. A blue-white flame also started on Michael's coat, where the blood spatter from the gunshots had landed on him. The pain from the burns finally forced Michael to release his cousin's charring head. Once he let go of James, he fell backwards, unable to stop himself from collapsing. Michael's head throbbed, a white-hot pain shooting between his eyes, blinding him.

The smoldering body, once free, fell backwards across the brown dry grass. As the flames grew bigger, all of them could hear the sizzle of flesh as James's body burned before them.

Jerold was stunned.

He watched his son's body burn as a growing hatred welled up inside him. He knew that they were all damned. He looked at the driver with mixed emotions, his face contorted as he watched his son's killer. The man had done what Jerold could not do. Silently he turned, walking back to the car where he had sat with his now dead son. The sadness overwhelmed him.

The driver and Adam watched him go; they stood over James as he burned. Michael rolled in agony a few feet away, having stripped off his coat, which was also now fully engulfed in flames.

Going over to the discarded coat, Adam started absently stomping at a few patches of flames that had jumped from the coat to the dried grass around it. The driver of the silver car stayed with the body, also stomping at any errant flames. Jerold got into the front passenger's seat of the bigger car, some one hundred yards away.

Within minutes, it was over.

In the open air, the body burned completely. Even the bones snapped and sizzled as they turned to a white ash.

Michael had stopped rolling and lay curled into a ball, holding onto his head like it would explode. The agony of the pain made him breathless and sick. After a while, Adam came back to the place where his brother's body had fallen. Once the dissolved bones stopped smoking, both of the men still standing started stomping the ash into the ground, trying to hide their secret for a while longer.

Chapter 6

January 13, 1.58 a.m.

In the darkened office, the priest and the scientist sat in pregnant silence. They both stared at the inanimate objects around them while curtains of snow fell outside the window.

The priest sat on a low sofa facing the fireplace, which now glowed with embers, but no real flames .

Both men had large snifters of brandy in hand, although the alcohol was bringing precious little relief to either one of them. The priest was the older of the two. Leaning back into the sofa, he contemplated the large picture over the mantel where a sailing ship plowed through a sea of oil paint. He had gone to sea as a boy, on his father's crew boat. He smiled at the feeling of great adventure, still able to remember the beauty of cold, salty spray on his face that made his senses slam to life.

His smile faltered slightly, as the present situation intruded on his reveries. His feeling of adventure was being replaced by a scalp-tingling sense of danger. The priest was scared. They were both scared.

He lazily rolled his head to relieve the tension in his neck as he glanced at the scientist behind the desk who seemed oblivious to everything.

The younger man sat at his desk, bleakly staring at the thin folder in front of him. Sometimes the brandy would penetrate the fog and he would pay attention to the glass, then return to his blank focal point. The manila folder sat there silently, seemingly harmless. Both men watched the folder, as if its sudden movement was imminent. Just as that thought crossed their minds, the old window latches failed, and a savage gust of wind burst into the room. The file swept toward the startled scientist.

The priest, also caught unaware, jumped to the window, fighting the billowing drapes around him. Pushing the window closed against the onslaught of winter, he flipped the latch, making sure it was secure this time. Silence settled around them with an uneasy weight.

From across the room, the scientist spoke in a voice tinged with fear.

"What are we supposed to do now?"

Looking out into the volatile storm, the priest was unsure what to say. After a long moment of no response, the scientist cleared his throat and continued.

"We can't keep this quiet, Father…It's bigger than I can imagine…"

Not turning from the window, the priest responded.

"We have to keep it quiet for now, until we know what we are dealing with."

The scientist slumped in his seat, sighing slowly, unable to turn away from the folder. Staring blankly into the night, the priest absently crossed his arms. He had to convince this young man it was in their best interest to stay silent.

Keeping his tone even, he started his pitch to make the scientist understand their situation.

"September 11th was so horrible for so many. If we can find out what all this means, then perhaps something…miraculous…can come from it. But you already know that someone is desperate to keep you quiet. Now, I'm sure that a secret this big must have someone guarding it…I think we both may be in danger…and only God knows who else may be. We must find out who tried to kill you today…"

The younger man shuddered at the thought of the bullets whizzing by his head.

"I know, Father, that's why I was thinking…um…if we go to the press, or the police…"

The priest turned, suddenly facing the younger man. He understood the torture this was putting him through, but for both their sakes, he had to understand what was at stake here.

"And tell them what? Are you out of your mind? That's what they will say, that you are crazy. A quack! …What do we tell them? Just march in and say, oh, by the way…I have God's textbook…?"

The old man's nostrils flared as he looked at his young parishioner.

"I have not reached this level in my life just to be dismissed as a heretic , or to be strung up as a nutcase."

Slumping down, the scientist tried again, weakly. ,

"We have this…"

He held up the thin folder, laying it back down on the desk quickly as if touching it had burned him.

"That? That is not proof! That is just a piece of paper. …You know damn well they will say you're a hoax! "

Now showing his own frustration, the younger man asked bluntly.

"Then how do we prove it?"

The old man turned back toward the window, rubbing his arms against a chill that refused to be brushed away. For a long moment, he let the question hang there in the air between them. As the thought came to him, he spoke it out loud.

"The only way to prove it…is to catch one of them alive…"

Startled upright, the scientist scowled at the old man's back; trying to protest but his mouth moved soundlessly, unable to find the words against such a notion.. His jaw literally dropped at the suggestion.

The scientist looked down at the folder as his stomach started to ache. As he curled back into his chair, he grabbed the brandy and started to drink from the bottle.

***

January 13, 2.00 a.m.

Diana sat upright on the huge satin covered bed, absently rubbing her expanding belly. Michael was lying to her. She was sure of it.

After they had made love that afternoon, she had drifted off into a nap. He had lain next to her for a long time, quietly watching the ceiling. As the time approached for him to leave with Jerold, he had made a phone call. Unable to contain his temper, his raised voice had roused her from her sleep.

Diana started toward the sound of his voice, which seemed to be coming from the far north corner of the dark penthouse. She stopped before she got out of the bedroom, straining to overhear his end of the conversation.

She listened, and learned of Alex's murder. Michael had told her it was a car accident.

It was not his father's much deserved murder that had her stewing, and the fact that he had lied did not surprise her. Suddenly, she felt that she didn't know Michael at all. Yet the lie had gone deeper; it had cut her to the bone.

Who in the hell was Anna? And why did Michael tell someone that he would always love her?

The wind tapping at the windows gave her no answers. Diana rubbed her belly as the darkness around her seemed to mirror her mood. Her shoulder-length chestnut hair curled in wild knots around her face and with her free hand, she twisted the locks.

Tomorrow, she promised herself. When the city came back to life in the morning, she knew that she was going to find out who this woman was, and how this Anna would affect the new life she was carrying. She thought about the words that Michael had used to describe his love for 'his Anna'. Balling up her fists, she shoved them to her eyes, trying desperately not to cry.

He had never spoken to her with such passion.

***

January 13, 4.12 a.m.

Hearing her name repeated brought Gail from her drugged sleep slowly, like floating to shore on thick waves. The pathetic little lamp between the beds was still on, but its energy didn't carry very far into the motel room. What light it did give seemed sickly, casting shadows that seemed odd to her in her confused state.
Then, she heard Joseph's name and a woman's voice saying that Matthew was wanted for murder.

As she finally opened her eyes, Gail saw that the television was on, and a beautiful Asian woman was talking about a sex scandal. A really terrible picture of Gail was magically suspended over the news caster's shoulder. Turning her head slightly, Gail saw that Matthew was very still on the bed, but he, too, was watching the TV.

Matthew's eyes were alert but narrowed with pain. He was crying, with no sound at all.

The cheap room had a remote that was plugged into the lamp table, and Matthew had obviously struggled to retrieve the little device. Several of the items on the table seemed to have been upended.

Gail brought herself upright, holding her wounded hand. It was no longer wounded. She wiggled her fingers just to make sure, nodding to see a perfectly functioning hand. She thanked God it had only dislocated. A broken bone would have taken her three whole days to heal.

Matthew did not acknowledge her presence, although she knew he was aware she had stirred. Moving the tacklebox-style first aid kit to one side, she knelt beside the young priest's bed, using the half-dried washcloth to try to wipe his brow.

His silent tears flooded his cheeks as she tried to comfort him.

"I'm so sorry, Matthew…It will be OK . Please don't cry."

As she said it, her own tears started again.

He pushed her hands away and held both his own palms over his eyes as she rubbed his arm. The bandages on his right hand absorbed his tears. After several seconds, he seemed to calm, somewhat.

"How?" Matthew asked from behind his hands.

"How was he killed? I thought…"

Gail swallowed hard. The pills had given her terrible cotton mouth. She knew what he had thought. He had believed that he had saved Joseph.

With stone in her voice she answered.

"When they were struggling, in front of the altar, Joseph had already been mortally wounded. " she told him plainly.

"In front of the altar?" he gasped.

Pulling his hands away from his face, Matthew looked at her directly.

"But I…I stabbed him. At the alter! …" His breathing became rapid again.

"I saw Joseph's eyes…He wasn't dead! "

Gail touched Matthew's forehead softly, trying to avoid his eyes.

"Shh… Shhh… I know…It was too late, Matthew, he was already hurt. I didn't realize he was stabbed, either, until.. After…." she couldn't speak the words.

Gail felt like she was choking.

The realization dawned on the young priest slowly, and a low, mournful cry escaped the man's damaged lungs. Putting his hands back over his face, his body was racked by painful sobs.

"Ohhhh God…OOHHH my God!"

Gail retrieved a blue pill. Holding it, she waited as Matthew adjusted to the terrible truth of what he had done.

"Oh God, I killed him for nothing!"

Trying to get through to him, Gail pulled at his bandaged hands, refusing to let him believe it. ,

"No…No…Matthew, listen. You didn't save Joseph, but you saved all of us. He would have killed us all, even Samuel! "

His arms became weak, and she was able to pull them down to his sides. She looked into his eyes as she reassured him.

"Not for nothing, Matthew…You saved us all…"

Not able to lift his arms any longer, he simply squeezed his eyelids as tightly closed as he could to block out the memories he still saw.

He had killed before, by accident, and now deliberately, too. Gail didn't know how to comfort him.

"Take this…"

She held the pill to his lips, and he obediently swallowed it. The apple juice was warm now, but the moisture still felt good to his parched throat. As she took the straw from his lips, he sobbed again. She was determined not to cry anymore.

After a minute, Matthew calmed down and looked at her drunkenly. He unexpectedly smiled, like a kid who saw an interesting bug.

"Why do you look so different, Gail?"

His smile lingered a moment as she smiled back at him.

"Oh…goodness…!" He looked confused.

"What is it, Matthew?"

"You…you look like…that lady…you know…that lady in the church…"

His eyes rolled slightly. His voice dropped to a drugged whisper.

"You know…that lady…I can't remember…her name…"

Gail felt her strength waning, too. She whispered it to him.

"Sara…Her name was Sara…"

With his eyes closed, Matthew repeated the name.

"Yes, yes…Sara…" he said, drawing out the name gently.

Just as he drifted away, he asked Gail one final question.

"I wonder…What was she doing in the…um…the confessional?"

Gail was grateful that she couldn't answer a man who had just lost consciousness.

***

January 13, 4.48 a.m.

The scientist's house was silent.

The man outside the house sat in his car watching the quiet structure, wrapped in the shadows of the street. He could see that the priest was still in there. Although the house was mostly dark, the study window still held a subdued glow. Every so often, a shadow would fall across it, and the man in the car would lean forward, squinting his black eyes, trying to make out the figure of his target.

His attempt on the scientist's life the day before had failed. He had failed. The man grimaced as he thought of James, his body burning. They all knew the boys birth meant there was no more time for mistakes.

He had left his cousin James to hunt down the young priest, and he had driven north to try to whack the scientist.

The missed opportunity to hit the scientist wasn't exactly his fault. He hadn't known that the man had been carrying his own pistol. The whole idea of making it look like an armed robbery was completely lost when the man had pulled own his firearm and fired back.

He had never let go of his briefcase.

It does not matter, the man thought to himself, he would make another chance. The car was as cold as a refrigerator, but he seemed oblivious to it.

Even if he did manage to get the scientist's papers, the man would still have to be killed, and quickly. The house burning down would ensure any original copies of his work would be hidden forever. But first he had to make sure the scientist was dead.

Watching the driveway to the house, the man felt a shudder pass through him when he saw the priest's car. What a disaster! The priest was not supposed to be there, but the scientist had obviously needed to confess and now the priest was just in the way.

The priest definitely knew their secrets, he was sure of it. Even though the killing didn't bother him, he was still somewhat put off by the thought of whacking the priest. He, too, had been a priest, once upon a time.

In the darkness, the man's face was lit by a beatific smile. Yes, he thought, I was once many things over many, many moons.

The snow had stopped falling some time back, and the new drifts gleamed like dull silver mounds. He knew that he would not get his chance to kill the scientist tonight; the new day coming might offer an opportunity, but he had to get this done quickly.

If Jerold and Michael could find Morgan and the boy, then this would not be necessary. It would still be prudent, but not necessary. Either way, he figured, the scientist had to go. But if they found the boy and his mother, then maybe he wouldn't have to take out the priest.

He knew it was wishful thinking.

The smell of James' body burning returned with such clarity it made him gag. He absently rubbed his hand, not able to shake the unconscious memory of the gun in his hand as he killed his own family.

Trying to force this walk down memory lane to end, he opened the door of the car savagely. He slipped into the darkness onto the icy pavement and closed the door very softly. The total stillness of the air seemed to mock his inner turmoil. A short walk in the freezing night brought his senses tingling to life.

Walking past the scientist's house, he saw the faint glow of the study window, deep in the recesses of the large structure. He kept walking. As he did, Morgan's face floated before him.

Her face always stayed close to him, haunting him. He had loved her for a thousand years.

The well-kept, large houses were all spaced widely apart. Set back from the quiet street, they reminded the man of angular sleeping giants. Obviously, the touch of the human presence forced onto the landscape.

The smile that touched his lips was bitter. Mocking Human. What a vain little joke.

In his mind he saw Morgan, in wispy white robes. Her presence in his memory made the bitterness both disappear and multiply. Damn her. She had betrayed him. She had betrayed them all.

A vision of Anna, also in white robes, both surprised and angered him. The very thought of Anna always made him spitting mad.

He could see her face so clearly; so beautiful. So deadly. He couldn't wait to stomp her face in. After a while, he returned to the car. He tried not to think of the Christmas gift she had somehow managed to send him every year for half a century.

For the life of him he still could not figure out how she even managed to find him to send him the same exact model car every year. Same color and everything, only with all 4 of the little tires ripped off. He actually blamed Morgan for it. It stopped being funny years ago.

Once more in the auto's dark interior, refusing to spend his rage on

Anna, he picked up the envelope on the passenger's seat.

The words on it read; Robert Gorin.

Inside the envelope were certificates and copies of awards of merit. Robert Gorin, P.H.D...Robert Gorin, M.D...The scientist had been a prodigy , graduating from medical school at nineteen. There were also copies of his parent's death certificates, children's birth records, and a divorce decree. There was a small portrait of Dr. Gorin and the ex-family. They all smiled so happily.

The driver looked back to the scientist's house.

The silhouette of a man was obvious in the study window. The light from the room behind him illuminated the large frame of the priest. He knew it was the holy man, because the scientist had a slight, almost anorexic build. If he rushed the structure now, he knew he would surely fail. The scientist had secured the house with laser sensors and one hell of an alarm. He would have to catch the man unaware, not on guard as he was tonight.

He knew that someone was targeting him; best to let the good doctor come to him.

In the silence of the waning night, he thought of Morgan. Morgan who had betrayed him. He knew she had not approached the scientist and the uncomfortable reality of that thought unnerved him.

Morgan had the baby they all feared, but she had not exposed them to this threat. In the darkness, he wondered who in the family had betrayed them all.

Still hearing the shots that had killed James, he wondered who else in the family would have to die to keep the rest of them safe.

He hoped Jerold and Michael would find the baby soon.

Chapter 7

January 13, 5.41 a.m., sunrise

They left Danny's body in front of an emergency room, although he was past needing any help a human could give him. Maria knew the man had two small kids, and she couldn't bear the thought of leaving him at a rest stop, as their new companion had suggested.

Come to think of it, the presence of this woman was also pretty hard to bear. Maria looked around the confines of the small clearing. The old mature trees stood close together, reflecting the amber light of the small fire they had built hours earlier.

No one spoke from the group of survivors, who were heavily bundled around the fire. They silently watched the flames, each of them thinking about Anna's thoughts on God's sense of humor.

Only Anna's face showed any emotion. The smile on her lips seemed amused and sarcastic as she glowed with health in the firelight.

The deep self-inflicted cut Anna had unexpectedly made to her own cheek earlier, had already healed, without even a scar remaining. They had no choice but to watch her go from badly injured to perfection in about one hour, as she had spoken of things none of them wanted to believe.

All of them looked at anything besides Anna's face. Even watching it heal with their own eyes, they had very few questions, only quiet looks of shock and wonder. She spoke completely uninterrupted for almost 2 hours.

After Anna had finished telling her tale, none of them responded as an unsettled silence rattled in the air between them.

In those hours, they each learned to fear this odd woman, but also, the awe of her bound them all tighter together in the taunt quiet of the forest. Not one of them even thought of simply walking away.

It was far too late for that.

Captain Edwards's face was blank as he watched a wet log sizzle and pop at a persistent flame. Doug's forehead was pinched, his eyes narrow as he watched the same log. Maria sat beside Doug, curled up to him, her attention on the glowing embers.

All of them had lost track of how long they had sat there. No one wanted to break the silence as a very real fear of the unknown hung in the air.

The fire hissed and spit at them, trying to consume the snow-covered log with a burst of angry sounds. Maria let herself openly stare at Anna's unmarked cheek.

Anna's eyes never moved from the fire. She had told them something none of them believed. None of them wanted to believe it.

Anna had cut herself so that they had no choice but to see it. She needed them to believe.

For a long time, Anna wondered if she had made a mistake when trusting these humans could mean the death of her family. But, what the hell, she thought. Her family was dying anyway.

The only thing that could save them now was the baby. And his human guardian.

As Anna again wondered about this young priest who may, or may not, still be alive, his brother looked sharply at her over the flames of the small fire. Doug also stared at the perfection of her face, thinking of the blue lights that had stitched her together earlier with a true chill up his spine.

She returned his gaze with no emotion, not sure how to make this any easier for all of them. Doug's mouth twitched with a hundred thousand questions that were left unspoken.

Finally, his voice calm and steady in the fire light, he asked the one question he needed an answer for. .

"Assuming all of this is true…" Doug began.

Anna's smile came back, both beautiful and mocking.

"If you are what you say…then what do you call yourselves…?"

Surprisingly, Anna's smile softened. She looked back into the flames with an expression of sadness. The captain and Maria, both watching her for answers, saw that the words came easily to her, as if the thought had been explained a million times already.

"We are what you are, Douglas. We are of the flesh, same as you. …' Anna sighed lightly.

"We love, we hate, we bleed. We are as God cursed us to be…We are called Mortals…"

128

The other three looked at Anna in awed silence. All of them knew the truth when they heard it. All of them watched her, desperate to see something that could contradict her allegations.

None of them wanted to believe her.

Her unmarred face refused to be challenged with reason, nor science. Doubt was not possible when they saw it to be true with their own eyes.

They were all three desperate to unlearn this knowledge. After a while, they all returned their gaze to the fire, defeated by a faith they were forced to accept.

She would let them stew on it a minute more. Anna knew she would need their help. If for no other reason than to let their deaths become a distraction.

With the priest dead or alive, it didn't matter. Anna knew what she had to do either way.

She would not fail the boy. She would not fail God.

Chapter 8

January 13, 9:07 a.m.

Abby held the baby close to his chest. The young FBI agent in front of him seemed fascinated by the newborn.

The agent asked his questions absently, glancing at Abby now and then to nod politely as the man became mesmerized by the sleeping child.

Abby had the very distinct impression that the Fed was trying to trap him. He held the newborn closer, refusing to be afraid. Careful to be casual, the cleric kept his voice even as he spoke. The baby slept soundly.

"Yes, I did drop by to see Father Joseph yesterday, as you already know…" Looking up to the older, more wrinkled agent, he said effortlessly, "I had missed Joseph…I spoke briefly to a large young priest named…um, Michael…No, Matthew. Yes, Father Matthew."

From his place on the floor, Abby kept his eyes averted to watch the child he held. The explanation came easily because it was the truth. He had missed Joseph at the church.

The well-dressed agent shifted his gaze from the child to the cleric.

"May we ask how you knew Joseph?"

The young man was standing over Abby, looking down on him. As he asked the question, he tried to lock eyes with Abby.

An involuntary shudder passed through Abby; the Fed's gaze reminded him of soldiers he had seen in the past. They, too, had pressed him rudely, looking him in the eye as they disrespected him. They had not been as obvious with his father…not until the next day, anyway.

Refusing to drop his eyes from the agent, Abdullah clipped his voice deliberately, the truth saving him once again.

"I met Joseph long before you were born, young man. We first met in Turkey, about forty-five years ago. He was young, in the seminary; we attended the same university. Theology was an interest we had in common. We met again in Italy, some years later. We had always been friends. That's how I know him. He is my friend…"

Abby allowed himself to break away from the Fed's eyes and again looked at the baby grimace in his sleep. He instinctively rocked the baby as he corrected himself.

"I mean, he was my friend…"

The two agents looked at each other. Webster bit the inside of his pockmarked cheek as the cleric fussed with the baby's wrappings. The old guy sounded sincere. Webster was naturally suspicious of everyone, but this guy seemed all right. Napoliss didn't believe him for a second. He watched the man on the floor a moment longer, and then once more switched his gaze to the baby.

The baby was an odd distraction; he had hoped he wouldn't have to press this guy head on while holding an infant Napoliss tried hard not to be in awe of the unusual beauty of the tiny child. He was gorgeous!

Napoliss asked evenly, "What were you hoping to see Joseph about?"

Abby looked at the man for an exaggerated minute.

"I was hoping to catch him and have a quick dinner with my old friend. I had to return to Boston; as you can see, I have other matters to attend to."

Napoliss knew a polite brush off when he heard one.

Switching his weight, he glanced at Abby before asking about the infant uncomfortably.

"Is, um, is he…um, she…yours?"

Now Abby lied smoothly,

"Oh, gracious no. Haha! No, this is my niece's child. As I said, I have other matters to attend to…"

He let it hang in the air. Neither of the agents could break the silence and, after a moment, they started fidgeting.

Finally, Webster interrupted with a polite send off.

"Well, sir, we appreciate your time…we hope we haven't intruded too much…"

Abby pulled up from his cross-legged position. He walked them to the door trying to remain casual.

"As I understand it, Joseph was already at dinner when I arrived. I'm so sorry I didn't wait for him."

Before Napoliss could speak, Webster responded thoughtfully.

"No, you're not, sir. You should not be sorry. Whatever happened to Father Joseph might have happened to you, if you had waited. …It was a good thing you came on back."

They came to the heavy front door of the mosque. It was beautifully carved with a sixteenth century Moorish design. A deep-red, solid plank of timber.

Abby held back some with a now restless baby.

With a nod, the rumpled agent looked solidly at the cleric. The baby started a high-pitched wail. As the two men measured each other, the baby started to flail, his cries becoming intense. Webster glanced at the baby and, with another curt nod of his head, turned and exited, slamming the huge door behind him.

Once in the Fed-mobile, Napoliss turned over the engine and let it warm slightly. He glanced at the busy Muslim neighborhood surrounding the mosque.

"Ok." Napoliss sighed deeply. "What next, partner?"

Without hesitation, Webster answered in a clipped tone.

"We need to turn this guy's life inside out..."

His young partner looked at him sharply.

"What? What are you saying?" Napoliss asked, confused.

"I don't like being lied to." Webster quipped.

Napoliss frowned, still confounded.

"Me, neither; what gives? What lies?"

"Turkey, Italy, whatever...I doubt that guy has any nieces..." Webster said flatly.

Napoliss narrowed his eyes.

"Huh? What does that mean?"

Webster became thoughtful a moment, then explained himself.

"He was open about trying to see Joseph...so why lie about having a niece...?"

The younger agent looked into the rearview mirror at the giant front door of the mosque. He did not question his partners instincts. If Webster had detected a lie, then Napoliss followed his lead immediately.

Without thinking too much, Napoliss pondered aloud.

"Terrorists? Maybe?"

These days, everyone jumped to stereotypes.

Webster looked at the clock on the dashboard before answering slowly.

"I don't know, partner. ...At this point, I'd believe anything."

Napoliss absently shook his head as he put the car in motion. Both of them thought about the hand print burned into the wall of St. Mary's as they drove out of town. The one in the alley burned into the brick also distracted

132

them both into complete silence. They knew whatever path they were on would test their own faith like no other case, no matter what they believed.

***

Morgan stayed in the deep shadows of the mosque. The Feds had assumed that Abby was alone. They had not seen the woman sitting in an alcove as still as a statue, holding her long silver sword.

Morgan knew Abby was terrified that there would be bloodshed in his mosque . Listening to her baby start fussing as Abby led them to the door made her breasts suddenly swell painfully, throbbing with milk that the baby was no doubt looking for.

She crossed her arms over her chest. The rapier gleamed in the sparse light. Hearing the door shut, she unconsciously breathed out in relief. She knew they were not safe here. Abby knew it too.

They knew the Mortal men were hunting them, determined to claim the special child. It was only a matter of time before they found Morgan, again.

The house in Salem Morgan had hid in during her pregnancy had been discovered by Jerold, along with the evidence of the baby's birth only minutes after the boy was born.

Morgan had been in labor for thirty-four hours. Her Aunt Sara had known they were coming. She had helped Morgan bear down, trying to deliver him before they were discovered.

Sara had prayed that Morgan was lying to her about the child's father. It was soon obvious that she had not lied at all.

After his first weak cry, the baby went straight to his mother's breast, both of them falling into an exhausted sleep.

Alex had hit the house within thirty minutes of the birth, hoping to kill Morgan before she could have the boy. In her sleep, Morgan had had been seized with the fever. Already weak from the extended labor, the fever made her helpless.

Before she could even open her eyes, she knew that she had been found. Alex was standing at the foot of the bed, watching them.

No, he had been looking at the baby.

As she came to, she saw the look of contempt that Alex couldn't hide. An involuntary sob escaped her as she recognized him. The baby slept on as she clutched him to her, praying that this was a dream.

Still hurting, still exhausted, Morgan had started begging him.

"Oh God, Alexander! Please, don't kill my baby! Oh God, no! ..."

Alex's eyes had hardened as he looked at her.

She started floundering on the bed, with Alex watching her. He understood that she was helpless. Just as he started to stoop down, the gunfire had startled them both.

From the front of the little cottage, Sara started screaming profanities. Alex put his hand quickly into his jacket, palming the little gold dagger. Morgan put the baby under her as much as she could, her legs still virtually dead from the hours of strain. She was terrified that she would accidentally smother her child.

Just as he had pulled the dagger free, his son Michael had literally fallen through the door.

Morgan never took her eyes from Alex as Michael fell at his feet, forcing the older man to pause his attack. As he bent to help his son off the floor, he saw Michael had taken at least two of Sara's bullets. One had struck the younger man in his upper left shoulder, the other catching him squarely in the guts. He rolled in agony. A gun that had been in his possession clattered to the hardwood floor under him as he flailed, trying to hold in his large intestine as blue lights burst from within him into the wounds.

Sara pressed her attack, in shock that Alex and his band of jackals had found them already. Running into the spacious bedroom, she had opened fire on the struggling men at point blank range.

Morgan grabbed the screaming baby and slipped off the far side of the bed. She lay over her son , instinctively covering her head.

Sara was screaming and cursing at them as she fired.

Michael had almost risen to his feet, blocking a clear shot at his father. Holding his son, Alex knew they were trapped. Sara started firing into Michael's back, his body jerking as the shots hit him. Alex instinctively started backing away, dragging Michael with him.

In front of the large ground floor window, Alex literally laid down backwards into the pane of glass just as he took Sara's last bullet in his forearm. The shattering glass rained down on Alex and his badly wounded son as they fell through it.

The bed was still bloody and wet with childbirth. As Sara scrambled over the bed, to the side where Morgan lay, she quickly scanned Morgan for any sign of blood from a bullet hole.

Morgan was trying to push the baby under the bed in a panic. As she scrambled from the bed to Morgan's side, Sara virtually ripped the small drawer open on the nightstand above their heads. Inside the drawer was a clip for the 9mm that Sara still held in her hand, still smoking from the barrel. There was also a small .22 pistol and, after slamming the clip into her gun, she grabbed the loaded smaller pistol as well.

A gun in each hand, Sara ran in a crouch to the broken window.

The long curtains that had billowed from it had been torn from their rod and ripped outwards with the men's bodies. Sara listened intently before risking a quick glance. The curtains lay in the bright morning sun, moving with a slight breeze.

Large spots of blood soaked into the silky fabric, and Sara could see more blood smeared in the snow. There appeared to be drag marks surrounding them.

Sirens were coming from a distance, getting closer.

Sara stood for a long moment, trying to figure out where the men had gone. She was pretty sure she had not mortally wounded that bastard Michael. She knew he would heal quickly, but she still prayed that she had hit him in the heart.

The baby's cries seemed to mix with the approaching sirens. Morgan was sobbing loudly, still trying to push the boy as far under the bed as she could.

Moving quickly, Sara had retrieved the baby, his cries of protest at this new world perfectly understandable. She asked Morgan in a harsh whisper.

"Can you walk yet? ...Or at least crawl? ... Come on, baby girl! ... Don't cry...Can you walk, Morgan?"

Morgan nodded weakly, not sure she could walk at all.

Putting a pistol in the waistband of her jeans, Sara had used her free hand to help Morgan to her feet, literally holding her up as her knees tried to buckle.

With an inhuman strength born of fear, Sara had half carried, half dragged Morgan to the attached garage. The sirens were still some way off, but the wash of sound seemed to surround them. Putting Morgan in the back seat, she almost threw the baby on top of his mother as she rushed around to the driver's door. As the garage opened, Sara was ready with the reverse, pushing the sleek sedan backward from its cave.

The lake cottages had been there for two hundred years, and Sara had owned hers since they were first built. The big rambling structures were spaced on wide lots around a large lake, which was now frozen in a winter slumber.

One of her neighbors, Charles, had heard the shooting.

He was standing in his yard looking across the divide between them, when the sedan had shot out of the garage and onto the wet street. Sara grinned, deliciously, as his eyes widened, a cordless phone stuck to his ear. Sara had known the old coot since he was a little boy at the beginning of the last century.

She could see he was excited and animated. Little Charlie-Boy was calling the police on her.

Sara took a road that curved away from the lake, away from the approaching sirens. She knew that no police would be able to find her in this forest.

As Sara drove, Morgan had put the baby to her breast again, passing out as he latched on. Sara watched her in the rearview mirror for a moment, remembering her total shock earlier.

Morgan had not lied to her. When Sara had seen that the child was a boy, as Morgan had known it would be, a terrible crushing feeling had hit Sara .

As she had tied off the cord, she was shaking with fear, with awe. Filled with a consuming terror , Sara had questioned Morgan sharply.

The exhausted woman had just stared at her with a quiet belligerence. Morgan was done answering questions. The healthy boy's very existence, said it all.

The baby was perfect. Sara shook her head at the memory of the perfectly formed boy slipping into her own hands.

This child could destroy the world., and it had been her own hands that had brought him into it. Sara felt awe and horror, not certain which was real.

As she drove, she prayed that she was wrong. She tried telling herself that the baby must be a girl, but she knew what she had seen. For the first time in many years, Sara felt true terror. And the real presence of the Divine.

They had driven for a long time, trying to decide where was safe. The only place that came to mind was the mosque.

Abby hadn't seen Morgan in almost ten years, but he had immediately thrown himself into the face of danger. The baby had also shocked him, but the joy he felt at seeing Morgan had made the man so happy that he was positively beaming as he took them both from the car.

Abby knew what this baby was, and yet caution was totally abandoned as he fell in love with the new baby instantly. He had hid them in the mosque until the night Abby and Sara had left to find Joseph. Only Abby had returned.

Now six days later, he stood in the doorway the federal agents had just exited from, unmoving and afraid.

Abby knew Morgan had slipped into the main floor as the Feds had surprised him, holding the baby. He heard her, but not the Feds until they literally walked up to him, on the mat strewn floor.

The baby was still mewling softly, and Abby bounced him absent-mindedly as he watched the door. They might change their minds and come back.

After a long while, Morgan could no longer stand the fullness in her breasts. Stepping out of her shadowed hiding place, she approached Abby from behind, knowing that he knew she was there. Turning to her, his expression told her that he was very aware of the danger surrounding him.

Morgan stared into his face with a tender acceptance of his fear.

"We can't wait for her any longer, Morgan…If we stay here they will find us." He said.

She shifted her gaze to the baby who was now squirming against Abby, looking for his dinner.

"Abby, we need the priest…"

She let the words hang in the air.

"We don't even know if Father Matthew survived! We don't even know if Gail survived, for that matter!"

His fear was making him edgy as he snapped at her.

Morgan looked at him, surprised and amused, holding out her hands for the baby. He instinctively let her take the boy. She handed off the sword to him as she snuggled the baby to her.

Now smiling, she chuckled at him.

"You should know better, Abby. If Gail has not been found, then she's alive."

She lifted up her thin shirt, exposing her breast, now hard with milk.

"Since the priest's body has not turned up, I suspect Gail is still with him. If he survives his wounds, then she will stay with him until he can move. I just pray that prick Jerold won't find them first. If the priest is hurt that bad…"

They both let the thought alone. If Gail was trapped, and the priest was wounded so badly he couldn't fight, then she could easily be overwhelmed and the priest killed.

They needed Father Matthew.

Walking back to the shadowed spot that she preferred, Morgan quietly sat down to feed the baby. Abby watched her walk through the large empty space, but he had hung back in the center of the building. The loud knock on the door they had just left startled them both.

Still holding the sword, Abby stopped dead still. The knock sounded again, louder this time. Morgan felt for the pistol in the back of her jean's waistband, flicking off the safety. She deliberately nodded at Abby from the gloom.

Turning back to the door, he stashed the sword in the fold of his traditional robes and swallowed hard.

Pulling the door open cautiously, Abby looked out to see a very short, very pretty young woman watching him.

He could tell she wasn't Arabic; maybe Puerto Rican, or maybe Native Indian, but she was definitely not one of his faithful. He frowned at her, confused by her presence and bold stare.

"May I help you?"

He asked it evenly, although he turned the sword's hilt in his hand within his robes.

"I'm looking for a cleric named Abdullah?"

The woman glanced around the street, trying to be casual.

"I am Abdullah."

He made no move away from the door.

The woman looked at him sharply, like she was deciding something. After a moment, he arched his eyebrows as if to say, "Get on with it."

"I need to talk to you, Abdullah…"

Again, she glanced around, taking one half step toward him. He did not move.

"I'm sorry, by Islamic law, women are not allowed in this part of the mosque…If you could…"

"Is Morgan allowed in there?"

She said it softly, but he reacted as if she had hit him. Before he could recover, she pressed on.

"I don't care about semantics right now, sir; we are all in danger…I'm here with a message. I need to talk to you. And Morgan."

She met his gaze of shock evenly, unflustered.

Not bothering to deny it, Abby was overcome by a sense of paranoia. He looked up and down the street, pausing to look into the crowd of

138

teenagers gathered around the store on the corner. He looked at her again.

"Who are you, young lady?" Abby asked with dread.

He could still deny everything.

"My name is Maria. I have a message from Anna. She is watching us now, sir."

Abby looked into Maria's eyes with only mild surprise. His sudden stiffening, though, brought a chill to her. She knew exactly how he felt. Anna had that effect on everyone, Maria thought wryly. Without a further comment, Abby stepped back from the door, ushering her in quickly.

Within an hour, Michael and Jerold also pulled onto the same street, parking at the store where Abby had seen the teens earlier.

They spent the next two hours terrorizing an old Arabic housekeeper. Michael had pushed his will into her, probing her knowledge. She had no idea where they had gone. They? Yes, they; Abby , the woman, and the baby.

Leaving the Arab woman kneeling in agony, Michael had been furious. Jerold accepted it as a dreadful feeling of fate. After ripping the place apart they sat in the car, watching the mosque, helplessly.

Michael thought about the scientist. His thoughts flashed to Anna. Everything was spiraling out of control. Jerold watched Michael and the younger man did his best not to flinch under his gaze.

"What now?" Michael knew the question was laughable.

"Wherever they ran, it won't be easy to find them. That bastard Abby is as resourceful as the women…We have to find the priest. Until we can figure out where Morgan is, we have to find Gail and that priest…They have to be taken out, now!"

Jerold sighed heavily.

"If your daddy wounded him badly enough, then we may not need to kill the priest, he will just die. … But either way, Gail still knows where to find the baby. We have to find her."

Michael had to be very careful. If Jerold suspected Michael's motives, he was not showing it.

Turning the engine over, Michael pulled back into the street, wondering where in the hell all of this would wind up.

Chapter 9

February 1, 1:14 p.m.

Matthew was drifting in and out. He had been in the backseat all afternoon, dozing as the miles passed. Gail had let him sit up front for a while that morning, but he tired very quickly. He had held on, but as the pain started again, he could no longer hide the sag of his once huge, powerful frame. Whatever pudginess he had gained as a priest, he had lost.

His injuries made him understand, as never before, how very fragile even the strong are. Not even shattering both arms in the wreck that had killed his parents had immobilized him like his encounter with the giant stranger at the church. For a long while Matt pondered on the man that had attacked him, the mental image of the man somehow making the pain of his wounded lung worse.

More and more, Matthew wanted the little blue pills. He silently struggled against it. He fought so hard; he had no strength left to try to hold off the pain of every movement.

The pain was sometimes soul-shattering. For a priest, Father Matthew did not like God very much at the moment. .

At one time, Matthew had been a pothead. He grimaced on the back seat. He had always understood addiction, addictive behavior. He had never lied about it. And then after…after his life, limbs, and family were shattered, it had seemed so easy to give up the drugs. . Sometimes, he had marveled at how the urge was just swept away; he had found God. He grimaced again.

First fate; and then God. Matthew had ran to God, begging Him to erase the final screams of his mother from his mind. Father Joseph had found him there, in the church, begging God to forgive him, and let him die.

Matthew had finally given in to the pain from his lung. After leaving the front seat, he had sheepishly asked Gail for a pill. The pain was making him gag. He wondered if she had witnessed his struggle.

When she had looked at him, her eyes had narrowed thoughtfully, unintentionally. After all, she had known Matthew from a child. She had seen his highs, literally, and his lows. Arching her brow, her eyes softened as she saw him quivering in pain. She was running low on the pills and his wounds were still horrible, crippling.

Gail knew her work on the massive wound in his chest was not sufficient, and that she needed help. She decided to seek it out, knowing the delay would make her sister come to her.

Gail thought about the mother and child in Anna's possession. Their cousin Morgan had placed herself, and new son, into the hands of God and perhaps the strongest pure blood Mortal ever born. Gail knew it would not be enough.

Retrieving the envelope from the glove box, Gail silently took out the little pill and put it in Matthew's palm. He had glanced at her, but she had already turned away, pulling at food wrappers and other assorted travel trash they had amassed. He drank it down with the last warm sip of his Dr. Pepper. He winced at the bitterness or the warmth; both of them were pretty gruesome. They had driven further south, stopping now and then as the morning wore on.

Matthew thought of the hotel room they had lived in for weeks, or years; in his drugged state he couldn't tell anymore. He knew he was wanted for murder. He opened his eyes and studied the ceiling of the car from the backseat. He was caught in something he didn't understand.

Matthew wanted to weep for Joseph, but he didn't like him right now, either. Father Joseph had lied to him. He was certain of it.

Looking at the back of Gail's head, he saw she had pulled her long reddish brown straight hair up into a ponytail. Matthew could see most of her right cheek and jaw line and he again thought, why the hell does she look so different?

Not different maybe…just younger. Much younger.

For the thousandth time, he thought, 'Impossible.'

He had known Gail for as long as he had been dragged to church, which was basically all his life. She had seemed old even when he was a child. He had recently started thinking that maybe Gail was Joseph's lover. He wondered if he could be wrong. Nothing made sense anymore.

Matthew didn't trust anything. He knew he was heavily drugged.

All Gail had said was, "We'll discuss everything when you're

141

stronger."

Perhaps she meant when he wasn't drugged up. Everything he saw was jumbled. His thoughts seemed detached and out of order.

Perhaps sensing his observation, Gail turned her head slightly, taking a quick look back at her frail patient; she paused when she saw his eyes, swollen and dreamy. He was fighting unconsciousness.

She smiled at him, giving him the weirdest image of her, bathing in a fountain filled with youth tonic. He giggled slightly at his own absurdities as she turned her attention back to the road.

Yep, he knew that she knew what he feared. She saw his struggle. In his foggy state, he was sure of it. Perhaps no one on earth knew him better than Gail, his mother's closest friend. The thought comforted him that Gail, of all people, had never given up on him, even in her own sorrow and rage. He was glad he was with her in the darkest of days.

As he drifted off, he felt a horrible panic. He felt that there was something important that he couldn't remember. He took a deep calming breath, forcing him to relax. He knew that between the shock and the drugs, his short-term memory was playing games with him.

He knew that if he just got stronger, it would ease up. He tried to be stronger.

Gail knew, too. He was relieved to realize that she knew! When he got stronger, she would tell him everything; that's what she had said. He waited to get stronger.

Forgetting what he was thinking about all together, Matthew finally succumbed to sleep.

Gail drove on carefully. Alert and cautious, she blended in with the rest of the traffic.

The southerly direction had led them into milder climates, and she marveled at the lush green expanses that remained in place even at this frigid time of year. She had forgotten how beautiful the south was. They had stopped in Mississippi, although Matt never came to. She had bought him some chili fries knowing he couldn't really handle a burger.

He had eaten some in Florida; for that, she had been grateful. She had stopped at a chicken restaurant drive-through, and he had downed a whole order of mashed potatoes and half the macaroni and cheese, but had fallen back into unconsciousness soon after. Gail knew that without further intervention, he would not heal quickly, nor even at all.

142

Not as quickly as Gail did, to be sure. She wished Matthew could heal as she did. She absently looked at her hand. Dislocating her knuckle had hurt like hell. But within a day , the bruise had completely faded. The abnormal swelling had disappeared. Sometimes, she was grateful for her mother's Mortal blood. Other times…well, not so much.

Gail never could decide whether she loved, or hated her mother. Even time itself had not sorted out that issue in her heart.

Gail had never known her real father.

Sara had been a landowner's wife in Jerusalem. Her human husband was not Gail's father, but it was obvious Gail's father was a human.

Gail's early childhood had seemed very normal, until the day she had accidentally discovered that her mother's husband was a homosexual.

Sara had tried to explain her marriage of convenience to the child, but she had understood only too well. Gail had pushed her mother about her own paternity; if not her husband, then who? Sara refused to answer.

Gail had become spiteful, calling her mother terrible names. Sara had slapped her, hissed at her, losing her patience.

She learned that her life and identity was a lie.

Gail smirked humorlessly behind the wheel. It had been not too long after that she had learned that her mother's life was also a lie, a big one.

The man Gail had always known as her father had cried and begged the child's forgiveness. He felt his sin had brought it all to bear. Gail had blamed him for years.

For a long time, she did not understand that it was her mother's lie had damned them all. Sara tried to tell her spiteful child the truth of whom she was. She had told her about her 'other family', called Mortals. Sara let Gail rudely question her, trying to explain the rules they must live by. A sixteen year old Gail refused to hear it, accusing her mother of being both a whore, and a liar.

Even her big sister Anna had been in on all the lies!

Gail refused to believe Sara. When her only earthly father had died suddenly, without her forgiveness, Gail's spite had turned on her mother.

The only thing Gail ever knew about her real father is that he was human. That was as much as Sara would tell her.

Gail was a half-breed. Her older sister, Anna, was a full blood Mortal, as was their mother Sara. Gail had resented the idea she was not a pureblooded human, or Mortal. She lashed out at Sara for it every chance she got. Gail knew better, though, than to confront her sister..

Anna had already been grown for millennia when Gail was born. She had encouraged her mother to have a child, for Anna had wanted one so badly herself.

Sara's marriage to the man had been purely political. He was a landowner and statesman; she was beautiful and worldly.

Sara had met him as a young man and had suspected that he was gay. She remained in the community, and after some years, she had met him again. He was a very eligible bachelor but apparently a hard catch. She had charmed him out of his secrets; she was a good listener, understanding. They made arrangements by morning; by the new month, they were married. They respected one another, staying very discreet, so as not to bring dishonor.

He amassed a fortune; Sara tried to spend it.

Sara had adored her husband. She was not attracted to him, so there was no unrequited love. They simply played by the rules and were happy.

One day, he recruited Anna, and in a drunken, festive, very loud announcement, they both declared to all of the partygoers that they needed an addition to the family and that Sara should get on with it. The crowd had cheered as her husband drunkenly lifted her and bodily carried her from the garden. The revelers had gone wild, clapping, and shouting.

He had delivered Sara to a room in the main house. Her husband had set her down outside the door and kissed her cheek lightly.

"I need an heir." He smiled at her.

She smiled back, cocking her head suspiciously toward the door. He produced a bag of coins and handed them to her.

"You will need these…"

Sara looked at it stupidly for a second, cupping her face as understanding dawned, making her flush.

"You bought me a stud?" She snorted with laughter.

Her husband, trying to talk quietly through the giggles tried to reassure her. ,

"No…No…Not 'bought', more like…um…'rented', actually."

They leaned against each other, laughing drunkenly.

Finally calming herself, she asked, "Are you sure you want this?"

As she said it, her husband's muscled young lover came quietly into the hall, looking at them expectantly, smiling slyly. They had smiled back at him. Her husband hugged her tightly.

"I'm the happiest man in the world."

She looked at him. He smiled gently, bending again, plopping a big wet kiss on her forehead.

"I need an heir, before I get too old to enjoy it! That stud will sire fine stallions!"

Saying that, he turned on his heel, leaving her alone at the door. Arm and arm with his lover, they had disappeared into the dark halls of the huge manor, leaving Sara alone to decide.

She had not taken a lover in decades, her mortal skin ached for the sensation of a human touch..

After only one second thought, Sara walked through the door with her bag of coins.

Her husband had good taste, very good taste. Within two weeks , Sara was pregnant. Their friends had cheered when her husband announced that he would be a father soon. She had excused herself to cry.

Exactly nine months from the night she was conceived, Gail was born; an eternal bastard to both races of man.

I In the car two thousand years later, Gail once again thought of how much people will do to have a child. She had tried many times herself. It had taken hundreds of years for Gail to accept that she was barren.

All half-breeds were barren.

Understanding her mother wasn't enough to dispel Gail's resentment. She glanced at Matthew again in the mirror.

He was out cold.

After her mother's husband had died, Gail inherited everything.

She had been a child of privilege, and in a time when women had very little, Gail was a powerhouse overnight. The rich, beautiful heiress refused many marriage offers, one from a crown prince.

It was said her only lover, was commerce.

Gail had tripled her inheritance within two years. She had denied the truth completely. Gail had been so spiteful; she had used her money and its influence to ruin Sara, and had chased her from the community.

Gail was sure that Sara had lied to her about everything; but, as the years had passed, Gail knew she was not aging. At age twenty seven, at the very height of her beauty and strength, time stopped touching her at all.

Gail watched her friends get old. In a cosmic irony, her eternal youth

145

made some believe that she was in league with the devil. Two childless marriages to human men seemed to confirm to the society around her that Gail was, in fact, bewitched.

She barely escaped the community she had lived in since birth. Even her friends had joined the mob to drag the fifty-eight year old Gail out into the sunlight, where all could see her unlined face and vibrant body. They had stripped her naked before throwing her into the road with no mercy.

Mortals were not even considered grown until they were one thousand years old. But by human time, Gail should have been an old woman. She could not yet control the power she had to make herself appear older. It took hundreds of years for Mortals to control such gifts.

On that day Gail finally learned that Sara was right, and that Gail should have moved on thirty years ago. Sara had warned her that her life would be in danger if she didn't. That day Gail learned to listen to her mother.

The entire village had stoned her. As Gail was dragged from her home, she begged God for a miracle.

When they had battered her body, she screamed at God. She asked for salvation, for deliverance.

As if in answer to her prayers, Anna had appeared on a huge black stallion.

The cold mud of the road had seemed to be a death shroud for Gail. The bright afternoon mocked her along with the crowd. The stones bashing her had suddenly stopped. She tried to crawl away.

The road slithered from the shadowed forest and as Gail crawled along it, she had looked up, seeing her beautiful sister astride the huge mount, slowly emerging from the wood.

Gail had collapsed face first into the mud.

Some of the elders of the large crowd remembered Anna from long ago.

They had stood open mouthed, in shock, watching the approaching figure. The younger people didn't understand, and one young man ignored the woman on the horse and rushed forward in the now mostly silent crowd. He kicked Gail as hard as he could in the left side of her head.

Anna watched them across the distance, as they tried unsuccessfully to kill her sister.

The elders of the group were staring at Anna and crossing themselves,

146

spitting on the ground. They retreated, somewhat, as Anna drew near Gail's shattered body.

The younger man, feeling a threat he couldn't understand, watched the newcomer, thinking she, too, would help them expel the witch in their midst. Anna stared him in the eyes as she dismounted. He blinked at her, not understanding her boldness.

The elders had gone silent, not knowing what this meant. A restless nervousness bristled the crowd. The horse, now unencumbered, did as it had been trained to do, and stood an arm's length behind Anna. The men of the group stood in awe as Anna removed her hood, revealing herself. The women stood silent, unsure of the evil, cowed by her beauty. Anna had slowly looked through the crowd, seeing faces she remembered. Finally, scowling, she had looked at her spiteful sister lying at her feet. The young man who had kicked her stood straight, not yet satisfied that his viciousness was spent.

Anna had bent over Gail. She would heal, Anna knew. Getting her spotless robes muddy, she gently pulled at Gail's shoulder. Anna watched the young man every moment. Gail had let out a low moan. Her mouth had been badly beaten and her teeth had cut halfway through her tongue. They had sawn off her long auburn hair. The mud and blood mixed in a sticky ooze, her eyes were swollen shut.

From her crouched position, Anna spoke to the crowd, quietly darting her eyes around them, waiting to be attacked.

"I'm taking this woman from here…Your fun is over…Go home…"

The young man had instantly started moving toward the women, furious.

"She be a witch! Touch her and Lucifer will hex you as well!" he spat at her.

Anna waited for him to come, still squatting. His angry momentum carried him within a step of her. As he opened his mouth again, Anna had thrust up from the earth, her fist catching him in fully the face.

The youth was about her height, built like a planter's son. His nose had caved under her blow. The audible crack echoed as he crumpled from the unexpected carnage of his face.

As soon as she landed the punch, Anna whistled high and shrill. Before the crowd could react to anything, the thunderous sound of hooves rattled through the now still morning. The horsemen came from all sides.

147

As they bore down on them, Anna shouted at the shocked crowd.

"You think the devil can be beaten from flesh? I say we shall see!"

The men on horseback, all cloaked in fine robes, shuffled in different directions as the crowd fled in a panic. Using whips and sticks they had cut in the forest, they hit anyone on foot that they could reach. One of the elders screamed as a horseman bore down on him, running him over with the huge chestnut roan. Anna had ordered them to beat the women of the crowd, too, and they were not spared the whip or the rod. Only the obvious youth were spared a savage whipping.

These men always followed Anna's orders. Without hesitation.

The melee around her in full swing, Anna had picked Gail up from the road. With her considerable strength she had pulled Gail up on the massive stallion. Holding her sister to her, Anna had left the townspeople to her men and rode hard through the forest. A major port city lay to the west, and by nightfall, Anna had ridden directly to the docks. Gail could barely move as they were approached by men who had been waiting for their arrival.

Someone asked Anna should they get the doctor, but she had waved them away. Gail covered her face so that the blue lights stitching her back together slowly could not be noticed.

As the men carried Gail up the gangplank, she could see the schooner was huge, a mermaid standing on the tip of the bow. Warm light glowed from the portholes.

By the morning, Anna's men had returned to the ship, noisily putting their horses into the hold. By dawn, they had disembarked.

The crew of sixty men seemed to bow to Anna's every whim. She handled them fairly, treated them with respect. More than a few looked at her with the shy looks of undeclared love. Gail was also treated the same way, except that she never tried to order them around. That was just as well, because they only obeyed Anna, anyway.

It had taken Gail four days to heal completely. Within a month, her hair was again to her waist. The sailors, not speculating about her recovery, had made jokes about the two most beautiful witches on the sea.

Gail grieved, not understanding how she could have lost everything she had ever known. Anna stayed quiet, understanding how upset she was. After a time, the sisters started discussing their secret in long, late night conversations. Gail was depressed, unaccepting. Anna let her be. She did not envy the rough lesson half breed's always learned to let go of their

148

human lives and ambitions. In many ways, Anna felt sorry for Gail, even if her own stubbornness had created a situation where Gail had lost everything, even her palace.

The first true intimacy of their bond as siblings on the ship produced a profound respect between them. A deep friendship was forged in the bond of the blood they shared. Anna watched her struggle with the truth. She didn't try to tell Gail what she thought of it all. The truth was something they all must decide for themselves. .

Gail had finally moved on after time. As new days kept dawning, she had eventually found that life had gone on. She had pirated with Anna for a few years; eventually she had gone on to study painting for many years, . For more than two dozen years, she had been a dancer, then a seamstress. Gail studied the law, medicine, religion, and history.

She had started a new relationship with her long-lost mother. Sara still blamed her, saying that the stress of Gail's hatred had killed her beloved husband. Gail did not feel sorry for her. She figured Sara had always known that she would outlive him. They agreed to disagree.

Gail became stepmother to seven children. Gail's new husband did not mind that she loved the kids more than him. Sara and Anna helped raise them; sometimes their Mortal cousin, Morgan, and her children would come to visit. Morgan had eleven daughters when Gail first met her. All of them virtual images of their mother. All of them half-breeds like Gail. All of them barren.

Morgan kept them happy, well-balanced. No one spoke of Morgan's mother. The woman had almost killed them all.

Because of Morgan's mother, one last savage curse from God had made sure that their race would die. Eventually. Inevitably. For over two thousand years, no full blood mortal child had survived birth. Only half breeds.

Morgan tried to fight against fate. She had had forty-seven daughters in her lifetime, teaching them all to adopt other women's human children. Making sure her legacy carried into many races. to date, Morgan was the mother of forty seven half human children she had borne.

Forty seven daughters. And only one son.

They watched the children Gail had raised, wither with age. She watched them die. Gail had become a writer, a teacher, and during a plague, a grave digger. She learned to play musical instruments: all of them. She traveled everywhere, spoke many languages. She married, and then buried human husbands. One husband she had killed in self-defense.

Gail nursed Anna after she gave birth to her third child. A dead son.

All three boys had been half human, perfectly formed, and lifeless. Unlike the other full-breeds, Anna seemed not to be able to reproduce herself with identical daughters. Only dead boys. The three of them had been born beyond saving, already blue.

Gail had held Anna down, holding her through the screams when she had lost her mind. They had buried the baby together. Anna tried to retrieve his body that night. She had almost killed Gail in her fury at God. She was actually trying to kill Morgan. The boy's grave was barely spared. Sara had thrown herself on the fresh grave, begging Anna to stop. Morgan and a wounded Gail had nearly beaten Anna half to death to subdue her. They had carried her, broken, from the family's cemetery, leaving behind Sara, who had collapsed in sobs. Sara stayed with the graves of her dead grandsons for almost two days.

Thankfully, the newborns of their race that are born dead do not incinerate when death takes them. They had all been able to hold the boys before burial and kiss their still faces.

After that, Anna refused to get pregnant. She became a spy, and then a soldier, a mercenary. Then a missionary. While Anna wiped blood from her sword, Gail fed poor children. Anna became a highway robber, giving her ill-gotten gains to Gail's food crusade. Gail became a nun; Anna went on the run in several countries for murder.

In one country, Anna was considered a terrorist. But, she always explained, even if the men were scared of her, the women there loved her. Behind their husband's backs, they called Anna a hero.

Gail waited for the years they could see each other.

Anna avoided kids; Gail sought them out longingly. They sought each other often, both desperate to hold off the loneliness of life. They spent time with Sara. They stayed months at a time drunk at one of Morgan's jolly homes. They had made friends, only to watch them grow old and die. At night, when she was supposed to pray, Gail instead cursed God.

She cried for the child she would never have. Her mother and Morgan had pitied her, and Anna for their inability to have children. Gail had hated them for it.

Gail drove into the afternoon sun with Matthew snoring behind her. She wondered how Sara had found her and Joseph, the infant she had kidnapped from Sara almost 70 years before. The only obvious answer was Anna.

Chapter 10

February 1, 2:21 p.m.

Michael watched Diana through narrowed lids. Lying on the enormous bed, he feigned sleep as he watched her. Her long frame had fleshed out pleasantly with his child. She was digging in the closet, pausing to look up at the shelf above her head. Her skin glowed in the faint afternoon light.

Michael thought she was breathtaking.

The slight filmy nightgown Diana wore exposed her creamy shoulders, gathering the filmy folds into a beautiful embroidered silk cascade. As she stood on her tiptoes to retrieve something from the shelf, her now very pronounced belly thrust out. He gazed at it with wonder. A half-empty box dislodged from beside her outstretched hands and plopped ungraciously on the top of her head.

From the bed, Michael snickered involuntarily.

Starting at his sudden proof of life, she retrieved the box from the floor and chucked it at him.

They seemed to be taking naps all the time now. Diana she was moody and restless lately. When she threw the box at Michael, he only laughed harder, and she stomped out of the master suite. She felt horribly pregnant. She frowned at the trappings of wealth around her. In the kitchen, on the immaculate counter, she found her letter holder.

Grabbing it and the checkbook, she sat down at the sixteenth century Spanish table to pay her bills.

She loved the huge, heavily carved table that Michael had given her. She knew that it had originally been commissioned by a prince in the 15th century. What she didn't know was that the 'prince' who had commissioned it was Michael. It had only ever had one owner.

She sat for a few minutes, paying her more personal bills from her trust fund account. She wrote checks for her nephew's birthday, a Valentine's Day present for Michael, and the private detective who was following

Michael also got a check.

Diana wrote out a shopping list for the housekeeper. As she was writing out a birthday card to her brother's kid, Michael bounded into the room naked, dwarfing the refrigerator as he attacked it. She watched from the table, giggling now and then at the top-heavy Dagwood sandwich he was making.

The pregnancy had influenced Diana's hormones and that morning they had already made love three times. Michael had lost track of time, working up an appetite. He had forgotten that death was waiting for them. Diana was not even aware of its presence, the life inside her kicking, making her feel alive in Michael's arms. He had finally collapsed on her, spent and shaking. They had fallen asleep like that.

In her slumber, she clutched him to her breast. He nuzzled them, dropping into dreams that at first seemed pleasant. The baby kicked at his imposing weight.

Diana had fallen into a natural deep sleep. Michael's dreams became disjointed, dark.

His father was there, saying words that Michael could not hear. She was there too; Anna stood behind Alex. She stared at him, saying nothing as if also aware this was only a dream.. She shook her head slightly. He tried to say something to Anna , but he, too, was only mouthing words that remained silent. His father became agitated, slapping him sharply. Anna simply shook her head; he longed for her.

In his sleep, he had pushed Alex back, not caring what he was trying to say. But Anna had magically turned into Diana. She was holding a baby. She held it out to him, smiling, wanting him to see. The baby was dead. He tried to turn away from her, crying with shock. Morgan was there. She too held a baby. He saw the baby was alive, but he had yellow eyes, and sharp little teeth. He spat at Morgan and her child. She also started shaking her head.

Michael awoke, still slightly covering Diana. He had been sweating, and as he tried to roll away slightly, the moistness of his skin pulled at her. She turned over once his weight was lifted off her, falling once more into a deep sleep.

He had lain in bed for a while, thinking about Anna. Her memory seemed to burn through him. He remembered her in many times and many places. She looked back at him from his memory, both chilling and inflaming his mind. He thought about the cruelty of the God who had cursed him, the God who had cursed them all.

Lying quietly, Michael had studied the expensive, impressive molding around the ceiling of Diana's luxurious bedroom. He thought about Morgan. Her mother also came to mind, and he could see the woman's face so clearly, even though she had been dead for over four thousand years.

Michael thought of his father, unexpectedly remembering the way Alex had shoved the blade into the woman. It had all been for nothing; the final curse had already been set down.

Jerold, too, had been there.

Alex and Jerold had ambushed the queen that posed as a human. .

Morgan had been just a child, and after her mother's murder was discovered, an army had taken the girl and her soon-to-be husband and fled. Morgan's sisters were taken to the desert and killed, though no one seemed to know by whom. Alex had also killed the man whom Morgan had known as her father, a heretic king, some years before.

Morgan and her child husband had stayed behind impregnable walls. The girl had no-one but her child love. She was unaware for many years why her parents had been killed.

The entire Mortal family had held their breath, knowing Morgan's position could be manipulated. They wondered if she would also have to die. It was obvious to them all that Morgan, herself, believed she was human.

After a while, Michael quietly rose from the bed. He shaved and showered and finally relaxed into the sauna. He tried to shake the memories, but they seemed to echo in the quietness. Again, his thoughts turned to Diana. He became emotionless as the endless scenarios ran through his mind.

The men of his race had to be very careful. He had not been, and his near-sightedness would bring death very soon.

Like the women of his race, he could only reproduce himself with a human mother. Any time his human lovers birthed a girl, it was always the same. The mother was spared her life but not the crushing defeat of giving birth to a dead daughter.

If a human woman bore one of the Mortal men's half breed sons, without fail, the mother died as soon as the boy was expelled from the womb. The human women simply did not have the strength to survive giving birth to a living Mortal child. None had ever survived it.

Half-human boys were as infertile as the half-human girls. All were exact duplicate copies of their Mortal parent. Only random differences separated the halfbreed clones from their Mortal parent, such as hair or eye color.

Like her mother, Gail had the same abilities as Sara, to appear very old. All halfblooded reproductions mimicked the gift of their Mortal parent.

The only significant difference between full bloods and half breeds, besides fertility, was the full bloods healed twice as fast as their barren children.

A child between two full-blood Mortals was an entirely different story. Michael thought of Morgan again, feeling sick.

No Mortal woman had given birth to a living son for over two thousand years. It was obvious to them all that Morgan's child could not be half human, or else it would have been another identical daughter.

Michael wept for Diana.

Thinking of the sixteen daughters he had already buried, Michael prayed this child would be a son, although he knew the terrible price of it. Without meaning to, he had learned to love Diana.

He was desperate to have a son even if it was half human, and even if the mother lost her life for it. Michael was going to hurt, no matter how it happened.

In the sauna, Michael wished for death, as he had every year for a thousand years.

Michael wanted to weep for Anna, instead he smiled, knowing that it would be an insult to her to cry for her sake. He missed her miserably. He wondered if she missed him. Before leaving the sauna, he cried for her anyway.

In the kitchen, Diana also made herself a sandwich of gargantuan proportions. They laughed, throwing pickles at each other. She had returned her bills to the counter cubbyhole; unthinkingly, she left her checkbook on the countertop during the food fight. They had decided to shop that evening, so Diana again approached the subject of finding out the baby's sex. She needed to know what color clothes to buy.

Michael easily lied to her.

"You know I think it's just wrong...I think the old-fashioned way is best."

Michael, in fact, was curious enough himself; he actually thought the new technology was cool. He steeled himself, remembering his first wife's death, his new son still trying to suckle her. He remembered his greatest sin.

The sandwich in front of him made Michael sick suddenly. He did not want to know the future. Diana watched him nervously. Throwing the remainder of his sandwich onto the fine china, Michael stood, abruptly.

"I've told you…why can't we just be surprised like everyone else?" he snapped, annoyed.

He started away from the table, unconcerned about his nakedness.

Watching his back retreat, she retorted. ,

"Michael, everyone else gets the ultrasound done and knows the sex beforehand…"

He completely ignored her, disappearing into the massiveness of the apartment. Diana also lost her appetite, staring blankly at the food on her plate. Finally, sighing, she stood and went to the utility room to retrieve her favorite maternity shirt from the pile of folded laundry on the work table. She didn't bother to take her clothes to the bedroom, where Michael had no doubt gone.

Diana dressed quickly, fighting back frustrated tears. Before leaving the laundry, she glanced over, seeing a few folded papers put to the side, on top of Michael's folded casual clothes. Looking around, she picked them up, unfolding them as she looked around again. The paper had been folded into fourths and had obviously been carried around in someone's pocket for a while.

Robert Gorin, PhD, MD…Scientist and government researcher. Second in command of DNA Victim Identification Team for the September 11th attacks. … His entire life history was on the four pages, even his police record. Paper-clipped to one page was a newspaper photo of the doctor; the article talked about his work at Ground Zero where he tried to give the families some kind of closure.

Diana turned the pages over, unsure of what this was.

Alex and Jerold were the owners of a vast medical research facility. That facility would now be Michael's also.

It was not unusual to find one of the family in the company of scientists, but this paper still seemed strange to Diana. On the final page, someone had handwritten notes about the doctor; listing his daily schedule.

155

His favorite restaurants were listed along with his children's schools. Diana frowned as she looked at it. Looking around the laundry guiltily, she deliberately refolded the paper, stuffing it into her bra. Leaving the laundry, she could hear Michael in the bedroom stomping around, roughly finding his clothes.

Calling out to him, she left the apartment to retrieve some packages her father had sent to her that were being held at the front desk of the building.

Michael finished his dressing and went into the kitchen to find his car keys. He pocketed them and re-closed the bread from their lunch. Wiping crumbs from the counter, he noticed her checkbook. With no regard for Diana's privacy, he automatically picked it up, looking at the register.

Michael smiled as he saw the check that had been written to the art gallery. So, she had bought him the Monet after all. He would have to feign surprise. She had written checks to a spa, the DMV, and her housekeeper.

One check had been listed as Raydon and Raydon. Michael froze. Feeling a sense of paranoia, he looked around the still apartment.

Raydon and Raydon. Why the hell would she have a private investigator? Even as he wondered it, he knew. Dammit!

He glanced through the register. She had written them several checks, starting two weeks before. Michael could barely hold his anger. The last thing he needed was this shit! He was so close to finding the scientist, and now this… He steamed, knowing he couldn't afford this to happen.

If Jerold or Adam found the scientist first, Michael would be killed for exposing them. Damn it. Damn it!

Hearing the front door open, Michael closed the checkbook again, being careful to replace it exactly as she had left it. He smiled through grinding teeth. He remembered the smell of James's body as it charred. Michael was unaware that he was not the only one who had found a secret that morning.

***

February 1, 6.17 p.m.

Jerold stood on the immense balcony attached to his office. The busy twilight street far below him was soundless at this height, and he thrilled at the twinkling million lights as the city came to life for the evening.

He was worried about Michael.

Jerold knew his nephew was in love with this human girl, Diana. He also was aware that Michael was anticipating burying someone he loved again, as the impending birth would bring horror either way.

The melancholy of Michael's moods had been disruptive. Yesterday, Jerold had had to step in between Michael and Adam, again. He knew if they ever went for blood, Michael would outright kill his son. There was no question about who was stronger.

Well, Jerold thought wryly, stronger physically anyway.

Michael seemed to be having an emotional crisis. No... a full on nervous meltdown was more like it. He snapped at everyone, except Jerold, that is.

Jerold's secretary was not spared Michael's ire and Jerold had lost his temper with him. The woman had been so upset she had fled the building in tears, calling her boss to quit that night. He did not allow her to quit, but instead gave her permission to speak to Michael in any way she pleased. After he doubled her salary, she agreed to stay on. Michael was told to live with it. Jerold doubted that his secretary was the focus of Michael's rage.

Leaning absently against the railing, Jerold breathed in deeply, calming himself. He was dressed in a tux, as he had a party to attend that night, somewhere down amongst the glittering lights. Showing up would be good for business.

Jerold missed Alexander. He hated himself for missing him.

Watching the dusk settle fully onto the city, Jerold thought of his older brother without emotion. Every day, including today, he wondered if the evil that had touched Alex was also his own failing. He had loved his brother. But Jerold had also hated him, in equal measure.

For most of his extended life, Jerold had tried to emulate Alexander. He had admired his boldness, his coldness. Until his death, Alex was considered the strongest of all the Mortals, possibly the smartest, as well.

The disturbing aspects of Alex's personality had been ignored by his little brother, blinded by hero worship. The night the brothers had killed Morgan's mother, it had all changed.

Jerold had loved her, as well. For millennia he had loved her. Alex had seduced her as well. Not because Alex loved her, but because Jerold did. Alex never failed to laugh in his little brothers face about the fact Jerold's true love, often warmed his own bed, when she wished.

Only Jerold had known that she was killed because of something that Alex, himself, had put into motion. He had not known it until the woman was both begging for her life and cursing Alex for manipulating her.

Jerold had been shocked, disbelieving, not knowing how to stop Alexander. She had fought like a lion, but Alex was determined to kill her, along with his own secret guilt in a plot that rattled Heaven, itself.

Turning from her as she begged for her life, Jerold discovered that Michael had followed his father into the temple. The eight year old child had quietly slipped into the room behind them.

From the shadows, the boy had heard everything. Alex had just laughed when he saw his son. Even now, Jerold could hear that strange laughter coming from his brother as clear as the day it happened.

Alexander had forcefully shoved her across the room, half dragging her as she fought for her life.

They had ambushed her at her bath, knowing that she would send away all of her servants. The beautifully tiled bath was as large as a room, but the pool was only four feet deep. Pressing his attack, Alex used his body weight to thrust them both into the pool.

Losing his grip on her momentarily, she was able to propel herself a short distance away from him. She had laughed at Alex and Jerold, cursing them both as fools.

Mocking, beautiful, with welts on her face, she pushed against the chest high water, toward the opposite end of the bath. She shouted at them in angry humor.

"You think to drown me?" She asked it over her shoulder, her voice shrill and sarcastic.

She played for time, knowing that her personal guard was on the other side of the door. She focused on getting to the door, wading desperately away from Alex.

Jerold, no longer stunned by young Michael's appearance, moved to intercept her, knowing how quick she was. He was in a panic. Just as she had put her hands on the rim of the bath, she stopped; Jerold blocked her escape.

Their eyes locked. Jerold's heart hammered, feeling as if it would burst. Looking down on her, for just a moment, Jerold stood in awe at her beauty. She was magnificent!

From behind her, slowly closing the distance, Alex hissed at her in the sudden quiet.

"Of course, I'll not drown you…wouldn't that be a waste of time?"

She had torn her eyes away from Jerold as Alex came in within arm's reach of her. She had tried to turn and face him. As she turned her upper body, Alex swung the little gold dagger into the left side of her chest, the blade finding its mark right behind her breast.

She had stiffened, feeling the puncture as it broke her rib and then pierced the heart.

She stood up rigidly straight in the water, starting to actually lean against Alex. She had looked Jerold in the eyes for only a second before her facial muscles relaxed, her ethereal beauty became a death mask.

Jerold's heart nearly burst, as if it, too, had been punctured; he had staggered and almost fell. As her eyes rolled upwards, she started sliding down and Alex wrenched the dagger from her body. A gush of blood hit the water and made it smoke. Alex let her fall. He had known that she would not burn in the water. He had wanted the pathetic humans to find her body.

Still in a state of stunned silence, Jerold had stood there stupidly, unable to move, while his brother killed and mutilated the only woman he had ever loved.

Alex turned to the opposite side of the room where his son cowered into a corner, holding to a painted column and shaking violently. The boy was wide-eyed, trying to curl into a tight little ball. Alex leered at him, smiling like a feral animal.

Reaching for her floating body, Alex had turned her over; in one quick motion he cut off most of her nose.

From the corner, the boy had started moaning, uncurling his body as he vomited. The sound of Alex chuckling echoed obscenely through the tiled room. Jerold had been horrified. He had fled the hall of the holy place with an eight -year-old Michael.

It had all been in vain. Within months, the final curse was laid that damned them all. The extinction of the Mortal race had been decided. .

Only Jerold and Michael knew that Alexander had betrayed the woman whom had defied God and brought death to them all. She took the blame for their plots of divinity, but every Mortal faced the consequences.

The humans had indeed found her mutilated and disgraced body. Their queen was dead. She never should have taken the throne of human power.

Jerold had been secretly grateful that young Morgan, one of the youngest full-blooded Mortals, was guarded by an entire nation. He had wept bitter tears when told that Morgan's sisters were executed. All six of the girls had been innocent half breeds. .

Morgan too, was an innocent, but simply by virtue of her mother's blood, most of their race vowed to kill Morgan for her mother's crime. . The new human king was not yet ten years old.

Morgan, the new queen, was only twelve. Jerold worried for them both as he had haunted the palace, hoping for a glimpse of the girl.

As far as Morgan herself knew, she was human. Her mother had not lived long enough to tell her the truth of her life, the curse of it.

Palace life had bred into Morgan a wariness of everyone except the human boy she had been groomed to marry since birth. He was a fun boy, thoughtful and sensitive. For all their youth, they were in love. The boy king always knew those around them could not be trusted. He had been only too right. One night, he was murdered by his highest counsel, before he could reach full adulthood.

Morgan had just turned twenty-one. The nation was stunned by the loss of their young ruler.

When the news came that the boy king was dead, Jerold had fled for the capital, hoping to gain an audience with Morgan. One evening she had dressed as a peasant, slipped past the guards and into the streets. Within moments, from behind her, a huge glow from the palace brightened the night. As she had hurried away, flames exploded from the inner temple. The roar of fire led to confused shouting. Morgan slipped into the dark tangled streets and maze of houses.

As Jerold came into her vicinity, the fever had hit them both, buckling their knees, warning of the other's presence.

Their entire race had received the first curse of fever long ago, and even the Mortal children suffered it. The fever was triggered by the awareness of a Mortal of the opposite sex in their presence. Though the curse was meant to punish them, over time it had become a fair warning system that made it impossible for a Mortal to ambush another Mortal of the opposite gender.

Morgan had desperately tried to flee, knowing danger lived in every breath she drew. The first curse came upon them both. It seared her flesh, and her mind for the first time, as she had never before seen a Mortal male.

Jerold had recovered fast enough to pin her down, telling her to relax and that the scalding of her skin would stop soon..

160

He fought urges that he didn't understand; he could barely see her through the tears of pain in his own eyes. As her strength had returned, she had fought, but he had the advantage. He struggled internally, trying to push away the sensation of the burning inside him.

His hands clutched her arms; it felt as if they were blistering her skin. After a full agonizing minute, they were locked together, both broken by the fever.

He held her pinned to the ground until she calmed down. He asked her where she was going.

Heaving, exhausted, Morgan could not find the strength to try to lie. She was running away; the powers in the palace were plotting against her. She had no one. She was terrified.

The cool desert air finally found them again as the fever broke. She had no idea that Jerold was her father that night. That truth did not come until later.

Jerold had spirited her away, hiding her from his brother and others in their race that followed Alex's orders. He had told her the truth. Morgan , as expected, hated him for it.

Morgan was the only daughter Jerold ever had before the final curse assured he would never have another. She was one of the last full-blooded Mortals to be born.

Jerold told Morgan of his sister Mortal, Sara Katherine, knowing that the woman would not kill another female of her own blood. He told her how to seek out Sara, warning her that her daughter, Anna, may not feel as kindly disposed.

The curse of Morgan's mother had already produced two dead sons for Anna.

Enraged by him, Morgan left without a word, and he had grieved terribly for her. Over the years, he had grown to hate her, like he had hated her mother. Without knowing it, he hated Alex too.

And now, because Morgan bore his grandson, he would have to kill them both. Jerold mostly hated himself.

From the balcony, Jerold silently cried as he watched the glittering cityscape sparkle like a jewel in the night.

Chapter 11

February 2, 10:10 a.m.

Anna put two more cases of beer on the counter, digging for the crumpled hundred-dollar bill in her jeans. The greasy tattooed guy behind the counter couldn't stop staring at her shiny black hair, her boobs. While retrieving the money, she wondered if she could get away with punching the guy; she quickly decided to stay cool. Putting the money on top of one case, Anna eyed the bottles of liquor behind the counter on shelves.

Seeing the direction of her gaze and desperate to keep this hottie here a moment longer, the clerk asked in a rough accent.

"Anything up there you need?"

He swept his hand in a gesture toward the bottles as if she weren't aware of where to find them.

Swallowing her annoyance once again, she said, "Yeah, a fifth of that Jack, and let's see...a fifth of the Tanqueray beside it."

The guy turned to retrieve them.

"Y'alls having quite a party tonight, huh?" He asked.

He was hoping for an invite. She was extra hot. His heavy Southern drawl sounded like syrup poured on dirt. He was amusing and annoying to her. Anna smiled her most beguiling smile.

"Not at all. No party! I'm just a terrible alcoholic, and if I don't get my bottles everyday then I go crazy and I run off all my friends."
She smiled sweetly. The guy looked at her, unsure whether she was serious.

He quickly rang up the purchases, tried to smooth out the wrinkles in the hundred and gave her the change. Her presence suddenly made him nervous, but he wasn't sure why that was so.

He stuck with bravado and offered to put the four cases in the car.

"I would LOVE for you too!" she cooed at him.

He blushed, picking up the cases and went out to the car. She carried the bottles outside, glancing quickly at the grungy guy, making sure he wasn't dropping her beer all over the rental car. Instead of approaching the car herself, she turned and walked to the far side of the parking lot where a group of Latino men were gathered, maybe seven or eight of them. As they watched her advance, in Spanish , she heard some of them say, "Beautiful."

One of the younger ones looked her over from head to toe, saying as she joined them,

"Ooh la la, mamacita!"

Anna chuckled.

"Hola, mi chabos!" She exclaimed. They greeted her back.

"Are you here waiting for work?" she asked it softly, not trying to insult.

One of the older guys responded.

"Si, pretty lady, you need help?"

With the promise of work, the guys had stopped leering, all of them listening intently now.

Again Anna smiled, but this time in genuine humor.

"Si, amigo, I have a cabin on Caney Lake. It has not been used for a long time. You know where the lake is?"

They all nodded in unison.

"What you need done , pretty lady?" The older one again.

Anna nodded, trying to speak clearly without the deep Southern accent that had infected her own speech.

"I need to get it ready; my brother is coming in two days, he's very sick…needs a place to rest. There's a hole in the roof, and the back porch needs to be completely rebuilt. . Do any of you know electrical?"

At this, two of the men nodded. The older of the two, unsmiling, stared into her eyes boldly.

Anna stared back, enjoying his pretty-boy Aztec face.

"OK, I need to make sure the wiring is workable; just make sure it won't burn my house down. Think you guys could do that?" she asked.

All of the men nodded, and she wrote down the directions in Spanish, She gave them the bottles of hard booze, making sure they had a ride, which they assured her they did.

" If you can have the job done in twenty-four hours, five hundred each…Si?"

The men all looked dumbfounded, each one of them hurriedly nodding at the windfall. She had no doubt they would show up.

163

Anna had learned a very long time ago that there were two types of people: those who pay to have something done, and those who get paid to do it. Anna was a payer. She would rather kill someone than dust furniture.

In her lifetime, Anna had collected fortune upon fortune. More than enough to pay someone else to fix the roof. .

Much of her stockpile of riches was buried, literally. She kept a good cash flow in currency, diamonds, gold, bonds, all in various safety deposit boxes around the world. The rest she kept close to the many homes she owned. In all, she owned over a hundred homes, two of them were more like palaces.

The number of false identities she used was countless. She had secured credit cards in all of them. All of the Mortals were hoarding just as many treasures as she, all of them were forced to play games with identity.

Anna knew that Gail would not be coming to the lake soon.

When she concentrated, she could feel Gail's presence, see the wounded young priest, as Gail saw him. She saw signs announcing the names of towns and their populations. She saw the route through Gail's eyes. The last time Anna had reached out, Gail was still a day away, trying to break a fever that the priest had lapsed into. She knew they were in trouble.

Anna had emerged from her connection to her sister weak, as usual, but sickened by the sight of the priest's ghastly wound: puckered and still crusted with blood. She had felt her sister's nervous concern, her helplessness.

Anna lay still on the motel bed, trying to think past Gail's thoughts, as they fed back into her own mind..

The captain, Maria, and Douglas played cards in the adjoining room, unaware that Anna had even returned from the liquor store. As her strength flooded back, she bit her lip at the sensation.

Pleasure and pain rippled through her as her mind fully returned into her own skull..

Through the closed door, Anna could hear Doug teasing his uncle about being a cheat. Maria good-naturedly was defending Edwards by hinting that maybe it was Doug doing the cheating. By laughing and bantering, all of them were able to momentarily concentrate on something other than the bizarre.

Anna lay quietly for a long while, studying the familiar room around her.

If the priest was still that bad off, they could be in serious trouble. For the first time in centuries, Anna asked God for a favor. Under her breath, she whispered to the ceiling,

"Please, Father, I'm begging you to let this man, Matthew, live...I don't know if we can protect this child..."

She let the thought linger as she lay there for a moment more.

As if on cue, the baby in the other room started mewling, not crying really, just an angry kitten type of sound. Someone was teasing Morgan, and in just a few minutes, the entire room seemed to burst with loud laughter. The baby had quieted.

Abby started singing in Arabic, an Islamic call to prayer, with his own beat added for accompaniment. Anna knew he was dancing the baby around the room. The others around him laughed, squealing with humor. Abby's religion forbade poker, but not dancing. The others in the room started to clap, trying to match his beat.

Anna was amused: 'rap' prayer, she thought. She lay there quietly, following the words of the ancient song.

Anna wondered how the Mexicans were coming along on her neglected cabin. It had been unoccupied for nearly a century.

Gail jokingly had said once that this would be their safe house, since she herself had gotten lost in the swamps trying to find it. Anna had taken her joke seriously and they had made an agreement.

North Louisiana was not exactly a spot where anyone would think to look for them. The thick forests and swampland had been their safe haven for almost two hundred years.

Once Anna had rolled out of the bed, she changed her clothes into something grungier. She was anticipating the old-age wreck her once quaint cabin had become. She opened the door to the other room. Abby had the baby over his head, doing a measured dance step to his song. They were all a little startled to see her in the doorway, not having known that Anna had even returned.

The captain, still holding his cards, took their sudden silence as an opportunity to lay down his hand, triumphantly calling out the other players.

"LOSERS!" Edwards shouted.

Full house, aces over kings. Maria and Morgan both did exaggerated double-takes as they watched him take the pot. Morgan left the table and

165

tried to wrestle her son away from a doting Abby.

As the captain raked in his winnings, Anna asked him if he wanted to ride with her and he happily accepted. Edwards smiled smugly, thinking of his fiery wife's reaction to his riding around with such a dangerous company. June would definitely not approve of his adventures, especially when the gang leader was such a stunning beauty.

The thought of his beloved wife made Edwards feel the sharp pain of frustration. The Feds had released her after the one hundredth rendition of "Henry the Eighth, I Am." He had been able to get a message to her to use their savings and take a vacation to her sister's house in Germany. She had not questioned him and had left immediately, thankful that he was safe.

The German consulate had told that federal agent to 'shag' himself when he had tried to explain WHY it was that he wanted her detained and deported back to the USA. Captain Edwards wondered if he could win enough poker hands to replace their savings.

He had tried to make it easier for June by telling her that every day apart would make the heart grow fonder. She had cried then; so did he. They had never spent a night apart in thirty-two years. The heart never had a problem with fondness: not with a woman like June.

In silent anticipation, most of the group looked expectantly at Anna. Only Doug looked at the cards, trying not to look at her.

Anna ignored him also, saying to the captain, "I've hired the Mexican army to fix the cabin. You're riding shotgun! "

With his winnings in hand, Edwards agreed enthusiastically.

"Hell yes, little lady! Any excuse to get away from these broke suckers!"

As he pocketed his winnings, he grinned pompously. Seventeen whole dollars!

Anna smiled in spite of herself. Still smirking, Edwards walked around the table in an exaggerated strut and simultaneously Morgan, Abby, and Maria burst into laughter. Doug watched his uncle's dramatic retreat with a slight smile. Shaking her head, Anna followed him on his way out of the door into the bright morning. As she had passed Morgan sitting on the bed, Anna glanced at the baby. Her smile tightened some and she and Morgan exchanged quick glances.

Morgan's own smile was filled with genuine affection even as her cousins face contorted with a grimace that attempted to disguise itself as an awkward grin .

Anna shut the door behind herself quickly as Morgan's smile faded. She was actually glad Anna was leaving for the day. The tension between them had become palpable.

After two and a half millennia together, Anna and Morgan still made each other twitch in odd ways. Morgan was always afraid of Anna, but now that shoe was firmly on the other foot, as Morgan considered how surprising it must be for Anna to fear her, for once. Like Sara, Anna was becoming ever more frustrated by Morgan's refusal to answer questions.

Looking at her son, Morgan's heart shuddered. Anna was not afraid of Morgan, but of the boy. Morgan was also afraid of him.

The child gazed back at his mother with a soft smile and unfocused eyes. Morgan prayed she would not have to kill her cousin.

In the motel's cul-de-sac parking lot, the quietness of the morning soothed Anna and Edwards as the sun warmed their faces. Getting into the rental car, neither of them spoke, both enjoying the peaceful silence. Edwards knew that Anna could spin one hell of a story, but for the most part she rarely spoke, choosing to keep her thoughts to herself. The captain was curious as hell regarding those thoughts.

She may be able to spin a story, Edwards thought, closing the car door, but damned if he wasn't sitting here caught up in something wondrous and dangerous. The old cop looked over his shoulder as they pulled away from their parking space, feeling exposed suddenly.

Anna never looked back.

Leaving the lot, they pulled past the office and onto the unpretentious two-lane road. Anna had surveyed the building as they passed. She could see that a screen had popped off a window in a room on the front wing of the unobtrusive motel. She made a mental note to have that checked when she got back. After all, Anna owned the place. Well, partly owned, she corrected herself. She had set up a dummy real estate company with her partner and had the management division listed as the owners. She sometimes forgot which fake name she had used. Need to write that stuff down, she scolded herself.

Her partner in the business had loved the idea because his family, at times, also needed a safe house. Of course, his family was mostly New Yorkers who liked to use fake names too. It had worked so well that they had bought other properties. Apartment complexes, motels, cottages in rural

167

towns, until the partner was making more money on real estate than on his other more family oriented illegal business ventures.

That was the only time Anna had ever turned a crooked man to honesty. She smiled as they drove in silence. Well, mostly honest; his family still needed an apartment now and then.

After several minutes, Edwards quizzed her casually about the trees, many of them already starting to burst with green again even with the chill air. He had discovered that Anna knew a lot about plants.

The rural landscape eventually started giving way to a house scattered here and there, finally coming to a two-block town. Edwards rolled the window down, breathing in the pine scent. Anna found herself rattling on about the native plants. She had spent much time here; her cursed heart was in love with the south.

Even when she prayed, she did it alone among the trees.

After passing a downtown area that was hardly the length of a football field, the conversation lulled. Edwards wondered how you fit an entire town into two blocks. He was a city boy after all. They passed more scattered homes and finally Anna turned onto a sturdier two-lane road. They drove a few hundred yards to a small wooden structure on an isolated strip of the world.

The huge sign on the roof declared it to be 'Bubba's Bar-B-Que'..."

Edwards's quick enthusiasm was brought on by the delicious smells blowing in the crisp breeze.

"By God, girl! I like the way you think!" He blurted.

Anna grinned as she pulled in to park on the gravel lot in front of the small building. Smoke from at least two stacks came from behind the place, floating lazily into the chill air. It was really more of a lunch stand than a restaurant, with nine or ten well-worn picnic tables clustered in neat rows close to the front window. Only one car was in the lot and no customers sat at any of the tables. Anna threw the car in park, the smells making her eager as well.

The large opening at the front of the stand allowed you to see pretty much the entire rectangular grillworks inside.

A young black woman sat on an unseen stool and watched them intently as they approached. Captain Edwards walked briskly, shivering and flapping his arms. Anna walked calmly behind him, almost forgetting there was any chill at all. The woman watching them approach didn't move an inch, still as a statue. Even though the opening she perched in was huge, the solid wall of glowing grills behind her kept her warm and comfortable.

In the summer, she swore everyday she would tell Bubba she quit. She threatened him with it often enough when they started having their moments. In the summer, the grill made the heat inhumane. She thought maybe she'd quit this next summer.

The captain made it to the counter first, his brisk step trying to outrun the cold front. He looked at the young woman, nodding to her with a smile. She nodded back with no emotion at all. . Edwards turned his full attention to the handwritten menus on large chalkboards hanging from the ceiling. Anna was three steps behind. His mouth watered; so did hers.

"How you doin' today, Kia?" Anna directed her question to the statue who watched them.

Kia quickly responded in a warn voice, a smile finally tugging at her lips.

"Pretty good, pretty good. What you up to, Annie May?"

Anna had no idea where the "May" part came from, but Kia had called her that since she was a child. .

"My uncle here is from up north. Can you believe he ain't never had no REAL bar-b-que?" Anna asked in astonishment.

The captain looked at Anna and the statue. Kia widened her eyes in horror, staring at Edwards like he just fell from the sky.

"WWhat? Never had real Barbeque? Go on, Girl. …That ain't right!"

Narrowing her eyes, she actually sounded indignant.

Kia looked at Anna as she finally stood up; and shook her head at the man, grinning slyly.

"Well, I think I can hook him up, Annie May." Kia stated helpfully.

Edwards saw that she wore a white heavy-duty apron over her simple dress. The apron was immaculately clean except for one large blot of obvious sauce close to her right thigh. He looked back to the menu, grinning like a wolf. He was going to enjoy this.

Kia looked at Anna with one raised brow.

"Girl, I already know…You want all of it! Just tell me how hungry you are?"

Anna grinned up at her.

"Very."

"I'll just make it up then. How's 'bout you, sir, whatcha think looks right?"

Edwards squinted, darting his glance all over the menu. Damn. It all looked right.

"Just make his up too, darlin', he'll be here all day deciding."

Edwards nodded his head, grateful that his struggle was over. Anna winked at him. She had learned over the past few weeks that he was as enthusiastic about food as she was.

Even though her race had never needed food to thrive, she savored every bite with gusto. Kia saw her often.

They watched Kia as she turned, going toward the back grills. Large trenchers of meat were strategically placed between the fires to keep them hot in juice filled bins. Pulling large plastic platters from a shelf, she started stabbing various meats. Getting another platter, she scooped veggies and cornbread, and biscuits onto it. Hesitating, she turned around to the hungry couple to ask Anna.

"Is he got what you do... that hyper... hyper..."

"Hypoglycemia?" Anna asked back.

"Yeah. Your eating... thing... It run in the family?" She looked at Edwards with her piercing eyes.

"Naw..." Anna shook her head, looking down. "Naw, he don't have it, he just loves good food."

Kia smiled hugely, showing perfect white teeth.

The captain smiled back at her, knowing enough to shut the hell up. He smiled bigger as Kia informed him.

"If you love good food, man, you will fall in love with me!"

In the spirit of their banter, Edwards kicked back the playful decaration.

"Just by your smell, I think I love you already!" he said

In an exaggerated motion he sniffed the air long and deep. Kia whooped with laughter. Anna chuckled, all of them caught up in the joy of good food and just being alive. Turning back to the grill, Kia's shoulders shook with ill-suppressed chuckles. After a few moments of comfortable silence, Anna saw the captain shiver at a small gust of breeze.

"Come on..." she said to him.

She turned to direct her words at Kia's still turned back.

"We're going to the patio, he needs to warm up..."

Kia threw an "All right" over her shoulder as Anna led Edwards around the corner of the building, along the side. Around the back corner, a large

170

latticework patio was attached to a wood shed. Two large cooking pits set into concrete were burning, as food skewered on spits roasted over them. Three tables sat around the perimeter of the latticework walls, each in its own area.

Anna led Edwards to the table closest to the pit and furthest away from the main structure. The warmth immediately soothed him; he held his hands toward it, trying to unthaw them. The see-through walls and mostly open ceiling gave the impression of being in a garden court. Anna didn't need the fire but she did position herself to be directly in the sun.

Unexpectedly she asked him, "What is your first name?"

Sitting up slightly he glanced back at her thoughtfully.

"My name is Douglas. Doug is named after me. Matthew is named after their father. ... Why? What is your real name?" He grinned at her wickedly.

She smiled back, a slight sad smile that touched her eyes.

"Anna." She said simply.

From the open back door, Kia whistled high and shrill, interrupting them. Like a Pavlovian dog, Anna bounded toward the door, her mouthwatering. After just a moment, she and Kia emerged, each carrying two of the pastel plastic platters.

Edwards jumped to help, shocked at the site of all that food. The women pushed him aside absently, setting the platters on the table.

As soon as she set down her platters, Kia turned, saying, "Go on...I'll get y'alls drinks."

Anna sat down. Edwards marveled at the mounds of food. Forks and knives were added, and they dove in, not waiting for the drinks. One of Edwards's platters was covered with veggies, the other heavy with all types of meats. Anna leaned over her food in almost a predatory manner, tearing at roasted chicken.

Between a biscuit and a huge chunk of brisket, Edwards asked her, "What's that about hypoglycemia?"

He tore at the meat.

Stopping to swallow, Anna looked toward the open back door explaining to him in a low voice.

"People don't like what they can't explain...it makes them nervous. When they see me gorge on food, they need an explanation of why I don't gain weight."

Edwards nodded as Anna added, "What Kia was really asking is are you a Mortal."

"She knows?" Edwards asked sharply.

"Yes." Anna confirmed. "She knows."

She tore into an ear of corn like a famine victim. Edwards nodded, understanding he was a stranger here. . Kia brought two huge styrofoam cups of lemonade. They attacked it too. Kia laughed and shook her head, leaving them alone to eat.

Anna secretly hoped that whatever happened, her safe place here would not be compromised.

With a mouth full of green beans, the captain wondered something aloud.

"If your kind doesn't need food, then why do you eat it?"

She sat for a moment showing no hint of emotion.

"The same reason you do…hunger." Anna answered matter of factly.

She popped three pieces of fried okra into her mouth.

The captain picked up one of the mushy golden-brown balls from his own plate.

"What is this exactly?"

He examined the food like a piece of questionable jewelry, holding it up to the light.

Anna absently said, "Fried okra."

Edwards looked at her, his brows pinched in a frown.

"So they do actually eat that here?" he asked.

He looked at the mushy ball again, unimpressed.

"Yep...just try it…you'll be surprised." Anna responded.

Finally, Edwards put it in his mouth, taking one small unsure chew, then another.

"Man… That's really good!" he exclaimed.

Anna smiled at him warmly, sucking down her baked beans with lemonade. He scooped a handful of okra into his mouth. Anna giggled warmly.

"You should do that more often, you know?" Edwards said softly, suddenly shy at the enormity of her beauty.

She looked at him, still grinning.

"Do what? Introduce you to regional cuisine?"

She picked up a stick of fried corn bread.

172

"Naw, you know…smile." Edwards said.

He felt shy. Her face relaxed and she let the comment pass as she tore up the bread.

They ate in silence for a minute, slowing their pace as their bellies swelled. Kia quietly appeared with more lemonade. She nodded approvingly at the captain's fast dwindling food supply, then disappeared just as silently.

Edwards had fallen in love with Kia for sure. He was sure his loving wife would have enjoyed this meal too. He missed June so badly.

"You said you are from the Middle East…Where exactly? That's a big place." Edwards said in a rush.

Anna stopped chewing for a moment as she became thoughtful.

"I was born in the region now known as Egypt. Most of us are from there, originally. Some from the area of what is now Israel, and Jordan. After the final curse…we all migrated along with humans, scattering…"

She let the thought trickle off, sure that she had answered his question. They both just picked at the food now.

"Now known as Egypt? What was it called before?" He asked.

Her answer surprised him.

"It was known as 'The Garden.' " Anna said with a shrug.

She sipped on her lemonade.

Edwards rubbed his lips, not sure what he wanted to know. He finally nodded, finding logic in an Egypt with no name.

"Umm…ungh…what year were you born?" Edwards asked, surprising even himself at his boldness.

As soon as he said it, Anna snorted with laughter, actually drawing lemonade up into her nostrils.

Captain Edwards tried handing her napkins as she tried not to choke and giggle at the same time. He grinned, unsure of himself, unsure of what she would share with him. Finally, she gasped, forcing herself to breathe calmly, chuckling at her own embarrassment. Anna looked at him, her eyes shining like a kid on a grand adventure. Edwards was humbled, floored by her beauty.

With a large smile she calmly explained.

"I was born in a year before there were years. Back then we didn't exactly have clocks…keep schedules…" She smiled at him sweetly, understanding his shyness.

173

This one, Anna thought, was strong enough to handle the knowledge. She silently prayed that his nephew, the priest, had as much strength. She was not usually impressed with humans at all, but she genuinely enjoyed Captains Edwards company.

Anna was pleased to see that the pure curiosity which the captain held in check so often, finally came flooding forth, unaware of itself. She had watched humans throughout all her long days, and she knew that the true measure of a human's intelligence could be seen in his level of curiosity. She had been waiting to see his blossom, and he didn't disappoint her.

"OK…look…um…Obviously, you don't want, or like, to talk much…I don't mean to pry, really I don't…I always say a lady can have her secrets! …But…um…I just want to know everything about you…So, well, just tell me up front what I CAN'T ask you about. And please, Anna, just feel free to tell me to shut up anytime…I don't mean any insult."

His unexpected gush of words had surprised them both. He seemed even more shocked that all those words had come from his mouth. She smiled at him, starry-eyed. He fidgeted with a paper napkin.

Anna leaned over the table, her voice soft and clear.

"I know you don't mean any insult…I can read your mind."

Edwards eyes went large for a split second. He bit his lip, looking into her eyes. An overwhelming sense of wonder made his old body tingle; pleasure rippled through him. In the two weeks he had known her, he had found complete peace. But some questions remained unanswered as his eyes locked with hers. He smiled at her.

Anna concentrated slightly, pushing her mind into his. Even if he could have struggled against it, he wouldn't have. The sudden images were peaceful and soundless. His mouth started working slightly, he wasn't sure why; he knew he was not speaking.

Edwards could feel her in his mind, just behind his eyes. A small presence, elegant and as solid as steel. He no longer saw her before him, but inside of himself as she took control of what he perceived and pushed her own memories into his mind.

He saw a man. He saw a man through her eyes. No, not a man, not exactly.

The creature appeared to be human, but not like Edwards, nor the Mortals..

This being was medium tall, a hunter, and Edwards could see there

174

were more of them, a family. He saw their faces. Their emotions needed no sound to speak. He saw a woman that he somehow just knew was Sara Katherine.

She was like him, but among these others. Sara smiled down at him, offering him something that smelled sweet. The non-men brought Sara offerings. She was their leader. In his mind, Edwards unexpectedly learned that these men were known as Homo-Ergaster. They were tool makers.

The odd trees tilted around them and then flew by in a blur, and Edwards joined the group again, they were walking across a vast plain. He and Sara walked in a family group with the tool makers.

Finally, men like him appeared on the horizon. Only, they were not men like him. They were perfect.

They were of all different flesh colors, all of them very tall. Edwards somehow knew they had taken the tones of the earth.

The sun and moon both hung in the sky as clouds rolled past, casting odd shadows across the plain. The tall men approached. A horrible fever exploded in Edward's mind.

At the table with Anna, his body swayed only slightly, his mouth still making small whispering sounds. Anna let it flow, not pushing deeply.

As the men like him came forward, the toolmakers scattered in terror.

Edwards stood beside a shaking, silent Sara. She looked down on him, smiling softly, trying to reassure him. The non-men ran for their lives.

Sara held him firm, standing her ground, knowing that they were trapped. She pushed his head, Anna's head, into the crook of her neck. The soft skins Sara wore felt like velvet in his mind. Her skin was also soft, her scent was earthy and light.

Soon their bodies started to burn, the heat melding them as one. Their flesh became inseparable as the fever pitched and rolled, making Sara stagger with the small child she held. He saw the cords of her neck straining as he tried pushing closer to her, needing her.

Sara fell to one knee, holding him up. In his mind, he saw the men not like him being pulled from the brush by the tall ones, the grass where they had fled no protection.

Edwards closed his eyes as the fever broke, leaving his body useless for a moment. Sara, too, started cooling, still on one knee with young Anna clutched to her. He felt Sara hug him tightly, struggling back to her feet. He opened his eyes looking over her shoulder.

Some of the tall ones had stopped their attack, also staggered by the curse, their awareness of Sara scalding into them all.. The Mortal males whom had recovered quickly had run after their escaping quarry, killing both men and children. The tool-maker women screamed soundless screams, trying to fight for their babies. He buried his face again in Sara's neck.

The images shifted again as if in blurred flight. Edwards saw setting and rising suns, the mountains, and icecaps that covered continents. He saw plants and animals he didn't recognize or understand.

Other men, also not like him, but not the tool makers either, passed before his borrowed eyes in a rapid succession. The skies stormed and thundered. Over a vast expanse of forest, he saw a campfire, pulling him to it.

They were men like him, none overly tall. Instantly, Edwards knew that they were the same type of human as he was. Modern man.

At the table, Edwards started sweating profusely. Anna never even twitched. Edwards was flying again through tropical jungles, overwhelming in their vastness. Oceans. Volcanoes. A desert.

There in the desert was a small town; buildings made of brick. Of stone. More humans like him. Many more. Bigger cities, palaces, man-made roads put in place deliberately.

Edwards saw three pyramids through her eyes. A river pushed beside them, unconcerned that it flowed against nature. He followed the river from above it, twisting quickly along it. He came to another large city in the middle of nowhere. He could see the city was brand new. Egyptian gods stood a hundred times larger than life and glittered with all the colors of precious jewels.

Without warning, he stood in a building. It was an artist's shop. There were earthen shelves built to hold sculpture. In front of him was a bust. The famous bust of Nefertiti gazed at him. Actually, two of them, identical to one another. The one he held in his hands was finished.

No, not his hands. Edwards saw the hands with which he held the finished sculpture. They were slim, feminine, with long tapered fingers. They lovingly caressed the fineness of the newly finished bust. They were the hands of a gentle artist. The wrists were adorned with expensive bracelets, golden rings on the long fingers.

The hands held the bust close to his face. He saw the beauty of

Nefertiti. She seemed so familiar to him.

The paint used on the face had been made with pure gold from Nubia. Edwards felt the sadness of the artist's touch. The desolation. The hands threw the bust onto the grass covered floor. It shattered.

The unfinished bust gazed at him, as the artist's hands hung by his side, feeling the broken statue in the joints. He felt shame coming from the one eye that remained unpainted on the unfinished sculpture. The door exploded inward. He was flying again.

On a lush tropical island, protected by an inland sea, he felt a pull toward another city. This one was different. The architecture was Moorish. Curved and liquid, unlike the symmetrical pyramid cities, Edwards knew he was going to his own home.

A grand house on a large estate pulled him to it. He somehow knew the layout of the house. He flew to an upper window as the new sun rose. He lay on a bloody bed, unmoving.

Sara stood above him. Frowning, sobbing, and frowning at the sobs. Morgan sat on a chair against the wall, muted cries shaking her. Sara fussed over Edwards as he lay helpless, stunned.

As he watched Morgan from Anna's eyes, he became enraged. The elegant hands that had smashed the bust fumbled to the table beside him. They grasped weakly at a lamp that still burned with a small flame; the tiny glass lamp was filled with oil. The hands flung the lamp at a curled-up Morgan, falling short in front of her chair, exploding into flames. Morgan silently shrieked as the fire licked at her long, flowing gown.

No longer crying, Morgan had put up her hands, as if to ward off the flames. All the fire instantly died.

Sara stood in shock, looking at Morgan. Her own gown was streaked with Anna's blood.

Morgan looked at the damage that the unexpected fire had caused. She stared at it, stupidly. Looking up, she looked Edwards in the eyes. Her lips drew up into a pout, tears once again poured from her. Morgan's face broke in silent agony as she fled the room. Sara looked back at him, concerned, hesitating. She wiped away tears Edwards did not know he was crying.

Sara steeled her chin, her eyes, her shoulders. The slight tremble of her lips betrayed her for only a second. She kissed him on the forehead, stroking his hair. Sara left the bloody bed and went to the little bed against the wall, carved with finery. She stared into it.

Edwards felt a crushing defeat. With a heavy sigh, Sara reached into the bed. A tiny bundle wrapped in silk was in her hands; blue silk. She hugged it close to her, kissing it. Turning to Anna, she walked slowly to lay the bundle beside the shattered body that Edwards lay in; he turned his head away.

Sara froze. Unsure. Soundlessly Sara begged Anna to look at her.

He studied the rich wall fabric, smelled charring from the lamp's fire. He knew that Sara was calling him, but he could not look at her. She held the bundle to herself again. He knew she was begging but he still could not turn his head.

After a long moment, Sara gave up and went to the arched doorway that led to an enormous balcony. The light curtains billowed beautifully in the tropical wind.

Sara wandered the balcony with her rejected bundle; sometimes crying, sometimes singing, sometimes silent.

Edwards knew the child she held had never drawn a breath.

Staring at the wall, he felt sleep descend on him.

He opened his eyes to another room, and another bloody bed.

This time he sat over Sara, in a dark room, rich with dark wood paneling. The night outside watched them with its moon eye through the window, as Sara strained on the bed. Her legs were drawn up and shaking. A man he somehow recognized as Sara's husband sat opposite him. They were both smiling. They watched the woman's struggle with impending joy already on their faces. They cooed to Sara . They promised her anything; they comforted her.

Into the hands that had thrown the lamp at Morgan, a newborn was caught, held firm by the thin fingers. The man had whooped soundlessly as his wife sat gasping. He smothered her in kisses. The hands held the baby close as it screamed for the first time at an unjust world.

It was a girl. It was Gail.

Before the hands even wiped the blood away, or grasped the cord, they had held the baby to his lips. Elation had flooded over him, then jealousy. He felt the air shift again as he was pulled into yet another era.

He stood at a grave of another dead boy.

Morgan stood nervously in front of him, twitching at the sight of the sword in the hands that held it in front of him. The hands that had caught the baby held the sword , threatening Morgan. . The sword was slender; the silver blade shone in the moonlight. Rage that was directed at Morgan flooded forth.

He swung the sword; he had to retrieve the baby. The baby was cold. He was drunk. He didn't care. Morgan cowered as the blade swung at her; when suddenly Gail was between them, catching the blade in her back.

Sara knelt at the fresh grave with more silent screaming as Edwards was pulled away.

He saw a man, very tall with dark hair. They were both caught in a fever. The captain recovered and willed him to stop his attack.. Edwards knew his name was Michael. He felt strange emotions.

He felt love. He knew it was forbidden. They both knew it was forbidden.

A man called Alex watched them. He caught them together and tried to kill her. Michael had stopped his father, betraying him. He took Edwards back to safety as the fever broke. Once more time flew away from him.

Edwards sat with Michael in an outdated art studio. They silently sat together, each bent to different tasks. Edwards laughed at Michael's attempt to mimic Monet's brushstrokes. They looked at each other across the room sometimes, long glances of respect and longing.

Without warning Edwards was again at the table behind Bubba's Bar-B-Que.

He was looking into Anna's face. His senses were still inundated and his body jerked as time pulled him back into the present. Edwards was shocked to realize that only a few seconds had passed since Anna had first looked into his eyes.

Kia was striding toward them as he slumped, exhausted, into the booth seat. The cook smiled, not understanding his exertions. She figured the meal had done wore him out; she thought it would.

Edwards involuntarily closed his eyes. The place Anna had been in his mind was still there, wrapped up like a ball of yarn. Her memories lay along the strands, lines of images she had given him. He could access them with his memory and could examine the images at will.

Kia was beside him.

"Looks like you been in a battle…"

She said it with a chuckle, looking at Anna, who had also slumped back. Anna grinned broadly, patting her belly.

Edwards blinked at the bright afternoon. Also weakly patting his belly.

He said, "I feel so full of… greatness…"

Anna nodded at his dual answer.

Kia beamed. "Y'all want somethin' else?"

She absently started removing the nearly empty platters, stacking them.

"Yes…" Edwards said "I want you to come home with me and teach my lovely wife how to cook."

He loved June with all his heart, but the woman was lost in a kitchen. He missed her so badly. Kia chuckled again, walking away from them with the remnants of what had been a great feast.

Edwards looked at Anna wide eyed.

She smiled slyly at him. "Sorry…"

It wasn't really an apology.

His own voice shaking Edwards asked , "What in the hell did you just do to me?"

He was still trembling, but regaining his strength. Anna shrugged and responded flatly.

"Sometimes, letting someone see , tells them more than they could learn by listening…"

Anna looked at him with a puckered brow; she hoped she hadn't given him too much. Edwards simply stared at her, touching that small spot in his mind. He was probing around its edges like a sore spot, but he felt the preciousness of it.

She watched him, emotionless. After a long while, Anna sat up straight and pulled at her painter's pants, fishing out a hundred dollar bill. She put it under the large salt shaker. From inside, metal crashed against metal in a burst of sound as Kia cursed to herself.

Anna looked at the open back door, quickly bristling. After a second, Kia walked by the door with a large trencher in hand, oblivious to them. Anna relaxed again, letting the salt shaker go.

To Edwards she asked, "Ready?"

His legs shook slightly as he said, "Oh yeah…"

The meal and the floor show had left him stunned and fidgety. He stood up weakly from the booth.

Hollering out to Kia, Anna announced their departure as they walked to the corner. Around the building once again, they saw the parking lot was still deserted. Edwards melted into the passenger's seat, the chill of the day seemingly gone.

As Anna started the car, he spoke.

"Sometimes letting someone see something, just gives them more questions to ask…to be answered…"

Anna grinned at him like she had just taken his wallet.

By God, she thought, I like this human. She pulled onto the road, heading into the deep wooded swamp country. She couldn't wait to get the Mexicans drunk. She felt like dancing.

Chapter 12

February 2, 12:14 p.m.

Napoliss got out of the Fed-mobile, cramping like a woman in labor. Webster also seemed a bit creaky as he climbed from behind the wheel. The crisp afternoon was deceptively bright, and they both squinted as they approached a row of battered picnic tables. The large sign above the small structure read Bubba's Bar-B-Que. The smell on the cool air made their mouths water.

They had been ignoring each other for about five hundred miles and both of them remained in a foul mood. The only bright spot in their trip thus far was stopping for meals.

A young-looking black woman sat watching them from the window opening of the structure. She sat as still as a stone statue. A huge, older black man was bent over a grill behind her, cursing loudly. Napoliss tried his good smile on her as he approached the counter.

Kia simply nodded, unsmiling.

Webster ignored her. They both stepped up to the counter, reading the large chalkboard menu. The man who had been cursing the grill became aware of their presence, and stopped cussing. He nodded to Webster, acknowledged Napoliss with a glance, throwing out a greeting in a deep Louisiana drawl.

"How y'all doin' t'day?" Bubba asked politely.

He frowned at his wife and part time worker who sat perfectly still on her stool.

Webster looked at the menu as he responded.

"We are fine, sir, how are you?"

The big man's response was, "Pretty good, pretty good...just holler when ya see what ya like..."

The woman studied these white men closely.

As they had gotten out of the car, Kia figured they were cops, but not from around here. Kia knew every cop in three parishes. She looked at the gun holstered on the younger, better dressed cop. Well, sort of better dressed. His suit was deeply wrinkled under his expensive topcoat. The gun on his hip was huge, a .44. She looked at the older cop with the mealy face.

Webster's topcoat was thin and obviously inexpensive; the suit under it was also cheap and just as as badly wrinkled as his partner. Kia could just make out the bulk of the gun holstered under his arm. The young one stood, hips tilted, with his huge gun on his waist, like a cowboy.

Kia rolled her eyes slightly. That's all the South needs, she thought, more white men with guns.

When the older one responded to Bubba, she heard the eastern tilt to his words. She stared at them. Finally, the younger one looked away from the menu, returning her stare.

Without hesitation, she rose from her stool asking, "What can I get for ya, sir?"

Napoliss watched her glide smoothly past the big man who had gone right back to his cussing the broken grill. As Kia stopped in front of them, she finally smiled. Webster thought she was beautiful.

He ordered a brisket plate; his partner ordered a roasted chicken feast. The woman went to the back, deftly stepping over her boss to get to the platters. At the counter, Napoliss and Webster gazed at the lonely road where a solitary car passed. They looked at each other.

Napoliss said, "Whatcha think?"

Webster studied the road. After a moment, he leaned against the elevated counter, sighing.

"I think we should keep going…The priest was spotted two hundred miles east of here, coming this way. Something tells me Gail Strappling is headed straight toward us…."

They both studied the quiet road again.

Napoliss returned to his question.

"If you think they are coming this way, why not stop and wait for them?"

He was desperate to get out of that damn car.

The last spot where Gail and Matthew had been confirmed to be had already been the scene of a two hundred mile grid search. They had made countless circles themselves around the area. The priest had gone to ground. Webster was sure that the running duo had stopped, though he couldn't say why. They had been on a steady course, the sightings putting them on a distinctive track, then nothing. The last sighting was three days ago.

They now knew that Gail was not a hostage, but in fact was seemingly in charge of a still-wounded Matthew.

Kia laid the food on the counter behind them. They turned around, amazed at the piled high platters.

Kia immediately said, "Fifteen forty-two, please."

Napoliss pulled out a twenty, handing it to her. She walked off to the register at the far end of the counter.

Webster asked the big man fixing the grill, "Have you seen any strangers around here lately?"

The man, who was still bent over the grill and cussing whenever he thought about it, seemed surprised by the question. He looked up with a puzzled expression, and seemed to notice the bad suits and holstered guns for the first time and frowned deeply.

Bubba didn't like sloppy dressers, and he didn't like cops. These old boys seemed to fit both areas to a 'T'. He made a show of thinking before he answered, unsure of what this stranger really wanted to know.

"Well...We gets lots a strangers through here..." Bubba said.

He stood up slowly, grabbing a towel as he rubbed at his enormous hands. He gestured toward the road absently with the towel.

"That there highway connects two interstate highways, so... There's always folks we don't know comin' roun' here."

Bubba leaned over his counter, comfortable that he was king here. He also had a gun, a sawn-off twelve gauge shotgun lying right below his hands, under the open counter in front of him. It was loaded with buckshot. He watched the men gathering their food, as if they were suddenly afraid that Bubba would snatch it back over to his side. He thought about doing it, for just a split second, just to mess with their minds. He thought better of it as Kia handed the young one his change.

"Anythin' in particular you lookin' for?" Bubba asked the men, realizing these cops were after someone.

He didn't want to serve no murderers, if he could help it; especially if it kept the damn cops away from himself. He passed looks with his wife Kia, whose face was set like concrete.

The younger agent tried to explain.

"Well, the man is big, hard to miss, and he may be hurt... You see

184

anyone like that?"

Bubba shook his head lightly, completely unfamiliar with the description.

From his pocket, Napoliss withdrew two pictures; one was of Matthew and the other was of Gail, looking pretty old. Bubba held the two pictures out, studying them closely.

The young man was obviously at a Christmas party, the moment frozen in time in front of a giant, glittering tree. Father Matthew grinned at the turkey before him, his face serene and boyish, although his eyes seemed to pierce the paper of the photo. Kia looked at them at the same time, stepping in close behind Bubba.

The picture of Gail had been taken in the garden between the church and Joseph's house. The summer scene seemed to catch the woman in a good mood on her bench. As she had looked up from a book, she smiled at someone who had snapped the picture. An older lady with deep lines around a pleasant mouth. Auburn-grey hair was pulled tightly away from her face, making her look even older.

Without thinking, Bubba said, "Man, that almost looks like Annie May."

Kia leaned closer.

Napoliss asked , "Who's Annie May?"

Kia started shaking her head. She looked harder at the picture.

"You trippin', Bubba. She don't look like Annie May at all! …" She paused, looking harder.

"That don't look like Annie…Just cause they're both women don't mean they look alike." She chastised her husband.

Still, she looked at the elder woman's photo a moment longer, frowning.

"Nope." She said matter-of-factly as she walked away.

Bubba remembered the Feds and looked up, handing back the pictures.

"Annie's a local woman who owns the hotel up the road some. But that's not her. That woman is 'bout forty years too old. . Never seen the man neither. Sorry." He shrugged casually; Kia came to rest again on her stool.

"What they wanted for anyways?" Bubba looked the older Fed in the eye.

Webster replied evenly, "Murder."

Bubba shook his head.

185

"Sorry I can't help no more, but never seen them around here…" Bubba looked down on the agents thoughtfully.

"Actually," Napoliss started, "You said there is a hotel up the road. We really could use some rest."

Picking up slightly on the drawl, he asked, "Whereabouts is it?"

Bubba pointed to a road that snaked off the main road that they were on. He gave them directions; it wasn't far, he said. After thanking him, they left three dollars on the counter for Kia and they walked off to a picnic table set about in the middle of a row.

They both sat on the same side, facing out, not turning their backs to the road. They discussed turning back and going another two hundred miles north.

Webster shook his head at his partner's suggestion. "They spent so much effort trying to get south, why go north now?"

Webster was bone tired. His partner kept him constantly on watch. They had worked well together for quite a while but the older Fed still didn't trust his John Wayne partner. Webster didn't really trust anyone, but Napoliss was supposed to have his back. The younger man made him edgy, feeling like he had to be twice as vigilant

Without meaning to, Napoliss became a smartass.

"Tell me again, WHY were they going south in the first place?" He ripped into tender roasted chicken.

"I don't know, smartass, WHY don't YOU tell ME?" Webster snapped at him.

Napoliss looked at him and stopped chewing at the sharpness of his tone. They were both tired and in a pissy mood. Napoliss sighed heavily, choking down the bite. He hadn't meant to upset his partner. He liked Webster, trusted him every day. He thought his partner liked him too. They shared a bond.

After clearing his throat, Webster grunted, "Sorry…"

They watched the road as they ate in silence.

Once Webster finished his food, he pushed away the platter and stood up, saying, "I'm going to stretch my legs."

Napoliss didn't respond, he was focused on his food. Webster walked slowly, going to the Fed-mobile; he reached inside and grabbed a crumpled pack of cigarettes. He leaned against the front of the car and lit a smoke, exhaling slowly into the cold morning, watching Napoliss take his time with his meal. Webster went to the trunk and opened it. Their hastily packed bags were a mess; they had been living out of the trunk for damn near five days now. He started to put things back in order, relieved to do anything that didn't entail driving or riding in that damn car.

In the trunk, he saw a manila folder that he pulled out and stood holding while he looked thoughtfully at his partner.

At the table, Napoliss finished his meal, wiped his mouth, and started stacking the platters. Webster came back up the slope toward the building and they both strolled casually back to the counter. Bubba stood from his completed task at the grill triumphantly, just as they approached.

Kia stood from her stool, and she moved automatically to take the dirty platters that Napoliss sat on the counter. Bubba greeted them again, immediately noticing the large manila envelope that Webster held.

He smiled guardedly at the Feds while Kia disappeared into the structure with her load.

Webster smiled back at him. "I was wondering if you could help me out one last time, sir."

Bubba nodded, waiting.

Webster pulled the two sketches from the envelope. Again, they showed him one man and one woman. The man's composite was on top. He was a dark-skinned man, appearing to be of Middle-Eastern heritage. The picture had been drawn by a top quality artist, catching every detail of his face. They couldn't find a recent photo of Abby, so they had had the artist age a photo slightly. He had caught the man beautifully in middle age. Bubba shook his head absently at the man's likeness. The handsome even features were completely unfamiliar to him. Webster pulled the other portrait from beneath.

Bubba froze.

As he did, the Fed told him, "They are probably traveling with a very young baby."

Bubba stared stupidly at Webster, stunned.

Forcing his jaw to stay closed and relaxed, Bubba shook his head, trying to keep it casual.

As Kia approached them, Bubba forced himself to speak solidly, convincingly.

"Sorry, sir. Ain't ever seen either one of them before, either."

Kia raised an eyebrow at him as she stepped back to them. She leaned

187

slightly, looking into a woman's face on the paper.

Morgan's face. Anna's face. It was impossible to tell which from the sketch as the cousins so closely resembled each other.

Kia went still as a stone, only her eyes widening a bit. She started shaking her head, remembering Bubba's last words. Bubba said a silent prayer and made himself breathe deep and normal. Kia stood back up straight, immediately going back to her stool. Her heart was hammering.

"What they wanted for?" Bubba asked it, dreading the answer.

He tried not to lean against the glowing hot grill behind him.

Napoliss shifted on his feet suddenly. Hmmm, what were they wanted for? …Indeed…Before he could start fidgeting, Webster answered the huge man.

Using his best FBI, 'I can arrest you' voice, he stammered only slightly on the lie.

"Well, they are…ungh…they are related to a…um… to a terrorist investigation… They may be material witnesses and we…ugh…don't really know at this time…But we need to speak with them."

Webster felt like screaming. This goddamned investigation was going to make him blow his heart valves and probably ruin his career.

The huge black man stood deathly still, he didn't even seem to be breathing. He looked hard at Webster, his stare as weighty as a fist on the Fed. Did he say…

"Terrorism?"

Bubba said it as if the thought itself were alien to him.

He looked at the face on the paper. This picture was not as detailed as the man's but it was definitely Anna. No, Morgan. Bubba shook his head, refusing to believe it.

Webster was twitchy. It was some serious shit these days for a federal agent to say terrorist. Webster had to be very careful. They had not reported the conversation with Abby to their superiors. They had hoped to pull one out of a hat. Abby had disappeared immediately following their encounter. They knew that his vanishing act had to parallel what had happened at St. Mary's. They just couldn't figure out how. Or why. There were no answers, only more questions.

Webster wanted to shoot something; maybe it would be Napoliss.

Webster kept his cool, "Well like I said, sir, we only want to speak with them. We think they may have seen something…"

Napoliss turned his back completely to Bubba's counter, trying to watch the road. He hoped his own career would survive this.

"Well, I appreciate your time…" Webster said briskly and then turned to walk back to the car.

" You folks have a nice day." Napoliss said as he also walked away.

From behind him, Bubba threw a "See ya…"

The couple watched the Feds get into their car in total silence. As they pulled out, another car was turning in; it was rush time and all the picnic tables would be full within an hour.

Bubba and Kia looked at each other.

Kia said softly "You's so stupid,Bubba!"

His eyes widened at his wife, as he realized the situation he had created.

They both knew that that one of them had to be there for at least another hour. Neither of them even dared to think about using the phone. the Federal agents were going straight toward Anna's hotel right now.

As a large woman with two angular teens came up the slope, Bubba said to Kia, "Pray."

Kia shook her head at him, both of them knowing that it was too late for praying. .

Bubba turned back to the grill, unsure of what to do. The woman and her kids stepped to the counter.

After a moment, Bubba said very loudly, "Fuck it!"

The white woman at the counter raised her brows but was not surprised. Bubba had a reputation for being crazy. Without explaining, he quickly darted out the back door. By the time he came around the side of the building, he was running toward his Jeep Cherokee. The woman and her kids watched in amazement as the Jeep jetted backwards in the lot, spewing gravel. Another car was turning in for lunch, as Bubba slammed it into drive and raced past the other driver at the road entry, whom had to slam on his breaks to avoid a collision.

Bubba's tires squealed as he hit the pavement, going in the opposite direction the Feds had taken. The astonished lady and her kids looked back to Kia, whose only movement was chewing on her lip. Kia smiled at them sweetly.

The driver of the newly arrived car parked and got out. Damn! Bubba could've killed him!

Oh well, he thought, Bubba's been crazy since he was a kid. But still, he shouldn't be trying to mow down his regular customers.

***

February 2, 12.36 p.m.

The scientist was very worried. So was the priest. They sat across from the dark, tall man silently until the priest introduced himself.

"Now that you're not trying to kill me, my name is Father Timothy."

The dark tall man looked at him like he was a bug.

"You may call me Miguel." The stranger said.

The quiet church around them seemed puzzled at the unlikely threesome.

Dr. Gorin was becoming a drunk. He was thinking of a few other addictions he could pick up, too, if he survived. Looking at the man sent to kill him, the doctor was certain he would die within the hour.

Father Timothy and Miguel looked at each other, their contempt silent but still very real between them. Miguel decided that he couldn't wait to kill this priest, after all.

Dr. Gorin poured another cup of rum. Yep, he thought, that's how you know you're a drunk: when you drink hard liquor straight from a coffee cup. Definitely an alcoholic. His knew his ex-wife would be so proud.

In a voice that Miguel thought was whiny, Timothy tried polite conversation.

"It's nice to finally meet you, Miguel... Now that you're not spending all your time trying to kill me."

Miguel smiled sarcastically. The priest flattered himself.

"I only actually tried to kill you twice, both times as an opportunity. ... You were never the original target, you just got in my way, Father. "

He drew out the title, mocking the holy man. The priest actually seemed more upset that he was not original.

Robert tried to ignore them both. He stared into his coffee cup. He knew he should have gone to the press. The church echoed with silence.

Miguel had known Doctor Gorin was hiding in the church. He had seen him enter the building last night. Miguel had cursed himself, tired of them both. He had never missed a target before; and now his entire hunt had been a failure. God, himself, seemed to be slanting the odds in Gorin's favor.

Miguel had finally, this morning, decided just to go in and approach them face to face. He had been thinking about his quarry. He had some serious questions. Miguel had long since figured that his curiosity would probably get him killed one day. He thought the whole conversation that was taking place in his head was sort of ironic.

Jerold had not told Miguel exactly why the scientist had to be killed. Miguel knew the family had been betrayed, but he wasn't sure why this man should die for it. If what he suspected was true, the doctor could tell him more in ten minutes than he had found out in thousands of years.

Miguel asked the man point-blank.

"Where did you get the sample?"

The doctor still stared into nothing, wondering if HE could fit into a coffee cup. The priest watched them both.

"Ground Zero." Gorin said miserably; he was miserable.

Miguel frowned deeply. He was seriously confused. He chose his next words carefully.

"As far as we know…no one in our family was in those towers. We were not there on 911." Miguel didn't like this at all.

The doctor looked at him blankly, then shrugged.

"Where at Ground Zero?" Miguel pressed him, aware that the doctor was as confused as he.

"The sample did not say. It was just in with the others…"

How could Gorin explain what he had seen in those horrible months?

"I just ran the standards tests on random samples… and… bam… there it was."

Miguel held his breath. "What standard tests?"

The doctor put the cup down, but still palmed it lovingly. He spoke absently, sure that he would die soon and not much caring.

"DNA, blood typing, genetic markers, and so on. When I returned to my lab, all my equipment had gone crazy."

He sighed heavily, remembering his excitement with a sad smile.

"To tell you the truth, I thought it was a fluke. I went to run the tests again and I took what was left and looked at it under the microscope…"

He drifted into his own thoughts as they waited.

After a moment Miguel said, "The rest of what? … What was the sample?"

Robert Gorin looked his wannabe killer in his eye.

"A finger...A man's pinkie finger."

Miguel rocked backward in the booth. It all made sense! He thought of his cousin; Michael. Miguel knew instantly that Michael had exposed them all.

Two weeks after September 11th, Michael had been missing a finger; a pinkie finger. Of course, the finger had grown back within a few days, but Michael had definitely been missing one. He had told his father and Miguel that he had lost it in a car door.

The giant research company they owned had been contracted to the federal government to do biological testing on the Twin Towersvictims remains, to identify them and give their families closure. Michael had tried to get lost in the masses.

Miguel understood that Michael had thought he could bury the results, and then hijack the traces of it. He struggled not to lose his cool. Miguel wondered why he hadn't thought of it, and then was glad he hadn't. There would be no closure for his family.

Miguel sat slumped in the carved back chair; the father's dining room seemed gaudy to him. The entire church seemed that way. All three of them stared at the gun that Miguel had laid on the table as a gesture. Before he did any more killing, Miguel wanted answers.

After a long moment, he asked the doctor, "You said that your equipment went crazy...what did the results say?"

Gorin looked ill, reaching for the bottle again, greedy about splashing it into his cup. He shook his head hard at nothing.

"The DNA sequence was impossible...I thought two samples had got mixed, that I was actually looking at two DNA helixes, but after...After I looked into the microscope, I went back and realized that there were many DNA strands....Like over six hundred! One finger with more than six hundred DNA combinations!..."

From his chair, Miguel looked the doctor in his watery eyes.

"Let me guess, Dr. Gorin, you found six hundred and sixty-six strands...?"

The doctor's jaw hit the floor.

"How did you know that?" Gorin gasped.

The priest looked at Miguel with his ferret-like eyes narrowed. Father Timothy swallowed hard. This was not good.

Miguel looked at the priest, unflinching.

"What did you see in the microscope?"

Miguel knew the answer to this one, too.

Robert Gorin sat straight up, abruptly. His eyes focused high up on a wall as his body swayed slightly. Quick soft smiles made the drunken man suddenly appear relaxed, beaming.

"Light. I saw…light." He said in a voice tinged with awe.

His smile deepened without him knowing it. Miguel frowned at the priest. He pressed on.

"In the DNA…What did you find out about the individual strands?" This time he didn't know the answer in advance.

Still staring at his spot, the doctor's smile disappeared.

"Half of the strands were male, the other half female. There were no genetic indications at all for any disease, the genome pattern was human, but…more! Much more. There were more genetic markers per strand than normal…Double I would say…All but one of the strands has its own identical mitochondrial strand…I've never seen anything like it…"

Miguel was staring at him again. His jaws clenched until his teeth hurt.

Miguel felt like he was about to faint. He asked the question their entire family would kill to ask.

"What of that one strand?"

The doctor frowned at the wall, slumping back again. He glanced at Miguel quickly.

"I think maybe I screwed that one up. The DNA itself was defective. It seemed to have a disease that involved folic acid…Like it…mutated them…I think I messed up the test."

Miguel put his elbows on the table, leaning in.

"Folic acids?" he asked, bewildered.

The doctor looked at him again and nodded.

"Yeah, you know, they are a basic building block for cell growth. Pregnant women need folic acid, it wards off deformities. But that female strand could never produce children, the way it deforms the folic acid would kill an unborn child."

Miguel stood from his chair with a start. He staggered away from the table. The priest and the doctor watched him with surprise, not sure what he was doing.

Miguel started pacing as his heart threatened to explode. In his mind, he was again in Egypt. He saw HER, Morgan's mother, so clearly. He turned on his heel pacing back and forth. The other two men watched him as he mumbled to himself. Understanding flooded through him.

Miguel knew WHY Michael had betrayed the family.

He understood HOW the final curse had been laid. He cursed Morgan's very bloodline.

Miguel also started cursing God there in the church. The priest tried to protest, he held up his hands to shut him up. Miguel's head hurt with the power of understanding. He thought of Morgan, again.

At the second thought of Morgan, Miguel stopped dead. His entire frame jerked with horror. Without knowing he did it, Miguel finally blurted out to himself.

"OH. MY. GOD!"

The priest and the scientist looked at each other. Before they could react Miguel suddenly jumped back to the table and grabbed for the gun. He snatched it up in one smooth motion. Robert Gorin hit the floor. He had been expecting to be executed. The priest had come to a half standing position and froze.

Miguel pointed the gun directly into Father Timothy's face.

"Dr. Gorin…Get up!" Miguel screamed.

No one moved. Miguel stared at the priest.

"Get up, now, goddamn it!" he demanded again.

The doctor rolled out from under the table. He stood slowly, trembling.

"I cannot tell you why right now, but you have to come with me." Miguel said in a calmer tone.

The room stayed still. Taking his eyes from the priest, Miguel looked at Robert fully.

"I promise you…I won't hurt you, Dr. Gorin, but you have to come with me."

In a shaky voice the scientist asked nervously, "Where are we going?"

Miguel thought about it.

"We are going to save my family."

The doctor's eyes widened, surprised. Miguel put the gun in his waist. Robert looked at it, understanding the gesture. He hesitated. Miguel nodded at him; he nodded back.

As they left the church, Miguel started praying to himself frantically. He had to find Michael. But before he could help Michael, he had to save that baby. He begged God to overlook their stupidity.

The only thing that was clear to Miguel in that moment, was that his Uncle Jerold had to die.

Chapter 13

February 2, 12.44 p.m.

Gail looked at Matthew. He was resting. She watched his breathing, slow and normal. He had had a bad night, but she was glad he was resting better now. She was once again dressed in her nun's habit.

Looking around the stark room, Gail was reassured by the simplicity of it. The simple metal-frame bed was full sized, and Matthew seemed to take up every inch of it. Above the bed there hung a solid silver cross, the one decoration in the room; the image of a tortured Christ hung on bare walls. The two simple wing chairs had a table between them. The only other thing in the room was an antique dresser that stood under the window. Daylight glowed through the window and touched the old furniture with loving fingers.

Gail had almost fallen asleep in the chair when the door opened. Mother Superior Frances Maria Salazar walked in. The young nun behind her was her own daughter, Sister Katherine. Frances returned Gail's groggy smile as Katherine, who was carrying a tray, went to Matthew's side. The older nun sat in the chair across from the one where Gail sat.

"Are you okay, dear?" Her voice was like warm honey.

Gail nodded, unable to hide her fatigue. Sister Katherine checked Matthew, ignoring the other women. She pulled at the bandages, checking to see if he was still bleeding. He wasn't. She nodded absently to herself, proud of her own modern surgical skills..

Sister Frances asked Gail, "Are you sure you won't rest in the next room...? The bed has been readied for you."

Gail looked at Matthew and shook her head.

"I want to stay here... With him." She said softly.

Sister Frances looked at Matthew, keeping her mouth from trembling by pursing her lips. Only a few of the sisters knew that the couple was here on the convent grounds. They had a vow of secrecy amongst them that anyone who asked them for help would be helped. The nuns would protect them here at the convent for as long as they could, but…Frances was not sure how long they would be safe here.

She looked at Gail. The woman had fallen asleep in the chair.

Sister Katherine had finished her exam of Father Matthew. She had been a missionary in a tribal hospital for much of her time with the church. This was not her first battle-wounded patient. But, Sister Katherine thought, he was the most special by far.

She stared at the handsome priest as he struggled to heal. She prayed for her patient.

Even if his purpose was hidden still from him, all of the women in the room knew what it was. Sister Katherine was in awe. The other nuns knew about their presence, but not of their reasons. Only that he was special, and wrongly wanted for murder.

Rumors of a child sent by God were just beginning to stir in the hushed corridors of the convent. Even if none of the nuns would dare tell an outsider anything, all of them were chatting amongst themselves as real excitement and mystery began building just outside Matthew's sick room.

The child with no name was on every woman's sacred lips, even if none could say for sure whom or where this child was.

Katherine tingled with pleasure, and with fear.

Both of the nuns looked at a slumped Gail, wondering how her head could lay like that in the chair. Frances sighed and Katherine shook her head again. With no agreement or even glances exchanged, both women moved toward Gail. Katherine held her feet up as Frances slid the other chair under them. They were more acutely aware of her certain discomfort than she was. Frances smiled to herself. Sister Gail had always seemed to go out of the way to make herself uncomfortable, almost like she had made it her penance. She would have worn a hair shirt if they had any handy.

The Nuns retreated from the room quietly. One of them would be keeping watch on the door at all times.

Sister Frances left Katherine to guard their patient, knowing that no ordinary threat could get past either of them. She returned to the cathedral to pray alone as she thought about Jerold.

***

196

February 2, 12.46 p.m.

Bubba sat outside the motel. From across the street, he watched the Feds' room. He had wanted to approach the door to the owner's apartments, but Bubba knew they would see him if he tried it. They had checked in, gone straight to the room. The agents had opened their curtains and stood, or sat, in front of the window ever since.

The door to Anna's apartment looked like a regular motel room door. Had Bubba never been in the space, he would have never known the apartment was there. One of the Feds sat in the window, watching the parking lot, a phone stuck in his ear. Bubba slid down a little in his Jeep. He knew the Fed couldn't see him, but he still felt exposed anyway. He prayed Anna did not walk out. He had no idea that she was at the lake.

Bubba knew that the cousin was in there, though ; the one in the sketch. The incredible similar looking women had come in together just yesterday for a late dinner.

Bubba thought long and hard about what the Fed had said.

Murder? Maybe. Terrorist? …Impossible.

Even as he thought it, Bubba asked himself, "Why would it be impossible?"

He knew the eternally young Anna was odd, even for a white woman, but a terrorist? He could not accept the thought.

He wondered about the woman Anna had called Morgan. Would Anna hide a terrorist?

Bubba looked into his mirror and saw both Feds silhouetted in the room's shadows. The mealy-faced one was wearing a towel and they seemed to be arguing. The young one disappeared and the one in the towel sat at the table in front of the window with a notebook and some envelopes. Bubba's foot jumped with nerves. He rolled his fingers in an odd drumbeat.

What in the hell was going on here? Bubba had no idea, but Annie May was his friend. She had helped him out once. He thought about the trouble these Feds' presence meant. If Anna was a terrorist, or hiding one, he would at least let her get a head-start before these guys got to her.

Bubba refused to believe it.

He knew why he didn't believe it. The Fed had lied to him. He was sure of it as he was of his birthday. Bubba trusted his friends, but not federal agents he already knew were lying..

197

Just close the fucking curtain! He wanted to scream it.

He tapped his fingers. He knew Kia would probably quit when he got back. If she hadn't burned the place down out of spite, that is. He smiled, thinking that he should have snatched the Feds' food back across the counter when he had the chance. He never had any fun anymore.

The last time he had any fun was when Anna had broken Bubba out of jail. He still couldn't figure out how she did it. Neither could the cops. By the time they came to arrest him again, they had realized their mistake. Well, they said it was a mistake. More like a damn frame up if you asked him. If you asked Anna, she'd say the same. Bubba rolled his eyes as the Fed at the table leaned over his work, seemingly enjoying his spot in the sun.

Keeping one hand on the door handle, Bubba waited. He watched. He tapped his fingers in frustration.

***

February 2, 12.54 p.m.

After leaving Bubba's, Anna and Edwards had taken a ride in the country. The captain was thrilled at the clustered landscape, admiring the huge stretches of forest. Even in the middle of the day, the interior of the woods looked dark. A line from one of the captain's favorite poems played in his head.

The woods are lovely, dark, and deep.

But I have promises to keep.

And miles to go before I sleep.

And miles to go before I sleep.

Edwards, too, had promises to keep. He thought of Matthew, then of Douglas. June's face had pushed away the countryside and the captain had ridden in silence. The huge meal was lying heavy in his guts. . Watching the path they were on becoming more and more heavily wooded, Edwards caught himself biting his nails.

He touched the spot in his mind that Anna had left there.

When it had first happened, he thought he had been flying. In pulling at the memories, he realized that the blurs from his original experience also had images in them. She has zapped me, he thought, not knowing how to feel about it.

Anna had been watching him closely, unsure of how he would react to her memories infusing his. He seemed fine so far. A little quieter than normal but that was okay. She, too, stayed quiet.

Anna drove the car like she herself had built it. Her familiarity with the roads had surprised him little. What did surprise him was that anyone could actually live in the swampy landscape they were passing. He could see deer and squirrels in the wood. He would swear on a stack of bibles he had seen a small bear looking back at him once. How did people even find out these places exist?

"How did you find this place?" Edwards asked unexpecctedly.

Anna seemed to be lost in thought. She shook her head slightly, pulling herself back into the interior of the car.

"About 1834, I was a married woman. My husband had inherited huge wealth from his father. He was like most plantation owners I suppose, arrogant. He had never reflected on the slaves handing him his food."

She sighed deeply, as if the thought still haunted her.

"We fell in love in Pennsylvania; he went to school there. I was so in love with him I never gave moving here a second thought…"

She let the thought drift off as Edwards stared at her with open fascination.

"You never gave it a second thought until what?" He pressed her.

She glanced at him as she slowed to take a turn.

"Until I actually got here." Anna said flatly.

She shook her head, like she was trying to throw off bad memories.

"The American slave trade was in full swing. Once, many years before that, I, too, had been a slave. I was a slave in Egypt, but it was very different."

"How was it different?" he asked cautiously.

To Edwards that made no sense. Slavery is slavery.

After a long moment of contemplation, Anna explained.

"Well, in Egypt they had laws against killing a slave, or maiming one. All slaves in my time as one, actually belonged to Pharoah, he just rented us out to the elite, or gave us as a gift that could always be revoked. Or used as spies. Anyways, as his property we could not be arbitrarily harmed by our lesser masters. The society was set up so that every slave had some hope of freedom,and could in fact become important people in the government…Even a ruler …. The American slave trade was different.

199

Slaves were not people in bondage here. They were scraps of meat chained to Hell and you could kill or main them as you pleased. There's quite a difference between what I went through and what I saw my husband's people do to their slaves. It was far worse than you could ever know from reading your history books."

Edwards watched the approaching hairpin turn, thinking about the difference a few laws make. Anna slowed only slightly, letting the tires grip ferociously. He nodded absently as he mentally compared slaves. He could see her point.

After the turn, Anna had continued, finally answering his original question of how she had come to know this lonely swamp in a meander of memory..

"Anyways... By 1842 my husband was ...not a very kind man. The cabin was built for him by his slaves. All this land once belonged to him, it goes on for miles. ...After he met a tragic, premature end, I used the cabin for a station on what is now known as The Underground Railroad. We safely housed almost four hundred slaves over the years. Almost all of them were sent to Gail or Sara, up north, who always had jobs for them. I had to marry another rich man to cover all the expenses, but at least he was much more humane. When he died years later, he freed all his slaves. Even though they were free most of them stayed with me for years, almost eight hundred of them..."

They turned again, this time down a dirt road, narrowly slicing through the trees. The bright afternoon was held at bay by the densely overgrown wood. Sometimes Edwards could see small patches of water in the trees.

He looked at her in the sudden shadows.

"Then what happened?"

She looked at him with a smirk.

"Come on, you know what happened... The Civil War? State against state...Brother against brother..."

She grinned at him tenderly, like a teacher does to a impeded student.

"The cabin was never found out, but it became too dangerous to keep the stop open, we were surrounded by Confederate soldiers in every direction.. Finally, it was too dangerous to simply remain at all. By the time the carpet baggers moved in to exploit the situation, I was in South America."

The shadows receded some, as the woods also seemed to pull back.

"What on earth were you doing in South America?"

Anna giggled and tossed him a look of amusement.

"I became what they call a 'coyote': a human smuggler. South America's slave trade was just as bad as the northerners. I did what I could, that is what I was doing down there. Whatever I could."

Edwards looked at her with a frown, unsure if he wanted to know more; he didn't.

Just as silence descended over them again, the woods finally gave way to a huge clearing. The cabin toward the back of the property was more like a four-bedroom house. There were Mexicans all over the place. On the roof, on the porch, one was cutting down a small tree beside the house; one man was under the porch, his feet sticking out comically. Loud Latin music echoed through the expanse.

Now slowing, Anna watched the house from the distance.

"Can I ask you something, Anna?"

She looked at him and nodded curtly before turning her eyes back to the cabin..

"You mention husbands…several of them…Um…um …how many of them did you actually love?"

Anna grinned at his hesitation, surprised by the question.

"I loved every one of them. Otherwise I would not have married them."

The sincerity of her answer surprised him back.

Anna pulled the car behind a battered old truck. Since there were no other vehicles here, the workers must have all come together in the truck. Most of the guys stopped only momentarily as they pulled up. The one Anna had negotiated with for the work was trying to come down off the roof. Anna had already had wood and other building material delivered yesterday. One small Latino was trying not to kill himself on a pile of shifting two by fours. He jumped out of the way just as gravity toppled the pile. Some of the guys whooped at him, yelling out in Spanish. They chuckled at his dance around the wood.

As she got out of the car, the man who led the crew came off the ladder, approaching Anna with a frown. She watched him come, putting her elbows on the top of the car.

" Hola, pretty lady. We have mucho problemos."

She cocked her head at him, "Si?"

"Si. The hole in the roof is…is…grande. Muey grande."

201

He held his arms out as far as they would go, trying to show her how much muey grande was. Anna simply nodded her head.

"Si, si, I know, amigo. I knew it would be bad."

The Mexican smiled, relieved that she already understood what they were up against.

"And we need more, umm, you know…the, um, wires, si? wires. You have the wrong ones here."

Anna nodded at the man and asked him, "Who can drive this car? Who has a license?"

The man turned back to the cabin, rubbing his lip thoughtfully. "Armando. He drives legal. He's under there."

He pointed to the feet sticking out from under the porch.

"He is the one who need wires."

Anna told him, "Tell him to come here."

As he did as he was told, Anna went to the trunk and Edwards moved to follow her. The music changed and a beautiful woman's voice filled the air, her words in Spanish perfectly understandable by her sensuous notes. Anna popped the trunk just as Armando and the crew boss came up to her.

They started grinning as they saw the beer in the trunk. Two cases of Tecante and two cases of Corona. Bags of ice covered the cases. They liked their new boss very mucho.

She saw Armando was the one with the bold stare, the pretty boy she had looked over in the liquor store parking lot.

"Can you put these on the porch?" Anna asked politely.

Armando and the other man jumped to do so. In Spanish, she asked the older one his name.

"Julio." He answered.

He smiled at her as he loaded his arms with Corona. Anna pulled a small toolbelt from the trunk. The hammer had a bright pink rubber grip on it. Edwards rolled his eyes as she closed the trunk. He chuckled as she started hanging it from her hips.

"Hey!…Don't I need a toolbelt too?" Edwards asked.

She shook her head at him.

"No, I need you to go with Armando. While he's at the hardware store I need you to go into the grocery next to it."

He frowned at her.

"All this work, and… um …You want me to go grocery shopping?"

He frowned harder.

"No, not for groceries."

She pulled a shopping list from a pocket and handed it to him. The list of contents looked strange to him. Boric acid? Gauze? He blinked at her stupidly.

She buckled the belt, grinning at him.

"Just trust me, amigo." She said as she walked away.

The Mexicans had seen the beer; they were talking loudly to each other and taking a well-deserved break. When Anna got to the porch, they all were indecisive when she asked what they wanted to eat. Finally, she just told Armando to get like twenty burgers and ten large fries. She handed him a hundred dollar bill. Edwards looked at the bill, no longer surprised. In their short time together, he had noticed she always seemed to have a supply of the large bills. She handed him one too.

Out of macho pride, Edwards started to protest.

"I can get it!" he had snapped, and she had looked at him with that…that… look…she had.

"I know you can get it, darlin'." Anna said sweetly.

She tried to ease the sudden tension as the men watched them.

"But if you run up your credit card, your lovely wife would hate me for it."

She had never even met June. The captain blushed with understanding. If he used his credit card, then the Feds would nail them.

He tried to make a joke as the edginess eased.

"Hell, in that case, I need more, this ain't enough!" Edwards admonished her.

The Mexicans laughed as he conned her openly. She grinned, watching him get bold. He held out his hand, joking, and the workers literally roared with laughter as she put a wad of bills into his palm. So, she did have smaller bills than hundreds. He smiled back at her as he casually pocketed all of her cash.

Anna shrugged. What he didn't know is that a giant room had been installed right below where her car was parked. It was filled with treasures he couldn't begin to comprehend. She opened a Corona, thought better of it and returned it to the ice, untouched. She would save it for later. She held out her keys to Armando, after confirming that he did in fact know the way back from town.

As they left, Anna entered the home her husband had built for himself. She was met by the ghost of their life together, the furniture literally hovering under white dust sheets, now yellowed with age. She started pulling them off, revealing the now antique furniture, crafted finely by the hands of artist slaves. The pieces were in perfect condition, if not somewhat musty. A bird had nested in the rafters of the tall ceiling. She had modernized the place back in the early seventies of this last century. The kitchen still gleamed brand new some thirty years later.

Anna had arranged for new mattresses to be brought out sometime today. Back thirty years ago, she had still preferred the feather beds, but they needed to be replaced. In all, there were three large bedrooms, all with giant four poster beds. Ancient mosquito netting still hung around one of the beds. Above it , the hole in the roof looked down on her.

One of the Mexicans looked back at her from the roof as she surveyed the room. She nodded at him, returning to the kitchen.

Her husband had told her the cabin was for his extended hunting trips. Anna knew he had carried out atrocities against his female slaves here. She hadn't told Edwards that part of the cabin's reason for existing way out here. She shuddered, hoping the ghosts would rest easy. All of the ghosts except his, that is. Pushing history out of her mind, she forced herself back to the present.

When Gail brought Matthew, he would need the room closest to the added-on bathroom. Anna saw in her mind his wound again; she felt Gail's worry. She started cleaning, keeping her mind on her tasks. Slowly, from all around and above the house, hammering and movement started again, quickly picking up pace. She scrubbed the bathroom until it gleamed.

She figured Edwards would be gone about an hour. As she swept the floor of the bedroom, she thought of her nice, clean little motel. Anna was completely comfortable in her apartment. She rarely came to the cabin. Anna found herself skirting the land her cruel husband had once owned if possible. After a hundred or so years, it had actually become a habit.

She often thought she had stayed simply because of the ghosts.

Anna had also thought that way about Egypt once. A land that bound her to it with the deaths of her most loved.

The thought of her last dead son floated through Anna's mind. She still went to their graves once a year, but as she stood there, she knew that even their ghosts had turned to dust. She wished for their ghosts to revive, even if their little bodies couldn't.

Anna thought of the new baby in her apartment: Morgan's baby.

Anger flooded through her as she swept the floor. She was oblivious to the dust cloud. Though she wound never admit aloud that she was envious of Morgan's motherhood, Anna knew her resentment of her cousin was based solely on Anna's own failing to ever produce a living child.

That Morgan could not only give birth to half breed Mortal daughters, but now a son, as well, left Anna feeling the white hot anger of unfairness.

Maybe she wasn't so eager to get back to the motel after all. Anna cleaned in a frenzy, trying not to think about the baby for at least a few minutes.

Chapter 14

February 2, 1:12 p.m.

Morgan and Abby lay on one bed with the baby while Doug sat in a chair. They were watching the news.

The church that Joseph had presided over was making headlines again.

The faithful, as well as the curious, were all flocking to St. Mary's. It had become an overnight sensation when the handprint was widely reported. The faithful saw it as a sign. The more skeptical still didn't know what the hell it was. Some claimed it was obviously the mark of the devil.

A guard finally had to be posted on the stairs as the unfaithful, or just plain ignorant, threatened to destroy it.

The trio in the room, three and a half counting the baby, knew the meaning of it all too well. The handprint was burned into their minds as deeply as it had burned into the stone.

Doug shivered in his chair as he remembered the small print burned into the wall and his soul. He felt sick all the time now. His stomach twisted in agony.

The public had also found the other handprint in the alley; they were photographing themselves beside it. Some claimed that miracles had occurred when they had put their own hands on the charred void. The street was literally closed down to avoid any tragedies in the two-block stretch. Doug was sure Joseph was rolling in his grave.

The sex scandal was still a scandal since there was no other explanation. They were all sick about it. The weirdness was mounting. Matthew and Gail were both murder suspects. Somehow Matt's brother, a judge, no less, was involved; so was their uncle, who happened to be a police captain. Then there was the coroner whom they couldn't figure out anything about, except that she was also missing and may have been involved in an inappropriate relationship with a high ranking official..

The police chief said he thought maybe the captain was running, but that no one should assume anything.

The man who had shot up the captain's house was wanted for attempted murder. He had been spotted twice; once outside the captain's house and again outside the church in full view of the cops. He had been shooting at a car that the missing persons were believed to be in.

Somehow, an unknown woman, whose description matched Anna, was wanted for the murder of Danny, the choir director.

They all started shaking their heads in the stillness of the room. Maria banged pots and pans around Anna's kitchen, needing something to do.

Douglas wondered if his brother had lived through the night.

Not surprisingly, the news never mentioned that a Muslim cleric was also missing. Abby told the room that they must have just forgotten about his plight. They all chuckled sarcastically.

In an unrelated story was the mystery of the vanished scientist. He had worked on the human genome project, and most recently at Ground Zero in New York City. He had told others someone was trying to kill him in the days before he vanished.

Morgan clicked off the television.

The silence fell onto them like shattered glass, serious and volatile. Doug continued to watch the screen, even though he only saw his own reflection. In Anna's perfectly clean kitchen, Maria made a huge mess to distract herself. None of them was aware that Bubba sat across the street, trying to keep himself from screaming.

Doug looked away from the TV to the door. He felt like running. Just opening the door and running, the way he had in basic training. Just run until his agonized guts twisted out, till there was nothing in his head but running. Douglas had involuntarily turned bulimic in the last week. The thought of food made him sick; when he actually got anything down, he didn't need to gag himself to get it back up. Looking at the door, Doug suddenly realized how unhealthy he felt.

All of his life, he had enjoyed perfect health and little faith. Now he had absolute faith and he couldn't even eat a piece of bread. He needed the sunshine on his face.

Getting up from his chair, Doug ignored Morgan and Abby's looks of concern. The man seemed to be falling to pieces right before their eyes. Doug avoided the kitchen as well, with the smells and Maria's looks of shock at his appearance. He went into the bedroom to put his shorts on and take a jog.

The fresh air would make everything all right.

***

February 2, 1:14 p.m.

Napoliss felt squeaky clean. Thank God! As he lay down on the freshly clean bed, he sighed, tiredly. Webster ignored him from the table.

Stretching out, Napoliss immediately started drifting. The bed seemed lumpy to him. He turned to his right side, then the left. After a minute, he turned to his belly and removed the pillow from under his head. It seemed to work for a while, and he drifted again. Webster glanced at him, jealous of his ability to turn off everything and just sleep, at any time.

Webster watched him for a moment more, reflecting on his own insomnia. After a second, Napoliss turned his head back over and squinted his eyes shut at the glare from the window. He pulled the pillow back up and put it over his own head. Webster thought about smothering him for a split second.

Finally, remembering his own weariness, Webster turned to the still open curtains. A few cars were parked in the lot but not many. A thin-framed, tall guy with dark hair came down the stairs wearing jogging clothes. The man stopped, facing away from Napoliss , and stretched his right leg, then his left.

Webster closed the curtains. After five days of being in that stupid car, he couldn't hold off the fatigue any longer. Napoliss was already snoring as Webster fell onto the opposite bed.

***

February 2, 1.15 p.m.

Bubba watched as the big man came out of Annie May's apartment door.

For a moment, he almost panicked as he glanced nervously at the Feds still open curtain. By the time the man reached the bottom of the stairs, Bubba was already halfway out of the Jeep, , but still hesitant. As the man in shorts started stretching, the Feds curtain had snapped shut. Bubba was

208

having a crisis at all the mixed signals. As the man had jogged from the parking lot, turning up the deserted country road, Bubba decided that if the closed curtain was a trick, he could still intercept the man on the road. He jumped back into the Jeep, pulling out of the restaurant parking lot where he had sat for almost an hour now. He checked his rearview mirror constantly.

Bubba pulled alongside the man, who had stepped off the road to let the car behind him pass. Instead, it slowed and paced him. Doug looked at the huge man who was automatically rolling down a window from a switch on his door.

Doug slowed a little and then finally stopped as the man called out to him.

"Hey man! Hey...Stop a second..."

Doug wondered if he was having car trouble.

When they were both stopped, the black man blurted out, "Where's Annie? Anna..."

Doug stepped back from the truck as a sudden paranoia made him start to twitch.

"Don't know what you're talkin' about, dude...Sorry," Doug blurted.

As he started to take off again, Bubba yelled at him.

"Stop!"

He let go of the brake and let the Jeep roll a few feet, keeping Doug framed in the window. Doug stopped again, putting both hands on his hips. He tried to look put-upon. It wasn't a hard effort. His heart was thumping wildly.

"Listen, DUDE...I know you know what the hell I'm talkin' about...you just left her damn house!" Bubba snapped at hm.

Doug looked at the stranger while taking a deep breath in, and then looked around the street nervously.

The giant man behind the wheel got right to the point. ,

"I'll just say this...if you is wanted by federal agents, then we have to go get Anna right now!"

Doug looked the man solidly in his eyes, now dead still.

"I'm not wanted by federal agents." He said softer than he meant to.

Bubba smiled at the duplicity of the response.

"If anyone else is in Anna's apartment, then they in trouble too. Men with badges just checked in downstairs. You walked right past their room!"

Doug looked at him hard, blinking rapidly.

Maria. The baby. Abby. Morgan.

Without hesitation, Douglas opened the passenger door of the Jeep and hopped in. They immediately started talking about ways to get past the agents' window with a large group of people that were all recognizable.

Bubba drove a long country block before coming back to the restaurant lot where he had sat for so long. They watched the doors of the motel, both of them worried.

Bubba pointed out the room the feds were in. He told the white man about the flyers, the accusations. By Doug's stunned face, Bubba knew he had been right. Annie May wasn't no damn terrorist. He was secretly relieved.

They watched the lower level window. The curtains remained closed. Neither of them could tell if a trap had been set.

Without knowing what else to do, they waited helplessly.

***

February 2, 1.26 p.m.

When Edwards, and his new best friend Armando, returned from their tasks, Anna was on the roof with three of the workers. The men seemed to be trying to outdo her pace as all of their hammers flew in a macho competition. The giant hole above the bedroom was almost fully repaired.

Edwards couldn't help but laugh at the little hammer with a pink grip that Anna used to batter the roof. Armando laughed too as they pulled up behind the truck once more.

The Latino guided the car expertly, smoothly, and Edwards found himself liking the young man. Their conversation in broken English had left them both laughing, enjoying each other's company. Edwards held the three huge bags of burgers as the crew stopped their work when the car approached. Laying down hammers and saws, they were more than ready for a beer and a burger.

Anna knew, without looking up, who was in the approaching car. As soon as she had heard the engine, she had concentrated, seeing the occupants in her mind. Before the effort could consume her, she had pulled back. Her hammer never missed a beat. After the workers lay down their

210

hammers, she too stopped; first to arrive, last to leave. To her, it was a game of stamina that she hardly ever lost. The Mexicans were killing her though. Her shoulder felt like someone had taken the pink handled hammer to it. She was glad for the break.

Edwards was already handing out the food as Anna came down the ladder. Armando was getting his roll of wires from the trunk and Anna could see the grocery bags in the back seat. She smiled at Edwards as he opened the back car door for her. He had been stunned in the grocery store when he realized that he was shopping for explosives. She grabbed both bags and carried them past the workers into the house. Edwards picked up a Corona, joining the men on the porch. After removing the toiletries and first aid, she was left with one bag. She left it on the counter.

Once outside, Anna also grabbed a Corona. She carefully took a sip, decided she could handle it, and gulped two swallows. The men tore at the food, ravenous from their efforts. Anna and Edwards both were still too full of Kia's cooking to be hungry. In easy spirits, the men joked, sometimes in English, sometimes in Spanish, as Anna and the captain relaxed into the group.

When half her beer was gone, she put the bottle down. She was already starting to feel woozy and decided she had had her limit. None of her race could hold their liquor. Anna hoped she hadn't drunk too much already. The chill of the afternoon had receded almost completely, making the day comfortable and bright.

As the men joked, Anna silently wondered about the young priest. She was seriously worried now.

She knew Edwards was worried, too. She hoped Gail would hurry. Anna knew that Gail had turned back into Mississippi the night before, but she hadn't told the rest of the group that. When the priest had started convulsing, Gail had had no choice but to turn back to where she knew she could find help.

Sister Frances was also a Mortal. Sister Katherine was a half-breed; They would help. Anna was not so much worried about Gail as she was about Matthew. His human frailty was evident when Anna reached out. She knew the man had been close to death, probably for a few days.

When Gail had moved Matthew from the motel, he had seemed okay enough, but the road had taken its toll. Anna had told Doug the truth about Matthew's fever but she didn't tell him they had turned back. She was at a loss about what to do.

She couldn't leave the baby unprotected. She could not allow him out of her sight.

Anna knew that she was wanted for Danny's murder, although it had been James who had killed the man. She shuddered as she remembered the warmth leaving his body after he had died in her arms. She had not known the man, but she knew he hadn't deserved to take her bullet. She swore that if she ever got her hands on James again, she would make him pay for killing an innocent.

Anna had no idea what it had already cost him. She would not have been surprised to know Jerold had killed his own half-bred son.

As always, the thought of Jerold brought Michael to her thoughts. Her fuzzy mind tried to steer away from his image but collided into it instead. The loneliness of her life seemed to crush her at times. Michael looked back at her from her cloudy memory, as clear and bright as the day around her.

The men on the porch barely noticed as Anna went over to the beat-up radio and started flipping through the stations. She thought of Michael's first wife, involuntarily flinching.

Anna had encouraged Michael to marry the woman, knowing that any future together between them was not possible.

The human girl had been bright and pretty; Anna had left Michael to his life when she had found out that the woman was pregnant. She fled the country, secretly humiliated that a human could give him something that she could not.

It wasn't until months later she had returned to find the disaster that had occurred.

The woman had given birth to a son, identical to his father, and then without reason or mercy lost her own life. Her frail human soul had given it's last spark to ignite the half Mortal boy with life.

Anna had not known that Michael had loved the girl so much. She couldn't comprehend what Michael had done when she died. He had gotten drunk.

In his rage at God, Michael had decided that they were all damned. He had raged through the house, tearing up everything as his wife grew cold in their bed.

In his drunken stupidity, Michael threw a torch onto the floor. The women who had helped deliver the baby had fled when he had started the destruction. After the torch had been thrown, Michael had deliberately passed out on the burning floor. He was sure the flames would consume him. His father Alexandet had seen the flames from up the road.

Alex barely saved Michael from the inferno. No one thought to take the baby, until it was too late. It had been the only son Michael had ever had.

Michael never recovered. They had to keep him in bondage for years until he was no longer suicidal. If one of their race tried suicide, the wound never killed them; it simply stayed open, and gaping.

Alex refused to let Michael do that to himself.

For all of Alexander's atrocities, he had cared for his son, as much as any evil soul was capable of. While she flipped the dials on the radio, Anna shuddered hard.

Armando must have been watching her because he walked up behind her and laid his thin jacket across her shoulders. He didn't understand that the cold would never bother her anyway. It was a sweet kindness and she smiled at him drunkenly.

The other workers, seeing his gesture, started making jokes and Armando blushed so red he looked sunburned. After a few minutes of ribbing, he finally had gotten up and crawled back under the porch with his roll of wire. Anna smiled sadly as they finally tired of the jokes and one by one went back to work. Only she and Edwards remained on the porch. She knew Armando was watching her, from time to time, from his spot below them.

Edwards looked at her silently, contemplating her ancient shattered soul.

She hid it from everyone, he knew. He had also been a cop long enough to see that people often lied to themselves about their own pain. He knew she was something different, totally out of his experience or imagination. Her heartbreak was clearly reflected in her eyes.

Edwards suddenly realized that he would hate to see her angry.

In his mind, he returned to the spot she had left for him, quickly coming to the image of Morgan trembling at the point of her blade. He saw Anna's nimble hands swing the blade and Gail step in to unexpectedly absorb the impact. Captain Edwards suddenly realized that Anna hated Morgan. He wondered how he had missed it. He saw the lamp again hurtled at a sobbing Morgan by those same hands. The Corona had made his mind loose and as they stared across the porch at one another, he decided to tackle it head-on.

"WHY do you hate Morgan?" He said it evenly, seeing Anna's eyes were puffy.

She seemed shocked at the question.

"Huh?"

Her eyebrows rose as she penetrated his flesh with her stare.

"I think you know what I mean…"

This time Edwards tone was softer, not trying to push, but his curiosity won out.

"Why did you try to kill her?"

Unexpectedly, Anna threw her head back and laughed.

The laugh was low and warm, turning into a higher pitch as she almost doubled over. Edwards was caught off guard by the way it sparkled and rolled across the clearing. He remembered his mother singing to him as a little boy. He had become accustomed to her smirk and was blown away by the beauty of her laughter. Some of the hammering around him stopped as the Latinos, too, seemed to pause to reap the gift of her laughter. After a moment, she ran out of breath, gulped hard, and laughed again.

Edwards looked at her like she had lost her damn mind. She finally settled down, still gulping and trying not to chuckle.

She told him, "I wasn't trying to kill her, I just wanted her to hurt, I guess. By God, Edwards, that's funny!"

He had no idea why it was funny. "Funny how?" he asked without humor.

Anna chuckled to herself, amused.

"If I wanted Morgan dead, she'd be dust by now."

She said it low, still somewhat merry, but the tone had chilled his blood. He knew she was telling the truth.

"Why did you want her to hurt?" He blurted, refusing to let her laugh it away.

The question seemed to sober Anna as she looked at him evenly. She took a deep breath, letting it out slowly. When she finally spoke again, her voice was so low he had to strain to hear it.

"I don't know…I guess I blamed her for what her mother had done…It just seemed so unfair…"

Anna looked away from him, sweeping her eyes across the clearing.

"At that time, Morgan was having babies damn near every year…I just wanted one …just one…of my own to survive. I just wanted her to hurt; I was not very good at losing, I suppose."

He knew it wasn't about losing. He became thoughtful before his next blurted intrusion.

"You actually held the bust of Nefertiti?" he asked in a serious tone.

Her eyes snapped to him as if he had kicked her. After a long moment, she again started laughing. Instead of a burst, it started out as a chuckle, growing louder until it seemed to literally vibrate him slowly.

After it had crested, she again spoke with only some bitterness. .

"Held it? Edwards. Please! I made the damn thing! It was always my work."

Before he could respond, Anna stood up, leaving him on the porch stuttering. She went into the house to make sure that the cleaning job she had done was sufficient.

Anna thought about the finished statue she had destroyed. She had always regretted smashing it . After all, it had been one of her best works, ever.

Chapter 15

February 2, 2.03 p.m.

Gail opened her eyes to find herself crunched between two chairs. Her long legs cramped and burned as she tried to lift them. She glanced across the sparse room and saw that Matthew was wide awake and watching her.

Sister Katherine had to repair the shoddy surgical work that Gail had done on his chest wound and Matthew seemed unnaturally pale as she met his gaze.

He turned his head away from her with set lips, deliberately looking at the ceiling. She knew he was upset.

Unkinking herself, Gail shoved the chair in front of her backwards, finally freeing her cramped legs. She went to the bed. Matthew refused to meet her eyes again. He started crying as she watched him. Not a sobbing heave, but a sad involuntary flood of tears. He turned his head further from her and watched the wall, turning away from her completely.

Gail felt his forehead and he seemed too weak to protest. She breathed a sigh of relief when she felt that his temperature was normal. She tried to comfort him.

"What's wrong, Matthew?" she asked softly.

At that, he slowly turned his head back to her. Locking his eyes with hers, he spat the words out.

"How dare you ask me that?" Matthew demanded.

Now she was the one who looked away. Her avoidance seemed to infuriate him.

"What. Is. Wrong? ... How DARE you ask that?" he hissed into her face.

Matthew trembled from head to toe with anger. He knew that he had been close to death. He had seen it coming for him, and here she was playing stupid with him.

He blinked at her face, unlined and perfect.

"Don't you think you should tell ME what's wrong? …Goddamn you to Hell!" He had screamed it.

Gail flinched at his fury. She knelt by the bed and grabbed his hand once more. He was too weak to pull it away, so he just turned his head again, studying the wall while openly refusing to respect her.

"I'm so sorry, Matthew. …Oh God, I'm so sorry. " Gail said, with genuine empathy.

Without turning from the wall, he mocked her. ,

"Yeah…right… Of course you are Sorry!"

Gail looked at him nervously, unsure of herself. She was not accustomed to feeling apprehensive, but his wounded fury at her filled her with dread. Mostly because she deserved it.

"You're right Matthew, I do owe you an explanation…I'm so sorry you are hurt."

Through clenched teeth, he demanded that explanation.

"If I'm going to die, I have a right to know WHY…"

This time he did turn and look at her again, his eyes showing no sign of the heavy drugs he had been under since surgery. Instead his eyes were wide, and clear as he glared at her.. He shouted at her.

"I'm hurt so bad! …They want me for murder!… I cannot go home… or even to a hospital! Why, Gail, why?"

Matthew's tears spilled rapidly down his face, hot and furious.

He looked back at the ceiling, trying to sustain the energy of anger, but failing.

"I am a murderer. … I don't know why. … Joseph is dead. …I STILL DON'T KNOW WHY!"

The last he screamed at the ceiling. He finally started sobbing, his broken body tortured by the force of his involuntary animation.

"Why, Gail? Why? … Why…can't…you…just… TELL ME, GODDAMN YOU!"

Matthew was almost in a panic even as he lay there completely unable to move. His face was red, his entire body shook as he finally fought back against it all.

Gail looked at the crucifix over the bed. She bit her lip as she held his limp hand. She stared at the impaled body of Christ, and she silently asked God for strength.

"OK! …OK…You're right, Matthew. You should know everything…

217

I'll tell you what I know...but I don't think it will bring you any comfort."

Matthew looked at her sharply. His eyes, already burdened with pain, seemed to narrow to just a sliver.

"Tell me." He demanded in a low growl.

Gail breathed out and dropped her head. Matthew stared at her face. She now looked the same age that he was. He knew now it was not a hallucination. She was no longer old. He hated her for something he couldn't explain.

Gail raised her head and stared into his eyes for just a brief moment. She tried to smile at him, but only it's ghost appeared for a mere moment on her full lips.

"Everything." He demanded.

"OK"

Gail let go of his hand and retrieved one of the wingback chairs that she had slept in. She pulled it close to the bed. Matthew watched her, unaware of how much everything was going to change for him.

*****

In the beginning, there was light.

God spoke the word and the universe was created.

He created the heavens and the Earth. He had made moons and suns and the universe was a garden of the Lord, Thy God. So fascinated was He by His own Creation that He, Himself, marveled at its beauty. He spent eternities there.

For a time, the Lord was satisfied. After many milinia , while walking amongst His creations, the Lord cried out in loneliness.

From His cry, a new creation was born. God was happy to see that creation take form from shadows and dust, and their perfection became His perfection.

He called them Angels.

They, too, wandered the universe, in awe of it. He made many of these Angels and was no longer lonely. They were of the spirit and honored Him as their Father. He blessed them with freedom, sure that He was in their spirits.

After eternity upon eternity, some of them changed, as awareness slowly dawned upon them. One of their elders refused God's will. He was known as Lucifer. Some of the others followed him, believing that they were as God was. They believed themselves to be God's equal.

Lucifer spit in God's eye and the Heavens split in a horrendous battle. To show his might, God cast down the rebel traitors and wouldn't let them back into His graces.

The Lord decided to change creation.

The Lord started again at the beginning. Perhaps, He had grown weary of the all the perfection, who can say? So, He changed the way He created.

He decided to make beings who would strive toward perfection; instead of being made so.

As His angels warred with one another, the Lord had gone to the Earth to weep.

From His tears, the oceans were born. From the oceans, new life came forth. Not perfect beings like the others, but confused, half-formed changelings, who grew up in many different ways to be many different beings. This new form of life was given the gift of being able to change, into something new, and better.

He gave this new form of life the ability to recreate itself, to reproduce.

Many of the angels became enraged at this gift. They could not recreate themselves! They had never known a child Angel.

Heaven split, again as even more Angels joined the Rebels in exile. To prove His point, God created an imperfect being in His own image. He called the being Human.

There were many different kinds of man, all of them human; all with immature souls. All of these humans were born with the ability to not only change their own fate, but to give birth to offspring that were actually stronger, smarter, and more perfect than their parents.

Aware of how wrong His first creation had gone, the Lord damned these men to be mortal, unlike the Angels who had never tasted death.

He blessed them all with life, and death. While the Angels were cursed to live forever.

Heaven erupted into all-out warfare as it became clear God now favored the humans.

The followers of Lucifer began poisoning the minds of the other Angels. He won over more and more, but many of them remained loyal to their Father. The two factions fought a battle that encompassed entire universes.

Then, there were the others.

These Angels had no wish to follow Lucifer, nor a desire to defy God, so they left His graces, so sure that, with all the madness, He would not notice their absence. While God was busy with the Rebels, the Renegades quietly slipped out of Heaven, in a fall that would be for eternity.

These Angels went to the Earth, now full of the life that God had made as a lesson to humble them. The renegade Angels marveled at the new creation called man.

They became envious.

While God waged war on the Rebels , these angels also played with shadow and dust, and then with blood and light, and unexpectedly took on the guise of a perfected form of man.

The first Angel to take the mortal skin of man was the strongest and most beautiful of them all. His name was Satan.

Once Satan learned how to add blood to shadows and dust, within hours the rest of his followers converted to the flesh as well. The fire of their perfect souls incubated them all to far surpass the weakness of this creature called 'human'.

In an instant, the moment they took to the flesh, they became the most highly evolved beings on earth.

The Renegades took all the tones of the earth, and both sexes.

They became spirits bound in perfect flesh.

There were six hundred sixty-six of them; half of them male, half of them female.

Once in the flesh, these renegade Angels became enraptured with their new skins.

They touched each other and learned emotions and sensations so strong it seared their souls. It changed them. The touch of a lover, and the wind in their different types of hair made each of them cry with joy at the rapture of it. Even tears twisted their souls in new ways, and every single renegade decided that this ripple of change across their souls could never be undone.

All of them refused to even try returning to Heaven. All of them chose to simply evolve. Here on this garden called earth, they were the New Gods.

They knew not hunger, but ate anyway, for the pleasure of it. The cold and heat could not break their flesh. Neither could anything else on Earth. They were perfect souls wrapped inside immortal flesh. They were unbreakable.

These earthbound angels gave in to all the demands of the flesh, wallowing in their pleasures. They became lustful and lay with each other just to feel another's embrace.

After a while, the three hundred and thirty three females began to get pregnant. Their perfected flesh reproduced itself many times as they suddenly became as fertile as the humans they watched.. For them childbirth was as easy and painless as any of their new biological functions were.

They never saw God coming; they were so caught up in their own creations and senses. Their children were born of Angels that had evolved, and all the renegades assumed this would please the Lord, if only He knew.

One day God returned to the Earth and surprised the renegades. He called to them, and they emerged from the grasses, ashamed and frightened.

God was furious.

They begged Him for the lives of their children.

God brought damnation on them all.

The six hundred sixty-six who defied Him were cast aside into the depths of Creation. They were torn from their flesh and their wounded spirits were consumed by Lucifer , whom lived in those depths.

God, however, looked upon their innocent children with mercy. But even mercy has its boundaries. These children were not supposed to exist, but even worse, they had already altered the rules He had laid down for all mortal life on earth.

Leaving their ill gotten immortality in place, God cast a curse among the children of the Angels. He told them that if the warmth of the flesh pleased them, then he would turn it into a fire that consumed their minds and scorch their perfect souls.

He set the males against the females, trying to keep them from one another.

The curse worked by awareness. When two of the Children of Angels of the opposite sex met, their simple awareness of each other would cause a fever in both so hot, that for many eons, these illegal angels of the flesh did indeed quit having children all together.

Couples that had been together for hundreds of years, fled from each other in horror, breaking up every angelic family line until the two genders stopped trying to seek each other out.

The curse of the fever drove them all mad.

Some became suicidal, yet it was quickly clear that casting off the flesh was not as easy as taking it. The immortal were not allowed to kill themselves.

The females turned on the males, pushing them away. . The fever numbed their minds and their bodies. Many of the males became violently insane. Unable to satisfy the demands of the flesh, they had turned on God's favored creation.

They started slaughtering humans.

The Children of Angels walked the Earth in packs, catching the human females and raping them. They cannibalized the flesh of humans, killing them in droves, just for sport.

The fever had worked but not completely as intended. God came forth to see them once more, and He was horrified at what He found.

For the second time, He cursed them. He gave them human hearts. He made them vulnerable.

In one whisper He stripped away their immortality.

The children of the angels were stunned. For the first time they understood Love, Hate, and Grief. They all cried and trembled in the presence of the Lord. They knew fear. They knew respect.

They felt compassion for the humans and the slaughter stopped. In time they stopped calling themselves the Children of Angels and began calling themselves 'Mortal'.

Their human hearts were indeed vulnerable, even if their lifespan still seemed to be indefinite. The slight imperfection of having a human heart, was clearly lethal to them as for the first time they saw their own kind succumb to the injuries of accidents and murder.

Eventually, in their own imperfection, the humans turned on one another. God allowed their struggle; allowing them to learn. They, too, cannibalized each other until only one remained.

Homo-sapiens. Modern man.

From the shadows, the now vulnerable Mortal children of Angels watched as this race of man developed an awareness of his own potential. There was no stopping him from ruling the Earth. Mankind became organized, anticipating his own needs. Humans had formed communities, which would become the first cities.

Eventually the humans had become so finely adjusted that they were almost indistinguishable from the Mortals. Some of the Mortals joined man, living among him, helping them.

Because of their human hearts, the Mortals again felt the need to seek out one another; those who were strong enough to bear the fever were still able to mate. Their children were born as they were, as a somewhat normal progression of the Mortal race continued on. After a thousand years the fever had become something they just learned to live with.

Some of the Mortals dared to have children with humans, hoping these children would not be cursed. They were no more cursed than their parents, however even then the half-Mortal and half-human offspring were all identical to their Mortal parent, and barren. Even before the curses, the human women that bore Mortal children, were never strong enough to survive the birth of a half-breed.

The Mortals learned to live in the shadows of man as the humans took over the planet. The existence almost seemed tolerable as life became its own distraction. Many millennia passed as the Mortal race found some semblance of balance among the human race.

Then came Nefertiti.

Nefertiti was born a full-blooded Mortal child. Both her mother and father had been cast down by God into the jaws of Lucifer. .

She resented God for it, in her human heart.

The Mortals were still having families, some of them very large families as they began to control the fever. A land known as Egypt came forth and the humans made marvels that were so beautiful, even the children of Angels were in awe. Humans became spiritual as they searched for answers. They created many gods to worship. Faith was a comfort to the humans, unlike Mortals who had no choice but to believe.

After a few thousand years, the Mortals had almost entirely integrated themselves into man's society. Nefertiti and Jerold were in love.

Alexander coveted his brother's woman. He started whispering ideas to Nefertiti. She foolishly believed him. Human politics became a game between them.

The man who ruled Egypt was called Pharaoh. In a human's near-sightedness, they became their own gods. Pharaoh was worshipped as a living god.

One pharaoh in particular was vulnerable. Alexander had a plan to get back into Heaven. The pharaoh's name was Amenhotep the Fourth. Nefertiti seduced him. He called her the most beautiful of all.

She told Pharaoh about the Lord, and he believed. He became a hieratic king, uprooting the entire system of Egyptian religion. He outlawed any other faith and Nefertiti cheered him on.

Unknown to her husband, and to Alex, she lay in lust with Jerold, and Morgan was born exactly nine months later. Pharaoh believed the baby to be his child. Morgan's royal name was Ankhsenpaten.

Alexander put his final plan in motion. He filled Nefertiti's head with the grandeur of God and assured her that the Lord could no longer punish them further. That God, owed it to them, to listen to their complaints and give them back their immortality..

Her husband changed thousands of years of history, just for her. None of them cared what the lesser humans thought. Not even their human demigod cared what his people wanted, or believed. Just as the humans began rebelling, Jerold and Alex decided to do something about it, sensing an opportunity to elevate themselves above all men.

Alexander killed the Pharaoh, leaving Queen Nefertiti with six daughters, five of them half human.

Alex told her that she could have all that was in Heaven here on Earth. As her children were still small, Nefertiti ruled in their stead.

Then, she got greedy, and foolishly did as Alexander suggested.

As a child of the Angels, Nefertiti should have known better. She took the title of Pharaoh Smenkhkare; she crowned herself a living God.

From the Heavens, The Lord God became enraged at her blasphemy. He walked the Earth again, bringing a savage final curse with him.

Without warning, three children of Mortals fell into a trance that lasted seven days. One of them spoke with the tongue of God, one of them spoke all the languages of man, and the third translated.

The other Mortals watched helplessly as their fate was passed.

God would allow them to bear children, but only with humans, and then they could only replicate themselves. The half-breed replicas would all be barren.

If they defied Him again and tried to evolve further with new life , the full-blood children of two Mortal parents would be born horrifically deformed, and already dying, or dead. No full-blooded Mortals would ever be born again.

God would never again tolerate their defiance. Their race was doomed to die. And just when all hope was lost, one last promise of mercy emerged.

Only one chance would be given to them to redeem themselves and prove they deserved to exist.

A prophet would be born to a Mortal. Not a replica, but a new creation. It would come in God's time, if they could survive that long.

The prophet would save the human race and the Mortal race, or he would destroy them both .

A human protector would be named for the child, by God and random chance. If the human guardian died before the child was raised, the prophet would destroy them all.

The baby's protector was foretold as a man of faith with a burden of sin in his heart. Before the child's seventh day, this human will have killed for him. A killer, who has not murdered.

Murder, after all, is a direct sin against God.

After seven days in their trance, the children who spoke the words of The Lord God unexpectedly awoke, with no apparent memory of the event. The full-blood children of Mortals suddenly started being born with horrific deformations,, birth defects so severe they died at birth or moments after.

When a Mortal woman gave birth to a child by a human father, it was always an identical female or a dead son. The Mortal males had sons or dead daughters.

The entire Mortal race vowed to kill Nefertiti. The two brothers, whom both loved her, did kill her. The pharaoh was dead.

The new pharaoh was the son of Nefertiti's husband with a lesser wife. He was known as Tutankhamen. By the human tradition, Morgan was married to him at the age of twelve. The boy was nine years old. King Tut was murdered in his own bed by the age of nineteen.

Morgan learned who she was soon after. She had fled the power structure of earthly gods. The entire Mortal race had been terrified that she, too, would take the throne for herself. Instead, she ran from it.

As the years passed, the number of Mortals decreased with no replenishment. Their race was dying, a slow agonizing death. After four thousand years had passed, only fourteen pure bloods remained on the face of the Earth.

The same month humans had discovered a female pharaoh's body in an Egyptian tomb, Morgan learned she was pregnant. As soon as she learned of the pregnancy, she became terrified, suspecting who the child's father was. When the boy was born, the others found out what Morgan had already feared.

Without warning, the mother's sin was visited upon the daughter. Morgan had been celibate for over a decade. Abby had been the only lover she had taken in almost eighty years. Abby himself knew instantly he could not be this child's father and he believed Morgan was indeed celibate when she had fallen pregnant.

Father Matthew had killed Alexander when the baby was just five days old. No murderer, but a killer none the less. If the baby were to survive, he would have to be protected at all costs, from both Mortals and humans.

God's time had come. So had the prophet. Father Matthew was the chosen one, if he failed, this baby would destroy the world..

The battle was just beginning.

Some of the Mortals, those Children of Angels, were in agreement with Satan who still called out to them in their dreams..

***

Matthew looked at Gail hatefully. She understood perfectly.

He glared daggers into her. His eyes were swollen and red. She had the distinct impression that if he could move, he would slap her damn head off. Gail wouldn't have been surprised to know he would have. She looked at him evenly, but she tensed up for his reaction. She was not sure she could hold him down if he reacted badly. He may have been hurt, but he was big and very angry at her, .

His long ago image as the 'side-walk bully' almost brought a stupid smile to her face; almost.

His look was deathly serious. Even though her heart broke for Matthew, she kept herself from crying, never allowing her gaze to waver.

Matthew thought Gail was beautiful. Her golden eyes met his hate-filled ones.. He hated her for being beautiful.

Mother Frances walked into the room, surprising Gail with her unexpected intrusion.. Her long figure in the black robe was thin, almost gaunt as she brought a tray of food into the room quietly. Gail and Matthew stared at each other, both silently cursing at God. Frances stopped, looking at them, startled into a sudden stillness. The tray lid had little droplets of steam all over it and a delicious odor started wafting through the air.

Again, the sudden image of the pudgy sidewalk bully flashed through

226

Gail's mind and she did allow herself a rueful smile at Matthew. The image was a hard to fit on the man she had come to know as a strong and faithful priest. The smile softened her eyes, her hair, and brow.

Matthew was breathless with the impact of her gorgeous smile. He hated her for it. She had just destroyed his soul. His shattered body ached.

He knew she was telling the truth. She believed in him, he could see it in her enormous eyes.

Frances cleared her throat softly, understanding the subtleties of emotion prevalent between them. She moved quickly to put the food on the table, trying not to interrupt any more than necessary. She was sure that the priest should not be awake so soon. He must be strong, she thought. Without looking at them she started arranging plates of food; Frances asked about Matthew without looking at either of them.

"Are you hungry, young man?"

Matthew was starving. He hated Gail for his hunger.

She smiled at him, stopping his pulse with her beautiful, hated smile. His body ached and he quivered with pain. His body had been shattered once before, and the old wounds hurt as badly as the new ones as his sins fell upon him with a body-breaking effect. The pain was making his soul wither.

Mathew wanted to die. Gail had lied to him all his life. The pain was too much. Every beat of his heart broke his spirit a little more in a relentless shattering drumbeat. Matthew started crying; so did Gail. She let the tears fall. He took his functioning left arm and put it over his eyes. Gail slumped back into the chair and wiped at the tears.

With velvet steel in her voice, Gail answered Frances.

"I speak for Matthew...Yes, ma'am, he's hungry. "

Frances retreated from the room with catlike agility and grace.

Gail still sat with her hands over her eyes as she tried to help Matthew through it.

"Would you like something for the pain?" she asked softly.

From under his arm, Matthew said "Fuck you."

After a moment, Gail rose from the chair to push it backwards, across the room. When it was back in its original position, she sat down and took the lid from her tray of food. She loved the nuns cooking. Gail ate silently while Matthew sobbed.

Chapter 16

February 2, 2.09 p.m.

Bubba stopped drumming his fingers. He just knew that Kia was gonna quit.

Doug looked at him and nodded, speaking with a shrug.

"Sounds good to me, man. I sure ain't got anything better figured out."

The huge man grinned; his perfect white teeth were startling against his smooth dark chocolate face. He nodded slightly in return. By God, this white boy had some guts! Bubba was only going as far as Anna's apartment, but if what the white man said was true, then this was going to be one hell of a visit. Bubba thought he was going to enjoy this.

He started the Jeep and rolled slowly across the deserted street. He watched the window of the room where the Feds were the entire time. Bubba rolled the Jeep right up next to the stairs that led up to Anna's apartment and parked in her parking space. They expected g-men to swarm them at any moment. As soon as the car came to a stop, both men were out the doors before the engine noise even died. Watching the still closed curtains, they quickly climbed the stairs.

Abby and Morgan were asleep as Doug and his companion burst in on them. Before they could shut the door, however, they both stopped, frozen dead in their tracks.

As soon as they had hit the door, Morgan and Abby had both come awake instantly. Abby had the gun pointed directly at Bubba's head. Doug's momentum had carried him through the door, and as Abby cocked the gun, Doug sucked in his breath sharply. The point of Morgan's slender silver sword was making a slight dent in his throat. The entire room froze.

Bubba smiled like he had won the lottery, and then he calmly turned and pushed the door shut with a light click. Yep, Bubba thought, this was gonna be a blast!

Startled by the sudden shift of activity, the baby started mewling softly on the bed.

***

February 2, 2.13 p.m.

Anna had drunk too much. She had scrubbed the floors of the kitchen till they glowed in the afternoon light from the window. They had delivered her mattresses, but she had never looked up from the floor, as Edwards had directed the delivery guys to the back of the house. While she had worked on the floor, she had taken a few sips to ward off the cold, at least two, too many. She knew it would pass quickly, but not fast enough. She inspected the floor. Anna had never liked being drunk and now she remembered why. She felt like she was drowning in a foul, liquid world; so, she decided to go to the car and sleep it off.

Without stopping to notice anything, Anna left the house. Coming into the weak sunlight, she raised her face to the sun. She opened the back car door and lay down across the seat as she closed her eyes. A slight breeze started blowing leaves into the car. It felt as though the car was rocking in the wind, but maybe it was all in her mind.

The captain had saw Anna go to the car and followed her. After he saw her lying down, he went to the driver's side door and got in behind the wheel.

Anna lay still, cursing the makers of Corona.

From the front seat, the captain asked, "Are you all right?"

She breathed deep, trying to sober up.

"Yes…I'm just worried… And I drank too much…"

Edwards nodded while he watched the Mexicans hammer away on the roof. Just as he reached for the door handle, Anna decided to divulge a secret.

"I didn't tell y'all something back at my apartment." She blurted.

Captain Edwards nodded again, not surprised; seemed like this little lady had more than a few secrets. The drunker she got, the more her speech took on the cadence of the southern drawl.

"Would you like to tell me now?" Edwards asked evenly.

He looked at the roof without seeing it.

"Matthew and Gail had to turn back last night; they're in Mississippi."

The captain snapped his head up, unsure where this was going. He had expected Matthew to be here by tomorrow morning. "Why did they have to turn back?"

Edwards kept his tone even, trying to disguise the sudden panic he felt.

"Matthew's wounds needed surgery again…Gail turned back because the place where she is now was closer than coming here. He was in surgery until midnight, last night."

Anna sighed heavy; she could feel the captain's tension.

"Did he…did he do…all right?" He was scared to hear the answer.

She comforted him from the backseat.

"Yes, he did well…He's very strong…I was scared that he couldn't survive, but he did. He will heal up nicely." She assured him in a hollow tone.

The captain squinted into the bright afternoon. His cheek muscle under his right eye started twitching.

"Where are they?"

"At my aunt's convent. I have a cousin that's a trained surgeon." Anna said flatly.

Captain Edwards frowned deeply, trying not to be alarmed.

"Didn't you tell me that Gail had gone to medical school?" he shot back at her.

He looked in the rearview mirror at her still form sprawled in the back seat. Anna wasn't moving but her tone became sharper..

"Gail graduated medical school in, like, 1500 A.D., or something! And we were all very proud of her, yes! But. …She needed help."

The captain lowered his eyes, looking at the dash panel without seeing it. He touched the spot in his mind that Anna had left behind.

"How is he now?" Edwards needed to know.

Again, Anna sighed, and he could hear the sheer fatigue in her voice.

"This morning he was very pale…he cannot use his right arm. I think my cousin Katherine did a pretty good job on his lung. Gail assisted her, but…"

"But…?" Edwards pressed her.

"They didn't have any anesthesia, only morphine. They tied him down; it was bad…he was in bad shape. I think I may have to go get them."

Edwards snapped his head up at that. He quickly realized that he didn't feel safe with the thought of her gone. He did not trust anything anymore. He missed June so badly, but he was glad that she was not here. He looked

230

at the house, watched a tree blowing in the breeze.

"When are you leaving?" he asked softly.

"I don't know. When we get back to my place, I can reach out to Gail again. I figured whatever happens…a few hours either way isn't going to make a difference now…if Matthew cannot be moved, we have no choice but to go to him. …"

The captain's shoulders sagged. His nephew's face passed through his mind, bright and lively. He could not bear the thought of that boy dead.

"Can I come with you?"

Anna smiled with her eyes still closed. She was glad to find strength in his bravery.

"Like I said, I dunno if I'm even going yet. I don't know if I can afford to leave."

On the front seat, he nodded absently. He thought that she was anticipating Matthew's death and if that happened, she would have to be here, to protect the baby.

Anna knew what he thought but gave no sign.

She felt sick. He didn't know that if Matthew died, Anna would not be protecting the baby, at all; she would have no choice but to kill him.

She could not afford to let Morgan get a head start. A mother would protect the baby, no matter what. However. If the protector died, then the baby had to die also, before he could have a chance to kill them all..

"You ready to get back?" Edwards asked her, unaware of her soul's struggle in the back seat.

She breathed deeply, letting the breath out slowly. Anna hated God in that moment.

"Yep." She said on a hard sigh.

She didn't want to go anywhere, actually, especially back into the child's presence.. Anna fished in her pocket a moment, pulling out the key to the car. She tossed the single key over the seat at the captain..

"Vamonos," she said, as he started the car.

***

February 2, 2.31 p.m.

Webster stirred slightly in his sleep. The small sliver of sunlight that came from between the curtains, disappeared, and then reappeared. He woke up, startled to realize that he and his partner were no longer alone. As he opened his eyes in the gloom, he saw a man standing above him with a pistol pointed right between his eyes.

Webster froze. In the shadows, he could barely make out the figure of Abdullah; the missing cleric smiled at him, as someone clicked on the light.

Rolling his eyes, Webster could see that Napoliss, too, lay still as a stone on his bed. The woman from the flyer was holding a sword to his neck. Doug Daniels watched the two men but kept his own pistol pointed at the floor. He stood between the two beds and Webster squinted up at him, unbelieving.

He looked up at the grinning cleric, unable to process this reality.

"You gotta be kidding me?" Webster exclaimed.

Abby cocked the pistol and the smile faded. The sound echoed softly, and everyone understood that this was no joke.

From somewhere near the bathroom, Maria, the missing coroner, approached Webster's bed with a roll of duct tape. Stooping next to the bed she instructed him firmly.

"Put out your hands."

Webster swallowed hard but the sight of the cocked pistol Abby held convinced him to do as she said. Napoliss tried to grunt, and Morgan pressed the blade of her sword gently, reminding him not to move.

Maria wrapped Webster up like a Christmas present. Abby turned the gun on Napoliss and Morgan lowered the sword. Maria bound him tightly, as well, adding extra tape to make sure. The younger Fed, now over his shock, glared at Abby's gun spitefully. Doug went to the door and opened it far enough to slip a 'Do Not Disturb' sign on the doorknob.

As he closed the door, Abby uncocked the gun. Both Feds breathed somewhat easier, as did Doug and Maria.

Abby stuck his tongue out at Morgan. When she frowned back at him, he spoke triumphantly.

"See, I told you we didn't have to kill them!" Abby said cheerfully.

As the stunned Feds followed the action back and forth, they watched Morgan stick out her tongue at Abby , blowing him a raspberry.

Maria smiled sweetly at the Feds. Doug grinned in spite of himself, glad they had stopped at kidnapping.

***

February 2, 2.47 p.m.

Jerold and Michael met Adam on the tarmac of the airport runway. They had boarded the plane early that morning, flying to several different cities by late afternoon.

They had checked Anna's place in New Orleans with no luck. Adam had been checking one of Sara's properties in Dallas. Jerold had sent Adam there knowing that he would find nothing. They checked Gail's farm in Houma. Jerold was getting frustrated, and he had been snapping at Michael since they left the farm. He now vented on Adam.

"Did you check both places?"

Adam had his hand out to open the door of the rental car; he stopped to turn to his father. He knew that Jerold was upset.

"Yes, Sir. ...the apartment complex too...Who knows how many properties she owned?"

Adam opened the driver's door and Jerold snapped at him.

"Well, we know she owns enough to keep your dumbass confused."

Adam froze as his father stepped into the seat directly behind his. The younger man looked over the top of the car at Michael. Jerold slammed the door. Michael met Adam's eyes and shrugged; he had been the target all morning and he was more than happy to let Jerold focus on something else. Adam got into the big sedan and started it. They drove in silence.

The city of Shreveport seemed to have expanded one hundred-fold since the last time Jerold had been there. Of course, the last time Jerold had been there was about a hundred years ago. The new casinos gleamed in the bright sunlight. The Red River Revel was in full swing. The riverfront was packed with amusement rides and people. They reminded Jerold of ants.

The silent trio passed from Shreveport into Bossier City.

Michael, too, had been to Shreveport in the past. He had never told his father that, though; he surely did not bother to tell his uncle now.

"How far is the motel?"

Jerold snapped, breaking the tense silence.

"About an hour or so to Sibley. ..." Adam said quietly.

Jerold relaxed back into the seat in a foul mood.

"If they are not there, we have to go to Colorado. Anna purchased an apartment building there." Adam said helpfully to no one in particular.

Jerold had known about Anna's real estate front for her properties. Well, one of her fronts, anyway. Jerold sat quietly fuming as he thought

233

about Anna . He could not wait to get his hands around her beautiful throat. In his mind, it was already being played out.

Jerold had been waiting to get that bitch for two centuries. He remembered the humiliation of their last meeting and flushed with hatred. He had walked right up on her. She had lain in wait for him. She was actually after Alex, but decided to have some fun with him anyway.

That night. Anna learned the truth about what Alex and Jerold had done had done to manipulate Nefertiti.

She had stalked Alex relentlessly; coming upon his brother was a bonus. Jerold's knees had locked at the unexpected fever.

Anna had already anticipated it, and was able to take him with little effort. As he had rolled in agony, she had swooped on him, forcing him to look into her eyes. Anna had pushed her will into him before the fever even broke. She made Jerold sit in a chair, facing her.

She decided to go much, much further.

Anna held his hands as she pushed deeper into his mind. She explored his thoughts, ripping memories from their resting place with no care of the pain it inflicted. In a full-out mind assault, she had mentally violated him. The more she found, the more she had to know.

Anna discovered that Alexander was supposed to meet Jerold there. Jerold's body twitched as she pressed further. He remembered the pain searing into his brain. She looked for, and found, his memories of what his brother had done to Nefertiti.

She also found something more serious. A suicide pact.

Jerold knew that Alex had met with Satan. Jerold had not committed the sins of his brother, but he hid the truth of his brother's secrets deep in his own mind. Anna saw all of it.

Sitting face to face, he remembered the ease with which she had taken everything hidden and private from him. Easy for her, that is. Jerold's soul had screamed as she pressed for more. His mouth was working, mouthing silent pleas as she tore at his mind. When the fever had hit her unexpectedly, she was still inside him and Jerold trembled in agony as they both experienced her pain.

Alex had triggered the fever in Anna.

Jerold was able to recover faster than she did. Her mind was still pushing and in the confusion of the fever, he began to get information back from her mind.

He tried to collect all the bits and pieces as his brother threw himself on the woman. Jerold got only disjointed images; he could feel her pulling back from him as her fever ripped at them both. The rape of his mind had left him broken and useless as she fought with Alex for her life. She had been able to throw the bigger man off, but he had gained the advantage. She suddenly stopped struggling, realizing that the only way to beat him was not physical. In his fury, Alex made the mistake of glaring directly into her eyes, unaware his own power could be used against him..

She locked her eyes on his and captured his mind, violently, before he could do the same to her. He rolled off of her slowly, his mouth working silently as she tore at his mind. Anna had been shocked at what she had seen.

Alex had not been the only one making deals with Satan. Michael had sold his own soul as well. Long ago.

Anna had been stunned. The images were clear, crisp, and she probed deeper. She felt the blackness inside of Alexander . A hole in his mind where emotion should have been was empty, a terrifying void filled with darkness. She had staggered away from Alex, releasing his mind abruptly. He rolled in pain, blinded by her violation. Anna had exhausted herself with the effort, and she knew that she had to get far away. Jerold was already trying to stand up from his chair.

As she fled the house, Jerold had reached out weakly, trying to grab her. She had slapped him so hard his body had rolled uselessly to the floor. She had shattered his jaw with the blow.

By the time the brothers had recovered, Anna was long gone. They had looked at each other, knowing that Alexander's secrets could get them both killed. Anna had wasted no time seeking out the others, telling them what Alex was doing. Before long, they had sent assassins after the brothers. They had cast out their children from the family. Alex and Jerold had killed many of their fellow Mortals . Alex killed seven of his own sons, Michael's brothers.

Jerold sat in the backseat of the car watching the city give way to lush green tree filled horizons. He could not decide if he had hated Alex or Anna more. It had been his brother's sin, but Anna had violated him in unforgivable ways.

If he could catch her, Jerold was going to make her pay.

Chapter 17

February 2, 2.50 p.m.

Bubba was emptying the dressers in the bedroom where Abby and Morgan had been asleep. Doug was emptying the closet. They were not worried about what stuff belonged to whom as they tossed clothes, diapers, and anything else they could find into the large duffle bags. Bubba was finding pistols and loose bullets in almost every drawer.

In the kitchen, Maria frantically piled bottled water, dry foods, and baby bottles into another of the huge duffles.

Anna and Captain Edwards walked in and froze, seeing Bubba kneeling in front of the dresser, inspecting a .38 revolver he had just found. Anna frowned as she looked at the huge man.

"Bubba, if you're trying to rob me, dude, there's better ways to do it other than broad daylight." Anna said with a slight shake of her head.

Bubba grinned at her from the floor. Edwards stood tense at Anna's back. He had never met Bubba and was bracing himself for the unknown. Anna shook her head again, speaking over her shoulder.

"Shut the door…It's all good." Anna said.

She put her hands on her hips as a grinning Bubba watched Edwards close the door. From behind the door, Doug emerged from the closet, having been blocked by their entry. His sudden appearance almost gave his uncle a heart attack.

Anna cocked her head, turning to look at Doug who was also grinning.

From the floor, Bubba said, "Annie May, if I was gonna rob you, I'd best come well-armed, that is for sure!"

He tossed the gun onto the bed. Edwards breathed easier. Without looking at him, she introduced the captain.

"Bubba, Edwards. Edwards, Bubba."

The two men nodded at each other curtly.

"Well, if you're not robbing me, please do tell me what the hell y'all are doing tearing up my house?"

On cue, a burst of sound came from the kitchen as Maria started cussing whatever she had just dropped. Anna rolled her eyes. She should go confront the little Latina woman, but thought better of it. Anna knew not to mess with a rattlesnake. Maria hated her, she knew, but she secretly thought the tiny woman was a breath of fresh air.

Doug addressed the captain.

"Believe it or not, Cappy, we have Napoliss and Webster tied up downstairs!"

Both Anna and the captain's eyes went wide. Edwards started laughing in disbelief.

"What?" Anna snapped.

They had already told her about the Feds and about the investigation at the church. Doug had grinned when Edwards started laughing, but he stopped at Anna's tone.

"Downstairs where?" she demanded.

"Room A13." Anna started looking around the room they were in. They had trashed her lovely apartment.

"Where in the hell is Morgan?" Anna demanded.

She was getting furious and not trying to hide it at all.

"She's in the room with them, Abby too." Doug sad defensively.

Anna still had her keys in her hand. Without further comment, she stomped past Bubba and into her own personal bedroom. At the back of her closet, a panel was already slid to the side. The rooms all had an unknown narrow corridor running along the back side of them. It was a great escape route and over the years Anna had found it had been most helpful for maintenance, too. She ducked into the dimly lit corridor, stomping down the crowded wooden stairs into the secret hall below. She could have found the room with her eyes closed, she was so familiar with the path.

The panel at the back of room A13 was also inside a small closet in the bathroom. As Anna stomped into the room, she stopped, looking at the occupants.

Morgan was standing casually by the window, inspecting her sword. Abby was sitting between the two beds on one of the room's modest armchairs. They both looked at her without surprise.

When Anna made her furious presence known, the Feds had turned their duct-taped faces toward her. Webster's eyes went wide and Napoliss quit breathing, literally. They looked back and forth between the two women, blinking hard. What the hell? They were not twins, but it was not far from it.

Morgan met Anna's smoldering gaze evenly. She put the tip of the sword to the floor, still holding it steady.

"Where is the boy?" Anna demanded.

Morgan's eyes widened at her tone.

"My son is with Maria, getting packed." Morgan snapped back.

Anna flinched inwardly at her possessive phrasing. She wanted to tear Morgan's damn face off. If she knew it, Morgan wasn't worried; her face would grow back.

It was the face of Nefertiti, but with a few exceptions.

Anna narrowed her eyes, unable to stop the muscle under her left nostril from ticking. The result was a twitching sneer.

"What in the fuck is…THIS?" Anna demanded.

Staring down her cousin, Anna waved one arm towards the bed, where the Feds lay stunned, not understanding anything but that they were bound like wild pigs. Anna never looked away from her cousin.

Finally, Morgan picked up the sword; slowly looking down on the Fed, she deliberately poked Napoliss in the bottom of his socked foot. He drew up like a fetus, eyes wide in horror.

Without looking at her furious cousin, she spoke with only a trace of a hiss.

"What does it look like, Anna?…It's lunch for you, you bloodsucking bitch!"

Abby's eyes widened as Anna launched her attack.

Skirting the bed Webster lay on, Anna jumped right onto Abby's lap as she scrambled over him; trying to use him as a launching pad to get over Napoliss' bed. Morgan watched Anna coming as she scrambled over Abby; and she too leapt onto Napoliss' bed, meeting her cousin in mid-air above the flinching Fed.

Abby was trying to retrieve the gun he had held on his lap, but when he flinched as Anna flew across him, the pistol had slid beneath his thigh. Clumsily clutching himself, Abby grabbed the gun wrong and almost dropped it, and then caught the fold of his jeans, almost dropping it again.

Morgan had tried swinging the sword at Anna as the older woman slid over Abby's lap, but her cousin was coming too quickly. As Morgan had leapt over the bed, Anna grabbed Morgan's wrist, easily disarming her and almost breaking the bone in the process. With her free hand, Anna went straight for the throat. Morgan landed two good punches directly to Anna's nose, shattering it. Anna used the pain to squeeze harder as Morgan tried pulling Anna's hands from her throat.

Morgan's momentum and her sudden collision into Anna threw them back, right into Abby's lap again.

They all three fought against each other as the chair toppled backwards.

The two women landed on top of him, locked in a death grip. Morgan was desperate to get Anna's hands off of her neck. Even though their race didn't need to breathe anyway, it was instinct. Morgan began to panic. She rolled her bulging eyes closed to keep Anna from violently entering her mind. She tore at Anna's head, her hair, finally putting her hands against the softness of Anna's own exposed neck. As she started to curl her fist around it, the sound of a pistol cocking stopped everyone dead in mid-motion.

From his position right below them, Abby had managed to put the pistol upwards, through their tangled arms, holding it right below Anna's chin. When he cocked it, Anna instantly released the pressure on Morgan, but she still held her throat as her hands froze. Morgan instinctively threw herself backwards along the foot of the bed.

Napoliss had fallen as well, taped like a piñata trying to get away from the bed he had fallen near Abby's feet. When he heard the gun cock, he also froze.

Morgan rubbed her damaged throat as she sat with her back against the door; Anna put her hands up in a gesture of surrender. She crossed her ankles, rolled her eyes toward the ceiling, and waited.

After a solid thousand racing heart beats Anna said, "Do it."

Abby uncocked the pistol. He laid the gun on his chest. Webster had scooted to the side of his bed; he stared down at them wide-eyed. These bitches were crazy! He blinked rapidly, his eyes as big as saucers.

From behind his duct-tape, Webster started cursing them viciously. They couldn't hear the words, but they knew what he said simply from his body language.

Anna looked down at Abby. As their eyes locked, Anna thought about it for a split second. She pulled herself back and her stare became blank. She had always liked Abby. Anna stood and turned deliberately toward Webster who was throwing a fit. He actually used his tied-together legs as a battering ram to kick at her. Anna leaned easily out of the way, and, leaning the other way, she slapped him right across his duct-taped mouth. He jerked his head right back around to glare at her.

Webster knew they were in serious trouble.

Morgan glared at Anna, watching her slap the Fed. Her throat was swollen, but she could already feel the electricity; a white-blue pulse working the flesh , soothing it.

The full-bloods healed one hundred times faster than the half-breeds. Anna's nose also throbbed and pulsated as both women began a healing process that would take only minutes.

Napoliss watched Morgan. She sat heaving and trying to draw air into her damaged throat. Anna glared back at Webster.

Without looking in Morgan's direction, Anna asked in a dangerous whisper.

"Who is the baby's father, Morgan?"

Morgan glared at her hatefully. She said nothing.

Still lying on his back with the pistol on his chest, Abby started laughing loudly in true amusement. Anna turned and stomped out of the room.

***

February 2, 2.59 p.m.

Father Timothy had passed out in his chair. In the gloom of the den around him, he had seen shadow monsters; finally closing his eyes against them, he drifted. Since the scientist had been escorted out of the church earlier, the priest had been drinking. In his dreams, he saw different kinds of monsters.

Forms, of all kinds, touched the edges of his dreams. The shapes were dark, smelling vile, making him breathless even in his sleep. Timothy never seemed to get a clear image of them as they swirled around him, ripping at him. In his sleep he mumbled drunkenly, his breath uneven and shallow.

The images tore at his mind. His clothes. His flesh. They seemed to taunt him deliberately, and he heard whispers he could not understand. He was pushed to and fro…scared of the whispering shapes that twisted around him. He wanted to run. In the chair, his body jerked and twitched. He was falling. He felt himself falling into a huge black vastness.

Father Timothy cried out weakly in the dark room as he screamed in his dreams. He felt the rough skin of the shadow figures rushing past him as he fell. Their skin was like harsh sandpaper, scraping him all over, taking millions of tiny pieces of flesh with them. He saw himself falling into a great expanse of black. The screams echoed into a thousand unseen caverns of darkness. He came back into himself just as he hit the ground, feeling the g-force both lifting and pulling him as he lay curled up on a floor of the expanse. He didn't land hard but the jumbled sensations left him shaking in the sudden stillness.

The ground he hugged desperately was sand-covered. Black sand-covered. He thought it looked like the volcanic beaches in Hawaii. In the sand were billions of tiny specks of glitters. Timothy lifted his head.

He stood at the feet of an angel: an angel with alabaster white skin that glowed faintly with an inner light. The angel was completely naked, with huge wings expanding from the back. The anatomically perfect female stood above him, looking down on him.

Set in the perfectly shaped cat-like eyes where the pupils should have been, there was nothing; not even an eyeball existed. There was only blackness, deeper than the expanse of nothingness around him. He gazed at her breasts, her flat belly, and followed the hips around, finally settling on the patch of hair where her legs met. The plumpness of the thighs spread down legs that were perfectly proportioned to her considerable height. Father Timothy shivered violently as he looked at her perfectly formed feet. The white of her skin virtually gleamed against the black sand she stood on.

He could feel the void of her eyes as he trembled. She lifted a foot, putting it on his head and forcing him to look upon her. He didn't meet her non-eyes, and instead focused on her perfect breasts, the nipples erect. He felt himself fill with lust.

Timothy didn't see the smile of contempt as she watched him. She put her foot down, making sure that her body swayed slightly. He became enflamed with heat.

He wanted to close his eyes. Timothy had learned to push away the female image long ago. But this was so real; he could not push himself to close his eyes. He hated those bitches that threw themselves at him at the church and at home, sometimes even during the day. He had conditioned himself over the years to see the filth of their flesh as they tried to lure him into filthy acts. He had become so convinced that he was literally phobic of the whores. He avoided them like the plague. All the women of his church tried to pass themselves off as right and holy, but he knew better.

Timothy could see even in nice clothes they still had filthy bodies. They still tried to tempt him. They smiled at him, mocking his needs.

He looked mesmerized as the angel swayed lightly again, making his erection painful and throbbing. He still stared at her body, sweeping his eyes down it. She was different, Timothy thought. She was his perfect angel: clean and precious. The heat from between his legs was almost unbearable as it flushed upwards into his belly.

His own nipples became erect as an electrifying charge passed into his neck, drawing up his scalp. The heat of it touched his mind. He finally looked at her perfectly shaped face.

She smiled at Father Timothy slightly, in contempt, and he twitched as he fell into the blackness of her eyes. She loved him. She knew his pain. He could feel it.

After years of mental angst, Timothy had finally given into his body. He knew that women had been forbidden fruit for a man of his calling and stature. One day, one of the thirteen-year-old boys in the choir had looked at him like his angel did: full of love. Father Timothy had been shocked at first. Then he had considered the boy's feelings. He knew people said it was wrong, but they did not know how much the boy had loved him, needed him. He hid it from the church and his parishioners quite well.

He told the boy that God would punish them both if anyone knew. Timothy had been clumsy in trying to return the boy's love. Someone had eventually found out, and one of the church elders had been alerted. Father Timothy had spent the next six months at a seminary high in the Utah mountains.

There were other priests like him there. He learned their tricks when they were forced to say what their sin was in group therapy. Timothy had hid it better at the next church. The church elders had believed him when he said he was healed from the ways of the flesh. They turned him loose on another community that sat unaware of his sinful nature. In all, there had been fourteen boys.

Looking into the depths of the angel's eyes, Father Timothy saw that she forgave him. She understood his needs. He was grateful at her pardon, awed to be in the presence of an angel. She looked at him with love, coming

242

from the black depth of nothingness in her eyes. She stooped, thrusting her hips close to his face, making him smell the clean scent of her. She lowered her hand and pulled him up gently by the chin.

When he stood, he realized that he, too, was naked. His erection stood between them, and she pulled his hands to touch her breasts.

Timothy resisted only a moment before he cupped them harshly, roughly, feeling her firmness. He squeezed the nipples painfully and watched as milk trickled slowly down his finger, hot and silvery white on his skin. He made a guttural broken noise as she touched his small penis. He loved it when she touched him.

They had been doing these many times over the past nine months, maybe a little longer.

Timothy moaned in the chair as she moved her nipple across his trembling lips. He pulled at it slightly as she rubbed him. Her wings expanded in full as he grew harder in her hand, impossibly hard. He lolled his head as she whispered to his mind.

Someone was coming to help him.

When he saw the woman, he knew what he must do. He would do it for her, for all of them. She seared the image of the woman into his mind, like a brand, as Timothy breathed harder, almost gasping. He was about to explode. The eruption came as the dream became too intense for Timothy. The strength of the orgasm woke him from the depths as he fouled himself, there in the gloom of the den. For a long time, he lay there, uncaring about the mess. He rubbed himself, feeling a shiver that shook his entire body. His angel made him feel so good.

Timothy wanted to go back to her feet. After a long while, he got up and went to his bedroom to clean up and change. As he pulled on his jogging pants, he heard a knock at the door.

Going down the stairs, he pushed the questions out of his mind. He felt like a boy again. He felt great! Timothy opened the door and froze. It was the woman he had seen in the angel's eyes.

He forced himself to smile at her. The woman was very pregnant.

"Are you Father Timothy?" she asked shyly.

He blinked hard at her belly, looking up into her face as he responded.

"Yes, I am." Timothy confirmed to her slowly.

She shifted nervously, looking around the street.

"One of your parishioners is missing...Is that right?" She bit her lower lip. "A scientist?"

Father Timothy narrowed his eyes at her.

"Yes. That's right." He said even more slowly.

Robert Gorin's face had been all over the news in the last day.

"I may know…um, I may know something that will help, Father."

He looked up the street also, trying not to twitch.

His eyes returned to the woman as he asked… "Do I know you?"

She shook her head lightly.

"My name is Diana. Can we talk some place quiet?"

Chapter 18

February 2, 3:31 p.m.

Anna lay on her bed, trying to focus only on Gail; she let her mind be pulled across a vast forest. She seemed to be flying across great expanses, the ground below whizzing by in a blur of color, and texture. She focused on the memory of Gail's face, and her voice. She felt her sister's heartbeat. Without warning, Anna was suddenly sitting in a chair in Frances' bedroom. From behind Gail's eyes, Anna saw Matthew.

His paleness had seemed to have improve a bit and he seemed to be resting comfortably.

Gail was aware of Anna's presence. She relaxed into the chair as her mouth started working softly with words that remained unspoken. She had been waiting for Anna to touch her mind. Gail was scared; she needed to know what to do. Anna gently probed her memory and, in an instant, understood that Matthew had been told. Anna was relieved.

The priest still had free will. He could still tell them all to get lost. Anna unxpectedy found a deep love inside of Gail.

The love that Gail felt for Matthew was not a shock to Anna, but she was startled that it had grown so strong. She left that piece of her sister's mind untouched. She found Gail's worries and pushed her own will slightly as she softly placed words in Gail's mind.

'I'm coming for you. Don't be scared. It will be okay. I am coming. Stay with the priest. I love you. Try not to worry.'

Gail started crying softly as Anna backed away from her.

Anna trembled on the bed, the effort of reaching out threatening to overwhelm her. She had to come back quickly, or she would be left violently ill. While she was bringing herself back from the expanse, she decided to circle her own location quickly. The earth flew under her as she looked down. Anna enjoyed the freedom of her mind slipping into the slipstream of time.

The car coming from the west drew her, suddenly, like a magnet. Anna had not expected it. Without warning, she was in Jerold's mind as he sat behind the driver, Adam. They were driving straight to her. On the bed, Anna gasped as she and Jerold simultaneously became aware of each other.

As one they both said, "Oh shit!"

She grappled with his will, trying desperately to pull back. She almost pulled away when she saw Michael sitting in front of her, looking around and behind him to stare into her eyes. No, not her eyes; Jerold's eyes. Almost instantly, Michael knew she was there. He squinted at his uncle as Adam, too, became aware that something was terribly wrong. He started braking hard, trying to pull to the side of the interstate.

Anna's heart pounded, and then stopped.

Michael. Her Michael.

She looked at him, in shock, as Jerold grabbed his ears, trying to literally squeeze her out of his head. Anna saw Michael reaching for her. He said her name in a jagged whisper as he reached for his uncle.

On the bed, Anna's heartbeat started again. She broke off contact without coming back to herself, first. The dizziness that hit her made her roll to the bedside as she vomited.

Morgan had stood in the corner of the room, watching her reach out. She was startled by Anna's abrupt movement. Going to her cousin, she bent down, holding her as the heaves shook her entire body. Anna was confused and sick; down on all fours, she had completely lost all sense of who or where she was. Before she could recover at all, Michael pushed his will upon her. With all the strength she had left, she pushed back.

Anna was much older than Michael. She was more experienced.

He was stronger.

As Michael pushed his way into her mind, she changed tactics and let him enter. She used his connection to suddenly twist her mind into his and take information from him. She saw that they were not far away. She saw Adam looking at her, as Jerold yelled at him from the backseat.

Go...Go...Go.

Michael pushed her mind violently. She would have been thrown upward if Morgan had not started to shake her to break the connection. Morgan had no idea what had happened, but she knew it was something terrible. Anna was halfway up on the bed and grasping at anything she could reach. Morgan knew of only one thing that she could do.

Anna grasped at the sheets, the pillows, trying desperately to push him away. Morgan concentrated, pushing her own will and the sheets in Anna's hands suddenly burst into flames, engulfing her hands.

The pain hit Michael as soon as it hit Anna. The crackle of the sensation forced Michael to pull back, and then let go.

Anna was totally consumed with self-preservation. As Anna beat at the flames, she felt Michael slip away, and even the pain could not keep her from slumping into a hollow soul. Hearing their struggle, Maria, and Bubba burst through the door as the fire started climbing up Anna's forearms.

When Morgan saw Anna's body go limp, she pushed out her hands, pushing her own will into the flame.

As quickly as it had started, the fire completely disappeared, leaving only the smell of charred flesh and sheet. Anna rolled away from the bed again as the agony of her mind and the wounds on her hands blinded her, making her gasp.

Bubba and Maria stood in the bedroom doorway stunned, mouths gaping.

The trained doctor in Maria clicked in after a few shocked moments. She ran around the bed, pushing the much taller Morgan out of her path. Anna was curled into the corner, shaking violently. She held her severely wounded hands in front of her, not seeing them. Some of the sheet had melted into her palms. Knowing nothing but pain, Anna cried out weakly. Maria grabbed her elbows, trying to see her damaged hands.

Maria e held the much bigger woman firmly as she looked at the charred flesh. Anna seemed to be collapsing.

Anna did collapse, backward. As she did, she said only one word jaggedly, forcefully.

"RUN!"

Morgan did just that. She hit the closet door in a dead run, almost falling down the narrow staircase. Through the winding hall she threw herself, determined to get to Abby and her son. As Morgan came into the room where the Feds still lay bound, she saw them gaping at her unexpected entrance.

Doug was holding the baby and Abby was sitting in his chair again, between the beds.

Without stopping to explain, Maria literally ripped the baby away from Douglas . He let her take him, trying not to grip at the baby and start a tug

247

of war. Morgan stopped long enough to catch her breath as she gazed, wide-eyed at the child. Maria came heaving into the room behind her. Abby had stood up when Morgan passed by him; he cocked the pistol, pointing it at the floor nervously.

The Feds looked back and forth between them, eyes wide.

Maria said as calmly as she could, "Get them in the car!"

She did not bother to explain as she turned and ran from the room again, back up to where Anna sat in shock. Her hands were already trying to heal.

Doug followed Maria back up. He saw the captain holding Anna by the elbows, trying to comfort her. Edwards looked at Doug with true fear in his eyes.

"We need a bigger car! " Edwards yelled at him.

He saw Bubba taking out the half-filled duffles from the apartment. Doug thought of the Jeep Cherokee with three rows of seats.

"We got one." He shouted back at his uncle.

Doug went to the window, pulling the curtains back; he scanned the parking lot. Bubba was already putting their duffles on top of the Jeeps luggage rack. . Doug breathed a silent prayer of thanks. He turned back to the captain who was trying to keep Anna's hands up, not touching anything.

She struggled against him slightly then lay back against the wall, chest heaving with the pain.

"What in the hell is going on?" Doug blurted.

Doug was trying to keep the fear out of his voice, heard his own words and realized he was failing miserably.

From the floor, Anna responded in a small voice.

"We have to go; Jerold is on his way...they know where Matthew is!"

Doug jerked like he had been shot. The fear became terror. His brother's face floated like a ghost through his mind.

"On his way here, or to Matthew?" This was from the captain.

Anna gasped painfully.

"Both! They will try to kill the baby first!"

"How long do we have?" Morgan asked, as she emerged from the closet holding the baby.

Anna shook her head slightly, her eyes remained closed.

"Maybe twenty minutes."

The captain looked at Anna, as she held her head back against the wall. He could already see the flesh of her palms flaking off the melted matter of

248

the sheet with a pulsating white-blue light.

Morgan knelt beside Anna, clutching the baby.

"Are you sure they know where Gail took him?"

Anna looked at the baby. Without wavering, she answered quietly.

"Yes…Michael just took it from me…He's in the car with Jerold."

Morgan's eyes flared slightly at Michael's name.

For the first time, Morgan thought that they may not survive at all. She ran to the car with her son clutched tightly to her.

***

February 2, 3.35 p.m.

Jerold sat in the backseat, holding his head as the pain passed. Michael sat on the front seat, trying to close his eyes at the agony in his own mind. He sat forward, holding his fists to his eyes. He wanted to throw up; he thought he might. Adam recklessly pulled the big sedan back onto the blacktop, pushing the auto for all it had.

From beside him, Michael said, "They know we are coming. …The baby is with them…The priest is in Mississippi."

From the backseat, Jerold nodded, a sneer coming to his aching face.

When he caught Anna, he was going to kill that bitch a thousand times over.

***

February 2, 3.41 p.m.

In the interior of her sleek sports car, Diana chatted nervously as Father Timothy listened. She told him many things. She told him what she knew about Michael's connection to the scientist, which was virtually nothing. Her PI had called her from New Orleans, where he had lost Jerold and Michael. Timothy listened to her, nodding here and there, a slight smile on his lips.

He forced the smile there; he could smell this woman. She was trying to pass herself off like the filthy women in his church, but he knew better. She was just as unclean as the rest of them.

Father Timothy thought of his angel. She had sent this woman to him,

249

so he went with it, not wanting to displease her heavenly spirit. As they drove in an aimless southernly direction, Diana told him her secrets as well. He was a priest after all, bound by the laws of the confessional. He smiled as she rambled, thinking that she was a piece of filth.

He wanted to scream at her that she was a whore. She was having a bastard child out of wedlock. As he listened, Timothy became aware of how special the child was inside of her. He quietly realized the bastard she carried was one of THEM.

She bemoaned her love, the liar; she asked him for direction.

"You will find Michael in Mississippi. He's on his way there now." Timothy blurted.

Diana had been almost as shocked as he was by this information. He knew the angel was telling them where to go. Timothy could see the convent in his mind, he somehow knew the layout of it.

Yes, he thought, the angel loves me. She forgave him. They shared a holy bond.

Timothy looked at the woman as her eyes narrowed in thought. She watched the road and decided quickly. At the next road, she turned left and went straight to the south-east on-ramp.

Timothy felt like he could rule the world.

Chapter 19

February 2, 4.09 p.m.

Adam and Michael tore up Anna's apartment. They found evidence of the baby and the secret pass in the back of the closet. They hurried, knowing that the women and their human companions had just left. In Anna's bedroom, above her bed, was a very old oil painting. It was of Michael. He stared at his own image.

He knew Anna had painted it; he knew her brushstroke better than his own name. He stared at the image of his own eyes, expertly captured by the artist. He knew she must have painted it from memory, as he had never had those clothes and had never posed in that position. She had created a perfect likeness of him. Michael cut it from the frame before Adam could see it. Rolling it, so as not to flake the paint too badly, he stuffed it in the waistband of his pants.

Jerold sat in the car, furiously anticipating catching up to the baby and its would-be protectors.

The men knew that someone had been in room A13. Michael had started going through some papers that sat on the table in front of the window. He had not been surprised to see federal documents and the IDs of the two men. He had wondered, only momentarily, what federal agents were doing with Anna.

Adam saw the roll of duct-tape, unable to discern what it was for, as nothing in the room had the tape on it.

Michael had stopped short when he found Abby's traditional robes. So, that bastard Abdullah was with them. Michael wasn't surprised, although Miguel's image floated through his mind.

Miguel would be pleased to know that Abby was, in fact, with them. Michael smiled slightly at the memory of the last time Miguel and Abdullah had met. He had never seen his dark-eyed cousin so furious or humiliated. For a moment, his smile widened when he thought of Miguel ripping the cleric from limb to limb. Abdullah would pay, the pompous ass. Miguel had been stewing for forty -five years.

Unable to gather any more clues inside the apartment, or from room A13, the cousins returned to the car where Jerold waited. As they approached the car, a giant black man emerged from the office at the entrance to the parking lot.

He started walking directly to them. Adam paid no attention as he slipped into the passenger's seat and shut his door. As Michael opened his own door, the man called out to him.

"Hey… Hey, man! Can I ask you something?"

Michael looked at him impatiently, as the man stopped about six feet away from him.

Michael showed his annoyance, "Yes? What?"

"Would your name be Michael?" Bubba asked him bluntly.

Michael's eyes narrowed to a deadly slit as he let go of the door and walked a few steps in front of the man. They were actually almost the same height.

"Who wants to know?" Michael growled it.

"Look, man, I'm just the messenger…." Bubba said, raising empty hands.

Michael raised one eyebrow. Seeing that he had the stranger's attention, Bubba went ahead.

"Annie May wanted you to know something."

Michael's scalp prickled. He was aware that Jerold had turned to watch him. Adam was slowly opening his door; his hand was on a pistol inside his coat. Michael dropped his voice to a whisper.

"What did she say?"

Bubba detected a true sense of sadness in the big, evil-looking white man.

"She said to tell you she is tryin' to save ya."

Bubba, too, had dropped his voice to a whisper.

"She said you could always change y'alls mind…"

Michael arched both eyebrows.

For a long moment he looked at Bubba, deciding whether or not to kill him. Bubba knew his life was being decided, but figured it would all work out. He nodded lightly at the white man. Bubba glanced to Adam who stood with a pistol at his side, not moving away from the car.

Looking back to Michael, Bubba told him the rest.

"She says if you love her...then you have to trust her."

Michael stayed perfectly still, even as his heart cartwheeled into his throat. He sneered at Bubba, who thought for a moment that he was a dead man. Michael looked him in the eyes, deciding whether or not to crush his mind . After a moment, when he still wasn't dead, Bubba shrugged again. He glanced at Adam as he turned and calmly walked back to the motel's office.

Michael let him go.

By the time Michael snatched his door open, he was furious. His heart and mind were totally at odds with one another. He hated her for his struggle.

As he sat down in the driver's seat, Jerold asked, "What was that about?"

Michael could feel the painting curl crisply as he sat. He frowned at the exterior of the motel.

"He was saying that Anna left a few minutes before four and asked if we needed help..."

Michael lied smoothly, and Adam nodded. Jerold glared at the back of Michael's head.

He knew his nephew was lying. Jerold decided not to push it. From the back seat he snapped, "Let's go."

Michael started the car, and pulled slowly out of the parking space. As they rolled past the office, Bubba stood inside the glass panel room watching them. He held up his coffee cup, as if waving goodbye , and he leaned casually against the counter inside.

Michael thought of his own image, staring down at him from above the bed, her bed.

As they turned onto the road in front of the motel, Jerold turned and concentrated. He focused on Anna's door for a split second and as Michael accelerated, the doors and windows to Anna's living spaces literally blew outward with an explosion of flame.

Michael did not slow down. From his place on the back seat, Jerold also targeted a propane tank at the corner of the building. The force of the explosion rocked the retreating car.

As the men drove in silence, Michael watched the smoke in the rearview mirror. He again thought of the oil painting laid against his thigh.

He saw the black smoke from above the tree line. Michael wanted to cry.

He didn't know if he could take any more of this existence.

***

February 2, 4.20 p.m.

Miguel called Michael's cell phone.

"Can you talk freely?" he asked his cousin.

Michael's voice sounded jagged, "No, not yet."

Miguel paused, "Call me back when you can."

"Did you kill that bastard Gorin?" Michael asked.

"Is Jerold there?" Miguel asked it guardedly.

"Yes." Michael didn't elaborate.

"Then tell him…yes…the scientist is dead."

Michael breathed a sigh, not exactly one of relief. In his mind, he saw the black cloud they had left behind.

Miguel continued, "I'm not joking…If you can…call me…As soon as possible. Understand?"

Michael said, "Affirmative."

"Where are you now?" Miguel sounded like he was having a crisis.

"We are about two hours east of Shreveport…Gail is in Mississippi with the priest."

From the other end of the phone Miguel said, "Oh shit."

For a second the line went silent, and Michael waited.

Finally, Miguel asked, "Are they with the sisters?"

He was referring to the nuns.

Michael said, "Yes…Where are you?"

"I'm about five hours from there…How long before you get there?'

"About the same; meet us there."

Michael cocked his head, waiting for his younger cousin to agree.

Miguel became antsy as his breath quickened.

"Listen to me….DO NOT hit them until we talk… DO NOT…Understand?"

Michael casually looked around; he braked at a curve coming back upon the interstate. Adam watched the road, listening to Michael's end of the conversation. He didn't see Jerold in the mirror, still staring daggers into

254

Michael's head.

"Yep…Got it…" Michael slowed exiting onto the ramp. "Meet us at the gates of the convent."

"Yeah…" was the only response.

From his end, Miguel closed his little phone, ending their conversation. From the beach , the roar of the waves soothed the earth itself. Miguel had bought the little retreat about ninety years before. He liked the easy life in the tiny panhandle of Alabama.

As he watched the water pound and retreat in an endless cycle, Miguel frowned at the beauty of it. Robert Gorin also frowned from the chair beside him. The doctor had just heard himself declared dead, murdered at that. He was paranoid.

His would-be killer handed him another beer.

Miguel said, "We're leaving in about ten minutes. Do what you need to…This will be over tonight."

Dr. Gorin gave him a long, sideways glance. He had been afraid that Miguel would say just that. He hoped he didn't mean his life would be over. The doctor still didn't trust the man who had spent weeks trying to kill him. He wished Father Timothy was here to guide him. He needed a rational voice.

Miguel let Robert study him as he sipped the non-alcoholic beer. He stared at the ocean, but in his mind, he saw instead the old gates of the monastery. He wanted to jump in the car and fly, but instead he sat calmly. He thought of Jerold. He shuddered inwardly. When Jerold found out that the scientist was not dead, Miguel knew he would be killed.

But only if he didn't get Jerold first.

***

February 2, 4.23 p.m.

The Feds watched Anna's lip quiver as she held her burned hands in front of her, upright. She laid her head back and closed her eyes, sick at the sight of her own damaged flesh. She was silently proud of herself for not puking again. If she had opened her eyes, she would have seen the pinkness of her new flesh. The memory of the pain was bad enough to keep her eyes sealed. The Feds couldn't take their eyes off her hands.

255

Morgan sat beside her, crunched up, trying not to touch her cousin.

She had tried to help already, and Anna had fought back with the only weapon she had handy: her teeth. The bite was already healed. Morgan rubbed at the spot absently, anyway, as she stared at the passing miles. The Feds lay on the floor, stretched out at odd angles at their feet in the rear of the Jeep. Morgan had removed the tape on their mouths after they had left the motel. She figured she could just reach down and kick one if he started screaming now.

They were too amazed to scream anyway. Both of the men stayed silent as they watched Anna go from severely wounded to fully healed in less than an hour.

No one spoke.

Abdullah drove the Jeep as fast as he could push it without drawing attention. Bubba thankfully had a radar detector, but Abby still went too fast anyway, loving the little gadget. Abby knew exactly where the convent was. He had been there several times for seminars aimed at bringing Christians and Muslims together. His mission had also hosted many of the events. Abby thought of Joseph as he gunned the Jeep. He tried not to miss his friend over the last days. He had failed.

Morgan caught Abby , more than once, emerging red-eyed from the small bathroom near the guest room at Anna's place. They had not spoken about it, and he was grateful she had left him alone.

Abby was mad at Morgan. He looked at her in his rearview mirror and smiled slightly. Yes, he was mad, madly in love.

He cursed himself for being a damn fool. Abby looked at Doug, who was riding shotgun. The man had changed rapidly in the space of a few hours. Before, Doug had seemed withdrawn, pinched with worry. He had lost at least twenty pounds in two weeks from his large frame, giving him a gaunt look.

Where before Douglas had been closed off and sickly, he was now awake and watching every detail of the Louisiana afternoon, eager to get to his brother.

Abby had questioned Mogan twice about the baby's father. Both times ended badly.

The only reason Abby had the second conversation with her was because the first one was so tedious and stupid that he never got an answer. He did admit that some of it was jealous curiosity. That was true. Abby had told her it didn't matter. The baby's existence changed everything.

Everything.

He smiled slightly as the radar detector beeped once, then twice as he rapidly decelerated. The baby's sweet face floated before him. He was so tiny. Abdullah had marveled at the tiny hands grasping his thumbs with surprising strength. Abby thought of the irony of the most powerful being ever born, was as big as a housecat.

He suddenly twitched at the wheel with an ill-suppressed chuckle.

On the seat directly behind the driver, the captain smiled as he snoozed against the window. Edwards dreamed of times long since past, that he could still picture so clearly in his mind. Maria sat curled up beside him.

Maria had turned around to watch the medical impossibility being played out behind their seat. She and the federal agents watched the lights in Anna's hands quit throbbing and twisting under the skin.

The baby lay sleeping in Maria's lap. She looked at the boy , wondering if he could heal that way. Maria spoke to the woman with a warm voice.

"Anna…you can open your eyes now."

Anna flinched at the thought. Morgan turned her head only long enough to observe the now healed hands. She turned back to her window, again rubbing the bite that once marked her arm.

Anna said with a grimace, "I don't want to open my eyes."

After a quick pause Maria retorted.

"All right…but can you at least put your hands down? You're really starting to freak me out."

Without meaning to, both Doug and Abby snorted with laughter. Morgan hid her grin behind her hand, trying to keep her shoulders from shaking. She almost succeeded.

Anna popped open her eyes, looking instantly past her hands to the little Latina woman who was staring back at her with awe. Maria put the baby to her shoulder, her own eyes meeting Anna solidly.

Anna studied the entire seated population of the truck, ignoring the Feds at her feet. She looked stupidly at her hands, pulling them closer to her face. She pinched her brow, examining them. God! That bloody hurt.

Looking back up, Douglas watched her from the front passenger's seat, grinning like a thief. Abby shook at the wheel trying to stay on the road as hey continued to laugh at her. Sitting between Anna and Doug, Maria watched her calmly, with no indication of the impending freak-out. She instinctively burped the baby as Anna glared at her..

Anna dropped her hands into her lap, then picked them up, crossing them over her breasts as she looked out the window, then glared back at Maria. The smaller woman met her gaze head on. . Maria had been raised in the ghetto; she wasn't backing down.

Anna looked back out the window as she said to every one, "Fuck you."

Maria frowned at her with a, "Hhrmmphhht!"

She turned back around, looking at Edwards who slept like as peacefully as the baby. . How could he possibly sleep at a time like this? Maria shook her head at Edwards still form, and met Doug's eyes. She was so glad to see him smiling. He looked at the baby in her lap.

Abby was beating the wheel in a fit of laughter.

Anna threw at him with ill-suppressed fury, "And fuck you too, Abdullah! I remember your little pistol trick earlier, asshole…You're lucky I fucking love you!…"

Morgan looked at Anna quickly, turning back to the window before their eyes could meet.

She was not surprised that Anna loved Abby. Abby was a good man. She was shocked that Anna had said it aloud. Even though they were family, Anna never let on that she even felt love, not even to her mother, whom had seen it anyway. None of them knew that she had left Michael a message, via Bubba. Anna seemed shocked too. She sat back, glaring out the window.

Abby was grinning like the damned fool he was at the wheel. With positive glee in his tone, he returned Anna's declaration. .

"I love you too, Anna! ."

Anna harrumphed. She flipped off the back of his head with a slender, lovely finger.

From the floor below the two cousins, Napoliss said, "Hey!"

Both Morgan and Anna glared at the Fed.

Morgan said, "What?"

Both women arched an identical brow in unison.

Napoliss said, "I have to go to the bathroom."

At the wheel, Abby's chuckle turned positively demonic.

***

February 2, 4.27 p.m.

Gail sat by the bed. Matthew had slept soundly all afternoon. The broth had brought some color back to his face and Gail was grateful. She held his working left hand as she prayed. She stared at the image of Christ for a long time, in eternal silent agony on the cross, looking down on them.

Gail knew the lance mark that pierced his silver image was no deception. She had seen the wound inflicted with her own eyes.

Christ had indeed been the human Son of God. But hs mother had been a Mortal. He was the first phrophet sent to save the Mortal, and human race.

The lance had barely pierced his human heart and it could not heal itself. Gail knew that was the only way Jesus of Nazareth could have been killed: a healer who could not mend his own heart. The child Gail had seen it all.

Even now, Gail wept at her family's failure to save it's own. She silently begged God to save Mathew . She would pay whatever price he asked.

Gail confessed her sins. She declared her love for her family. She told God she had accepted that no child would be hers.

She apologized for calling Him names in her thoughts.

She asked for a miracle.

She believed in Matthew; she believed in Him.

She loved them both, so much.

She told God in the silence that she would trust He was there, but He had to trust she would do what she had to do.

She asked God to forgive her mortal sins.

She asked Sara's ghost to forgive her, for failing her.

She asked Him to protect those she loved.

Wiping the tears crudely from her eyes, Gail looked at Matthew's adored face. She kissed his hand as it rested limply in her own. She got her breathing back under control as used her sleeves to wipe away the tears. She stilled the severe shaking of her legs.

Gail breathed deeply as a total calm slipped over her.

She placed Matthew's hand gently back onto his chest. She gazed at him, her face soft when she knelt at his bedside. From under the bed, she pulled the long duffle bag up, twisting to get the unbending bag onto the chair. Laying it across the steep arms, she unzipped her bag and stood looking at the contents. From the loose depths of it, she fished out two gold daggers. Gail looked at the blades. She studied the ruby set into the hilt.

She frowned, inspecting the emeralds around it in a peculiar pattern.

Gail had pulled the bigger one from Alex's body as it burned.

The smaller one gleamed in the late afternoon light. She got a lump in her throat as she remembered Joseph trying to weakly pull the dagger from his own chest. Holding Alex's knives, Gail started crying, but didn't stop a moment more for the tears.

Turning to a sleeping Matthew, she gazed at him as she held the blades close to him. She put both daggers in her left hand, using her right to roll his body slightly onto his right side. He never stirred as she placed the small dagger under his waistline. Letting his body roll back, she rolled up his left hip, placing the bigger one under his left thigh.

As he rolled back onto the blades, he stirred slightly. Matthew's eyes snapped open with a pained look into his soul. He worked his mouth as his functioning left hand twitched under Gail's breast. She immediately checked him for fever. He seemed a little warm, but otherwise normal.

He saw Gail and closed his eyes.

Matthews's forehead drew up as he hissed in a gulping breath. He started nodding his head for no apparent reason.

Gail asked, "The pain?"

He nodded now more rapidly; without moving much, he started squirming on the bed. He couldn't stop nodding.

He said breathlessly, "Oh God, help me!"

Gail went to the table between the chairs. The small drawer was almost ripped from its place as Gail slammed it open, scattering the two loose little pills that bounced wildly off the edges. She snatched one up. Matthew was trying to pull himself off the opposite side of the bed. He was now shaking his head in a slow constant movement.

Gail went around the bed and knelt in front of him.

He was trying to get his legs to move over the edge of the bed. She stooped in front of him, pushing him back easily. His eyes were wide with a terrible twitching blankness. He started sobbing dryly. He had no more tears left. She pushed the pill between his bared teeth. He bit down on it reflexively, barely missing her finger. She pulled her hand back abruptly. The full-bloods could grow back body parts, but not the half-breeds. If she lost a finger, she just lost a finger.

Gail was already missing a toe. But, it was a little toe , as Anna had helpfully pointed out with a dead serious look on her face.

Gail smiled slightly as she watched Matthew calm down on the bed. His eyes rolled up as his good arm stilled. He kicked at nothing once, then twice.

Gail pulled the thin blanket up over his feet, back to his upper chest. She was careful not to disturb the large bandage.

After a long moment, when she was sure he had stopped flailing, she retrieved the glass of water from the bedside table. Matthew was smacking at the bitter residue of the pill. He closed his eyes as he licked at his dry lips. She let him take a long pull on the straw. He made little breathless moans between swallows. Finally releasing it, he opened his eyes only slightly. He plopped his head down, unable to barely lift it to begin with.

He finally opened his eyes all the way after a moment, watching her put the glass back on the table. She turned back to him. He saw her eyes were full of gentleness.

With his tongue sticking oddly to the top of his mouth, Matthew asked her, "How do...How come you're not...old? How did you do that?"

She smiled at him as she took his limp right hand in hers. She was relieved to feel him squeeze her hand faintly.

She said, "Shhh...That's my little secret."

Gail involuntarily thought of her mother Sara, whom had passed the gift of aging onto her identical half-bred daughter. She looked absently at Matthew's bandage as the memory faded.

Though the smile lingered, Matthew could tell when the ghosts of sadness swept across her. He closed his eyes on Gail's beauty, not able to cope with the enormity of it. He started drifting, feeling warm and fluid.

He gave her one tiny squeeze from his wounded right hand, chuckling quietly. As he passed out, he spoke with slurred words. .

"I love you, Gail." His hand went limp again.

Within two thousand crazy heartbeats, he was snoring softly. Gail put her head down and wept. After a very short moment, she let go of his hand and stood up quickly. She got mad on purpose. She thought of her mother again, Sara aways made Gail angry..

The deliberate thought worked as she frowned sharply. She used the sheet to dry her face, welcoming the roughness of the material. Going back around to the bag on the chair, Gail dug with purpose into its recesses.

She pulled out a small pistol in a leather holster. She bent down, using the Velcro straps to secure it to her right ankle. She reached into the bottom of the bag again. Gail pulled out two larger holsters from the bag and untangled them. The two holsters strapped around her back, fitting snugly into her under arms. The leather holsters were stitched together with an angular weave of black material that matched the thin bullet-proof vest she wore. Her white long-sleeved dress shirt contrasted brightly from beneath it. The cuffs of the shirt were stylishly wide.

Gail grinned as she thought of the secret wardrobe of Sister Katherine. It was funny. The younger she looked, the younger she felt. She actually flushed warmly as she thought about Matthew's drunken words to her.

Gail grinned with joy.

Still smiling hugely, she pulled out two matching nine-millimeter pistols to fit the holsters that lay flat against her ribs. She checked the safeties and put them in the holsters. They were lightweight, with full clips of ten chances each. From the back of the chair, Gail retrieved a smart tan jacket with a zippered front and cropped waist. It covered the vest like a glove. She zipped up the front, staring at the bolt that was thrown into place, securing the room's door.

The door was wide and thick. It was also tall, about eight feet. Gail studied the beautiful carved flower relief on the door frame as she fumbled with her collar. Her smile faded somewhat. As she re-adjusted her cuffs, she thought of Sara. She swept her eyes away from the door, resting them on the floor.

She thought of Joseph: her mother's adopted son.

Joseph had been Gail's brother, her adopted brother. Gail had taken him from their mother when he was just a baby . Their mother died in her lost child's bed and Gail wondered if Sara had found peace there. Gail was only a moment too late going into Joseph's room to ask her mother's forgiveness.

Gail had heard, through Anna, that Sara had vowed to kill her for taking the human boy that Sara had adopted. . Gail had simply taken Joseph from his crib one day and disappeared.

Sara never discovered Anna had actually arranged the kidnapping. Sara assumed Gail had done it because she wanted a baby so badly. It was never true. Sara would never admit that she had grown abusive towards a young Joseph. His frailness as a human had demanded an intervention.

Gail had taken him to a Guardian church and buried her escape in the bonds of confession. The Guardians had hid them well.

The human network that chronicled the Mortals' existence was bound by the covenant. These humans were bound by sacred oath to collect, and protect, the secrets of the Mortals, from other humans. Since they had been called Children of Angels at the dawn of man, before their immortality was stripped away, these humans had only one duty, to document the life story of every Mortal.

Stories that were never complete, as humans shorter lifespans required every Mortal to chose a new Guardian at least twice every century.

Usually they chose exceptionally neutral members of the clergy, but Mortal's like Anna were likey to simply chose those most loyal to her alone.

As only fourteen Mortal's remained alive, so was that the exact number of Guardians left as well. Each Mortal knew the names of their chroniclers, and some of the Mortal's were so close to their human observers they actually kept them like pets in their own household. Conveniently on hand to talk to during the loneliest years and eras.

The Guardians could never reveal their secrets in their lifetimes, not even to the other Mortals. Joseph had been chosen as Gail's Guardian, he had been writing her life story since he was 14 years old.

Joseph had given his life to protect Gail's secrets, moments after the only mother he ever knew died in his arms.

The federal investigation into St. Mary's already had a copy of Joseph's memoirs that they had found in the confessor's side of the confessional.

The Feds could not read nor destroy it. They didn't know what the hell to make of it. The press was already getting subpoenas to release evidence in the strange happenings at St. Mary's.

Gail knew it was just a matter of time before the humans broke the ancient code it was written in, and the story of her entire life would become public.

Gail had helped Joseph through his life. She had raised Joseph as her own, watching him become a fine, strong man. She hadn't seen Sara in the fifty years she had been with Joseph the boy, and Joseph the man, both as his protector and his subject.

Before Gail could cry again, she reached into the bag, grabbing handfuls of loose bullets and putting them into the pockets of the close-fitting jacket. She zipped the dainty pockets closed. She bent over the bag again and pulled with one hand on the small swords that had lain across the arms of the chair. Finally limber again, the bag crumpled into the chair.

Gail laid one sword beside Matthew temporarily as she lifted the mattress edge. She put her shoulder into it, heaving his dead weight, holding the mattress up with her back. Gail carefully laid one of the little razor-sharp swords in between the mattresses. She felt the guns under the jacket shift slightly.

Pushing the chair back to its original position, Gail slid the other matching sword behind the chair. She pulled the duffle bag out roughly, covering the hidden blade. She sat in the chair beside it and watched the door. She stared at the bolt. She started breathing deeply, trying not to sweat.

In her mind Gail saw Sara screaming drunkenly at a one year old Joseph. She watched the boy of her memory cower in fear from their mother. Gail winced at the silent memories.

She refused to hear them.

Gail stared at the bolt, sometimes studying the relief carving around it. She studied Matthew. She rubbed her lips, her forehead. She stared at the door.

After a minute, she heard the bells in a not-so-distant tower ring once, then twice, calling the nuns to dinner. Gail sat upright in the chair. She looked at the bolt.

Gail knew that Sisters Katherine and Frances would be bringing their dinner soon. She looked at Matthew once more and stood, walking the distance to the door, quickly throwing the bolt free. She unlocked the ancient latch on the handle. Matthew needed the food to get strong.

Gail realized that the door was her goal. Whatever happened outside this door, she would not let it get in here. Whatever the cost, she vowed.

She returned to her chair. She watched the door. After a while, it seemed to watch her back. She thought of Alex, then of Michael. She glared at the door, defying its gaze. She looked at the unsecured bolt without seeing it at all.

The nuns of the convent had quickly spread the word to each other in whispers. They knew of this man's presence. That he was special. Gail usually felt comfortable surrounded by the faithful.

She watched the door. It stared back at her hatefully. She knew she would have to cross that threshold soon. She dreaded it.

Even if it meant her life, nothing was getting to that door; nothing mortal, anyway.

Gail flinched. She started clenching her fist, then her jaw.

She took comfort in the thought that the other nuns knew of this man's sacrifice. There was rumor that a special child had been born to Father Matthew and that he had accepted in blood, sacrificing himself.

Gil put her chin on her chest, slumping in the chair. She had no more time for tears, and there was strength in numbers.

She knew Satan was shopping for Mortal flesh. The baby's birth signaled his return. Matthew was already defrocked of his robes. He was wanted for murder. The prophet had indeed returned.

He had been born once before, but gave his own life so that God's favored ones would be given one more chance.

God's favored ones killed him with a lance to his human heart, while he was impaled on a cross. .

His human wife Mary had collected his blood in a cup, trying to do anything to keep every part of him together, and whole. She had failed.

The women who had loved him wept at his feet, jeered at by the lost. The men who had followed him had fled, living in fear. In the end, it was the women who loved him, who bore witness to his final, mighty struggle.

The Mortal woman who bore him, and the one he loved above all others, stayed with his shattered body for days, weeping. Gail studied the crucifix on the wall above Matthew remembering the women trying to shield her young eyes from the execution of the first prophet by crucifixion.

His name alone had spawned a profound legacy. Gail remembered her childish limbs stretching, trying desperately to touch his impaled, blessed feet.

Gail remembered his cold blood dripping onto her tiny sobbing face. She could still feel the drops splash onto her and roll down her cheek.

She wondered, for the hundred-millionth time, why those who wrote of it had left out the part about the rain.

Gail looked at Matthew as she thought about the torrential rain that had flooded over the women at his feet. The life-giving rain had been a sign of God's acceptance of the sacrifice.

Life rained down on the fools who knew not what they had done.

He had been sent to save the world. . No one had counted on the human's reaction to him. She thought of the sheets of water that cooled the body of the savior as he died on that cross so long ago.

Gail stared at the door, remembering the blood on her being washed away by the rain. She had been no more than 5 or 6 years old, just a baby.

She smirked as she suddenly thought of the baby born to Morgan. The smile faded somewhat as she considered the door.Gail was feeling trapped. She hoped Anna and Morgan would get here soon.

Something wicked lived in this holy place. Gail knew it as surely as she knew the rain.

She could feel it in her bones.

She watched the door. It watched her back.

Chapter 20

February 2, 5.00 p.m.

As soon as Miguel heard Jerold's voice, he started stuttering. Surprisingly enough, Jerold did not think this was strange, as the boy had always choked up on him. Jerold knew why Miguel feared him. . It was his gift; the gift of fire.

The Children of Angels had only one real and present fear. Each one of them feared fire. Most of them were actually phobic. Even Alexander had feared his little brother's Mortal Gift of hellfire.

Jerold understood that Miguel was afraid of him. . He frowned in disgust at the stammering idiot. He had never liked his nephew, whom had the distinct privilege of being the last full-blooded Mortal to be born alive. Miguel had been 6 months old when Nefertiti declared herself a god.

"Where's Gorin's body?" Jerold asked bluntly.

Miguel snapped out of it. He hadn't figured on Jerold answering the phone and it had thrown him for a second.

"I brought him here to my house in Alabama."

He told the lie with only a few hitches in his breath.

"He's a part of my garden now." Miguel swallowed hard. Without pausing, he went ahead. "I just planted him."

It was good to let Jerold think Miguel was being led,

Jerold took a second to consider the boy's loyalties. With Miguel, you just never knew. He gave him the benefit of the doubt reluctantly.

In a tight, forced voice Jerold asked, "Did you have any contact with the doctor?…Did you …um…leave any trace?"

Miguel froze. He had to be very careful.

"Um… contact, sir?"

"His scientist friends will be all over the place… did you speak to him, what dd he say to you?"

Miguel left himself a wide margin.

"No, sir…I caught him in an alley while he was going to his car…I made the shot from maybe one hundred feet. You would have loved it… Anyways, the house and his home lab is already in ashes."

Miguel deliberately deceived Jerold knowing the cost of it, and he held his breath. Miguel wanted to scream. Instead he controlled himself to finish the fake update in a casual tone.

"I drove up, trunked the body. I buried him here in Alabama. …and it's a done deal." Miguel forced his breath to stay even.

"There were no witnesses." He added.

Jerold couldn't find an angle. He sighed heavily.

"Very good… Did you call for a reason?" Jerold asked.

The question caught Miguel off guard.

"Uhm… uugh, yes, sir. I thought I would speak to Michael. We are supposed to meet at the gates."

Jerold twitched suspiciously. He didn't trust Michael anymore. He had never trusted Miguel.

"Here he is." He responded flatly.

Jerold thrust the phone over Michael's shoulder. Michael took the phone, holding it to his ear with one hand while still holding the wheel steady with the other..

"Hola."

Miguel told him quickly.

"Remember me when you get a sec…"

Michael smoothly replied. "Yeah, I'll call you when we get to the gates."

Miguel measured his words carefully.

"If you get there first call me… Just stall for time. Don't approach them until we talk, ok?"

Michael frowned and measured his own response. God only knew what Miguel was up to now. He had always had the chaotic human habit of unpredictability. Michael had aways admired him for it.

"Si, amigo. I will do that."

Michael hung up the phone. In the seat behind Michael, Jerold played with a bullet. He glared at Michael's head.

Jerold knew more than Michael gave him credit for, Jerold thought to himself. He had known for weeks that Michael had betrayed them. Jerold's eyes narrowed with fury. He played with the single bullet.

He should have died for it, but Jerold needed Michael, for his own ends.

He could not believe that Michael had taken such a stupid chance to hand a Mortal body part to a scientist. Even in his anger though, Jerold knew why he did it.

Michael didn't want to lose another love, or another child.

It really was all for the best, Jerold thought. The end could not come fast enough for him..

After Jerold had intercepted the results of the tests, he had been going back, checking Michael's car door amputation story. That's when he had found her.

Morgan... Jerold's only daughter. The daughter of Nefertiti. Had Michael not betrayed them, the chance encounter would have never happened. Her secrets would have remained hidden.

She had been coming out of the medical plaza office buildings as Jerold was walking in. As soon as he saw Morgan , they both seized with the fever of their blood.

She had felt it coming, though she had not yet seen her father when it hit her. As it had overcome her, Morgan stumbled on the empty staircase she was climbing.

She started looking around frantically, knowing a Mortal males awareness of her had just triggered them both.

Morgan's eyes met her fathers below her on the ground floor lobby entrance. , just as he slumped against a towering glass wall behind him.

Jerold was stunned at her belly, her VERY pregnant belly. In an instant he could feel his grandchild's rapid heartbeat. In that moment Jerold knew what this child was as his own heartbeat merged with theirs.

The electricity that passed unseen in the air between he and Morgan carried images and sounds from all three of their minds.

Jerold was almost too stunned to even feel his body burning from the inside.

The fever hit them like an unexpected burst of hellfire. Because of their shared gift, the heat became more intense than normal between them, fusing their three souls together with pain.

The glass that Jerold leaned against started to crack around his body, and web outwards, as the glass began to shatter from the intense heat of him.

He staggered away from it , watching as the super-thick glass spiderwebbed upwards and out with a terrifying cracking sound. Jerold threw himself to the floor just as the twelve-foot wall exploded over him. The tiny chunks that rained down cut his flesh with thousands of teeth. He covered his eyes as the pieces got bigger, tearing into his clothing. The sound had been deafening. By the time he had been able to roll over and look for her, Morgan had already stumbled away.

From everywhere, people had rushed over to him, holding him down. He had tried to get away, but the flood of people the explosion brought made his exit clumsy and in vain.

Jerold started tracking her from there. Her mind had given him the exact image of the house she was hiding in. It only took a few days to find out it matched one of Sara's many homes.

Jerold also found out that same day, that Michael had lied to him about his finger.

If Michael had not betrayed them, then Morgan would have had the baby in secret.

Jerold knew that some of the players of this mortal game were being protected by higher powers, but surely if God was slanting the odds in the baby's favor then God would have not let them find the boy just minutes after he was born. He used that as a way to rationalize that it was indeed God's will that they should destroy the boy.

Jerold was certain God wanted an excuse to burn it all, and start again.

He sighed heavily as he mentally tore Michael's head off. Jerold had friends of his own protecting him here on earth. He thought about the nun.

As he watched the miles go by, Jerold decided to forgive Michael.

After all, Michael's time was coming soon. Promises had been made. Michael thought he would have all he desired on this earth. Jerold thought Michael would be dead by midnight, and whatever silly promises he clung to would be a moot point..

As he played with the bullet, he thought about killing Miguel, as well. He looked his own son.

Jerold shuddered as he studied the side of Adam's face in the front passengers seat. The boy had always been slow. Jerold was disappointed in his one living son, but that was also a moot point. Jerold knew if it all worked out well, Adam would rule the world by tomorrow morning. Not Michael.

As the miles rolled past, Jerold was glad that it would all be over soon.

***

February 2, 5.06 p.m.

Abby pulled into a rest stop that was little more than a picnic table set in some trees off the road. The highway was deserted, and in its condition, it was probably not well-traveled at the best of times. Abby and Doug walked the entire perimeter before going back to the Jeep to haul out the Feds. Morgan sat in the front passenger seat as Anna and Doug pulled the younger agent out of the truck. They left Webster on the floor.

Cutting the tape from his feet, Anna stood up facing him. He looked at her, glancing at the hands where she held a small knife. He dd not even see the knife, only her hands holding it. There was not even as scar from her severe burn. Like it had never happened.

Anna looked Napoliss in the eye, poised to cut his hands free. He stared at her, almost mesmerized. Anna spoke to him in a low and deliberate voice.

"Understand this…trying anything stupid gets your partner a bullet in his head…got it?" Anna said flatly.

Napoliss paused before he nodded.

Anna frowned.

"You both are burdens to this little adventure…I'll think nothing of leaving you both here dead. …Say 'yes, ma'am' if you understand." Anna demanded.

Morgan smiled down at the baby, shaking her head.

Without hesitating again, Napoliss said, "Yes ma'am."

He really had no choice except to stay on this ride until the end. He looked at his partner, who watched him back from the floor of the Jeep. Doug cocked the pistol as Anna cut the tape.

Napoliss looked at the cocked gun in Doug's hand. He blinked hard, absently rubbing his raw wrists. Doug motioned with the pistol toward the woods.

"Let's go."

Napoliss did as he was told, walking stiffly after being tied up for so long. Edwards joined them as they crossed the clearing. Anna also pulled out a pistol and sat at the open door beside Webster's head. She watched the place where the three men had disappeared. Webster studied her hands. He barely noticed they held the gun. He silently prayed that Napoliss would not do anything stupid. Webster thought of his wife.

He asked Anna, "Can you make a phone call for me?"

Anna glared back at him, narrowing her eyes. She looked to the clearing as Maria emerged from the opposite side from where the men had gone. Abby started walking that way too, needing to relieve himself. Anna looked back to Webster and shifted the pistol.

The federal agent could not stop watching her hands.

"What's up, Agent Webster…? You need a pizza?" She shifted again.

Webster swallowed hard and looked her in the eye.

"No… I want you to call my wife; tell her I called you from the field and that I'll call her tomorrow morning."

He sighed heavily as he looked at her face.

"That is assuming I'll live through the night. Please just tell her I love her…?"

Anna frowned at the woods, waiting for the men to escort Napoliss back to them. Webster's words fell on her with an uneasy weight.

Anna looked at the mealy-faced Fed and saw the fear in his eyes. She looked over at Morgan, who had shouldered the baby and was looking at Anna expectantly over the back of the seat.

Suddenly, with a growl, Anna asked him, "How do I know you're not trying to set me up?"

Websters sudden look of surprise told her that he was being honest. She shrugged and looked back at the woods, uneasily. He kicked his tied feet as he tried to get closer to her.

"Please. I swear I'm not trying to set you up! If I don't call, her she'll know something's wrong."

Agent Webster would have start begging but instinctively he knew it would just make her more suspicious.

Anna thought about her last husband. The image of his cancer-ridden body growing cold in her arms made her flinch inwardly. He, too, had called her every day, if only to leave her a message. She thought of his laugh, his beautiful landscapes, his poet's heart in the fragile body of an earthly warrior. He had fought the cancer like a lion. He died as lions do: crying out in agony.

Anna never cried until it was over, then she had burned their childless home to the ground. Well, Morgan had helped.

Anna stood up, pacing nervously, the Fed's look of confused acceptance suddenly making her angry. Morgan had turned back around, not wanting to be a part of this conversation. With a sigh of relief, she saw the threesome emerging from the woods. Studying them through the windshield, Morgan spoke to the Fed who was helplessly watching Anna pace.

"Hold off on that a minute, Federal Agent Man. ."

Webster rolled his eyes. He breathed in a frustrated burst. He thought of the woman's hands. He would not have believed it if he had not seen it with his own eyes. His frustration died as he thought of her blackened flesh becoming whole. The woman who had burned her had not seemed to notice the miracle; she just sat beside her, silent and blank.

No one bothered explaining to the Feds exactly how the woman had gotten burned in the first place. Doug and the captain brought Napoliss back to the truck. Edwards was secretly grateful that Webster was still alive.

Anna told Napoliss, "Sit."

He obediently sat on the floor of the truck, his legs still touching the ground outside the open door. Maria was waiting with the duct tape.

Napoliss tried to protest. "Oh man. Please!No!"

He tried to shield his legs from the tiny woman.

Maria stopped. She wasn't about to get kicked. She looked over at Anna. She actually felt sorry for the poor dumb bastard. Anna looked back at her while she was deciding. Napoliss held his hands out as if he was trying to stop her from crushing him. Anna finally shook her head.

They couldn't risk it, so Maria started man-handling his ankles.

Anna looked at the defeated man. "Sorry, dude…that's the way it has to be…Our paths seem to be in direct conflict…" she let the thought trail off.

Napoliss started to say something as Maria moved the roll to his wrists. He already held them together as if about to plead with Anna. He watched her hands twitch on the pistol as he fell silent.

Anna tried to sound comforting.

"I know you're not comfortable. … Just understand this, that killing you is no benefit to me, but I surely will if you force me to. You'll be released when this…" She paused.

"…When this is over."

272

Both of them looked at her, wanting to believe her.

Napoliss was returned to the floor of the vehicle and Webster was hauled out. The same warning was given to him as before, though this time Anna went to the extra lengths of putting the pistol to Napoliss' head. She wanted Webster to see it; she knew he was the stronger of the two. She wanted to make sure she had his attention.

Webster looked at his wide-eyed partner begging him with his eyes not to do anything dumb. She definitely got his attention.

This time, all three of the men, Doug, Edwards, and Abby escorted Aent Webster into the woods. Anna approached the passenger door. She opened it slowly so as not to startle the sleeping baby on Morgan's shoulder. Without looking at either of them, Anna started digging around Morgan's feet.

As she dug, Anna asked in a subdued tone, "Where's the wallets we lifted?"

Morgan immediately leaned forward, reaching for the glove box on the dash. Anna waved her hand away, beating her to it. Morgan lay back into the seat, looking at Anna's long black tresses. Morgan smiled at the back of her dark head as her cousin retrieved the wallets from the recess. Anna shut the box with a snap and turned to shut the door. Morgan deliberately focused on the just-closed dash, expecting her cousin to shut the door.

Anna froze.

The baby's soft head rested on Morgan's left collar bone. The tiny baby had his eyes wide open staring directly into Anna's eyes. Morgan felt the attention and shifted her son uncomfortably, glancing at Anna. The baby's enormous eyes held her entire attention. Anna could not turn away.

He was still somewhat wrinkled looking, as he was not yet three weeks old. He was growing into his skin rapidly, though. His tiny bald head was covered with a thin layer of fuzz, the same deep chestnut as his mother's flowing locks. . He stared at Anna, demanding her attention.

Anna flinched finally as the thought of Matthew came upon her. She prayed he wouldn't die. She shook her head at the baby's beauty. She almost became sick.

Oh, God! Let the priest live. She would pay any price; anything.

Finally coming back to her senses, Anna looked at Morgan. Morgan seemed to understand the effect that the baby was having on Anna's peace of mind and she merely nodded.

Some things cannot be put into words; they just are.

Palming the wallets, Anna dropped her eyes and slammed the door unintentionally. Without stopping to feel guilty about it, she stomped off to the nearby picnic table that qualified this oasis as a 'rest stop'.

Abby and Doug accompanied Webster back to the truck as Anna set the first wallet on the table. One of them was obviously more expensive: calf-skin leather, finely grained and top stitched. She was fairly certain that it belonged to the younger agent . She opened it up and inspected his license. Marcus Napoliss; what a name, she thought. She found a picture of one pretty girl, then another. She counted his cash: forty-five bucks. She unfolded little scraps of paper from the large cash pocket. On one of them she found what she was looking for.

Paul Webster 462-1583 cell 297-5951 wife's cell 297-7406

Anna laid the scrap aside. She opened Webster's cheap trifold wallet. The plastic inside was as worn as the exterior of the wallet. As Webster was being taped back up at the truck, he stared at her. Inside the wallet she found his family portrait. Agent Webster was caught in a rare smile as he embraced his smiling wife. Anna looked at the woman and the obvious twins in her lap.

Tracy, P.J, and T.J. declared their identities on the back pf the photo. A child's hand had scrawled, 'Merry X-mas Daddy'.

Anna scooped up the wallets. She walked to the truck where Webster was being rolled back into the floor of the vehicle. She grabbed a cell phone from inside her thin jacket. The others started piling into the truck in various seating positions; Abby had opened Morgan's door and taken the baby from her as she hopped down. Abby rocked the baby, swaying slightly, as Anna leaned against the Jeep.

As Anna dialed the numbers on the scrap of paper, she glanced at the baby. He had twisted his little head around and was gazing calmly at Anna. She shivered, turning away as the phone started ringing at the other end.

A woman answered. "Hello?"

Anna greeted her warmly,

"Hello… Is this Tracy?"

The voice said, "Yes… This is she…?"

"Yes, I'm calling for your husband on a secure line, one moment…"

Anna turned and looked at a wide-eyed Webster on the floor. She pointed her pistol at him. Using her free hand, she put the phone to

Webster's ear. He stared at her hands.

To his wife, he said, "Hello, baby…Yeah, I know, I'll fix it. …OK, I'll be there in the morning."

Webster looked at Anna's face and she flicked the pistol, showing her impatience.

He looked at the gun, inches from his face.

Webster told his wife , "I'm in the field right now…"

He scrunched his forehead at Anna as he said, "Yeah. Yeah. I'm sorta… tied up… right now. But I will be home tomorrow."

Anna looked at him with a sneer. He dropped his eyes to her hands.

"Yeah, I just wanted you to know, I love you, baby."

Anna held the phone tightly.

Webster watched her hands.

"OK, I'll call you in the morning… Kiss the boys for me…" He almost choked up as he said, "Tell them Daddy loves them… OK… bye."

Anna snapped the phone closed as she lowered the gun to her side. Webster looked at her from the floor.

He quietly said, "Thank you."

Anna walked back to the passenger compartment and put the wallets in the glove box again. She was already scared of having to call the woman to tell her where to find her husband's body.

Morgan emerged from the woods as Anna, also, took her turn among the trees that were now mostly shadows in the approaching night. When she emerged, the sun had almost completely gone. In the dusk, Anna squinted at the Jeep. Abby sat in the passenger's side of the front seat, holding the tiny baby. Anna studied the cleric as he held the baby up, telling him how strong his little body was. She smiled softly. She had respected Abby, even when he was a young man. The thought of Miguel in Baghdad suddenly flashed through her mind as Anna snickered Almost fifty years before Miguel had found Morgan in Iraq just as she had started falling for the young cleric named Abdullah.

Miguel had gotten drunk in New York and by the time he got to Morgan he had been high on weed, too. The stopover in Amsterdam made him stupid with suppressed passion . He marched into the university in a foul mood.

Abby and Morgan were sharing long exploring glances across the lecture hall when Miguel stumbled in loudly calling her name.

Morgan's jaw had dropped. Abby's face was registering little more than disgust at the manners of the drunken intruder on the campus. Morgan had jumped up to run out, too humiliated to sit still. She ran past the shocked professor and grabbed Miguel by the sleeve as she went. The fever hit them both at the same time; Miguel was so anesthetized by alcohol and drugs he really wasn't feeling the full brunt of the burning curse. . He was stupidly grinning with love and grimacing in pain at the same time as Morgan bodily dragged him from the room. She managed to get him into the hall before the fever made her knees give way.

Because of her Mortal gift of fire , Morgan was able to hold off the fever better than most Moral's could, but it still left her hugging the wall and trying to breathe normally in the deserted hall. Unable to hold Miguel up any longer, he fell to the marble floor of the hall, too drunk to fight it. He lay flat on his back chuckling through gasping breaths. As the fever passed, he felt the overwhelming compulsion to laugh, so he did.

Abby came busting through the door like a cavalry charge; Morgan thought that he reminded her of an avenging angel.

The young student looked boldly down at a giggling Miguel who was wallowing on the floor at his feet. Morgan clutched the wall, determined to look relaxed. It didn't work as well as she had hoped; Abby frowned at her. He looked at the stranger at his feet.

In perfect English, Abby asked Morgan "Is there a problem here, Miss?"

Morgan scowled at Miguel. She was too humiliated to look at her classmate.

Still scowling viciously at Miguel, Morgan said, "No... No... It's okay, Abdullah..."

Miguel laughed harder.

The future cleric watched Miguel roll around on the floor, not sure what was happening, but certain that there was more to it than her explanations. He looked at Morgan who was slumped against the wall.

She said in a faint voice, "It's okay, Abdullah...Really."

She drew herself upright and turned to look at him. He stood in the darkened hallway like a beacon drawing her nearer. He gave off the essence of absolute integrity and her human heart was lost to Abby from the first glance.

Miguel was a thousand years too late.

Morgan blinked hard as Abby winked at her. Quickly and deliberately, he smiled and turned on his heel, and then he went back into the lecture hall, leaving her to whatever it was that had brought the man to lay at her feet.

The class ended a few minutes later and Abby was the first one back out of the door. He found them both standing; Morgan was hissing at Miguel as he stood looking at the floor. A group of students paused in the hallway to watch as Miguel grabbed Morgan's arm and she smacked him soundly.

Miguel saw Abby watching them, showing subtle contempt for Miguel's lack of control. He tried to grab hold of Morgan again, but she shrugged him away.

"Please...Morgan...Listen to me!"

"Go home, Miguel..." She snapped at him.

She avoided Abby's bemused gaze.

Miguel looked at Morgan , dumbfounded.

"I...I...I flew around the world today to come and get you!"

Morgan snorted at him, forgetting the young Arab watching her.

"I'm not going anywhere with you, Miguel!"

Miguel pointed towards the far end of the hall, started to speak, then forgot what he was about to say. He looked at the hall then pointed again.

"I have a car right outside for us. ...It's parked at the stairs..."

The group of mostly male students looked at the drunken stranger, puzzled. They all wondered how he could be parked at the stairs.

Morgan didn't care where it was.

"Good...you have a ride...Now go home, jackass!" she shouted at him

She was furious.

Miguel pointed again. He dropped his hand as Morgan turned to walk the opposite way. She didn't look at Abby as she passed him, but her face was bright red with embarrassment. Abby stood still, with his arms crossed over his considerable chest, and watched her pass.

He thought she was adorable.

She had walked about twenty feet when Miguel started howling.

"Morgan... MOORRGGAANN!... Where are you going?"

She turned her head to look back at where Miguel was kneeling on the floor. He smiled in agony as she turned to face him again. He dropped to both knees as the men in the crowded doorway watched him.

"Moorrggaann...I...LOVE...YOU..."

Miguel put his palms together, pleading.

"I LOVE YOU, MORGAN!…Please, come with me?"

Morgan's mouth dropped open in humiliation. Flushing from head to toe, Morgan closed her eyes in horror and started shaking her head in disgust. She fled down the hallway despite his continued begging.

Abby never lost his grin. He tried not to laugh at the pathetic man in love with the class hottie. How low love will take you…Abby thought of the hottie's golden eyes.

The stranger rose from the floor where he had been groveling, finally running after the woman who had crushed him. Abby and the guys behind him burst into cheers watching him disappear down the hall.

As one, most of the group ran the other way to check out the stairs.

The stairs actually descended onto a portico that was the front entrance of the school. In front of the stairs was a lush expanse of grass with a fountain in the middle of a small inner garden.

Sure enough, a little red sports car with two dainty seats sat between the fountain and the stairs. The young men burst into laughter as they ran out to check out the car. They could see that the small driveway flanked with plants was all torn up with tire tracks going over the curb and then the grass, leading straight to the car.

Abby retrieved the keys from the ignition, looking at them thoughtfully. After a moment, he walked around to the trunk. He opened the trunk and took out a lug wrench. The young members of his class cheered him on as he loosened the heavy nuts on each of the tires. The group helped him replace the hubcaps.

By the time a defeated Miguel had returned to his car alone, Abby had already backtracked to find Morgan. She was sitting on a bench in a small garden area at the rear of the campus.

Abby had often laughed with them about the fool who was in love with Morgan. Miguel had been furious and self-destructive, and Michael had found it expedient to retrieve him. Abby would admit to being in love, but he would never let them think he was a fool.

They never thought he was.

However, since then Anna made it a point to find out where Miguel was every Christmas to send him a model car. The exact replica of the car he was driving that day arrived every year, with all four tires meticulously attached, and then ripped off before being carefully wrapped. As Anna returned to the Jeep, she froze. Morgan looked at her expectantly from behind the wheel. Their eyes locked with a frigid intensity.

In a loud voice, rolling her head on her shoulders, Anna objected loudly.

"Ooh…hell no!" She snapped.

The occupants of the Jeep looked at her in confusion. Anna marched to the driver's door, opening it roughly.

"Get out, lead foot…I'm driving!" Anna commanded.

Anna glared at Morgan , daring her to refuse. Morgan finally got out reluctantly as Anna threw at her.

"I'll be damned if I let you kill me before I can even get to the fight!"

Abby's snicker turned into a snort of laughter. God knows, he'd had experience with Morgan's driving and wasn't anxious to repeat the experience.

The baby stared at Anna from Abby's arms. She wanted to touch his face. She wanted to smile at his soft sweetness, so she deliberately scowled instead.

As the moon came above the horizon, the Jeep lurched and lumbered back onto the highway. Webster shifted as the car started rolling. He looked at his new view under the back seat and scowled. For the next few hours, the agent would wonder about the voodoo doll that stared back at him from under the seat.

Chapter 21

February 2, 5.59 p.m.

Father Timothy marveled at the helicopter. The nimble little blades were already whirring around, pushing gale force drafts into the people who waited to board it. Timothy looked at the pregnant woman.

After they had taken the interstate, they had gone directly to the small airport. Diana had tried calling her father to see if he would loan her his corporate plane, but he had refused his daughter. Timothy smiled as he thought, 'poor little rich girl'; though he did admit that chartering a helicopter was quite inventive, for such a stupid woman. He looked at her belly and wanted to throw up.

Father Timothy felt the sin of her flesh and the vile scent of it made him sick. He smiled as she returned his gaze; he had to do what the angel told him. He would not fail his perfect angel. Timothy had to string this creature along for only a while more, and then he wouldn't have to be sickened by her unholy presence again.

In the twilight, the door of the chopper opened and a man carrying a clipboard approached them, crouching under the blades.

He approached the pregnant lady, asking loudly above the wind, "Are you the folks going to Mississippi?"

Diana started nodding her head vigorously as Father Timothy watched the air machine again.

"All right, miss... I looked up the location; we should get there between eight and nine..." The pilot instinctively looked at her swollen belly

"You need anything before we get going?"

Diana said "NO" very loudly, so as to be heard over the rotating propellers. The pilot nodded at Timothy, putting his arm over the filthy woman as he waved him to the craft as well .

Timothy almost crab-walked to the chopper as he was being careful not to stand erect. The pilot opened one back door, expecting them both to get into the back compartment. Timothy scowled at the rear rotor blade. He was tired of this rich, vile, nasty bitch of a woman. He saw his angel among the blackness of the sky. The stars reminded him of her silver-white alabaster skin. Timothy took his place beside Diana , trying not to cringe. He smiled pleasantly to cover his revulsion.

His angel had promised anything; anything he had ever desired would be his, if he did this holy thing. The thought of it made him sick not too long ago; but lately...

Diana smiled back at him. She was grateful for the roar of the propellers. She was starting to feel very pregnant, even if she did have a long month left to go. She sighed heavily, watching the ground retreat as the pilot took it up with one smooth, expert jerk. She was silent for a while, wondering who Anna was. Timothy said that Anna would be there, too. Diana wondered why Michael would be going to a monastery... And why on earth would he take his secret girlfriend there?

Diana was glad that Father Timothy was with her there to guide her. She thought about the confrontation that would be coming soon. She HAD to make this 'Anna' understand some things...

Timothy said they are supposed to meet there at ten, with the scientist. Diana was glad she would have a chance to rest first, because the fatigue, worry and all the tension lately had made her feel especially vulnerable. She thought that having this baby might just kill her yet.

If Michael loved another woman, Diana hoped she would die anyway.

She was glad that Father Timothy was there to guide her.

Timothy thought of all that would be his when his angel was pleased.

***

February 2, 6.03 p.m.

Kia watched the sedan as it left the gas station. The two younger men who had blown up Annie May's apartment seemed to be in an argument at the gas pump. They were literally screaming at each other over the top of the car. Kia's dark eyes rolled up into her head.

She rolled down her window but was too far away to actually hear the words. Eventually, the older-looking man who was in the back seat got out of the car and within a few waves of his hands, both men had shut up. Kia watched their body language.

She thought about her husband Bubba, whom had barely escaped the inferno at the motel. He had been lucky to only have a severe burn on his back and a busted ear drum from the force of the explosion.

Kia looked at the voodoo sacraments on her dash, and hanging from her mirror . She swore to God right then that she would take vengeance on these men, no matter what rules Anna had taught her about not interfering in Mortal family matters.

The older man from the back seat and the front passenger, who looked just like him, finally got back into the car. The driver with the dark hair stood for a tense moment, watching the cars on the interstate next to the station. Kia had no idea where they were going. On the interstate she could hang back slightly, but she was afraid that soon she would have to follow them down into some damn country-side where she couldn't hide as easy.

Kia waited until the dark-haired man had apparently stewed long enough; he jerked the door open with suppressed rage and got in.

She watched the brake lights glow momentarily, then go dim as the car rolled back out into the night. Kia rolled with them. She slipped in her favorite CD, trying to keep her sense of detachment. She had no idea where this would all wind up. She thought of Bubba.

Kia adored her husband. She was not going to let the men that wounded him slip away. When she found Anna and brought her back, he would forgive her; he always did. But this time she was quitting for sure.

Anna was her responsibility. Kia had been Anna's human Guardian since age 17, chronicling the life of the legendary Mortal.

Kia had lived her entire life in Anna's shadow.

Most of the time, Kia had no idea where Anna was. . Hell, that girl was so good at getting lost, that most of the time Kia would have to wait and figure out a way to get her secrets from her after she returned home.

Kia was a hand-picked chosen Guardian, and therefore bound by the bonds of confession. But Anna was a literal clam when it came to giving Kia the facts of who did what. Mostly Kia had to rely on the mountain of texts the had inherited from the long line of Anna's previous Guardians.

The Book of Kia was only one chapter in the Chronicles of Anna. In all, Kia had almost two thousand years of Anna's life story in her possession, some of it written in Ancient Egyptian, though the bulk of it was in Latin. However, Kia knew even that two millennia span of documents was less than a fourth of Anna's actual story.

At one time the Chronicles of Anna spanned another two thousand years further back in time, before Nefertiti, but Anna herself had destroyed her own history, leaving whatever she was before the final curse, comletely untold.

When the Feds had left the BBQ stand earlier, with Bubba hot on their tails, Kia had waited at the restaurant because she knew where Anna was: at the cabin. Kia was not allowed to interfere.

Guardians could follow, and observe, but no direct action was allowed by the humans to interfere in Mortal's family business. . Kia thought about the vows she had taken. No direct action. But the vows didn't say anything about indirect action.

The vows didn't say anything about the baby's birth, either. Kia shook her head in disbelief as she thought of the child. All of Anna's Guardian's had feared this child. Kia still had trouble believing he had come in her own short lifetime.

Things were about to change forever. If Satan had his way, ten thousand years of his reign would start tomorrow.

If the Mortals that she watched over failed the boy, it would start tomorrow. She prayed to God they would not fail. She begged God to protect the boy.

Kia shuddered at the crucifix that was hanging from a chain on the mirror. It had a big fat ruby in it, with a strange circular pattern of emeralds surrounding it. It was the emblem of the Guardian. As Kia glanced at it, she hoped she would not die tonight.

The only way a Guardian could be killed by a Mortal was to break their vow of silence, or the vow to not interfere. If a Mortal killed a Guardian without this provocation, the consequences were immediate and lethal. None of the Mortals would tolerate another Mortal targeting their scribes or their secrets. It was simply forbidden.

With the exception of the human mob crucifying the first prophet from Nazareth in a political execution, Matthew killing Alexander had been the first time in almost three thousand years that any human had killed a full-blooded Mortal.

Whatever else was in store for the rest of this lifetime, Kia knew nothing would ever be the same again.

Kia had a blast following Anna through the years. There was usually a path a mile wide, lined with kicked asses in her wake. Kia smiled to herself as she thought of Anna, but it quickly changed to a frown as she watched the long sedan pull onto an off ramp. She twitched as she followed. She would have to follow closely now and pace the large car, but it left her more visible.

Kia thought of her father. She thought of the notes she had retrieved after a Mortal killed him for interfering between Anna and her Mortal family when he got in the way. According to her father's writings, Anna had been an enigma since day one for him as well. He had also served Anna for his entire life and Kia wished she could tell him about the boy.

She thought of the baby, and prayed harder . She sure hoped God was listening. Kia accelerated and kept the larger car at a safe enough distance ahead of her. Her unoccupied leg started jumping from her sense of danger. The thought of the baby calmed her.

Now was the time to interfere; Kia would not fail the boy if she could live that long. She would not let Anna fail, even if it meant Kia broke all her vows before dawn.

Again, she prayed silently for Anna. She knew that Anna would not fail. She believed in her. Kia stayed with the car like a shadow.

***

February 2, 6.05 p.m.

Gail jumped slightly as the footsteps echoed in the hall.

The door opened just a crack wide and a grey head poked in. The calm serene eyes of the nun were visible through the crack as she surveyed both Gail and Matthew.

She nodded and asked Gail, "…May I come in?"

Gail nodded as the tiny nun stepped through the door. She walked swiftly to Matthew, the quick energy of her movements belying the calmness of her eyes. Stopping at his bed, the elderly nun looked down on Matthew and smiled.

Gail was aware that Sister Elizabeth had been a nurse in her former life; before the convent that is.

Sister Elizabeth had retired as a RN and had planned a perfect retirement until her husband had unexpectedly passed away in their garden. Her one daughter was grown and gone, so she had turned to God. Elizabeth still dreamed of her husband though; she missed him so badly.

The woman turned her smile to Gail, and she returned it. Gail needed to believe that she wasn't alone right now, as it felt like the pistols against her ribs weighed tons. Sister Elizabeth started talking as she walked across the room.

"Oh my. …You look pale, child…"

She sat across from Gail as Matthew started snoring loudly. They both looked at the young priest, startled. Sister Elizabeth chuckled.

Dropping her voice to a whisper the nun said, "Other than sleep, is there anything that you need?"

Gail started to ask her for a thousand warriors of God, if that were in the asking. She instead shook her head at the elder woman.

"No, ma'am…Now it's up to the clock." Gail responded softly.

The former nurse looked back to Matthew. She knew he was special; she knew that very well.

Sister Elizabeth asked Gail, "Think I could just sit with you for a bit…?" The woman nodded her small head toward the priest. "I'm so glad you brought him here…"

Gail said nothing. She only thought of getting through whatever was coming.

She forced a smile to her lips. "Yes, Sister…You're welcome to sit with us…"

The nun settled back into her chair. They silently watched Matthew, although Sister Elizabeth knew that Gail watched her every second, too. Eventually, they both drifted into their own thoughts as more soft footsteps echoed in the hall. They passed the door, going both ways as the sisters returned to their private rooms to get ready for evening mass. After a few minutes, most of them faded away into the recesses outside the door.

Gail watched the door. Sister Elizabeth sat slightly between her and the door, and she also eventually started watching the door, too. Gail listened with every ounce of energy to every noise outside the door, no matter how small or seemingly insignificant it was. Sister Elizabeth turned back to the priest on the bed. They sat in an uneasy silence that left them both even less willing to speak. The old nun lost herself in thought.

Gail watched the door. It watched her back.

Finally, firm footsteps echoed down the hall. Sister Katherine opened the door and Gail almost had a heart attack at her sudden entrance. Seeing Sister Elizabeth gave Katherine a start and she lurched backwards quickly; a steak knife dropped from the tray, or her hand, Gail could not tell which. Elizabeth had already stood to help her retrieve it when Katherine swooped down to grab it. Gail stood, bracing herself.

"Oh… Hello, Sister Elizabeth!…" Katherine was nearly whispering so as not to disturb her sleeping patient.

She walked to the table between the chairs and set the tray of food down . Gail held her breath as Katherine stood back up with the knife still in her hand; they both looked at it.

Katherine said, " I'll bring a clean one…."

Gail nodded her head, reaching out casually for the knife.

"Five second rule…Don't worry about it…"

Katherine considered the knife in her hand for a long moment. Finally, she placed it in Gail's outstretched hand, handle first. Gail forced herself not to snatch the blade. Katherine and Elizabeth looked at each other. Katherine spoke to the woman who appeared to be years older than herself; Gail knew how wrong perception could be.

"Will you be joining us for Mass, Sister?" Katherine asked.

Elizabeth looked at the young priest and nodded carefully.

"Yes, child…I just wanted to pray over him…" She nodded toward Matthew.

Katherine smiled tightly and, without another word, she left the room as abruptly as she had entered. Gail looked at the knife.

Leaning over, she opened the domed lid of the tray. Yep, a nice lean cut of steak, with beans and corn. There was also a small bowl of broth for Matthew. Sister Elizabeth looked at the knife in Gail's hand for a moment before she came to her feet.

She looked down on Gail. "Is it ok if I come by after Mass to sit with you?"

Gail simply nodded her acceptance.

"Yes, Sister, I would like that." Gail said softly.

Just because she was paranoid didn't mean she could excuse rudeness. Elizabeth smiled back at her gently as she turned and left through the large door. Gail waited a full thirty seconds before going to the door and throwing the bolt into place.

She went back to the tray to get the broth for Matthew. She stopped a moment and thought about it before retrieving the last morphine pill from the drawer and dissolving it in the liquid.

If things went badly tonight, then Gail wanted Mathew to be literally feeling no pain. She prayed that he would still be alive by the time it wore off.

Gail knew that Satan was heading directly for her, and she was certain that some of his agents were already here. She took the drugged bowl to the bed.

Before she woke him to eat, Gail told him that she loved him.

In her mind, she tried to think of ways to beat the devil and there were not that many. When he took human flesh, he was only stopped momentarily if you killed the body of the sinner he took. In spirit, he was severally limited, but if he could be forced into the body of a Mortal or a human, he could be killed as they were.

I Inside the baby, though, through him, Satan would be reborn to take over the earth. In the baby's flesh, he would again be immortal.

Gail wished that Anna would hurry.

***

February 2, 6.23 p.m.

As Michael drove, Anna was his only thought. He could see her standing on the Nile's bank, her perfectly sculptured hands and arms decorated with bands of beaded jewels. In his pre-occupation and on unfamiliar roads, he missed his turn. After cursing himself and telling Adam to shut up, Michael pulled into the mouth of a hidden dirt road to turn around.
The otherwise silence inside the car seemed a living presence and haunted the moods of all three of them, putting all of them in a foul mood.

Michael thought of the painting that still was rolled against his thigh. He hoped he was not creasing the old painting. He thought of the image of his own face staring over her bed, and he wanted to rip the steering wheel off in his hands.

Michael thought about her message. She wanted his trust. She was trying to save him! He almost snorted out loud with laughter.

In the mirror, Michael saw a car that had been behind him also flip the same odd turn that he had. Michael squinted into the mirror, watching, and wondering what it meant.

Jerold and Adam ignored him.

Anna flashed through his mind, again, as he came back to his missed turn. He slowed but still took it too fast, braked and slowed as Jerold and Adam looked up. Michael ignored them.

So, Anna was trying to save them. He sneered at the sentiment. Anna was always trying to save something. She didn't save his son; she didn't save her own sons. He watched as the car that had turned with him before was again turning and following his route.

Michael thought of his father, and about the priest who had killed Alexander. He wondered why Anna had not tried to save her mother. Michael was tired of Anna trying to be his savior.

He thought about her black eyes, flecked and ringed with gold. Michael's jaw clenched as he thought of over five hundred years of Anna deliberately frustrating him, trying to save his damn soul!

He hated her for it. He absolutely hated her for it!

Michael frowned at the car in his rear view. He considered it for a long time before deciding that he would deliberately miss his next turn as well . He watched the headlights, even as he kept the road in sight. He would know soon if he was being followed. Anna's eyes stared at him from his memory, her tender mouth drawn up into a teasing grin. Michael felt like he was trying to swallow his stomach. He watched the lights as Adam absently stared out the opposite window while Jerold was doing the same thing from the back seat.

Michael looked at his uncle in the mirror; he clenched his jaw.

He wondered where Miguel was. He thought he knew why Miguel wanted him to stall Jerold. Miguel had the scientist. His cousin held the test results that Michael had hoped he could bury. Michael knew that his uncle had found out about his deceptions, and he felt like a wild animal that was trapped in the hunter's snare.

The results must be startling for Miguel to risk being killed by Jerold. Michael knew he would find out very soon what the test results revealed, but it hardly mattered any more. .

Everything was different now. The prophet had been discovered among them; promises had been made. Michael shuddered deep in his bones.

Michael knew that he would be having his own son, soon. No more dead daughters for him. Promises had been made.

Diana would bear him many living sons and daughters. Michael had demanded assurances that it would be so.

Anna's ever-present ghost flashed through his mind. He thought of her standing over the ancient graves of her own dead children; she still couldn't let go... not even after ten lifetimes, or even a hundred. She refused to let go of her pain. Michael got angry as he thought about her trying to save them; she was putting herself directly in his path.

He looked at the car behind him and he was now sure that they were being followed.

Anna wanted to save them. He silently prayed that she would be able to save herself from him.

Michael had promises to keep.

Chapter 22

February 2, 6.53 p.m.

Anna drove dangerously fast while keeping alert for the beep of the radar detector. The image of Michael looking back at her numbed her brain. She saw the expression on his face when he had realized she was there, in Jerold's mind.

Anna thought of the painting above her bed; she had painted it just so she could see his face every day.

Anna hated to love Michael . She also loved to hate him. She wished she could touch his beloved face, and slap it for good measure.

Beside her, Abby kissed every inch of the baby's face and head. She had almost laughed out loud to see the little baby actually grinning at Abby. His toothless rapture was the most endearing thing Anna had ever seen.

She scowled and watched the road.

She could feel Michael's hands over hers, directing the paintbrush. She could feel him at her back. She could see him standing on the banks of the Nile long ago, his arms and fingers, and even his toes, banded in gold rings and chains. She wanted to scream at the road that flew beneath her tires.

Anna could feel him holding her head, kissing her throat, and herself pushing him away. She despised him for the soft caress of memory. She hated him for her own unfufilled need.

Anna begged God to change Michael's mind, and change his heart. She caught herself praying and gave up on getting God to listen to her. He had never listened to her. She had quit wondering if God cared about her, long ago. .

She respected Him, but simply left Him alone, as He had left her lonely. She needed God to listen to her tonight, but she was still afraid He didn't care.

Anna wondered if she screamed loud enough, would He listen to her now?

She glanced sideways at the baby, now lying on Abby's shoulder. In the glow of the inner lights, she saw him staring at her again. Anna shivered. Abby petted him absently as he sang Muslim prayers softly. The even, loving tone of the cleric's voice made the baby smile softly.

Anna watched him from the corner of her eye, letting her mind relax into the beautiful, ancient rhythm. Without meaning to, she saw Michael standing in her mind, the memory so real that her heart almost ripped from her chest.

Anna saw him as he had been once when she had first seen him in Egypt. It was the first time in her life that Anna had seen a Mortal male with the same gift of will as she. His familiarity istantly captured her mind.

Michael was much younger than her, but he had grown very quickly into a wickedly clever man. She clutched hard at the wheel, feeling his eyes on hers and the battle of wills that always followed. She almost always won in those days.

After a few hundred years, , she had started to realize that he was stronger than she. She finally didn't fight it and let him into her mind.

After so long in the darkness of age, for the first time Anna had felt the warmth of sharing. She took comfort in the fact that he had grown stronger than she. She could still trip him up though.

Anna smiled, sort of, at the toothless grin of the baby on Abby's shoulder. She watched the road closely; the convent was not far now. She watched the shadows of the trees closing in on the sides of the roads.

She watched Michael in her memory as his eyes filled with love, respect, and savage desire for her. She saw his face twist into hatred as she gave him full access to her mind, but denied his physical passion.

For centuries she denied him, knowing it would cost both of them their souls.

From somewhere in the back, the Agent Napoliss, started asking questions about Anna's miraculous recovery. At first, Morgan tried to answer his questions, though she was obviously distracted. As the miles wore on, Morgan had finally started telling them things they didn't want to believe.

Webster had rudely scoffed when she had mentioned "Satan." Morgan had bared her teeth at him, calling him a fool.

"Who are you?" Morgan sneered at him, "Doubting Thomas? …You saw with your own eyes. You knew when you saw Sara's handprint burned into stone that you were out of your depth here. ..."

At the wheel, Anna's brow curled into her usual frown. Hmmm...

Anna started laughing. At first, it was a cold hard sound, like ice breaking, but it changed to a full-bodied laugh that left them all looking at her. The still tied up federal agents tried to strain their necks to see what the woman at the wheel found so amusing.

Abby smiled, and in a stage-whisper, he asked, "What's so funny?"

Anna roared with laughter and floored the gas pedal, eager now to see what Fate had in store.

"I just realized who these guys are..." She giggled sarcastically.

"Meet our hostages...Marcus Napoliss...and Paul Webster..."

Abby looked back and down blankly. Edwards and Maria looked at each other, not understanding.

"Meet... Mark... and Paul." Anna said in glee.

From the back where she had been watching a wide-eyed Napoliss, Morgan snorted in laughter. Doug rolled his eyes as Maria shook her head.

Edwards said, "Damn...This is getting downright biblical."

Abby's laughter shook the baby on his shoulder. Anna tried not to run off the road.

February 2, 7.12 p.m.

Gail watched the bolt she had relatched when Sister Elizabeth left. She sat in the chair, watching the door from Matthews's bedside. His double dose of drugs had him passed out beyond any natural sleep. His loud snore echoed through the small chambers stone walls. Gail studied the patterns of the old bricks. The convent had actually been built as a fortress and its sturdy construction was a marvel of man's ability to protect himself. Gail wondered about man's inability to protect himself from within.
Behind the thick walls of the holy place, Gail shivered in the chill of the quiet. She wondered if God was anywhere near.

Since she had first come through the doors of the convent, Gail had heard the whispers of panic. At first, after dragging Matthew's body into the room, his screams drowned out all of the night.

But after it was over...She heard them again.

From her chair, Gail looked at the door for a long moment. She couldn't ignore the whispers, but she was sure they were urging her to flee. She again looked to Matthew. If she tried to move him again, it would kill him. Gail knew she would not leave his side until death came to her. He smiled in his sleep; she smiled back at him, shy and tender. She prayed that he would live.

Gail flinched, wondering who in the convent was going to try to kill them both. She felt it coming like rain in the air.

She unzipped her jacket. The pistols rested comfortably against the Kevlar vest. Gail again counted the bricks in the wall. Inspecting the door with swollen eyes, her only concern was how she could fortify the large plank of cedar. In her mind's eye, she could see the sitting area outside the door. On the same wall the door was on, a large hall extended both left and right, with the sitting space extending directly in front of the door.

Gail considered the door that closed off the seating area and one hallway. It was not enough to hide behind.

There was no way to block the north hall; it was impossible. Gail felt trapped. She prayed that God would turn away from what was about to happen. She looked at Matthew, startled to see him staring back through drunken eyes.

He whispered to her as she leaned forward and grabbed his hand.

With a goofy grin, Matthew said, "It's OK, Gail…I think…everything will be OK now. …"

His smile was huge and serene. She grinned back at him, trying to comfort him back.

"How do you know, silly?" Gail asked, teasing him.

His face twitched slightly , his eyes were open but clouded as he smiled beautifully.

"I had a dream…" Matthew whispered breathlessly.

Gail raised an amused eyebrow.

" Oh yeah? Did you dream of me?" She smiled tightly, shyly.

Matthew chuckled.

"No, haha! …you're funny. …I saw…I saw…an… angel…"

Gail's smile froze.

She frowned at him as he closed his eyes, still smiling in rapture.

"She was beautiful…She told me…um…she said it was all going to be OK."

His voice started fading as he again fell into the warm drift of sleep.

Gail stared at him, trying not to panic.

In a breathless, dreamy voice, Matthew said, "She was so pretty! She wasn't as beautiful as you, though ..." His voice drifted away as the drugs again took him under.

Gail closed her eyes, trying not to hear the whispers coming from the stone walls. . She let go of Matthew's hand and stood. Stooping back down, she kissed his forehead.

At the door, Gail stood listening for a long moment before she was satisfied that there was nothing beyond it. Breathing deeply, she looked at Matthew. She believed in him. She switched the safeties off on her hidden pistols and threw the bolts on the door.

February 2, 7.24 p.m.

Timothy felt like his body was shaking apart. The constant vibration of the chopper was driving the feeling deep into his bones. The woman sat beside him; too close. He could smell her expensive perfume trying to cover the foul smell of her water breaking.
Father Timothy knew that she was in labor.

Diana stared into the night sky as the priest scowled at her back. She was trying to hide the pains in the dark interior of the confined space, but Timothy could feel the involuntary heaving of her body. She had taken some deep breaths and turned toward the window, trying to mask her struggle in the roar of the propellers. If he had not been forced so close to her, he may have never noticed.

As Timothy sneered at her back, his angel appeared in his mind. She smiled at him, and he no longer saw Diana's shape in the dark. The priest smiled suddenly as the black void of the angel's eyes pulled at him, easing his tension. He relaxed into the seat while inspecting the back of the pilot's head.

The angel's image filled Timothy like an overflowing vessel with a warm liquid. Her alabaster skin glowed from the blackness of memory. She loved him; he knew it. He felt it shining on him there in the darkness. Timothy loved her back.

The angel, his angel, told him things. She put into his mind whatever he wanted to know. He asked and she gave. To him, it was never odd that he suddenly just KNEW things. She showed Father Timothy images of such beauty that often made him weep with wonder. She encouraged him to explore his fear. Things he had always been scared to approach in thought were, unquestionably, without warning, just THERE. She didn't judge his more secret longings and dreams.

Father Timothy had been saved; he was sure of it.

Why else would God have sent an angel to him?

Why else would God be ready give Timothy a child born of angels?

Father Timothy had always known he was special, destined for great things. When the angel had told him what God expected of him, he was sick at heart, but he BELIEVED. Surely if God had an earthly servant, it would be a man of faith, like himself. Timothy smiled in the dark, thinking of all the unwashed masses that would never see the glory he was now flying toward. All that he asked would be given.

Timothy knew he would be rewarded by angels, and by God, himself.

Next to him, the woman's body was seized by labor pains. He did not look at her again, choosing to let her believe that her deception was not yet noticed. He could hear her panting over the engine and prop noise, and he smiled to himself; let her think she's hiding her pain.

Timothy had already known that the baby would be coming tonight. His angel had told him this perfect boy would be his, a gift from God.

All Timothy had to do was kill the other child. The angel assured him it was God's will. One small blood sacrifice, to prove Timothy was worthy, and all the world would be his to command.

Timothy filled with joy as he thought of the promises he had been made. .

***

Michael was sure that the car was following them. Adam had also noticed. The two cousins looked at each other silently now and then. Jerold slept fitfully in the back seat, unaware of what the men in the front seat knew.

Adam whispered to Michael, "What do you think?"

Both men stared at the road ahead of them.

Looking quickly in the mirror at Jerold's relaxed frame stretched across the back, Michael winced.

In a soft tone, he said, "I dunno...I doubt it's Miguel..."

He stopped short. He almost said Miguel and the scientist. He flicked his eyes to the car's lights in the mirror then back again to the road.

295

Adam casually said, "Could be a Guardian…?"

Michael looked at him with a quick, sideways glance. As he clenched his jaw, he gripped the wheel tighter. They were still at least two hours from the convent. Michael knew he had to kill the priest while he lay helpless. They would not get another chance.

Michael again glanced at the lights in the mirror. The car's driver seemed to sense that they knew they were being stalked, so the car followed them openly. The dense woods crowding the lonely highway made Michael feel claustrophobic. He exchanged glances with Adam again.

They looked at other in perfect understanding, and, without warning, Michael engaged the brakes, skidding onto the shoulder of the road. Jerold was thrown bodily into the backs of their seats. They could hear the tires of the car behind them also slamming to a stop, the forward motion carrying the following car to within seventy-five feet of the back of the sedan.

Jerold had started to curse from the floorboard but as soon as he heard the tires of the second car, he had simply started struggling to come to his knees. They were illuminated faintly by the headlights. For a long moment both cars sat idle, no movement coming from either vehicle.

Michael and Adam watched from their mirrors. Without speaking, both men started toward each other, trying to squeeze past the other to change seats. The car behind them didn't move. Jerold watched the unmoving car, trying to figure out what he had missed.

As soon as Michael was once again seated in the passenger's seat, he relaxed into it, immediately sending his mind toward the unknown presence. Michael could feel himself being pulled to the person at the wheel and almost immediately he sensed it was a female. As he pushed his will into her, he was vaguely aware of the symbol of the Guardian hanging from the mirror.

Kia's free will was taken from her easily as Michael slammed his presence into her. Almost immediately, he was aware of Anna's connection to the female.

Adam looked back and forth from his cousin to the car in his mirror. Adam flinched slightly as Michael's eyes closed and his body heaved from the concentration.

Michael saw Anna in Kia's memory. He saw her as he had never seen her before: curled on a couch, relaxed and happy.

He saw Anna dancing in a tiny fringe-covered red dress as all the males on a dance floor tried to gyrate closer to her. Kia tried to push Michael away from her mind and he pushed back harder, astounded at his visions of Anna. He saw her crying, holding a bloody sword.

The images came fast and furious, some from a child's perspective, some from an adult's. Michael ripped the memories from Kia , crushing her thoughts into a blinding pain. Michael saw Anna standing in front of his portrait with a pallet knife, poised to slash it. He saw her covered in blood and gulping for breath. He pushed harder. He saw Anna at the BBQ stand, helping Bubba roast meat on the open fire pits.

In the car behind the sedan, Kia screamed as Michael ripped into her mind. He tore Anna's confessions from her thoughts. She held her ears, screaming as her body arched stiffly up, meeting the steering wheel.

Adam frowned at Michael as the man started snarling in his concentration. He glanced around nervously. Whoever was in the car would surely be under Michael's control, but Adam was not sure how many people were in the car. Michael could only enter one person at a time.

Adam finally wrenched open his door, holding his pistol at his side as he quickly approached the still unmoving car. Coming closer, he could see only one shadow and quickened his pace. He opened the door, holding the pistol in a shooter's stance. The woman behind the wheel was rigid, her face thrust upwards toward the roof of the car.

Kia's mouth worked soundlessly as she sat helpless. Adam held the gun level with her head as he studied the religious articles scattered across the dash. Hanging from the mirror was the familiar ruby and emerald pattern of the Guardians. Adam instinctively started backing away as the woman seized even harder. Her hand clenched open and closed into a repeated fist.

Adam loped back to the car where he had left his door open. Michael was starting to ball up and tremble.

Breathlessly, Adam exclaimed, "Stop it…! She's a Guardian…!"

From the back seat, Jerold looked at his son sharply. Michael moaned as he violated every part of Kia's mind. From the car behind them, the woman screamed in agony. Michael saw the cabin. He learned that Anna had forbidden Kia to speak of Michael.

Adam looked at the car. He ground his teeth at the pained scream.

"Stop it! Stop it…! You're going to kill her…!" Adam insisted.

Jerold looked out the back window, then back to his son.

"Perhaps, son, that is the whole point…"

297

Adam looked at Jerold quickly with shock.

"You know the cost of it!" Adam screamed at him.

Leaning over his seat, Adam grabbed Michael firmly by a shoulder and shook him hard .

"Stop it...! Stop it...!" Adam yelled directly into Michael's ear.

Michael sat up some and the scream from behind them faded within a breath. Without being able to stop himself, Michael started crying.

The sobs made his mind pull back convulsively into himself. Michael wanted to beg God for one more moment with Anna; instead, his sobs became broken, any words lost in the agony of his mind returning into it's own lonely shell once more . Adam looked at him with a frown as Jerold sat back into the large backseat. Michael's cries seemed to stun the other two men as they watched him collapse into unspoken memories.

Finally, Adam walked back to the other car.

The woman was slumped sideways in the seat, her arms wrapped around her head as if trying to ward off a blow. She was also sobbing, but it was weak and soft. Adam started looking under her seat, in the console. Her helpless body was roughly pushed aside as he checked the glove box. He took the keys from the ignition. Walking to the back, he opened the trunk and searched every inch of it.

If she was a Guardian, Adam knew she had a journal that chronicled the secrets of the Mortal she followed. . He found nothing. Adam returned to watch the woman as she lay curled where she had fallen. He could feel the pistol in his jacket. He watched her for a long moment.

The Guardians could not be killed for their secrets. The other Mortals would not protect one of their own who broke this tradition. But there was no rule about stealing the Guardian's journals, if a Mortal were lucky enough to be able to find the damn things.

Adam returned to the larger car, getting in behind the wheel. He still had the woman's keys in his hand. They could not kill the Guardians, but they surely could do everything to slow them down.

Michael tried to quit sobbing as Jerold frowned at him from the back seat. Leaving the car behind them silent on the dark road, Adam pulled away from the shoulder and drove as fast as he dared to a fate that had already unknowingly been arranged for him..

Chapter 23

February 2, 7.34 p.m.

As soon as Gail threw the bolts, she pulled the ancient handle in a controlled jerk, stopping the swing before it opened shoulder length. She had one hand in her jacket. The door to the south hall had already been shut and latched into place, forcing Gail to crane her neck hard to the left to survey the unblocked northern corridor and the sitting room immediately in front of her. Understanding what she saw took longer than it should have, but the sight was pretty bizarre.

Her cousin, Sister Katherine, was kneeling face-first, her forehead pressed to the seat of a sofa in the sitting area. Slumped forward was probably a better way to put it. She was wearing a long nightshirt type of robe and her shaking was evident even in the dim light. The deep green of her robe seemed darker in the light cast by the glowing embers in the fireplace beyond the couch. Katherine held a sword limply in her left hand. It scraped the floor softly with each shudder that passed through her body.

Gail stepped closer to the frame and gripped the pistol on her left side with her right hand. Looking down the long north hall, she saw Sister Frances, also sword in hand, standing erect with the sword touching her nose. She stood on tiptoe, chin up, eyes closed. Her breathing came in ragged gasps. Gail knew that the women were in the throes of the fever.

Very quickly, she stepped into the shielded doorframe, snapping the door behind her with her free hand. She hoisted the pistols while watching Frances trying to control the burn. Now that Gail was aware of the nearness of a Mortal male, she too felt her knees go weak as the sensation started scalding its way up her thighs. As her hands started shaking, she used her left hand to turn the latch of the old door behind her. She put the key into the back pocket of her stiff new jeans. She had to lower the gun and her head as the fever burned up her arms. She heaved, turning her head slightly to watch the north hall. On the sofa, Katherine's shudders intensified.

The long hall was pocketed with doors lining both sides of it. This was the nun's private housing wing of the sanctuary. The doors looked small against the vast height of the ceiling. Frances stood about halfway between Gail and the end of the corridor. She was still a full hundred feet from her aunt. As she tried to control the pain, Gail heard voices coming from the very end of the hall, coming down another hall that intersected this corridor. Frances dropped from tiptoes, slowly looking around to the far end, then back toward the door and the sitting room. Katherine was pulling herself up from her crouched position in front of the couch; she used the unsteady sword to help push herself to her feet, though she still used the couch as leverage.

Gail's scalp prickled painfully as the voices seemed to drift to her from far away. She could hear Sister Elizabeth's voice, high-pitched with concern. The sound did not seem to be coming closer. A man's voice was also in the mix of noise coming from the corridor. Gail's breathing slowly returned to normal, as she saw Frances move quietly from her hiding place. She moved slowly up the left side of the dim hallway. Thankfully, the fever in Gail was evaporating with each gasp of air that she took in. Katherine stood as still as a statue by the couch and stared at Gail. Her dark eyes seemed moist and bright as she watched.

Katherine asked quietly. "Are you OK...?"

Gail nodded at her, waving the pistol in her hands. She hoped she wouldn't shoot herself in the foot. Now deliberately smoother, basically faking it, Gail nodded more firmly. Katherine turned her dark eyes back to her mother, who was about three-fourths of the way down the hall. She had her palm firmly against the upright sword, holding it against her right shoulder. Francs walked soundlessly.

A man's voice carried down to Gail. He was saying, "Please..." It was softer, more pleading.

"Please...I need to speak to Gail..."

As the voice of the elderly Sister Elizabeth was lifted in protest, Gail froze.

It was Miguel.

Gail cocked the pistol in her hand, causing Katherine to look back at her in alarm. Her attention was immediately drawn back to the north corridor. Frances stopped as she, too, recognized the voice.

Sister Elizabeth's voice carried well as she argued solidly, "I'm

300

sorry...I don't know who you're talking about...There is no Gail here...You cannot go this way, sir!"

The pitch of her voice sounded louder as footsteps and shuffling sounds drew nearer to the opening.

As Miguel stepped hurriedly around the corner, he stopped in shock as Frances suddenly lunged toward him, sword raised for a strike. Miguel involuntarily threw up both hands as Frances closed the distance between them quickly. She jerked to a stop about seven feet from Miguel and held her poised sword toward him. The stop was so sudden that the tip of the blade still swayed.

The woman simply stopped as Miguel used his own Mortal Gift to turn the air around Francis into a wind trap that refused to let her move any further through it.

Miguel watched her with some concern as Frances froze in mid-stride and mid-swing. Holding his gaze steady, he spoke to her with ragged urgency.

"I'm not here to hurt you, Francis...I need to see Gail."

Frances' eyes tried to focus as she heard his voice from far away in time. He couldn't hold her much longer.

The scientist and Sister Elizabeth had frozen in place when Frances had launched her attack. Dr. Gorin stepped back slightly, hugging the corner block of the hallway intersection.

Frances was trying to move; her body trembled as Miguel concentrated. He was desperately looking down the hall past Frances. His voice was strained as he spoke to Sister Elizabeth.

"Where is your priest, Sister?...I want to call a truce under the bonds of confession." Miguel blurted out.

Frances, still standing with the sword poised in mid-swing, narrowed her eyes as Miguel backed away slightly. He let up the mental pressure on her somewhat as he took half a step backward. He hissed at Sister Elizabeth.

"Where is your priest?"

Elizabeth finally looked away from the woman frozen before her.

"Our priest is not here. He had business on the coast..." Elizabeth proclaimed.

Miguel let go of Frances slowly. Her arms sagged again with the weight of the sword pulling at her. Miguel looked desperately at Elizabeth.

She said to him quickly, "I can take your confession..."

As Frances lowered her arms, she scowled at Miguel. She could not touch him now that he had publicly asked for a truce. By tradition, she was bound to accept it. After all, they were all family. She hissed at him as he looked at Elizabeth. The old nun pulled at the collar of her gown as she withdrew a necklace with a small gold pendant that glittered in the dark hall. The huge, fat ruby in the center of it was surrounded by emeralds in an odd circular pattern.

Frances scowled at the old woman, her elegant face caught in a contemptuous sneer. Elizabeth, indeed, was able to take their confessions. She was a Guardian .

Katherine breathed deeply as the nun brought out the pendant. She looked at her mother's back nervously as Frances turned on her heel; clutching the sword. Francis gave her daughter a look of disgust. They would have to talk about it later, if there was a later.

Katherine knew her Guardian was dangerously close to interfering.

Frances snapped back around as Miguel picked up the diminutive Elizabeth by her elbows and propelled her backwards away from Frances. Robert Gorin stood hugging the wall behind him, still in shock at the nun's unexpected attack with a sword. His wide eyes went back and forth as Miguel disappeared down the hall and turned into a bathroom with Elizabeth in tow.

The doctor stared down the hall where Katherine stood, her sword pointed toward the floor. He glanced back to Frances and asked her in a shaky voice.

"Are you one of…them?"

Frances hissed at him, " One of whom?" She snapped it.

He seemed to flinch.

Gorin tried to explain quickly, "One of…of… the…um… Family?"

Francis almost spat at him as she turned on her heel and started walking back toward the seating room, where her daughter and niece stood. She hefted the sword onto her shoulder, coming down the hall casually as she frowned at Katherine. Katherine shrugged as if mystified and looked to Gail, who shook her head quickly. Katherine looked back to her approaching mother then at the scientist beyond her. Katherine felt a little disgruntled because she knew he was a human, and only God knows what Miguel had revealed to this guy, or how he had been caught up in all this.

Katherine absently shook her head, thinking of Miguel's crazy thought processes. Ever since he was a kid, he had been crazy.

The doctor stood away from the wall now that the armed nun was retreating. He shifted his weight nervously, watching her and the woman at the end who looked just like her. Well, almost.

As Frances neared the end of the hall, the door to the restroom came open and Miguel came out, with Sister Elizabeth following. The old Guardian was as pale as a ghost and seeing her face didn't make the doctor feel any better. They walked hurriedly back to the intersection of the halls. Miguel put his hands up to caution the doctor to go slow; no problem there. He stopped in front of Gorin as Sister Elizabeth went ahead of them, walking quickly toward the three women at the end of the hall. All of them were frowning at her. She walked as fast as her arthritic feet would carry her.

Elizabeth looked at Gail over the other two women's shoulders. She glanced nervously at a still sour Frances and a seemingly emotionless Katherine. She spoke directly to Gail.

"He needs to see you, Gail…He has information that some in the family…would kill for," Elizabeth swallowed hard.

Gail blinked , trying to not look surprised but failing miserably. She rubbed her limp wrist against her chin, the pistol still in hand.

"He asked for a truce…He confessed his sins." The old nun gazed upward at Gail, trying not to say too much.

Gail spoke slowly, her mouth dry as hundred-year-old dust.

"I'll see him now…Right here…" Gail responded.

She swallowed hard as her aunt and cousin both looked at her.

"Bring him here…If my family needs to hear this…then it should be heard by us all." Gail insisted.

Frances turned and looked at the two men down the long hallway. Gail looked too, still unsure if this was a trap.

"Only Miguel…Tell him to leave his boyfriend where he is." Francis retorted.

Elizabeth shook her head, refusing.

"No…no…He needs to come too." Elizabeth said quietly.

Gail showed surprise but the little nun's lips were pressed tightly together. She nodded at Gail silently, reassuring her that the human had to be included. .

Gail finally nodded back, agreeing to whatever this was. Having humans involved in any of this was a bad idea, especially since they killed the first prophet. In the two thousand years since, Gail had very little reason to believe humans had evolved much since then.

Sister Elizabeth turned to walk back down the hall as the women stood watching her. Gail holstered her pistol and wiped the sweat on her palm onto her jeans. She gripped the gun again, thought better of it and left it in the holster. She looked at Katherine's sword, feeling only slightly better.

Elizabeth approached Miguel as he watched the threesome. She spoke low to him, and he pulled Gorin along as he started in their direction. Sister Elizabeth walked behind them closely.

The old nun wouldn't have missed this for the world.

***

February 2, 7.43 p.m.

Morgan glared at the federal agent. . Napoliss glared right back.

From the front, Anna said, "If he kicks his foot one more time, cut his toes off."

Morgan smiled at him as she said, "OK."

Napoliss's eyes narrowed as he thought of going toeless for the rest of his life. Webster shook his head absently in the gloom of the dark Jeep.

From his place beside Maria, Doug listened to everything, seeing nothing. His thoughts were on his younger brother, the brother he hated, the brother that he worried for constantly. Doug hoped that they could save him. He glanced at the baby that Maria was holding. He hoped he could save them both. For the first time in his life, Doug regretted all those years that he did not 'believe'.

Knowing now that there was indeed a God filled him with no joy, only an infinite sadness he could barely contain. Doug knew, wholeheartedly, that he would die to save the brother he hated. God's presence had immediately humbled the young judge. Blessed are those who believe; he thought. Doug wanted to weep.

From behind him, Napoliss addressed a still smirking Morgan.

"Look…Why do you have to be so mean about everything? …We were just doing our job!" He sounded indignant, self-righteous.

304

Morgan blinked at his arrogance. Her face seemed to shift as she held his gaze steady. She knitted her brow a him.

Speaking softly, Morgan replied "We are also just trying to do our jobs."

At that, Napoliss virtually spat at her.

"Job?… Job? What the hell kind of job would that be?" Napoliss blurted in disbelief.

Morgan's eyes narrowed at him as a look of disgust cleaved her brow.

"You pathetic little human!… We are here to protect your existence!" she shouted into his face.

She had to resist the urge to kick him in the face. Instead, she became enraged.

"Fucking humans! Of course. there's always the question of who will protect you from yourselves!… Look at you!"

Morgan waved her hands fast and tight at the bound agent laying at her feet.

"Just look at you!… He gave you everything and you kill it!…The very water He brought you from has been poisoned by you little bastards!" her voice was a snarl.

Morgan crossed her arms, now huffing, her annoyance rose up and took over the silent interior of the vehicle.

"Your presence was supposed to humble angels! And just look what you've done!… You were just doing your JOB? … You make me fucking sick!"

Morgan glared at Napoliss as he squirmed on the floor. Beside her on the bench seat, Captain Edwards tried his damnedest to stare at only the blackness beyond the window. He too felt like a very small human.

Morgan continued, her anger barely spent.

"He gave you paradise, you burned it! He gave you life and death and still you deny his power? He gave you blessings as far as your imagination can take you, and you piss it away policing each other! That is your JOB Agent Napoliss!" She harrumphed like a disappointed mother.

"Tell us! Oh please, Federal agent man!…Do tell us, why are you here? Why would God favor any of you? …WHAT DO YOU BELIEVE? " Morgan taunted him.

Her beautiful face was contorted by her passionate anger, making her look feral. The moonlight gleamed on her bared teeth. She looked as if she

305

would like to launch herself at him.

Napoliss apparently thought the same thing, as he wiggled back, trying to put some distance between them. He dared not look away from her ferocious eyes.

The captain leaned closer to the window. He reached out for the spot that Anna had left in his mind; it immediately soothed him. Doug leaned up as he and Maria looked back quickly at Morgan. Matthew's face floated through Doug's mind: his own face, the face of his brother. His hatred for Matthew flushed through him, compounding his feeling of guilt.

From the front seat, Abby concentrated on the dark miles passing. Morgan stared down Napoliss, daring him to answer her.

The agent stuttered as he took a moment to think about his response. .

"I believe... I believe... we're all... um... going to die." Napoliss said in a voice soft with fear.

Morgan widened her eyes at his comment. Without warning, she snorted with laughter. From the driver's seat, Anna also burst out in a cold flat chuckle. The sound of it chilled Doug's blood.

From his place on the floor Napoliss asked numbly.

"Why is that funny?"

Anna answered as Morgan started shaking her head.

"That may just be the smartest thing you've said yet, Agent Man. " Morgan laughed harder without humorAs fast as the sound had burst forth, it faded as she once more glared at Napoliss. . The captain glanced at Morgan beside him , trying to find any trace of hope in her gorgeous face. He found nothing but the truth staring back at him. Facing down Satan was not a sure way to extend one's life.

Without being able to help himself, Edwards asked Morgan quietly, "What do YOU believe?"

Morgan looked at Edwards slowly, deliberately. She had a strange look of longing as she swept her eyes over him and spoke solidly.

"I believe also that we are all going to die. And I believe it is all my mother's fault. But at least I wasn't a damn Virgin when my life was sacrificed for human's sake! Thank God for that."

Morgan lifted a brow as Edwards blinked rapidly in consideration. He knew she was not trying to be coy.

From the front of the Jeep, Anna spoke to no one in particular.

"We're about fifteen minutes from the convent...I'm pulling over."

The truck slowed to a laborious stop on the shoulder of the dark road. Abby and Anna switched places and within a minute, they were again moving back onto the black top. Abby was sure handed at the wheel, familiar with his destination. In the passenger's seat, Anna laid the seat back as far as it would go. Her head came to rest beside a crowded Doug. They looked at each other and Anna winked at him. Doug blinked hard at the unexpected gesture but before he could respond, Anna closed her eyes and forced her breathing into a steady rhythm.

Anna reached out with her mind, concentrating on Gail. She could see her sister in her memory, and she focused on it, pushing her will into the direction of the convent. She breathed rapidly as she felt herself being pulled. Reality drifted away as her mind twisted through the night beyond. The sensation of uncontrolled flight made Anna's breath stop and her body trembled slightly at the effort. She quickly saw the priest's chamber; saw him sleeping heavily as she was pulled to the large plank door. Her mind was pulled through the wood and without warning she was looking out through Gail's eyes.

Anna moaned. In her mind she saw Miguel seated beside another man. Anna was shocked to see Miguel. Gail was focused on the other man and a moment of confusion touched both sisters as they became aware of each other. The awareness of Miguel triggered the fever in both Miguel and Anna, and Gail flinched as she felt Anna's pain enter her body.

Anna was aware of a dark presence close to Gail; not from the men in front of her, but from beside her. The sensations set off conflicting agony for Anna as she tried to roll her mind away from Gail, to spare her the fever.

Anna knew that she had just put her sister in mortal danger.

Through Gail's eyes, Anna saw Miguel look around as his body started jerking. Anna rolled away from Gail; the vision faded as Anna's mind once again snaked through the night. On the seat, her temperature skyrocketed suddenly and Doug watched as her eyes rolled back into her head. He instinctively pushed Maria and the baby back with his body, as Anna's teeth bared. Abby watched the road, throwing a few nervous glances as the windshield started fogging slightly. Before long, Captain Edwards and Morgan also strained to look.

Morgan immediately knew that a Mortal male had just triggered Anna's fever. Her own temperature was unaffected because she did not know where he was, or who he was. She knew Anna was scouting ahead, but had no idea where the danger was. She watched Anna, ready to help her break the connection if it was Michael. She was relieved to see her older cousin come back quickly into herself, holding her temples as the fever rolled into her forehead with a hammering effect. Anna tried to sit up, faltered, then lay back down as her scalp drew up into a million points of pain.

Abby slowed the Jeep, trying to decide if he should pull over. The humidity inside the truck was fogging up all of the windows. Abby swiped at his windshield, slowing even more as he tried to stop. The cleric rolled his window down trying to capture the cold air of the night in the opening. The wipers thumped uselessly as the dew formed on the inside of the glass.

Anna pulled herself first left, then right as her head came to rest somewhere between the passenger's seat and door. She relaxed into the seat letting the heat roll off her. Anna could see the stars and she focused on them as her breathing struggled. Her eyes teary and blank, she watched as one star seemed to be moving. Slowly, like in a dream she realized she was seeing a helicopter flying low in the dark night above them. Even as she was realizing what it was, the lights disappeared into the blackness of the night sky.

Abby kept the Jeep steady. He was relieved to hear her breathing returning to normal.

Chapter 24

Gail involuntarily sat forward and sighed as Anna slipped away from the edges of her mind. Although she had not felt the heat of Anna's fever, she had felt the pain as it registered in Anna's mind. Miguel watched her lean up and instinctively cover her mouth as she gasped.

He scooted toward her, anticipating that she might fall face forward. Because he was already in the presence of Mortal females, the fever that Anna triggered in him was no more than a flush of heat up his spine.

Gail unexpectedly slouched forward just as Sister Frances stood up abruptly on her left. The nun pivoted toward her niece and swung her heavy sword in a wide arc, aimed directly at Gail's throat.

Gail was still trying to shake off the effects of the mind link when she felt Frances' sudden rise. As the nun swung the blade, Gail instinctively started to rise also, her eyes still blurring. Miguel saw the trajectory and threw himself backward as the blade sliced the air in front of his face.

Gail never saw the blow coming as she half stood.

Instead of taking Gail's head, a glancing blow landed across her chest; directly across both breasts, bound tightly by the Kevlar vest. The blade hit the vest slightly broadsided and the Kevlar crunched under the force of the blow but did not slice all the way through. Gail's body pitched to the side and the sword slid across her unprotected upper left arm; cutting it all the way to the bone across the front.

She had not expected the assault and so Gail was flung backwards and to the right by the impact. Katherine had been sitting on the arm of the couch and as Gail was pushed over, she landed squarely on her cousin. Both women toppled to the floor in shock. Frances snarled in frustration as they fell, her eyes wild and vicious.

Francis could sense how near the others were, so with a savage growl she spun around, intending to take Miguel quickly.

Miguel had watched in horror as the two women were taken down with one blow. Robert was beside him and he panicked and jumped to his feet, just as Frances changed direction.

Gorin made a large target of himself, so Frances swung the blade at him. Miguel reacted without thinking, both pulling down and pushing on Gorin as he tried to pull past him. He got his arm around the scientist's body and screamed as the sword chopped into his elbow and forearm. Before he could scream again, Frances ripped the blade from his arm and swung at the scientist who was trying to disentangle himself from Miguel's arms.

This time her aim was true as she fully hit Gorin in his left side. He caught the blade between his hands as it hacked into him deeply, right below the ribs. He couldn't even scream as he felt his body almost sliced in two.

A gunshot exploded in the small room: a sonic boom that shattered the air of small stone chamber.

Gail extended her right arm and shot Frances in the head above her right ear.

The force of it staggered Francis as she pitched forward and back, although she didn't go down. She jerked her hands to her head, blindly. Frances was stumbling, trying to stay on her feet, when she was shot in her throat and chin. The second shot produced a sickening sound as the bones in Frances' lower face shattered. She blindly jerked towards the open hall of the north corridor and in the confusion, slipped quickly from sight as Gail was again thrown off balance by her struggling cousin..

Katherine was trying to scramble up from the floor, but her movement pushed Gail off herself and they both fell once more, entangled.

Gail rolled off her cousin, rushing back to where Gorin still stood.

One foot on the ground, one leg bent at the knee along the couch, Dr. Gorin was trying to hold his side together, though the sword was still stuck in his body. He was panting, tightly looking straight ahead. His mind refused to let him look down, even though he knew instinctively what had happened. Gail reached out to touch his arm as she stared at the sword with horror.

She pulled her hand back, not knowing how to help him.

Miguel sat on the couch curled up against the far arm. He too could not look away from the sword. He was only numbly aware of his own severely wounded limb that he cradled to his chest. He was bleeding profusely, but the faint blue pulses had already started electrifying the wound.

Katherine was crying as she brought herself off the floor. She held on to the couch as she became violently ill. Her stomach twisted impossibly hard as she realized that her mother had just betrayed them all.

Gorin faltered, almost fell, and gasped to no one in particular. "Oh, God... Please. Help. Me."

Each word was a gasp, hard and desperate.

Gail lowered her eyes as Gorin tried to focus on her. "Please... Please..."

The hand covering the wound let go and his bloody fingers reached for Gail. With no hesitation, she gripped his hand. As she closed her fingers into his , Gorin started to collapse. Throwing the gun to the couch, Gail used her other hand to hold his elbow as she tried to guide him onto the floor.

Miguel sat forward, getting his feet out of the way. He silently stared at the carpet, cupping his wounded arm. Gail could see that he was crying.

Gorin's eyes started blinking rapidly, looking back and forth from Gail to Miguel. He let out a terrible growl that turned into a moan. A spastic twitching came across his face as he broke into a dry heaving sob. Gail was right beside him, gripping his bloody hand in a pathetic attempt to comfort the man. Gail looked to Miguel.

Miguel swept his eyes down from the man's shoulders and shuddered at the sight of the tip of the sword protruding from his back. He looked at Gail in confusion, but she was looking at the floor and shaking her head. Katherine lowered herself into the seat across from them. Their eyes met across the space; he knew that her mother's betrayal had surprised her as much as anyone.

Katherine looked to the corridor where Frances had fled with a blank stare.

The blood Francis had left behind was wet and dark, not burning or even smoking. Katherine knew that her mother was already trying to heal. The heart had not been stopped. Without warning, Miguel picked up the pistol Gail had thrown down. Silently asking for forgiveness, he put the barrel to the back of Dr. Gorin's head and pulled the trigger.

Both Gail and Katherines jaws dropped in shock. Sister Elizabeth, sank against the far wall where she had stood silently.

The man was out of his torment, but their struggle was just beginning. The devil was loose and walked among them already on this night..

Miguel dropped the gun onto the couch beside him and started crying as the pain in his arm finally registered. Within a few minutes his arm would be functional.

Katherine stood, picked up her sword, and started after her mother. As

311

she came to the door, she stopped as Gail called to her quietly. She turned to hear the only thing that Gail could say.

"I love you Katherine. …Please, Be careful."

Katherine eyes watered as she heard the words. She opened her mouth to say something, but finally just pressed her lips together.

She couldn't look at Gail as she told her, "I love you, too."

With a curt nod, Katherine spun out the door and out of Gail's view into the north corridor. Gail looked helplessly at Miguel. As he stood up, still holding his arm, he smiled down at her. She grabbed his unwounded hand and kissed the tips of his fingers.

Now it was Gail's turn to tear up as he said softly, "Good luck, Gail…I'll see you after."

She smiled at him as tears spilled forth, unchecked. Before she let go of his hand, she addressed him a final time in a croaking voice.

"Thank you, Miguel." Gail said sincerely.

He winked at her. Without further comment, Miguel walked quickly after Katherine. He would make sure that her mother did not escape.

Gail looked at the dead body before her. There was no way she could leave the man's body like this. Sister Elizabeth saw struggling with his remains and went to help.

The two women silently bent to their task with the highest of respect. The old nun knew the man would be remembered as a hero among the Mortals.

Because Miguel had brought Dr. Gorin here, in just their few minutes of conversation, Gail had dared to hope for things she had not dreamed of for centuries. Though they had failed to protect him from their own, it was possible that the message he had brought would restart the evolution of both humans, and Mortals.

If either species survived this night, that is.

Hopefully there would still be some of them alive if they won this battle. Satan must be beaten, first. The baby would be arriving any moment and Hell would follow right behind.

Gail returned to Matthews's bedside to pray. The final battle had begun.

As she stepped towards him, a great vibration started under her feet. Before she could react, Matthew screamed from the bed, his good arm suddenly thrust upward.

Arching his back, eyes tightly closed, Matthew reached for the ar above him as he screamed.

"I accept life. …I choose only life! Oh God, please. I want to live!"

As he slumped back into a deep sleep, Gail ran to him before the shrug of the earth beneath them flattened her to the cold stone floor. .

***

From his exile in Hell, Satan trembled.

The long bondage of slumber was suddenly lifted as the Devil found himself awakening fully for the first time in two millinia.

From the bowels of the universe, a great thunder rumbled across vast plains of time. Every planet and star felt the vibration of it tremble their moons and mountains.

The words that echoed across Creation were immediately understood by everything it touched. Even the trees and insects heard it in their own known languages.

Satan cried out as the fire God had used to forge his soul erupted forth and the cry became a scream. A great weakness brought him to his knees, quite literally. . The burn of awareness that the fever brought to his spirt scorched his vile soul. No longer hearing his own screams, the boom of the voice in his mind threw Satan to the black sand floor with a power so great his own will was instantly taken by it.

With a roar that echoed through time itself, the thunder spoke.

"I am the Lord, Thy God. Thy life is mine to command."

The words split through the heavens and pushed past the planets in a terrifying vibration.

"Your own will be done! …Go forth, Children and seize the fruit of thy soul. "

As the sound shook through Satan, he grasped at the black sands around him. He remained for a long moment huddled within his own awareness. In a million eternities, the sand quit shaking but the echo of devil's scream went on and on. Around him, in the blackness, the shadows stilled as ten thousand demons took to unseen caverns, shaking and in pain. As his scream rolled away, the blackness stilled into a deep void. Satan trembled hard as he opened his eyes to nothingness. His empty eyes burned as tears of fire fell from them.

Satan instantly knew that the boy and the Guardian were now standing

313

on the same holy ground. He had been expecting it. The trauma of the event had made him reflexively extend his massive wings. With a struggle, he pulled them in and folded them around himself.

He missed his human flesh, the flush of sensations it triggered.

For the first time in thousands of years, the Satan was fully awake. He stood with a roar, once again extending his wings as he reveled in the awakening. The demons slipped from their hiding places, drawn by the call of their master. They swirled around him like frenzied shadows, their rough skin sliding harmlessly over his immortal flesh. He petted them, laughed at them.

His time had come.

Hunger filled Satan, then thirst. The thirst drove him to madness as he greeted his slaves. The devil smacked his lips in glee. Only one thing could satisfy the soul-searing burn. He smiled as his depthless eyes lightened in glee.

Once Satan had feasted on the baby's blood, he was going to take over the entire earth.

As he took flight from the nothingness of Hell and rejoined Creation Satan flew straight towards earth to take back his family and his flesh.

He could not wait to meet Anna. Again.

Chapter 25

The moon stared down on the massive iron gates, making them gleam dully in the night. The cold bright air froze the iron; the long, tapered bars stood locked together, blocking the jeep.

A security box was hidden in a recess of the wall, to the right of the gate. Inside the vehicle, the unusual group of travelers just sat and looked at the gate, silently.

Abby sat behind the wheel with Anna beside him. They looked at each other out of the corners of their eyes, and then both swept their eyes across the massive bar that slid between the two sections, locking it into place. These had been the original gates, built when the convent was new, needed to fortify it from a lawless river port. The solid iron bars were twenty feet high and stretched an imposing fifty feet across.

Abby broke the silence, his voice neutral and low.

"Well, I guess that leaves out ramming it, then?"

Anna half-grinned. She knew the cleric would love to try anyway.

They could use the call box and announce themselves, but Anna insisted they were walking into a trap; they all knew that she was probably right.

Morgan held her son close. She stared into his beautiful tiny face with true wonder as he slept peacefully at her breast.

Just the sight of the gates made her flinch, and in the silence, Morgan started to tremble. At first, it was just a quiver, and then fear began to roll across her in waves that lapped at each other. In reaction to the fear, she started to sweat heavily, and her tension was relayed to the sleeping baby.

The baby, unaware in a blessed slumber, began to stir and fuss as his mother squeezed him tighter. He was uncomfortable and agitated by her compulsive gripping; he roused more fully to let them know he was not a happy camper. Morgan juggled him from side to side, suddenly unsure of how to hold her own child.

She lay him down on her lap, and then put him on her shoulder. As he wiggled against her, she put him down on her lap once again. The baby tried kicking his tiny legs and mewing shrilly, still only half-awake.

In the brightness of the moon, the gates of the convent shuddered as the lock disengaged itself without warning.

The massive panels swung away from the car, slowly inward, seemingly all by themseves.

Anna and Abby blinked hard at each other.

Anna jerked upright and watched the gates as they silently removed themselves from their path. In the backseat, with the baby once more sleeping, Morgan stilled. She watched the gates in disbelief, her dry mouth tasted like cotton balls.

Both Maria and Doug turned from watching the gates inexplicably open to stare at Morgan. Almost immediately, their eyes were drawn to the baby resting on her lap.

Edwards simply stared at the boy with awe. .

Abby had the rearview mirror pointed at Morgan, and he watched as the others all turned their attention to her, then to the baby. He looked back at the gates, standing quietly open in the bright night. He glanced back into the mirror, wishing that he, too, could gaze at the baby.

Anna still studied the gates. She turned her gaze to Abby, who returned her questioning stare. Deliberately, Anna tilted her head sharply to the narrow road in front of them.

Abby turned on the headlights and rolled the Jeep past the gates. Once the car cleared the panels, the gate started moving fluidly and gracefully, closing securely behind them.

They were now on the grounds of the convent. The main building itself lay in shadows, nearly half a mile away. The lights from its many windows glittered to them through sparse trees ringing the building.
The main cathedral had the only windows that were fully lit in stained glass panels that were illuminated like a jewel from within. Doug, Maria, and the captain all felt the impact of its beauty. The federal agents , still in the floor, could not see what had left everyone speechless.
The Mortals felt the impact of what happened next, before their human companions did.

The fever hit them as it had only once before when the final curse was laid.

Affecting them all at the same time, the crushing on-rush of hellfire caused seizures so severe that even the strongest Mortals screamed out in agony.

The heat that seared their flesh traveled swiftly along nerve endings, turning their minds into an inferno of pain.

Awareness usually triggered the fever; however, this fever triggered awareness as the Children of Angels screamed in terror at the voice that cleaved into them. .

Abby slammed on the brakes as Anna violently jerked from her seat as it hit her. She started screaming and flailing so hard that Abby was screaming too, terrified by her pain. As the truck lurched to a stop, Morgan too, was screaming.

Edwards, stunned for a moment by Morgan's outburst, instinctively reached out and barely caught the baby as he was thrown from his mother's lap. Snatching the baby up to his chest, Edwads was trying to turn away to shield him. Morgan's uncontrolled jerking brought her hand up and her knuckles caught the captain squarely under his right jaw. Unable to hold them both, Edwards curled around the boy, as she clawed at the inferno inside her own head.

Kicking out violently, she caught Webster's foot with hers. He tried to squeeze back into Napoliss as the captain slid down into the floor with them, pressing the boy between his own body and the side of the Jeep.

The sky rumbled with thunder.

It said "I am the Lord, Thy God...."

At first, the vibration seemed to come from the Earth, itself, as it literally shook the ground. The crest of the rumble increased as the two women started to come from under the fever's hold, both of them falling into a giant weakness as the thunder seemed to envelope the earth and sky.

"Thy life is mine to command."

Over all the continents, the rumble shook the planet with massive force. In some places around the globe, the Earth shifted along fault lines; mountains trembled, and several ancient volcanos again sprang to life after a million years of sleep.

The waves of the oceans stopped as the vibration shook them flat. The terrifying rumble became a roar as all living creatures tried to shield whatever ears they had from it. It was impossible to block out.

"...Seize the fruits of thy soul."

In the Jeep, all the occupants hugged one another as the sound became an unbearable pitch. Their teeth rattled as they were shaken to their very

317

bones. Just when they were sure their very flesh would be stripped by the roar from the skies, it rolled away and was gone.

The profound silence that followed was almost as deafening.

Shaking, Abby lifted his head from the steering wheel. The only sound was the harsh intake of breathing by all the occupants of the Jeep; they sounded like they had just run a marathon. Quiet sobbing filled the void and the sound steadily increased.

Except for the baby, who smiled sweetly, all of them were crying. All of them were completely weak with terror and rattled teeth. .

The convent stood directly in front of them. From the corner of his eye, Doug saw a light flickering to his left that had not been there before. Trying to focus, he squinted into the darkness and saw small flames dancing, maybe a thousand feet away.

A few crowded trees made the shadows hard to distinguish. Doug squinted hard, trying to understand.

It took a moment for Doug to realize that he was looking at the crumpled remains of a helicopter.

***

When the fever seized them, Adam had been turning onto the final stretch of road leading to the convent. The sensation hit them all so hard and fast that none of them noticed as Adam lost control of the large sedan. As they all screamed, the car lurched away from its intended turn and rolled wildly across the intersection. An oncoming car saw them veer off course , just in time to slam on the brakes. The sedan bumped crazily into the far ditch as the other car screeched to a halt.

With very little impact, it rolled head-on into a pine tree that shuddered as it was bumped by the car, stopping its motion.

The hapless driver of the other car opened his door and took a few steps toward the sedan. As the full impact of the thunder hit, the man was thrown violently to the pavement as the earth shook beneath his feet. Trying to shield his head, the driver squirmed in mortal terror, forgetting the sedan on the tree. Even after the sound died away, he lay like that, as did most of the Earth.

The men in the car sat shaking and gasping for long moments after. They all avoided looking at each other.

The forest on either side of the road was awesomely silent; the very human sound of crying was actually a comfort in the silence. Could they have seen through the dark trees, they would have realized that all of God's creatures were huddled where they had fallen, most were also crying as well..

The terrifying thunder assured even the wicked that they had just witnessed an act of God.

By whatever name you may use to describe God, every heart knew His power.

Adam squeezed the water from his eyes, took a ragged breath, and gently put the still-running car into reverse. For several minutes the angle of the ditch refused to let them out easily. After some maneuvering, he put the car into drive silently, nosing it back onto the shoulder. Pulling back onto the blacktop, Adam was about to give it gas when the night exploded behind him.

From the night sky, a single bolt of lightning shattered the pine that the car had impacted. The top of the large tree was sheared off as the men jerked around in shock. Most of the treetop fell with a crushing boom down to the exact place where the car had been. Shards of broken pine pelted the car, raining down wooden shrapnel.

As the quiet aftermath descended over them, they looked at each other. None of them spoke. Adam touched the gas and returned to their path quickly.

Jerold thought it was a good night to die.

***

After Gail stopped shaking, she knelt beside Matthew to pray. The young priest had been pulled from his comatose state to semi-conscious awareness by the sound; he never realized that it was not a dream. He would almost achieve awareness but that would lead to an immediate slide back into his dream state. In his dream awareness, he heard Gail screaming, but no impression lasted long enough for it to become a clear thought. He drifted in a swirl of mellow oranges and yellows.

Matthew communed with the angel in his dreams. Well, one of them anyway; he didn't like the other one.

He started to shiver as Gail whispered unintelligible prayers for their safety beside him.

The one angel came to him in soft clouds; her beauty was warm and so alive. In his dreams, she sat with him as his body was racked with pain. When his shattered mind turned inward, she was always there, calming him. Sometimes when it was truly unbearable, she would cup both Matthew's cheeks lovingly and stare deeply into his eyes. In those moments, he would fly away from his body into a jewel-blue sky. Matthew tried to be strong for her, as several times she cried beautiful tears for him. He felt unworthy of her blessed tears.

She always said the same thing. over and over, "…God chose you. You are loved."

No one had loved Matthew at all since the horrible day he had caused the accident that took his parents lives. Even his own brother Douglas had turned away from him. The only person that had been willing to speak to Matthew afterwards, was Father Joseph.

The angel assured Matthew that he was forgiven.

He was grateful and humbled by her. She knew his sins but never judged him. Her kindness renewed his faith each time she comforted his fears.

She had wrapped her wings around him and held him as they both cried tears of joy. She whispered to Matthew that the blood of lambs would redeem him; and there would be no more sorrow.

He held on to the thought, desperate for that redemption. Desperate to not hate himself any longer.

In his more aware moments, Matthew wondered again…Why does that angel in his dreams look so much like Gail? As he faded back into a warm darkness, he again thought of the angel's eyes that were exactly like Gail's.

Gail begged God for courage. As she swept her eyes across the man in front of her, Matthew's eyes suddenly popped open. He was struggling mightily to stay awake.

Simultaneously, they smiled at one another.

Matthew said proudly, "I love you, Gail; every day."

He rolled away again as the smile left her lips. She stopped in contemplation and began to smile again. She held his limp hand and beamed. Miraculously, Gail felt all doubt leave her. The fear it caused was also gone in a rush; only faith remained.

Gail thanked God for His greatest miracle of love.

Chapter 26

Miguel quickly caught up to Katherine, following her mother's blood trail. They looked at each other without speaking.

Katherine shook her head. She followed the narrow staircase into the basement storage room with Miguel less than a step behind her, constantly glancing back to protect their rear. Both of them knew that the unburned blood must be followed. Miguel tried not to flinch at the small sobs that escaped Katherine every so often.

When the sound of the shattering earth reached them, it crushed them to the floor. They had just come upon the stairs and they both almost rolled down the stairwell as the seizures hopelessly entangled them. In the violent nature of their struggle, Katherine had accidentally stabbed Miguel in his right upper hip as her little silver sword flailed. Although not a serious threat to him, it was a large gash.

He actually didn't remember it happening; his mind had been consumed by the words of God. Hers, too.

In the quiet that followed, Miguel was silently thanking God that he had the chance to choose a different path before it was too late. As he had heard the words of the Lord, Miguel had been filled suddenly with a sure, overwhelming faith that he had chosen wisely.

He automatically thought of Michael and his old soul ached. Migual prayed. He knew in his soul that it was too late for Michael. , He didn't know what else to do except pray, and hope that his cousin, his one true confidant, had changed his heart before the thunder had struck.

Ignoring Katherine's small gasps, Miguel was lost in his own reverie, unaware of his own moaning. He knew Michael well, too well. Michael was the closest family he had left, since Miguel was an orphan, and had no siblings. He had been raised in Jerold's home and had been a small child when the young Morgan had fled from the murderers of her boy-king husband.

Miguel bore the distinction of being the last full-blood born to this world.

In his deepest soul, Miguel's heart trembled with sadness. He knew Michael would keep his promises, however misguided they might turn out to be, and now it was too late. He wondered if the humans understood that Judgment Day was at hand.

He doubted the humans understood at all. They never did.

The simple door that stood across the huge old storage space stood ajar, illuminating a path through the room. In the bright moonlight that spilled into the void they could see Frances' robe, crumpled and blood-soaked outside on the glistening grass.

Pushing quickly around shadowed shapes of forgotten boxes and furniture, the duo threw back caution and hurried their pace. They knew the baby had arrived. They pushed the pursuit of their quarry into the bright moonlight.

Because of their close relationship, Katherine was almost identical to Morgan physically. And in turn, Anna's close resemblance to them both had long prompted all of the Mortals to simply refer to them as 'The Triplets', even though they were all three from a different set of Mortal parents and could only be cousins, at best.

No Mortal had ever given birth to twins or triplets. Though they often wondered aloud about it, only God could know why.

The Mortals all looked alike, that was true, however; a few of their features always developed in slightly different ways. The nose, the chin, ears… Personality also was reflected in their individual features; where some had more of a pinched look, others were more supple or rounded. No matter the variation, all of them remained beautiful far beyond a human standard.

Miguel had often thought Anna was probably the most beautiful of them all, yet her constant scowls could be hard to swallow. He loved Anna dearly, but her intensity drove the others away. He often thought that she did it on purpose for the solitude.

Almost every family member, except Gail of course, wanted to kick Anna's ass. Anna, in return, let them all know they could try it anytime they got up the nerve. Everyone knew where Anna was, yet no one ever tried to find her. She preferred it just that way.

Miguel followed Katherine to the grove of trees on the far side of the convent. He tried hard to avoid staring at her resemblance to the love of his very long life. Miguel knew Katherine had long been in love with him for a millennia. She had never forgiven Morgan for being the one Miguel chose over her, even though Morgan herself rejected every advance Miguel ever made.

The tangled love lines of their family was a spiderweb of loyalties and broken hearts.

As Katherine hunted her own mother, she also looked at anything besides Miguel.

The trees were sparsely spaced, and no underbrush grew up to entangle them. The underbrush had been cleared to make it easier for the sisters and the guests to wander among God's creations. The trees embraced them under an umbrella of pines needles caught in the gold of winter slumber.

In the shifting shadows, Miguel watched as Katherine tracked her severely wounded mother.

He thought of Morgan as a frigid blast of air blew over him, unnoticed. The chill was not bothersome, but the gust pushed at him. Leaves and pine needles were scooped up into a startled, frenzied dance as he instinctively put up a hand to shield his eyes. The arm was nearly healed from Frances' earlier attack. As he put up his hand, he pushed his will slightly.

Though he could not stop the wind, he could direct the stabbing pine needles and whipping leaves directed at himself. He put his hand down as the objects slid past and around him but not into him.

Like their looks, the Gift varied for all of them, depending on family line. The curses made them weak, sure, for even they could not defy the laws of nature.

But after centuries of life, Mortals did learn to control their will and harness the power of the mind. Each full-blood Mortal child was born with the same mental gifts as their father.

The half-bred girls mimicked their Mortal mother's gifts. However, the half-bred males, mimicked their human mother's gifts, which was to say, they got none at all.

As Katherine stood up from her stooped inspection of the ground, the dimness of the loose canopy made her seem to be an exact duplicate of Morgan. Unheard over the wind, Miguel sucked in his breath. He had longed for Morgan though many lifetimes. Katherine did not need to hear his reaction to see it. She knew he saw her cousin in her face.

Katherine accepted that it was real to him at those moments. But she still hated Morgan for it.

She tried to ignore it as she asked," Should we split up?"

As she said it, the words were ripped from her lips by the rough wind and tossed to Miguel. Shaking his head to clear away the momentary vision, he frowned and shook his head harder. To be heard he raised his voice.

"No…We can circle back first…She may be trying to lead us away…" he said stiffly.

They both knew enough not to be led. They couldn't leave Gail unprotected or she'd be slaughtered, along with the Guardian.

A great sadness made Katherine's eyes close as Miguel waited for her opinion. He knew she was mourning what her mother had done. He felt outraged and sick that she had been forced into this position.

Reaching across to her, he gripped her thin shoulder, saying, "Are you gonna be ok?"

She smiled at him sadly.

"No." Katherine said into the wind.

Miguel smiled back, forcing Morgan from his mind.

He gripped Katherine's shoulder tightly in a true display of empathy before releasing her. He turned slowly, looking back the way they had come. Standing close to her, Miguel felt her stiffen as she watched the path in front of them.

Turning his head but not his body, Miguel also froze.

Morgan stood in the path before them in the moonlight, watching them. She held a baby to her shoulder.

As Katherine and Morgan locked eyes across the distance, Morgan slowed her hurried momentum and stopped dead in her tracks. The hand she used to support the baby's back also gripped a pistol. The other hand dangling below his tiny diaper held a sword pointed loosely toward the ground.

As Miguel turned his head toward her, Morgan turned her eyes to his.

A raw heat flushed through her groin and thighs. Far above the wind, they heard her keening moan as she gripped the baby tighter. The pistol slid from her grasp as she reflexively opened, and then closed her hand. The moan formed the words, "Oh my God!", as her voice faded into the gusting wind.

The fever made Morgan stumble, first forward slightly, then back.

Before Miguel or Katherine could move, she staggered to one knee at the upward flush of heat. Miguel's own fever did not trigger at all. Neither did Anna's as she rushed to Morgan's side. Miguel had already triggered Anna's awareness of him.

Anna snatched the baby from his mother as Morgn fell to her knees onto the soft earth. She never took her eyes off Miguel as she knelt quickly, giving Abby a clear shot over her head.

Had Abby not been trying to hold on to the pregnant woman at his side, he might have gotten that shot. When Anna ducked, he had already pointed the gun, bringing it level with Miguel's heart.

When they had left the Jeep, just a minute ago, Anna and Abby had started running for the convent on either side of Morgan and the baby, as Edwards, Doug, and Maria had run past them to the burning helicopter.

When they reached the tree line, the group had seen a pregnant woman in the wreckage desperately grasping at saplings to pull herself towards the lights of the church. They had run their group right into her, snatching her up as they went.

Diana's clothes had been torn in places from the impact of the chopper's hard landing. Pulling the survivor with them, they did not bother to make it easy for her as Anna and Abby basically dragged her behind Morgan.

The woman, who said her name was Diana, was already in full labor. Within moments along the trail to the church through the woods, Miguel and Katherine had appeared in their path.

As Abby aimed at Miguel and squeezed the trigger, the human woman beside him threw her body upright as she felt a thousand tons of nature dragging her upward, taking her breath.

The shot went wide, off to Miguel's right, biting into a tree less than two feet from him. The pine-bark shattered, and Miguel flinched at the chunks that sprayed over him. Seeing Morgan there had caused him to forget about shielding himself.

Abby cursed in Aramaic and tried to right himself as Diana folded into the ground.

As the shot rang out, Morgan tried to come up out of the fever. Her knees locked and she sat down again hard, her mind on fire.

Katherine, startled by the shot and their sudden appearance, threw up her arms, waving them wildly as she stepped in front of Miguel.

Katherine screamed at the cleric, "No! No! Stop!"

325

Abby leveled the gun at her. Diana's fall had pulled him down into a stoop. He freed his hand from holding her and stood up straight. Abby hesitated as Katherine stepped between shooter and target.

Abby blinked hard, looked at a duplicate of Morgan in the moonlight. It only made him hesitate further.

Anna was pulling Morgan up, scrambling to retrieve the dropped pistol. Even in her distress, Morgan was already feeling around for the sword that had fallen the other way. Anna leaned away from Morgan to retrieve the gun. l.

Katherine, hands still up, started rushing across to them. It was apparent to them all that she was protecting Miguel, using herself as a shield. Abby lowered the gun, glancing quickly down to Diana, whose face bore mute testimony to her suffering. She was crying, huge tears running down her cheeks as Abby tried to lift her by her arm. He prayed Allah would be merciful to this poor woman.

He did not know that Satan had already promised mercy for her, as payment to Michael. A promise easily broken.

As Abby pulled at the woman, she cried out in what could only be called a howl. Since the premature baby had not fully turned, the contractions tore through her uselessly as her body was tortured.

All the fury that God had unleashed in a whisper seemed to manifest itself in Diana; even though the woman had never given birth before, she knew something was terribly, horribly wrong.

Diana had tried all her life to be brave, like her namesake, the goddess of the hunt. Her father had always said she was more fearless than any son. As the cleric, who was a stranger to her, pulled her up, she completely lost any thought of courage. Or hope.

Diana honestly attempted to stand, but as her hips unbent the horrific pain exploded into screams that shook her.

In a whoosh of heat, she felt like her water broke again , and as she fell once more , Diana looked down at the unfamiliar sensation. Her light khaki colored maternity pants were awash all right, not with amniotic fluid, but rather with purple-red blood. In a gush, it soaked her pants all the way down to the ankle cuffs.

The literal torrent of blood made Diana become frenzied in her cries. The contraction was causing her to curl up, the crush in her abdomen cutting and clipping the screams as they kept coming.

Anna had stopped reaching for the pistol as Diana screamed out. The shrillness of the scream caused Anna to clutch the baby tight as she turned swiftly on bent knee. Her gold-flecked black eyes grew enormous as she too watched the impossible gush of blood from the woman.

Morgan sat swaying, legs splayed in front of her. She was shaking her head, shaking off the fever. The fever they had experienced in the truck had already left them all shaken. This one sapped her strength as she tried to focus on the screaming. Even though Diana was directly behind her, she knew the sounds of a woman in the throes of childbirth. Just three weeks earlier, Morgan had wanted to scream that same way during the birthing of her own son.

After Sara showed her the perfectly formed living male child, Moran did scream just like that.

Turning back towards Morgan, Anna fumbled with the baby and her own gun which she still held. Anna tried to shove him into Morgan's arms. She still flailed them weakly as her skin started cooling. Anna had to get to Abby and help him drag the pregnant woman inside.

It never occurred to Anna or the cleric to leave her behind.

Katherine, with Miguel one step behind her, was ten feet away from them when Frances stepped out onto the path, holding the sword that Morgan had lost. Anna was next to Morgan, although her head swiveled back and forth to check on Abby, Anna did not see the attack coming.

Frances had retrieved the sword from the trees and she stepped out beside them on the path. All the groups focus was behind them, so they were unaware of her presence for a split second.

Only Katherine and Miguel saw Francis emerge from the treeline.

Katherine stumbled as bile rose in her throat, cutting off the scream. None of the others saw Frances as she hefted the sword off the ground and brought it up to her shoulder like a golfer in full swing.

Katherine saw the tiny figure of a dark-haired human woman running right at her mother, though still quite a ways behind Abby.

Maria, coming from the opposite direction, had also seen Frances step out. She realized that the group was unaware of the threat, and she started running as fast as she could in the darkness. There was no way to get to them in time, so she started to scream at them to get their attention.

"Look out!" Maria screamed, as a shadow fell across Anna face.

Maria stumbled on something and hit the ground, hard, a distant witness to the carnage that followed.

The words had registered in Anna's instincts before her mind comprehended the threat; Anna snatched the baby from Morgan and started rolling with him curled into her chest.

The sword sliced at the exact spot where the baby had been, leaving no doubt that this was a direct attack on him.

The sword bit into Morgan's left thigh and she did not react as the flesh was laid open to the bone. Still shaking off the effects of the fever, she had seen Frances as she had swung the sword at her son. Without time to react, the wound itself was emotionless for her. In an instant, Frances withdrew the sword and took a short, measured hack at Morgan. Now that she had wounded her, Francis intended to finish it. Anna had flung herself and the child far enough away so that she was not within easy reach, so Francis went for Morgan's head, instead.

Morgan, still fever-weak, saw the second blow coming. Helplessly, she splayed her hand up and intercepted the blade with her palm. . It suddenly occurred to Morgan that Frances had just tried to kill her son; her baby, the Prophet, whatever he was, he was still her child.

As the blade cut deeply into her hand, a hatred welled up in Morgan so strong that all her features literally contorted with rage.

Morgan curled her wounded fist around the flat, fluted blade. Picking up her straightened leg, she twisted her hips around and used the side of her shin to sweep Frances' feet from under her. Morgn pushed on the sword as it cut deeper into her hand. .

Frances gave way. The blade twisting in her hand made Morgan gag, but she pushed harder. Just as Francis's feet flew from under her, Katherine and Miguel arrived from the opposite direction; within a heartbeat Katherine straddled the woman, battering her.

Morgan, her leg and hand bleeding profusely, used her shoulder to push Katherine off her mother. Her lame leg forgotten, Morgan went for Frances' throat as Katherine was pushed back to Miguel's feet.

When the attack had happened, Abby at first tried to cover Diana with his body. His gun had fallen into the folds of his robe as he crouched beside her. In an instant, Morgan had caught the second blow and taken Frances down. Abby knew the first blow had made contact, but he was not sure how badly Morgan was wounded. As he watched her scramble and push her way onto the fallen Francis , he saw the wound to her leg had exposed the bone.

328

In his own body he felt the pain of it; he felt its agony in his heart.

Morgan apparently didn't feel it, or didn't care; either way, she did not hesitate as she went for the woman who just tried to kill her baby.

Frances was literally being shaken like a ragdoll by the enraged mother , yet she was smiling. Francis and Jerold understood each other. They both longed for death; in her mind Francis wished Jerold luck.

Morgan picked up the sword with her free hand.

Katherine started screaming and bucking against Miguel as he held her to his chest. He knew it was best this way. If Katherine lived, she should not have to remember killing her mother by her own hands. Frances made a half-hearted attempt to ward off the blow. Morgan sank the blade deep into her chest as she thought about her son.

Her son. The Prophet. The Savior. His son.

Morgan spat into her face as she killed her.

Frances went slack under her, and then jerked upward to meet the blow. Katherine screamed and clawed at Miguel's hands. She kicked back with her feet, but he held her fast until her strength ran out.

Morgan hauled herself off quickly as heat started rolling off Frances' body. Her leg didn't seem to work properly and she finally felt the ghastly pain.

Katherine collapsed as the smoke rose from her mother's body with tiny hisses and splats.

Abby helped Morgan back to a seated position. The shock of both fevers and the blood loss, the unexpected killing of her aunt, and the pain of it all, was too much.

As Frances' hair licked into blue-yellow flames, Morgan's mind went numb from shock. She began blinking slowly, as if in a dream.

Anna was picking herself up and Abby left Morgan's side to help her with the baby. As Anna came to her feet, she passed the struggling baby to him. Checking her pistol quickly, Anna took in the horrible scene; one body on fire and another body racked by convulsions. Anna squinted at Diana, trying to understand the woman's injuries.

Morgan's blank eyes stared directly across the distance into Miguel's, as he held her virtual twin. To Morgan, time seemed to stop, and the shock pushed her into a soft place where this was not happening.

Diana had lost consciousness where she had fallen. Maria knelt beside her; the woman looked bad, very bad. Her skin was cold to the touch, but she was breathing.

The white-blue electricity flooded through Morgan's hand, and her thigh.

Having hung back slightly to inspect the chopper for more survivors, Edwards, Doug, and the federal agents came up the trail toward them at a run.

Edwards, propelling Napoliss by his elbow, breathed, "Oh my God!" as he automatically counted the fallen: Morgan, an unfamiliar pregnant woman, and a man and woman he did not know.

Edwards stopped and freed Napoliss from the tape that bound his wrists, as they, too, gazed at the burning body.

Webster saw the palm print in his mind on the wall of the stairwell in St. Mary's, and the smooth skull on Joseph's bed. He knew whatever internal fire that Francis burned with, was the same force that had scalded a perfect print into stone.

Anna grabbed a large portion of Frances' robe that was not yet burning. The dead woman lay horizontally across the trail. With a heave, Anna twisted her and slid her over to the side of the path to clear their escape route. She tried to be cognizant of the woman's daughter, who was still watching. Anna tried to throw her as gently as possible.

Anna had no idea that Father Timothy also watched her from the forest . In the darkness, his eyes opened unnaturally wide, as Satan watched through them also. The priest's large frame twitched in the dark as he watched Anna through the trees. In his stricken mind, Timothy saw that it was the face of his angel; the angel who loved him.

Chewing viciously on his lips, Timothy's mouth watered.

Satan's thirst had become a raging fire. He could have slipped into the priest's body but he dared not. If Timothy were killed, he would be sent back to hell with him. . If Timothy lived, it would only be for minutes, as Satan's soul of fire would consume the human body rapidly. Even Satan had to play by the rules.

Timothy grinned in the darkness; soon Satan would be the one making the rules. Satan pressed his will just enough to use the flesh of Timothy's eyes to watch the horror unfold with glee..

The smell of burned flesh enveloped the woods. A look of rapture crossed Timothy's face as he watched Anna from afar. The priest knew that he had been blessed. He never was aware of the fact that he'd gone insane.

In the bright night, a phone rang out, alien and shrill.

Startled, Miguel answered his phone on the second ring. The group watched him, unsettled by the unexpected noise. Katherine stilled her quiet sobbing to listen.

Trying to control his voice, Miguel said into the phone, "Yeah?"

He looked at his feet as he said "Yeah…OK…Wait for me at the gates. I'll be there in ten minutes."

He snapped the little phone closed and looked at Anna, who stared at him openly.

"Michael… and Jerold…Are pulling to the gates now."

Anna's heart burst, but she was so still that even her breathing seemed to cease. She looked down at Morgan, knowing the healing had already begun, knowing she couldn't carry her.

Morgan jerked her head around to Anna almost screaming, "Run!… Take him… Run now!"

Without a moment's hesitation, Anna grabbed Abby by the arm. The cleric tried resisting, gripping the baby as Anna hauled him into a trot. He twisted in her grasp, looking back at Morgan as Anna almost dragged him by the sleeve of his robe. Once past Miguel and Katherine, he gave up trying to turn around and started to push past her. On the trail behind them, the rest of the group was trying to pick up Diana and Morgan. Miguel prayed they had even five minutes.

He knew Jerold would not wait long.

No one saw Timothy, angling through the darkened trees to intercept Anna and Abby.

Chapter 27

Jerold and Michael stood in front of the large sedan, studying the gates. Adam stood beside the driver's side door, also inspecting the gates with rather subdued awe. They were massive. The only other time any of the men had been here before, they had been invited guests and the gates had not registered as an impediment. Jerold was unaware that the one person who had been expecting them was already dead in the woods. The gates stood locked, silently mocking them. A savage gust of wind ripped at them fiercely, though none of the three paid attention to its cold presence.

Without warning, the security box burst into flames and the bolt locking the panels together slid back with a soft scraping sound. They were all so stunned that none of them so much as flinched as the gate started swinging slowly away from them.

Michael knew that SHE was beyond those gates. He silently cursed Miguel, frightened by the consequences of his betrayal. Michael didn't know exactly where Miguel was, but he felt his presence nearby. When Jerold found out about Miguel's change of heart there was going to be hell to pay.

Michael knew that his cousin could not undo it now, even if he wanted to.

Michael had struck a deal of his own, one where changing your mind was not an option. Judgment had been passed. The only thing Michael could do now was to make sure that he was on the winning side. His part of the deal was going to be quite impressive; after all, as the Devil had paid highest of all for his cooperation.

He flinched as he thought of Morgan. He feared and loathed Morgan's gift of fire.

Michael turned his head towards Morgan's father.

Jerold watched the gate open fully and stop before he turned and grinned at Michael. The younger man tried not to grimace. Jerold nodded and turned abruptly around, walking past Adam to return to his chauffeured seat in the back of the car. Adam was rubbing his chin while inspecting the gate and he and Michael just looked at each other in consternation.

Michael turned around quickly, going back to the passenger's side front door. As he walked, he watched the ground while thinking about Jerold's suicidal glee.

The Mortals, like humans, could go truly mad. Like humans, the Mortals also were very paranoid of the insane. In his logical mind, Michael knew anyone suicidal must surely be insane; yet even as he disapproved of his uncle's death-wish, he understood it. He understood only too well.

Jerold had been millennia old before Michael had even been born. The thought of living so long could make any one insane.

Unlike Jerold, Michael had no wish for it to end. It was change that he was after. As he opened the car door, he saw Anna in his mind wearing a red fringed dress, dancing like a poetic demon. When this night was over, Michael intended to rule the Earth. It was not the heavens he wanted, he'd never seen the heavens and had no wish to; all he had ever wished for was this existence. A life with HER.

He became angry. The angels had taboos that humans held too. Some things were just against the law of natural order.

Michael thought of all that had been forbidden to him. When he reaped his reward, he would offer the Earth to Anna. When she refused it, as he knew she would, he would have the power to command her soul.

Through the blood of the baby, all the angels in Heaven could be commanded; all the angels on Earth as well, including Michael.

Michael made sure the new rules were slanted in his favor. He never realized he had already been tricked into slavery. In his rush to have her at his will, he had forgotten that the Devil never bargains fairly.

Adam drove the car past the silent bars of the gate.

***

In her room, Sister Elizabeth wrote in her journal. She recorded the secrets of Robert Gorin and his sacrifice. She wrote quickly of Frances' betrayal and of those who hunted her. She knew not yet of the woman's fate. The old nun shuddered there in her chair. Sister Elizabeth had suspected Francis of being suicidal, for years.

In secret, when Katherine confessed, it was apparent that she, too, had suspected something. They never speculated about what it was that

333

disturbed them both, but they did discuss fleeing sometimes. Katherine talked her out of it many times, and Elizabeth knew why. It was the church. Katherine would never leave it.

After her husband died years before, Elizabeth had given into Katherine's charge and joined her at the convent. She had never regretted it. The old woman felt at peace here with the faithful.

Elizabeth wrote of Gail and Matthew. She smiled as she thought of those two. Some things she didn't write down, knowing that life worked out in funny ways. Elizabeth did not know if the priest understood that Gail was in love with him.

Elizabeth paused over the tattered old journal as she thought of the baby.

She wrote about the thunder.

She wrote down every detail that she could think of that remotely related to the baby. She knew that he would be here soon.

Elizabeth thought of Sara in that confessional.

Because the FBI now had the Book of Joseph, from the Chronicles of Gail, Elizabeth did not know if Joseph had been able to bear written testimony to the boy's birth. She wrote down the story exactly as she heard it.

Elizabeth

Had the shot not rang out, Elizabeth may not have heard the screams that followed. The wind, already howling, would have masked it.. She laid her pen down sharply and got up on her old feet. Going to the shuttered window, Elizabeth listened to the eerie cries. The horror they conveyed shook her wise old soul.

She hid the journal in its hole in the stone wall.

Going quickly to the door of her private bed chamber, Elizabeth listened. Opening it, the nun scanned both ways before stepping out and then rapidly closed it behind her. She walked on arthritic feet, as fast as they would carry her to the young priest's room.

Elizabeth knocked lightly. She jumped in surprise as Gail threw open the door and leveled the pistol to her nose.

Gail blinked, in shock at what she had almost done. Just as her elbows locked upwards, she reversed their direction, lowered the gun, and took one step back.

Very calmly, Elizabeth said, "Someone outside is shooting and there are screams…"

Gail wrinkled her forehead as she looked into the grey eyes of the smaller woman. The wind carried more screams that peaked into mournful howls.

Gail lowered the gun. "I know," she said.

She pulled the old nun into the room and slapped the door shut behind them. Returning to her perch beside Matthew's bed, Gail sat rubbing her lip and calmly considering the young priest she loved.

Matthew slept soundly. When the thunder had smashed all of creation, the wound to his useless right shoulder had vibrated violently along with everything else. Fresh blood had seeped into the large bandage, slowly blotting dark, wet spots.

Elizabeth waited by the window but stepped back as the shutters rattled hard against their latches. As the wood creaked from the onslaught of the frenzied wind, the old woman turned and went to the opposite side of the bed. She stood over the young man, looking at his slack face.

Quietly, the nun said, "Is there anything you need?" Elizabeth shifted as she avoided eye contact with Gail.

Gail understood that she could not offer to help. Only one Guardian would be allowed to intervene.

Gail looked back to her beloved Matthew.

Now avoiding eye-contact as well, Gail chose her words carefully.

"Well, for one thing, take out your crucifix."

Gail wanted Elizabeth to be identifiable by the other Mortals. Perhaps they would not kill her if they knew she was a Guardian. . She displayed the necklace; the emblem of the Guardian gleamed in the candlelight of the small room. Gail found the light comforting.

Softly Gail continued.

"I suppose the sitting room would be a good place for you to be, sister…A good place to…'observe'…before they can get to the door. You can ask their names personally, so that your journal remains detailed."

Elizabeth brightened. Asking their names would alert Gail before they could pounce into the room.

Not that Gail would, or had, asked her to interfere. She smiled at the woman.

"I think I'll do just that." Elizabeth said softly.

335

Gail smiled back at her like a fellow conspirator.

Elizabeth crossed herself and leaned down slowly, putting her old cheek to Matthew's forehead. She smiled again at nothing as she allowed herself to linger.

With a wink at Gail, Elizabeth turned and neatly disappeared out the door. Gail studied Matthew's bare feet, free of the blanket. Sighing, she got up and threw the bolt on the large door. Going to the table, she plucked the small bottle of baby oil up from the assorted medical debris.

Matthew's feet had become dry and cracked in his extended weakened state. Gail took off the tan jacket, exposing the double shoulder holsters fitted around the Kevlar vest. She rolled up both of the overlarge cuffs on her borrowed shirt. To calm herself, Gail anointed Matthew's feet with the oil. As she rubbed the moisture into the dry flesh, the smoothness of the motion soothed her.

The wind battered at the shutter as she prayed.

Clearer than before, but still a mere whisper, Gail clearly heard her mother's voice say, "Run!" "

She blinked back tears, her hand still resting on Matthew's foot.

Without meaning to, Gail remembered the cold blood of Jesus of Nazareth dripping onto her cheek and her hair. …as the women around her flailed in agony. They had all reached to touch his impaled feet.

Gail rubbed Matthew's feet in a gently hypnotic motion. She stopped as a baby's cry pierced the volatile winds. The prophet was here!

Without warning, the wind stilled with the cry. Its sudden cessation was abrupt and complete. Gail watched the shutters and she let go of Matthew's feet. Reaching behind the one chair that still remained in its original position, Gail shoved aside the empty duffle bag and retrieved her small but deadly sword. She returned to the bedside chair and sat as still as a statue. Her gaze was now focused on the door.

The total silence of the night chilled her. Gail prayed that the baby was still alive.

***

As Anna fled away from them with Abby and the baby in tow, Edwards and Doug watched them for only a moment. Edwards removed his small pocketknife and grabbed Webster by his still duct-taped hands.

Over the wind, the captain shouted at him, "Get inside the convent as fast as you can!" With no further ado, he sliced the tape neatly, freeing the relieved federal agent. .

Before Webster could even draw down his hands, Edwards shoved the small knife to him. He shouted loudly, "Get your partner and go!"

Edwards went to Doug, who was trying to help the bloody, pregnant woman. As Webster cut the bonds of Napoliss, Doug hefted the unconscious woman while Maria steadied her head. Edwards reached for Morgan, still sitting flat on her butt, in shock.

Edwards was glad to see the glazed look had somewhat left Morgan's eyes. Ahead of them, Miguel had reached out to Morgan as well, trying to help her stand.

Sister Katherine rose slowly. As the agents ran past her, she paid them no attention.

Katherine watched her mother's body burning. Aided by the wind, the flames had consumed Francis rapidly and completely. . The blue-white flames sometimes burst into a sudden yellow, only to sparkle back to white. Katherine involuntarily sneered at Morgan as the men helped her to her feet.

The sneer disappeared when Katherine saw the wound in Morgan's thigh gape open, splashing fresh blood in uneven spurts even as a fresh burst of blue white lights also seemed to spill from the wound as she tried to heal.

As the men tried to lift her to her feet, Morgan gasped with her mouth hanging open; involuntary tears filled her eyes as she made a weak cry into the savage wind.

Katherine felt the crushing horror of what her mother had done. She had secretly known for years that her mother was probably suicidal. Never once did Katherine think she would go this far.

The heart of a Mortal that is pierced always brought death. Any other wound they could heal.

However, anytime the intent was suicide and the wound self-inflicted, even a blow to the heart would not do it. The human heart God had cursed them with would simply gape open and bleed.

If the other Mortals did not finish them off, they could walk around that way for years, and indeed centuries. God would never allow the children of angels an easy way out of life on earth.

Katherine knew why her mother had volunteered to kill the boy. Even with its purpose clearly defined, it was a suicide mission. Satan had promised Frances mercy in return. She would have been his slave instead.

Jerold had made the same nearsighted agreement in exchange for a single death. But he had offered far more than Francis had.

Katherine turned her head to look at Morgan. The men were clumsily trying to drag her and hold her up at the same time.

The identical faces locked identical eyes. Morgan's head lolled as they shuffled her forward. She never broke the gaze. . Passing Katherine, Morgan mumbled, her tongue feeling swollen.

She said to Katherine's face, "I'm so sorry…"

A look of hatred contorted Katherine's face as Morgan's own broke into a horrific mask of sorrow and pain. The shuffling of her badly wounded leg was almost more than she could bear. She knew her cousin Katherine already hated her for Miguel's choices and she knew, in her heart, that their family bond had been broken forever. Morgan loved Katherine, always. She regretted the way it had all turned out. Because of their startling sameness, Morgan had always been fascinated by her cousin.

As the men carried the wounded Morgan past Katherine, Doug rushed a step behind them, still carrying the petite pregnant woman. Before turning to follow them, Katherine looked at her mother's body one last time. The face she shared with her mother was now charred to the bone of the skull.

Katherine hoped Morgan would live to face the Devil.

As she turned to follow the others, the baby cried out in a scream that only the newly born can make, both terrified and confused. Though the sound lasted for only a second, it seemed to roll forever into a devastating abrupt silence.

The wind left the trees as if it had never been there in the first place. The sudden stillness made everything alive stop in startled reverie. For an eternal few seconds, nothing moved.

The baby did not scream again. Anna did.

Chapter 28

Anna and Abby broke through the tree line, still two hundred feet from the front right corner of the convent.

A gentle upward slope of grass was all that stood between them and their goal. The moonlight was intense in the clearing ahead and flooded the grassy area so that they could see their path clearly.

Abby and Anna ran for their lives as fast as possible, desperate to get the boy to Matthew. .

Just past the last tree to the right, Father Timothy stepped directly into the path in front of them and swung the broken limb like a baseball bat. He directed it upwards, deliberately aiming the limb at Abby's head.

The cleric had the baby folded into the gathers of his robe sleeves when the limb hit him squarely in the face..

Anna was so close behind Abby that their heads were nearly in the same space as they ran. Her slight height advantage put her nose to the right side of his crown. Guns in both hands, Anna pushed Abby's back from behind with her chest. He knew that she was literally using herself as a shield.

As the limb arched at them, Anna instinctively grabbed Abdullah around both shoulders and tried to twist herself around him.

Abby still took the brunt of the impact as Timothy stepped into the moonlight. . Instead of taking the blow directly across both cheekbones, as had been the aim, the branch caught Abby's right cheek and jaw. He distantly heard his own face shatter in unison with the blow that also hit Anna in the head, splitting her scalp above her ear.

Abby's head was thrown back into Anna's face and as the branch impacted her also, the back of the cleric's skull shattered her nose.

Their momentum and the blunt force of the unexpected assault threw both of them off their feet. Both Anna and Abby were pitched backwards as the baby, its forward momentum unstopped, flew straight out from Abby's arms as he reeled backwards.

As the startled baby flew through the cold air, he screamed at the sensation of uncontrolled flight. Pitched forward into the clearing, the baby dropped and then slowed, almost suspended in mid-air as the sound of his cries seemed to dangle with him in a sudden stillness.

The violent wind stopped completely; the baby floated downward slowly to land softly on the cold ground.

The silence of the wind dying was immediate and profound.

Father Timothy stopped as the wind stopped. With eyes unnaturally wide and reflecting the yellow of hellfire, the priest and his shadow watched the nearly naked baby burst from Abby's sleeve and then gently touch the earth.

The small baby's exposed skin was flushed a warm healthy pink. The freezing blanket of dried grass where he landed started smoking in humid puffs as it immediately started thawing visibly around the child.

The baby kicked the gentle stillness with a tiny cooing sound.

Timothy blinked his yellow tinged eyes hard at the miraculous landing before he swept his eyes over the still outstretched branch.

The priest thought, 'Wow!…That was cool! '

Timothy had enjoyed hearing Abby's face collapse. He looked at his two victims. He giggled as he threw down the limb.

Both Anna and Abby had been laid on their backs by the assault. Abby lay motionless where he had fallen. Anna had unknowingly brought her hands up to her shattered face and head. For a long moment, she knew nothing. The moment lingered; the blow had injured the brain itself. Her eyes and senses were filled with the tiny shards of light, already stitching her back together.

After the wind died, the complete silence finally made its way into her awareness. The pain awoke her memory as her brain and nose started fusing itself together again with a terrible burst of agony. The wounded soft tissue in her head healed rapidly.

The bones around it would take more time.

In Anna's newly repaired mind, an image of the boy forced her battered eyes to snatch open. For the first time, she saw the priest who had hit them.

Father Timothy was looking away from her, into the clearing. Anna knew in her gut that he was looking for the baby. She tried to roll her shoulders as she winced at the pain. She saw Abby lying motionless beside her as her eyes began to clear. His head was turned away from her, but his entire body was slack.

Anna's heart broke for Abby; she refused to look at him again. She stared up into the tree canopy and the clear sky above the clearing. She tried to focus as the itching in her nose became acute.

Not able to pick up her shoulders, Anna rolled them instead, twisting her body away from Abby's while watching their attacker.

The priest walked into the full moonlight. Anna's arms weren't responding as she twisted again and saw the baby lying in his path.

A light warm mist had formed over the grass in the clearing and the baby seemed to be suspended on a wispy moonlit cloud of it. The grass around the child was not only thawed, but green shoots had began to appear in the golden winter hue of the otherwise dead lawn.

Father Timothy stepped up next to him and looked down with awe on the unaffected infant. From her place on the ground, desperate to get up, Anna screamed out without meaning to.

The sound startled the priest for only a moment, and he looked back at Anna's helpless struggle, smiling widely. She flailed on the ground beside Abby's stillness. Sure that she was no longer a threat, Timothy focused on the baby lying before him.

Stooping quickly, the priest picked up the tiny infant as Anna's helpless scream intensified at the dawning of her failure.

Cradling the baby to his chest, Father Timothy's eyes glowed with yellow light and pulsated in the darkness. The baby's loose-skinned forehead wrinkled as the flickering eyes mesmerized him.

The man gasped as the tiny baby smiled hugely into his face. The calm grin was toothless and wide, making his captor almost tear up at the beauty of him. The boy blinked hard, watching the yellow light dance behind the priest's eyes.

Still flailing, half blinded, Anna managed to put her hands to her shattered nose as she screamed at Timothy's retreating back.

Timothy started humming as he embraced the child and casually walked across the large sloped lawn to the corner of the convent, intending to walk to the back of the structure and through the unguarded rear entrances.

Anna's scream came to an abrupt end as she used her breath to focus on heaving herself up, instead. Every movement of her head sent a dizzying shockwave over her, making her gag. She willed herself to not hear her body's screams of protest. As Anna finally came to her knees, gripping the

341

tree, Napoliss and Webster ran up to her.

Webster went to Abby whom still had not moved. Looking for a pulse, Webster , fingered Abby's throat under a sagging shattered jaw. He felt nothing. Looking at Napoliss, who had given up trying to help Anna, the older Fed shook his head slightly. The younger man flinched.

Napoliss didn't believe these women at all, but even he knew whatever this was, the stakes had just been raised to lethal.

Webster had known instinctively that the women were telling at least some of the truth. The image of Sara's handprint haunted him. Unlike his partner, Webster's heart, though tough and suspicious, was humble.

The handprint on the wall had humbled him. The tears had sprung to his eyes upon first seeing it, all doubt left his soul. The tears came from knowing, surely and soundly, that there was something bigger than him; something BETTER than him.

Webster realized with a start that the baby was not with them.

Looking around quickly, he saw the back of the retreating priest who seemed to be holding something small and precious. His jaw gaped as he realized what it was. Webster was immediately sorry that he had been a doubter.

Looking down at Abby, Webster's mouth worked soundlessly as he saw the gun in the man's limp hand. He focused on it. The renegade priest was disappearing around the building as the agent snatched up the gun. Napoliss was once again trying to help Anna regain her balance. The woman weaved drunkenly, grasping for support.

Webster ran after the man with the baby.

Realizing that the baby was gone belatedly, the younger agent asked her loudly, "Where's the baby?"

Anna pointed blindly, her newly repaired facial muscles working oddly. She gritted the words through clenched teeth.

"There! There…He took him! …" She shrieked it.

Napoliss finally noticed the priest as he disappeared around the corner with Webster already running after him.. His partner had already closed half the distance. Napoliss reached down and retrieved one of Anna's loose pistols and ran to back up his partner. Anna gripped the tree, barely standing. She stumbled as she tried to follow and grabbed the tree harder.

She was having a lot of trouble keeping her eyes open long enough to follow their path.

Anna stood there in the moonlight, awash in shame. She had failed. The less she moved, the faster she healed. She tried to simply remain still a moment, to get her bearings.

The blessed and sanctified human hands that Satan needed to kill the baby held the boy, even now as Anna stood shaking, helpless.

She looked down at Abby's still form. Knowing she was going to stumble anyway, she fell in his direction; with her knees bent, she put her hand directly to his wounded face. She knew he could not feel it.

For the first time in a thousand years, Anna prayed.

From her still-bloodied lips, she said softly, "Allah be merciful to this man, he is loved. Have mercy." "

Anna cried moonlit tears from the black-flecked golden depths of her eyes. She kissed Abby's face as she felt her knees strengthen. She was healing very rapidly now; well, her body was anyway. She knew her heart would stay broke forever. From the gloom of the trail, Edwards and Miguel emerged with a now slightly limping Morgan still between them.

The three had seen Anna and Abby illuminated in the moonlight as they approached the clearing. Just outside the shadow of the tree line, it was very apparent that Anna was praying. Still touching Abby's face, the woman had lifted her head to speak directly to the full moon, to cast her words directly to the heavens above her.

Whatever color Morgan had gained since she was wounded, was lost as she saw Abby's still form on the ground. Almost at a full run, Morgan nearly fell, then slowed completely. Edwards and Miguel, feeling her pull back, unthinkingly grabbed her from either side again propelling Morgan forward.

She was literally being dragged to the horror she knew she didn't want to see. Morgan tried to stop but they pulled her forward. Her eyes froze on Abby and she finally leapt forward towards him on her still-throbbing leg. The reality of his utter stillness sank in, and Morgan screamed as she pulled at him clumsily.

Anna turned to face them. Morgan collapsed beside her and started pulling at his head and shoulders, seeing the massive wounds.

Staring at his face, she gasped, "Oh God…No! Abby please no!…Oh God, baby!…No!"

Abby never responded. He could not heal as she was doing even now. When the lightning started, Doug was barely clear of the trees.

***

When Father Timothy picked up the baby, from his shadow Satan laughed into the void of nothingness that he was. From the shadows of the priest's eyes, Satan squealed in glee. The pig-like sound of it echoed faintly in Timothy's own ears, exciting him.
Satan backed out of the shadows of the man's insanity but left images in his mind to hold him and bind him to his task.

Images of an angel, a black-eyed angel with gold flecks of fire in them, filled Timothy's mind. As he shuffled with the baby, his eyes dimmed as his thighs burned with lust. Glee overtook the possessed priest as he boldly approached her image in his mind.

The raw power that coursed through Timothy's mind he took to be a blessing that God only bestowed to the strong. As the priest had approached the convent, Satan grinned in nothingness as he viewed the humans with the woman from Timothy's shadow.

Satan knew he couldn't enter the Mortal's flesh without their permission.

The Devil smiled again. He actually preferred non-believers, anyway.

From the edges of Father Timothy's shadow, Satan's gaze immediately settled on the humans. Like a magnet, he felt himself drawn to Napoliss, who had just started running across the clearing.

As Satan jumped from Timothy's shadow, a larger shadow pulled from the moving shape. In an instant, the darkness virtually erupted from the spot and swept the entire clearing in its enormity.

A third of the way across the grass, Napoliss still ran after Webster as the shadow leapt at him. He only had time to snap up his gaze to try and anticipate it as it descended on him in a shapeless, weightless mass.

Napoliss hit the ground like he was sliding into home base. One leg out, one knee under him, he caught himself, curling his outstretched leg back as he skidded on both knees. Almost at once, Napoliss felt the darkness slip into him through his mouth and nose. The young federal agent grabbed his throat, struggling to breathe.

The blackness burned into his mind and his closed throat convulsed violently as he emitted a haunted guttural scream. The scream came from

344

his bones as his soul was consumed by fire. A fever started in Napoliss' feet and through his groin as the flaming sensation traveled up into his belly.

The human creature known as Napoliss was changed, and ceased to be, as his essence fell into an everlasting void. The vileness he became had no name. In a sound that caused everything in the night to become still, he shrieked with demonic laughter.

A hard yellow light began to flicker from behind his eyes.

For a moment, the universe swayed as it tried to re-balance itself through the onslaught of unnatural energy.

Lightening snaked through the night sky into the clearing. Not even two feet in front of Napoliss, the lightening exploded into and up from the earth. The dried grass flash-fried as the electricity sparkled it into ashes. He reveled in the power that came from his new being. Destruction was a thing of beauty to his new eyes and all around them, the powers of Hell strove to find a foothold. With each new explosion, he squealed louder.

Without warning, three more bolts of lightning slammed into the clearing; their impact seemingly targeted to just the clearing. .

The sight was awesome and the boom deafening. The group of survivors now included Maria and Katherine. They all jumped and flung themselves to the ground as the skies opened in a terrifying display.

As the pain of the fever swept into the forehead of the body he now owned, Satan's mouth locked open in pain. The million, jagged pinpricks seared the Devil's mind in a beautiful agony as he infected the flesh with his spirit. He roared at the flush of heat.

Lightning rippled across the walls of the convent as the energy spread outward in all directions.

The trees around the survivors became a maze of zigzagging white-blue slices of light. Two, then four bolts, slammed into the pines immediately flanking them. The slender trunks exploded; first the bottom, and then the tops. The ones who huddled there screamed as log-sized shrapnel rained down on them.

The electrical storm expanded deeper into the trees as the skies randomly took revenge on the Earth.

When the first bolt hit, they had all been facing it. The pounding thrust of the lightning's shockwave impact had hit Anna squarely in her still half-broken front teeth.

Morgan grabbed Anna's shoulders at the first strike. They still sat dumbfounded beside Abby. As the secondary bursts of lightning struck the trees over and behind their position, Morgan pitched herself forward using her body to cover Anna.

Anna heard screaming and realized it was her own as the trees above them was bombarded with a series of rapid lightning strikes. A large branch hit both women harmlessly on their legs. A million pine needles exploded into them, biting their flesh.

Anna felt the impact of the large piece of trunk that fell across Morgan's back. She saw Morgan's face as the crunch registered and the log rolled off of her broken back. Under her, Anna was relatively unharmed. As she started trying to roll from under her cousin, small sticks and leaf fragments hit Anna's upturned face.

The storm of energy moved away, further into the tree line. Anna rolled over to change their positions and as Anna swung her weight off the woman, Morgan gasped. Huge tears were rolling down her face, hot and blinding with pain.

Anna had broken her back once in a horrible accident. She understood the ghastly look. She tried to comfort Morgan as best she could.

"You'll be fine…" she said tightly.

Morgan nodded absently as she lost all feeling below her breasts. Morgan knew she would heal, but first she would be bound by the hideous paralysis.

Anna gripped her hands tightly and Morgan managed to squeeze back somewhat.

As she stared upward into Anna's concerned face, Morgan begged her.

"Please go save my son… Please!"

Anna looked toward the now slumping Napoliss in the center of the moonlit clearing. The man's body shook with laughter as the lightning pounded away from him. He rolled in rapture on the grass.

Anna looked Morgan in the eyes. Both women smiled as Anna kissed the back of Morgan's hand and folded her weak arm across her chest. Leaning over her fallen cousin, Anna retrieved the only weapon she saw amongst the broken trees. She picked up Morgan's sword and left her side with a teary-eyed, determined nod.

Anna never bothered to see if anyone else had survived.

She knew the Devil stood between her and the baby and there was going to be hell to pay.

Chapter 29

As they rolled into the grounds of the convent, the three men spotted the abandoned Jeep about a third of the way down the long drive. They pulled up behind the silent vehicle, noting the still open doors.

All three exited the car and the two cousins quickly searched the inside. They had never seen it before. Jerold didn't bother looking through it. He stood at the rear of the Jeep and looked longingly at the huge panels of stained glass that gleamed from the cathedral. The sanctuary was the largest part of an enormous structure and Jerold smiled slightly at its glittering, colorful beauty. It reminded him of his balcony in the city, the night there alive with light and depth. How many times had he longed to jump from that very balcony?

On the air came the scent of burned flesh. None of them commented on the smell, though it was strong enough to make them gag. Separately, all of their thoughts touched on James. Adam's mind had lingered on him.

Adam scowled at his father in the darkness. His father never noticed. His father never noticed him at all. Adam had learned not to care over many centuries.

He had no idea that his father had made a deal to give him a starring role in the grandest of all his designs. Adam knew his father thought he was lazy, and his cousin dismissed him as outright stupid. He had learned to accept that, too.

Adam was neither lazy nor stupid. Sometimes he just confused things. He controlled it mostly, knowing it was the same curse many humans had. The simple learning disability was not serious by far, but his entire race had branded him as 'simple' or 'stupid'.

It was a simple flaw of the flesh.

Adam knew about many things that would surprise his father. He knew many things ABOUT his father. The man never saw Adam study him.

When the lightning hit on the far side of the building, they all stopped and watched the awe-inspiring flashes.

A pig-like squeal of laughter rolled past the explosions.

Their eyes widened as more strikes, seemingly concentrated in one area, pounded rapidly. Abandoning their own car, all the men started in the direction of the lightning. The trail ran far down the slope to their left. Their view of the corner of the building was slightly obstructed by a thin arm of forest that hugged the loose slope.

Drawing their weapons, the three men walked fast, headed toward the open area; they all sped up to a trot as though on signal. The slope seemed to push against them as they ran toward the shrieks that echoed from the trees in front of them.

Adam and Michael outdistanced Jerold, running full-out across the cleared slope. The band of trees stretched before them, and Michael could see the entire perimeter being bombarded by bolts of lightning from the clear inky-blue sky. It became apparent that the storm was expanding and rolling as it attacked the earth in a barrage of white hot light. As it left the trees in front of them, the wall of lightening actually rolled deeper to the left and into the woods that enveloped the slope. The line of crackling energy rolled straight into them, then over them as they huddled on the frozen ground.

Jerold watched it come; he had sucked in his breath as it crackled through him. The sensation rolled past him and around him rapidly. He was blinded, momentarily, by the flash of white-blue light fizzing in his eyes. Jerold blinked hard and started to rise. Michael and Adam were already up on their hands, looking back at him.

As the roll of energy hit the cars, one huge lightning bolt split in two. Both cars simultaneously exploded upward. Without time to even see the burst behind him, Jerold was picked up and thrown forward by the shockwave.

The sedan flew upwards and back as the lightning impacted its hood. The large luxury car flipped perfectly backwards in an effortless flip-flop.

The hit to the Jeep, catching the back of the truck, became a direct shot to the gas tank, and it was the added explosion of it that propelled Jerold. The truck actually twirled on its rear left corner as the second explosion pitched it up and to the left in Jerold's direction.

Jerold hit the ground hard and as he landed, he flung himself over onto his back. He watched helplessly as the car started a fast furious roll towards him. He could see that the momentum of the roll would not reach him, but even so, he cried out from the sheer terror of it as it came directly at him.

Twenty-five feet from him, it rolled to a lurching, sliding stop.

In the quiet aftermath, Jerold looked at the Jeep burning on its roof. He was gulping out of sheer reaction. His old heart slammed crazily against his ribs. He was stunned into doing absolutely nothing.

Michael and Adam lingered only long enough to see Jerold cheat death. Before the Jeep had even stopped shuddering, they were off again, running to the trees.

It was their way; nature's way. If you could not keep up, you got left behind.

The sparse tree line sprawled all the way up the slope to the convent walls, but was not that deep. As they came into the shattered rows of pine, both men scrambled over debris. In the center of the sloped clearing that lay before them, they saw a human on his knees.

The young agent Napoliss held his head as he laughed. Satan felt his blood tingle. He had gained the sensation of touch, smell, and taste. Not just the feel of it, but the feel of it in flesh. The taste of the windless air on and inside his cheeks almost satisfied his thirst.

From his stomach a deep hunger exploded. A great bloodlust built in the flesh of his guts.

Their blood.

His blood.

The baby's blood.

Satan squealed a maddening swine sound from the mouth of Napoliss. He tried to rise but stumbled back to his knees. Just as Michael and Adam paused to listen, a figure slipped from the shattered tree line into the moonlight. She was still a long way off but they both recognized the woman instantly.

Michael's heart broke. It was HER.

The awareness triggered the fever in both men.

As Adam gasped loudly, Michael stilled to his soul. The heat in his thighs scalded like hellfire as the woman calmly, quickly walked into the clearing. A small rapier-thin sword gleamed silver in the moonlight.

Anna was walking straight towards the human, hefting the sword. From their covered positions, they sank unnoticed into the throes of the fever. Michael held himself upright as long as he could. The heat had almost instantly closed off his throat. He grasped a sapling as he unconsciously registered the feeling that something horrible was coming. The visionless premonition manifested itself into his burning guts, making them twist with sickening effect. Trying not to fall, he actually vomited, but it never made it past the locked throat muscles.

From his position above her, Michael watched as Anna charged the man who was turned away from her. The man had his hands on the ground, trying to push himself up.

It was obvious that Anna had the advantage; but even so, Michael still screamed. He didn't expect the sound to leave his throat but it did. It burst forth into the stillness, giving away their position.

Anna, in mid-stride with drawn sword, heard the scream from her far right. She recognized the voice that made it. Him.

Her blood chilled as her soul remembered itself, and it's agonizing loneliness.

Anna clenched her teeth against the slam of her heart but did not hesitate as she swung the sword.

Michael could not believe his fevered eyes as he saw the man standing, looking face to face with Anna from three yards away. It was impossible…

Adam, too, blinked rapidly as he threw off the gasps of heated air from his mouth.

Michael did not see the man stand. He did not see him turn to face the woman. He just suddenly…was. If Michael's brain had registered the image, his eyes didn't. He jerked backward with the realization that the human had moved faster than the eye could perceive.

The swing Anna made was perfectly aimed and perfectly timed to take Napoliss' head. Her soft step was perfectly executed by someone who was a master swordsman. As the blade was millimeters from the back of his neck, a blur of color flew away from her blade and suddenly he was over there, watching her with eyes of fire.

All of Anna's considerable strength had been placed into the blow. As she sliced harmlessly through the empty air, she prematurely halted her step and stooped as the velocity of the blade came to an abrupt end on the ground.

Anna froze.

She was trapped in the moonlight with the Devil.

A shudder coursed through her as she slowly shifted her eyes up the length of the borrowed body. Napoliss was lean and muscular on a tall frame. His heritage gave him a classically good-looking face. Anna took in his full lips and straight nose. He stood upright, watching her carefully, arms resting behind him.

From her stooped position, she stared into the eyes of yellow flickering flames.

Rationality fled from her mind and a fear that was deep and primal found a spot inside her. Anna's lips opened loosely as her eyes clouded. Centuries of conditioning finally kicked in and she used sheer will to make herself react in exactly the opposite way that she felt. It had almost always saved her ass.

She knew there was no escape this time as she deliberately blinked back the glaze of shock. Unable to look away from the flames, Anna forced her face to sneer at her adversary.

In a deep rumble, she said, "Balimos…?"

Anna tilted her head questioningly as her heart screamed in terror. The fire of his eyes made her skin start crawling in fear. Her nostril twitched.

Satan smiled at Anna. He deliberately tilted his head to study her.

From her gut, Anna growled, as she took the only chance she had…Forward and up.

As she came up with the sword, Napoliss almost serenely brought around her own gun. Her momentum threw her forward as he shot her in the center of the chest. The sudden crack of her sternum thrust her back, but she willed herself forward.

The hand of Napoliss unloaded the .38 into her chest.

Michael's screams echoed in her head like a hollow memory.

Anna staggered under each blow but refused to fall. The flaming eyes danced in delight as the last shot slammed into her ribcage. She forced her feet forward.

The sword fell from her limp hands as Anna lost control of both of her arms. She forced herself forward by sheer will as she pushed herself into the arms of the creature who had murdered her.

Of the six bullets, one had found the mark, just barely. It only took a needle prick.

Anna stared into the eyes of fire that terrified her. Napoliss had no choice but to catch her as she flung herself, empty-handed, into his arms.

He caught her slight body against his sturdier one. Her weight caused him to cradle her close to keep from falling himself. He watched her search his eyes of nothingness with a horrified wonder. The Devil thought she was beautiful. He smiled at her lovingly with his handsome face. The effect of his eyes was mesmerizing. His smile softened and he allowed himself to be drawn into a staring contest with his victim.

Anna swallowed hard and hesitated only slightly.

Now that she was dying, she suddenly had no fear. Inside her wounded body, she found contempt in the eyes of flame. Using all the strength of her mind, Anna used every ounce of the gift at her disposal and she entered Satan's mind.

Once inside his thoughts, Anna found herself in flames. Satan saw her presence too late. She ripped into the flames of knowledge and damnation in Satan's memory, seeming to split the marrow from the core of the fevered brain of Napoliss. The federal agents stolen eyes led the way like a springboard, directly into the mind of Satan.

They both screamed as Anna burst into his thoughts like the tormented, frantic soul she was.

Satan closed his eyes, trying to ignore her will as he struggled to throw the woman away from him. Anna's was repulsed by the things she saw in his mind and tried to flee it too late. As she tore away from his images, she lashed out and grasped impressions of his thoughts and chunks of memory.

Anna screamed from the darkest recesses of terror, as images of Hell shattered her mind.

Though the connection between them broke mentally, he held her in his arms only a moment longer. He tossed her aside easily, pushing himself back to unsteady feet.

Anna screamed, even though one of her lungs had been pierced by two bullets. Lying on the ground, she was no longer aware of the five wounds that knitted and healed with a bluish-white wet fire. Her body was working furiously to save her from death. Five of the bullet wounds burst with a swarm of bluish lights. .

The one wound that her body could not repair bled a steady small stream, slowly taking her life.

Before her death could come, Anna found herself in Hell.

As Satan's stolen memories forced themselves into the chain of her own, Anna's screams turned to cries that produced a rapid sucking noise. The cries became a strangled whimper. The open wounds rippled with tiny bolts of light trying to repair the damaged flesh; all the wounds, but one.

Anna fell into a great blackness as her dying body still twitched with the confused determination of a tenacious life.

As her body stilled, Anna saw distant visions of Heaven itself. As she was pulled into consuming nothingness, the visions faded as Hell closed in around her.

From the stolen thoughts, Anna learned the secrets of Satan.

***

After Anna had left Morgan's side, Miguel tried to push a large log off of himself. His newly-repaired arm was shattered once more, as were all the ribs under it. The large piece of tree refused to budge. Miguel gulped in pain.

A huge gash across his forehead burned as the tiny fragments of electricity almost burst from the wound. Turning his head slightly, making sure his neck was not broken, he spit at the dirt and debris that had found its way into his mouth.

Miguel froze, seeing Morgan lying somewhere out past his toes.

Morgan lay in the moonlight on her broken back, with her pale face staring down an even paler moon. Miguel's heart broke as he cried out. The pain in his mind and body felt exactly the same. Crushing… trembling… crippling.

Her face serene and calm, Morgan did not try to move, but he could see her blinking. Miguel watched her breast rise, then fall evenly.

As he lay there watching Anna's shadow recede into a long sliver, he studied the face his heart yearned for; Morgan, his Morgan.

Miguel suddenly remembered Katherine. He had no idea where she was or what had happened to her. From somewhere far away, Miguel heard Michael screaming.

Morgan heard it as well , and stared at the stars above her with a slight smile.

Twitching, and then violently jerking, Miguel fought against the log that entrapped him. The mixed signals and tearing of his heart by the mixed loyalties caused him to sob in fear as the log stayed fast. He pushed at it with his injured arm, but it refused to move. He watched Morgan's lips move silently in the moonlight as she mouthed silent words into the still air above her.

When he realized that she was praying, he noticed for the first time the utter stillness of body. Now in a panic, he used the good arm to push against the earth while using the injured side as a wedge to shift the log.

Miguel shook, crying out in pain and frustration as he pushed harder. The gunshot froze everything momentarily in a deafening blast.

Before they could react to the first blast, five more shots rang out. Each blast caused him to shove out blindly, now truly in a panic. The large section of trunk finally gave way.

Pushing it aside with a growl, Miguel tried to force little packets of air into his crushed ribcage as small, clipped moans escaped with each breath. He sat up, intending to go to Morgan, but he realized that Katherine was still lying where she had fallen just a few feet away.

Miguel cried out in agony.

Forgetting Morgan, but seeing her face anyway, Miguel forgot his pain as he watched Katherine gasp. She, too, was lying face up, looking at the moon in the now clear unobstructed sky before her.

When the lightning had started in front of them, Miguel had instinctively pushed Katherine behind him, as everything froze during the terrifying display in the clearing. Unthinkingly, he had pushed her back into the loosely-spaced slender trees. When it became apparent that the storm would not be contained and actually started to roll, Miguel had only an instant to grasp at his will and protect himself from the worst of the damage.

The clearing was still taking vicious strikes as the tree Katherine was hugging had exploded with a gigantic white flash. Now looking back up into the night sky, the same sky that had sent her destruction, she did not cry. Katherine did not call out in any way. She simply gasped. In…out…sharp and hard.

A large piece of shattered pine impaled her upwards under her right ribcage.

Anna's distant scream took all hope from Miguel's heart. He tried to scramble to Katherine, but something seemed to be wrong with his leg and he fell several times. Anna's scream vibrated through the silence with the fury of frustration, and the desolate hollow sound of failure.

Katherine gasped, her body jerking with the effort. She had curled both hands around the protruding piece of wood in her as if she thought to pull it out. She gasped. In… out… tight… and fast.

Dragging himself by his one undamaged arm, Miguel twisted his shattered body over to lie beside her. A slight mist of smoke started rising from her as he brought himself close to her. Katherine's eyes focused one last time on his face. She was glad Miguel was with her for the end, even if he could never love her. She died still loving him.

Miguel heard Michael screaming from down the slope, close to the building's corner.

Katherine gasped a final time as Miguel tried pulling her closer to his side. Michael's scream was not of pain, or of rage. Miguel shivered, as he tried not to think of the dark place inside his cousin soul where a sound like that could even be imagined.

Miguel looked up in time to see Michael break through the tree line to his far right and into the clearing. Adam struggled behind him, trying to negotiate the debris of broken trees.

Michaels screams were curses as he ran.

"You bastard…you bastard!"

He was charging blindly into the field as Adam wisely seemed to hang back out of caution.

Miguel turned his eyes back to Katherine to see her eyes had already glazed unnaturally. The wooden shrapnel piercing her heart started burning.

She still lay partially over Miguel's leg; through his tears, he pushed her off him. His face was so wet from his tears that he had to wipe them on his arm before he could check to see if her blood was still on him. He was paranoid of the flames that waited for every Mortal. .

Morgan was alive, but still motionless, as Miguel started looking for the others. He cried out at the carnage behind him on the path.

Edwards had frozen a shoulder length beside Katherine when the tree exploded. Her body had shielded his from most of the shrapnel, except for his head.

Miguel knew the old man would not be getting up.

The large tree from which Timothy had launched his attack from still stood to Miguel's immediate left. As flames started licking at Katherine's lips, Miguel heard crying from under the debris of large branches that had been sheered off and rested at it's base. He grasped at pine needles, still attached to their small branches from the very tip of the tree. .

Using his good leg to scoot back from Katherine's smoking body, Miguel stopped and grasped an inner branch, propelling the light but bulky mass away from the still standing trunk.

Diana and Douglas were exposed at the foot of the tree, completely

355

untouched by the projectiles.

Because of his close relationship with Michael, Miguel recognized Diana instantly, , and in one painful glance he could see that Diana was dead.

He could also see she was no longer pregnant.

When the lightening started, Doug had gripped her fiercely and tried to protect Diana from the violence of the storm around them. He heard her say that the baby was there as they crouched for protection from the lashing limbs falling all around them. Before Doug even realized that she had stopped breathing, he had flung her down and started ripping at her blood-soaked trousers. The tip of the tree sheered off above him and harmlessly landed across his back as the foliage on it worked to cushion it's fall and envelope the duo beneath it.

Now in the harsh glare of moon, Doug whimpered as he held the bloodied just born baby to his face. At the sight of it, Miguel began crying, too.

The boy was premature and tiny, but still an exceptionally beautiful child. He had taken the best genes from two extremely good-looking parents and combined them to form his perfect, unique little self. The baby hung from Doug's grasp, the warm, wet fluids on him chilling quickly in the moonlight.

The unnatural stillness of the baby caused Doug to feel pain like he had never felt before; it was a confusing combination of frustration, love, and anger.

Unconsciously, Douglas shook the baby lightly, his heart refusing to believe what his hands and eyes knew to be true.

"Baby!" Doug said oddly, as if trying to make the newborn respond.

Douglas sook the child again, gently, refusing to understand.

Miguel was devastated by the tragedy playing out in front of him. His tears became hot fat drops that washed his face in agony. He tried to pull himself upwards but his legs refused to move, still. Even though he could not feel it, Miguel knew his hips had been broken by the tree that had fallen on him.

If Miguel lived, he knew he would have to tell Michael that his son was dead. The boy he had prayed for, for an eternity, almost lived.

As Michael went screaming across the clearing, Miguel jerked around to watch him.

With a profound sadness that cleaved his heart, he realized that Michael, himself, was not going to make it.

Doug shook the dead baby, refusing to accept it and clearly in shock. He had not yet even noticed his beloved uncle, Captain Edwards, was also deceased, some twenty feet away.

Everyone that watched the clearing knew that Michael's rage was going to be the death of him, as well. .

Chapter 30

After Elizabeth left her earlier , Gail threw the bolts on the door again. She started back to Matthew's bed-side when she heard the first scream; instantly she knew it was Anna's voice.

The sound of her sister, screaming out in terror, rippled through Gail's soul. Just as she decided she must join the fight now … The sky opened up in a terrifying display of displaced energy. The single first bolt jolted the very bricks of the walls around them.

The bolts of lightning that followed made her jerk and gasp, as the electricity crawled over the walls of the convent like giant, long-legged, white-hot spiders. The shuttered window gave off eerie, faint throbs and pulses as the sky split and the lightning gavels struck the earth so hard and fast she leaned over Matthew, afraid the roof may be compromised above them.

Gail grabbed Matthew's limp hand in hers, amazed that he wasn't jerked upright by the quaking booms.

Matthew slept like a heavily drugged baby while the earth shook.

Gail looked at the sword in her lap and dug her inner arms into the suspended guns that dangled from the holsters. The sensation did not reassure her. Clutching Matthews's hand, Gail's heart cringed as the echoes of pig-like screams cut through the explosions.

Gail knew that Satan had come for them, had probably already taken to flesh. The squeals of laughter echoed through the night as the storm rolled away.

The sound of gunshots stilled Gail's heartbeat, momentarily.

First one shot, then five more in a rapid burst.

Because of Anna's gift and the bond they had shared from the womb, the two sisters had always been able to feel each other, even across vast distances. Like a whisper of presence, the one constant in Gail's life, besides God, was Anna's shadow, always there watching over her. The blood of the mother that they shared was always reaching for itself, touching it's own familiarity. Because of that bond, Anna had many times appeared in her life, just at the moment Gail needed someone the most.

For all the eternities she had lived, Gail had never once lost faith in either God, or Anna. Nearly from her first breath, all of her memories were colored by knowing that Anna was there. Anna had deliberately planted a small presence in Gail's mind on the day that she was born, so that her sister would always be able to go there and find her, so that Gail would never be alone.

Gail had always been guarded by the strongest of all the full-breed children of angels, that watched over her day and night. It was well known that Gail and Morgan were the only true friends Anna had. Even if their other extended family members avoided Anna like the plague, all of them agreed on one point.

Anna never failed.

No matter what goal or the barriers, Anna never, ever walked away defeated.

Just moments before the gunshots, Gail had felt a gush of shame from the soft, unobtrusive presence she loved so dearly. She had been shocked and unsettled by it.

Anna had never felt shame before in all the thousands of years they had bonded through blood, and the presence of that emotion coming from her confused her sister deeply.

As the rapid burst of gunfire sounded, Gail felt the phantom gouging pain of Anna's mortal wound pierce her own unwounded heart. Coming to her feet, not knowing or caring how she got there, Gail cried out sharply into the still room.

"Anna!" Gail screamed reflexively.

Gail's hands went blindly to her own chest, groping the sliced Kevlar over her breast. In an instant, she was both gasping and trying to control her breath.

She cried out again, "Anna!", and as she said it, Sara's voice echoed the name with her, from beyond the ghostly layer of reality.

Both voices were weighed by sorrow as they mingled together. Gail knew that her mother was there in spirit, watching them. She was grateful for the haunting.

Still clutching at the smooth Kevlar, Gail's fingers lost strength and instead splayed flat against her chest. For a moment, she couldn't breathe as she felt Anna presence draw away from her, and back into itself, for the first time in thousands of years.

Gail gagged on the sob that broke her will; she lowered her head, the tears rolling into the damaged body armor. As her sorrow manifested itself in her body, she heard Anna's scream again, this time frantic and horrid.

Without pausing a moment more, Gail went to the bed and retrieved her sword. Picking up Matthew's right hand, she kissed the knuckles and allowed herself one last look at him. Her old heart flip-flopped painfully.

Gail winced as the screams purged the stillness. She headed out the door to do battle, hoping with all her soul that Anna had not failed.

Gail had to believe that Anna had not failed.

She knew that if Morgan's son was dead or dying, they would all be killed anyway, just to satisfy Satan's bloodlust.

Because of the role he had been designated to play, Matthew would be Satan's next target, after the baby.

Gail wanted to believe that Anna was still fighting as she ran to help. The vast emptiness where Anna once had been inside her mind, the wasteland left in her soul, cried out like an abandoned baby. Anna's spirit had, in effect, amputated itself from Gail's essence. In her human heart, Gail refused to consider the obvious reason why.

She wanted to believe that her sister's will would keep her from failing, but Gail never honestly thought it was true. Her heart wanted so badly to BELIEVE IT!; however, her mind knew differently.

As Gail moved out the door to intercept Satan , she was crying like a baby.

***

Jerold had come upon Adam and Michael in the tree line as both had faltered forward, still shaken by the fever. He, too, was weakened by the flush of heat when he saw Anna step out to take the human.

As the heat had melted his muscles into weakness, Jerold had seen the eyes of the human sparkling with a yellow glint through the night.

Jerold smiled, pleasantly contemplating the arrival of his own long over-due death. It never should have been this hard to die.

The death he had been promised had no Heaven or Hell. As the flush of fever cramped up Jerold's facial muscles, he sneered, thinking that he would never bear this branding iron of pain ever again. He had known no true pleasure for years, only pain, as life had ground to a tasteless bitterness with his every breath. Not a day went by that he did not wish he were dead already.

Now with the fever gripping him, Jerold watched with a ripple of genuine satisfaction as Anna swung the sword and missed her target. Had his throat not been closed tightly, he would have cheered. Even the searing pain could not dent the hatred that welled in him; his hatred for HER...

Jerold heard her clearly say "Balimos?" in his burning ears. As the gunshots jerked Anna backwards, Jerold smiled in ecstasy.

He watched Alexander's only daughter take all six rounds on her feet. Anna's half-brother, Alexander's son Michael, quivered before Jerold, screaming like a banshee.

Jerold's smile was cramped as the fever pulled at his scalp, forcing his eyes to water. He watched Anna throw herself into the hands that had shot her. Jerold knew in a flash that she was trying to take both bodies to the fiery death they all anticipated. He closed his eyes as they swelled from pain.

Michael screamed in horror at the scene being played out in front of him. He never saw his uncle standing behind him. Jerold wanted nothing more than to knock the boy's brains out, anything to shut him up.

His stomach turned as he listened to Michael scream for that bitch... That bitch Anna! Daughter of Alexander. The sister Michael loved incestuously.

Jerold, too, had fallen into the same sin. His love for his brother's only daughter had turned vile in his insanity.

When both of Anna's Mortal parents had died in the same night at St. Mary's, Jerold had wept for his brother even as the thought of Anna being flushed out of hiding made his mouth water.

In his mind, Jerold saw his Alexander looking at him with disgust. Jerold smiled back at his memory, no longer caring it was forbidden.

After Nefertiti was betrayed and then killed by Alexander, Anna had started tracking the man who was a stranger to her. She had no idea that he was her father. Sara had let her walk right into it, blindly. Nna did not know whom Alexander was to her, but Alexander knew too well exactly whim Anna was to himself. Sara knew that Alexander would never hurt his own daughter. Even if she agreed the man was just evil, Alexander welcomed he pursuit, eager to finally meet and teach his daughter whom she could be.

Sara had borne her child in secrecy and thought she would be safer that way. Alex let her go, knowing they would meet again, some day. His spies kept track of their every movement.

Sara had fled with Anna into a great, nameless desert soon after her birth. Since he had never fathered another female, Alexander had become enthralled by his daughter. Time upon time, he watched her from the shadows. When it came to his ears that she was tracking him, he let her follow his false leads for years.

Anytime he chose to look, he could find her. He could touch her mind without Anna even knowing he was there.

Realizing that Anna did not know who he was, he had started playing games with her, leaving her messages to taunt her during the wild hunt. He did not reveal the truth to her, merely watched to see how she handled it.

Alexander had been impressed with his first child and only daughter.

As time went on, he also left other things that he thought she might need or like: a chest of treasure, or jewelry he had imagined giving to her. She took it all, thinking it was loot. More than once, Alexander had made sure to leave fresh food to feed her after she had tracked him mercilessly; she had been hot on his fake trail for days. He had been delighted to see that after she had eaten it, she had savagely torn up his table. Once, he had even contacted Sara to come to rescue their daughter, the time Anna broke her back.

Many times, when Alex had to go away, he left Jerold in his place to track her movements. Jerold had been captivated by her clever beauty. The presence she created had cleaved into him in a much different way than her father had reacted; ways that were forbidden.

Incest was strictly forbidden among the Mortals. Any Mortal caught breaking the taboo faced an instant death sentence.

Within a few decades of the hunt, Anna had several times come across Michael's trail. It had taken her years to realize that Michael was the son of her target. The first time she decided to follow his trail to the end, she had been shocked to come face to face with him.

They were immediately drawn to one another as the fever hit them the first time they became aware of the other. . That they looked almost identical to one another, stunned them both.

As Anna did not know Alexander was her father, she did not know Michael was her half-brother, at first.

362

She had never actually seen a male of her species, except once in the desert, but she had been only a small child then. She knew that those she hunted were Mortal males, but seeing one up close and in the flesh had sent her senses reeling and all her rationality scattered. .

The games had begun.

They struggled against each other in a battle of wills designed to steal the very memory of one another.

Since Michael never knew of her, she found no memory of it in his mind. Since it didn't exist in her memory either, it never occurred to her that it could even be so.

Fascinated by their shared gift, she had become hypnotized by identical eyes that reached back. For eons she had been alone in her mind. For the first time that day, someone not only met Anna's gaze fully but boldly burst into her thoughts, questioning.

She won the first struggle, and he was smitten. She had humbled him as no other had ever done before or since. To Michael, the meeting was fate.

His clumsy immature caresses of her mind had not gone deeply enough to find that she hunted his father. She had been able to sheath it in the steel of her mind.

Seduced by longing and images of sharing love just once in her lonely life, Anna had moved toward him, needing him . She knew he would lead her to her quarry. She dared to hope that, as a fullblood, he had answers Sara had withheld.

Jerold had found them together , but not before the bond had been set. It had cemented into the fire of their souls. He did not know Anna would not allow the relationship to be set in flesh; not yet.

Michael had fallen in love, But Anna was far more reserved, knowing to wait for the unknown to surface before losing herself.

All her instincts told her that she could use this Mortal male to find her target, but she was not prepared to let him become confused about their relationship. She had many good excuses to keep him at arm's length, but she kept the best reason to herself. She knew full well the danger of reckless bonds.

Jerold had seen them together before the fever hit them. He did not dare approach either of them, so he fled.

Jerold knew full well who and what she was. He cursed Sara to hell for lying to the girl, or at the least, withholding the full truth. Stunned, outraged, and confused, Jerold had stumbled away to contact his brother and told him about his children; both of them.

Alexander had come immediately.

In the battle that followed his arrival, Anna had been an innocent; however, it was she who lost the most. She had never again trusted a damn word her mother said. Helping Gail kidnap Joseph was a simple choice for Anna . She had never lost a moment of sleep over hurting Sara after that. Alex had saved Anna from his brother and protected her escape.
Anna had seen the passion of hate in Jerold's eyes as he had wounded her. She knew he would ALWAYS be the enemy. She had no idea of the love he felt for her. A forbidden desire that stalked him as surely as he had stalked her.

Alexander was furious. He forbade the family's males from approaching his daughter her at all. He and his son had struggled over it for centuries. Michael knew it was forbidden. After many years he no longer cared.

When Jerold dreamed, he dreamed of her; perfect as an angel. A black-eyed angel he had been denied. . Anna's memory drove Jerold insane as she stole his imagination, yet remained ever untouched by him.

Until one night, the image of her in his dreams touched him back, wings and all.
As Jerold watched Michael run into the clearing, he laughed at Anna's still figure laying in the moonlight. He was glad she would die with him tonight. As he ran to her, in his own mind, Michael saw Anna as he had first seen her. The curses coming from him burst forth as he raised the pistol in mid-stride. The human reeling away from Anna's body looked up.
Surprised by Michael's appearance, Satan smiled as he watched the enraged Mortal run into the clearing..

Michael bore down on him as the man-creature stood up and started running away from him, impossibly fast across the slope. He was running as fast as his unnatural human legs would carry him and the creature was steadily increasing the distance between them by leaps and bounds so fast he was barely a blur.

Michael screamed, firing shots that he knew would not hit his target but unable to think of anything else to do. Satan made it to the corner of the building , angling slightly in front of a startled Adam whom had popped up from the treeline not forty feet from the body Satan had stolen. Satan

364

slipped to the opposite end of the structure from where Timothy had gone, with Webster close behind.

Satan grinned through cracking lips as Michael's last bullet hit the wall beside him. He slowed instantly to a walk. Grinning, still moving too quickly, t, he tried to slow down, knowing his inhuman strength was burning up Napoliss' frail human body.

The grin left Satan's face as he thought about timing. It took an extraordinary amount of strength to jump from one body to another, even for something as powerful as he.

Satan calculated that he would make one more jump, into the Mortal body prepared for him, and after he drank the blood of the baby, there would be no boundaries left.

All the Angels in Heaven, itself, would fall under his command completely as his immortal flesh evolved again to eclipse any human achievement or strength.

The grimace that passed for a smile ratcheted his face into ways it was never meant to move.

Hugging the silent wall, Satan hurried around to the layers of staircases floating from the front of the immense cathedral like terraces. His mouth watered as he thought of the altar that lay inside. Again, he giggled in a short pig-like burst. How like the women, he thought, to be caught where a church is handy. He scoured the now silent grounds around him as he lurched up the first of the stairs that went up to the impressive front doors of the sanctuary. The panels of huge colorful stained glass hung suspended in the wall above him; he was revolted by the display of twinkling beauty.

The mad priest had been instructed to bring the baby to the altar of God. In exchange for empty, greed-filled promises, the priest had agreed to sacrifice the baby in the name of that very God.

Bleed him on the altar of God as an offering from sanctified hands.

Satan giggled at the foolishness so rampant in all fanatics.

As the fevered body of Napoliss approached the door, he realized that the handles of the enormous planks had been wrapped with a chain and padlocked.

Satan held the lock, examining it. He wondered what they had tried to lock in? He knew full well what they were not locking out.

With a savage jerk, he pulled the steel lock apart as he ripped it from the chain. The effort involved almost dislocated the shoulder and fingers of the weakening body. Satan knew he must jump again soon, before the body burned itself up.

He had to find the body that was prepared for him quickly. In his blind run for the wall, Satan had not noticed that the body he was promised had been right there in his path. He had gone right by Adam as he had ducked Michael's bullets.

Satan thought of the baby as he unwrapped the chain from the flute-shaped door pulls. The human body he used was parched, burning inside. The added heat of his eternal thirst inflamed Satan's mind into a fever pitch.

He knew the blood of the baby would sooth the cries of his burning soul.

As he jerked on the doors, Satan licked his lips.

Once he took over Adam's body. he would satisfy his terrible thirst for knowledge. As he threw the doors aside, he hurried forward.

If the altar was still empty, he would have to go find Timothy before time ran out.

Satan's time of free will on Earth was limited before he would be pulled from his mortal flesh and back into nothingness. As he walked into the sanctuary, he could hear his clock endlessly ticking down.

Silent row upon row of habited nuns turned as one to watch the intruder. The women had been locked in since the beginning of mass under Gail's order. Katherine had done as she had been bidden, not needing to be told the reasoning. They knew what was coming; Gail was afraid the sisters would panic and flee into the path of the Devil. She could not have known the altar among them was Satan's goal in the first place.

Satan could not use his own stolen hands to cut into the baby. The hands had to be volunteered. They not only had to be willing but BLESSED by the church; sanctioned to do Gods will.

The nuns realized they were locked in from front and back after the thunder had forced the Earth itself to cower. Being faithful and sure of the powers that held them together as a close-knit group, when the pig laughter had started all the sisters had fallen silent. The praying yet still fearful nuns accepted, with little struggle, that the Devil had come to Mississippi.

As Satan threw wide the doors, he shrilled in outright glee.

"Ahhh NUNS!" he exclaimed in mock surprise.

366

The women froze as they saw his yellow eyes flicker impossibly bright, bursting with sickly light.

Satan seemed to gain immense pleasure at the sight of the startled faithful, allowing himself to smirk at their distress.

With Napoliss' burning throat, Satan said with a huge grin, "Helloo laaadies!"

The doors slammed shut with a giant swoosh. The nuns remained dead silent.

***

Timothy paused near the rear door of the building. Looking inside the open door , he could see the vast hallway that ran both ways nearly the full length of the structure. A simple stone stairway split the hall to his right in halves. The heavy staircase went straight up to the second floor and opened fully into a gallery that faced down to where he stood. The right hall narrowed into a passageway past the stairs.

Father Timothy never looked to the left; he spun right to go down the narrow corridor. The angel told him that the altar lay that way. As he stepped forward, his insanity marveled at her understanding.

The agents of Satan were trying to take the baby that God had instructed Timothy to sacrifice in HIS name. The demons trying to get the baby could not possibly understand the mind of God. It never occurred to Timothy that he couldn't either.

He never saw the foolishness in his blinded faith. He was righteous among men; Timothy KNEW he was! Without any doubt. He smirked as he cuddled the tiny baby close. Three steps further away from the door and the priest froze, as a very tall woman rushed unexpectedly onto the staircase above him. She seemed startled that someone was there, and her head jerked backwards in reaction.

Timothy froze; so did Gail .

He was a step away from the bottom step, looking face to face with her as they both stopped to stare at one another.

Timothy saw in an instant the slim sword in her hand. She also had shoulder holsters hugging around her from her back, dangling under her arms. One of them was empty.

Her right hand held the missing pistol.

Gail couldn't move; every ounce of her attention was focused on the baby.

Gail's intuition forced herself to look at Timothy. She had no idea whom he was, or his role in this, but his hollowed eyes of madness said it all. She raised the pistol very slowly. Timothy's eyes widened slightly, and he shifted the baby in confusion. Unsure of her hesitation, sudden understanding dawned, and he raised the baby in front of him as a shield.

Gail lowered the pistol at once. Timothy grinned and, still raising the baby, he ran into the narrow hall beside the stairs as she was forced to run the opposite way to get down.

As she got to the bottom three steps, she hurled herself down, trying to turn just as the door opened again and a human stepped in.

This possible threat being immediate, Gail was forced to abort her attack and put the new threat in her sights.

She almost reflexively shot Webster in surprise. As his gun came up, he threw it downward again, as he recognized her face. Not her face, the face of the crazy chicks that had kidnapped him earlier.

Seeing him lower his piece, she hesitated and didn't shoot him.

Webster said in a hiss, "Don't shoot, lady! I'm with the good guys!"

He looked at her, still sure she'd shoot anyway.

Gail said, "What makes you think I am?"

Webster gulped, fearing that he was a dead man. Gail lowered her gun. He breathed out and felt his sphincter relax.

He asked breathlessly, "Are you Gail?"

She nodded at him, and Webster tried to continue as he stood up straight.

"I'm…"

He stopped, forgetting his own name.

Gail said, "Yeah, I know, one of the good guys."

She turned away from him and started after the priest. She didn't have time to make new friends. She had to get to that baby. Gail ran into the empty passage in front of her at full tilt.

The baby had to make contact with Matthew or they were all dead.

In Gail's faithful heart, she knew that when they made contact, a miracle would happen. She did not know what form it would take; she didn't care.

Whatever miracle it would spawn could not come fast enough. Gail only could be certain that if the baby could not be saved, everything she loved would die or be enslaved. Staring with Matthew.

The shattered man that now lay upstairs was utterly incapable of defending himself if she failed. Gail pressed her pursuit into the dimly lit passage to get that baby, whatever the cost.

He was Matthew's only chance.

He was the world's only chance.

Chapter 31

Anna descended into Hell, as terrified as any soul could be.

As the shadows swiftly moved around her, against each other, terrible sounds of whispers invaded Anna's ears. The sound was touched by the tenor and pitch of the mad, the insane. Anna screamed outward into the oblivion she had fallen into. The shadows closed around her, ripping small furrows into a million parts of her flesh. Like being scratched by needles, the sensation shredded her soul as she spun into the downward unending vortex. The whispers around her grew frantic and insulting.

Anna never stopped screaming. As snatches of her mortal memories fled in rips and shreds, the image of her mother made her cry out "Momma!". She was thrust away from Sara , back into the darkness of the shadows tearing her into pieces.

As Satan's memories burned into her own, Anna was propelled back to her mother.

To the desert.

The toolmakers they lived with fled in horror as the band of perfected Children Of Angels males crested the horizon.

As Homo Ergaster, with their immortal queen, Sara, had come face to face with the perfected men who bore the blood of angels, they had bolted as a group. In their newly formed higher thought, they understood perfectly who was higher in the food chain. The smartest of the group could almost understand why, but he could never quite make the connection.

To Homo Ergaster, it was simple; they were the food of the Gods. It was just that way: natural selection. Even the females and babies fled, understanding an animal reaction to danger.

The smartest of the Angel males smiled, as he saw Sara standing with a four-year-old Anna cradled to her neck. Even as the angels had mimicked the tools of human creation, their children grew as humans did, though with none of their weaknesses. At full adulthood, around their twenty-seventh year, age no longer touched them. Anna was as normal as any four-year-old human child.

Most of the group of fifteen perfect men had all laughedat their sister Angel. Some of them snorted in disgust at Sara whom had just been caught living with the foul little creatures that were running for the grasses.

The fever had consumed the men's minds as Sara staggered into her own inferno under the desert sun, asking God for mercy.

Mercy is for God, not for a wolfish pack of Angels who took what they wanted, when they wanted. And oe unto anyone who stood against them. They attacked with not the slightest thought of mercy.

Jerold held back in pleased surprise; he had finally caught up with his brother's bitch, and his daughter.

Jerold became crazed with bloodlust, and he howled with laughter as the fleeing little human creatures tried to get away from the pack. They were not as important to Angel males as the lowest cockroach that crawled upon the earth; the only thing that they needed was the blood.

Their only value lay as a blood source. The Children of Angels had developed a tase for human blood. Every time they drank it, the change that rippled across their flesh was a rapture of strength and progress, as the power and intelligence of their prey fused into their own skin.

The first curse had just been laid. But not the second, or third. Only the fever could stagger any of the Children of Angels, and as they had not yet learned to control it, the burn was still an event most of them had avoided at great cost.

Since they had never known pain, the men's violent reaction to the fever forced the Angel women to flee them, or fight them for the safety of their own lives and that of their children. Sara had ran from Alexander to escape the torture of it, breaking their Angelic family line forever, unable to simply remain beside each other. She had taken Anna and fled to the desert where the Angels rarely hunted.

The Angel male's hungers had raged beyond control, not able to satisfy the demands of the flesh, feeling only the sin of it.

Every one of the creatures Sara led and loved as her pets, was slaughtered, torn asunder, and their carcasses molested in vileness that was unspeakable.

Jerold had taken Sara himself; as , the leader of a pack he had some entitlements and Sara was the only worthy prize worth taking that day. He had wounded Anna badly in the head, as he had beaten the child from her mother's desperate grasp.

Sara's gift of aging was no match for Jerold's gift of fire. Nor could she match his natural strength advantage, but even so, she had fought like a lioness.

Anna slept, unnaturally jerking, convulsing, as the attack went on. Her little head burst with thousands of tiny bolts of light. The height of the sun had not lowered when Anna finally opened her eyes to the shadow leering above her.

Swaying above Anna, Jerold had watched the child twitch as she came to. Her mother lay behind him, completely split from her ribs to her still exposed groin. He knew he could not kill Sara, as they were all yet still immortal, , so he gutted her instead, knowing it would take hours for her to heal enough to move. He did it because it was extra painful for their kind to be disemboweled.

Jerold smiled down at Anna in his drained, drunken satisfaction. He knew his brother would not care about him harming Sara. Alexander often spoke of harming her, himself, after she had ran away with his daughter.

As Jerold hovered over the child, he thought about violating her as well. He swallowed hard as Alexander's image flew suddenly to mind. The taboo on incest was already strong among them. Jerold wisely hesitated as Anna's tiny fingers began flexing in her unnatural seep..

Though they were both fullbloods, Alexander were actually half-brothers, born of different fathers. Their mother had been one of the original six hundred and sixty-six who had distanced themselves from God and His war with Lucifer.

Jerold knew their mother would be outraged at the violation of this child. . Still, he was more worried about retaliation from Alexander than over some perception of right or wrong.

Alexander may not care about this woman, but the child was a different story.

Jerold grinned as Anna rolled her eyes with only the whites showing. Alexander had become a father with one glimpse of his firstborn. Jerold had seen the pride in his brother at the sight of the newborn. Snatched from the womb, Anna had screamed and Alexander had cried as he had become a father for the first time . His brother, who had never shed his perfect tears, cried when he pulled Anna into this world with his own perfect hands.

Now, four years later, the child lay helpless on the ground, quaking and trying to wake up. Jerold moved closer, intending to sit beside her. His brother would reward him handsomely for his daughter's return.

The child's beauty was spectacular and as he leaned over her, she reached up between them suddenly and rammed a small, sharpened stone tool directly into his heart.

As the shadow had shifted above her, Anna came fully awake. The small stone tool that she always held came up as she struck out, mostly a reflex reaction. Going smoothly between his ribs, it took only a solid slight thrust to cleave his perfect heart in two.

Jerold's blood splattered, and then gushed into Anna's eyes. Her nose and mouth were instantly filled with the hot mass of it.

The shadow flew backwards up and off of her as the still severely wounded child twisted and crawled away, gasping and gagging. Anna never looked back. She was a child of the desert. The law of the jungle applied here as well: kill or be killed. It was just that way. She crawled to the tall grasses, choking and blinded by Jerold's blood.

Inside her head, the bright sparks exploded with a green-blue infusion of light. As Anna swallowed reflexively, the blood hit her stomach, and as she disappeared into the grass she staggered and convulsed.

The knowledge of Jerold's blood worked itself outward in an electric pulse, infesting itself through her tiny veins. Young Anna understood questions she could not possibly have known to ask.

A fire grew in her mind as the instructions for his unintentional gift buried itself inside her wounded head; a fire she feared.

The knowledge of the blood became the knowledge of the mind.

As the second curse had not yet been laid, Jerold propelled backwards, sitting on his haunches in shock as the child staggered away, unimpeded, choking on his immortal blood.

Dazed, Jerold looked at the tiny stone tool protruding from his chest. At first, he just frowned at it dumbly. Sara groaned in sobbing disgrace behind him, and he grinned drunkenly at the little flint handle sticking out of his chest.

As he curled his hands around it, Jerold almost laughed. By God, that little bitch not only looked just like her father , she also acted like him, too!

He plucked it from his chest just as little blue dots of light started rending his heart back together. It itched badly.

Some of his men staggered back from the grasses, covered in the blood of the humans they hungered for.

Some of them laughed at Jerold as he pulled the stone from his heart. He scowled, flushed in humiliation. Wounds to the heart were disgraceful to them, as it spilled so much of their blood.

Everyone assumed that it was Alex's woman who had stabbed Jerold . He stomped to the tall grass where the child had disappeared, furious. Anna was still missing as he looked at the bloodied wallowed grass where she had collapsed. The clever little girl had disappeared completely. He had put his men on the hunt after he had grown frustrated. She stayed gone.

After Sara had healed, she had fled back to Alexander, empty arms dragging like a million tons of grief. Alex had been angry at his brother's lack of control and dragged a wailing Sara to Jerold's father.

Though very sick, he had allowed them an audience.

Satan had listened in secret glee at the details of his son's brutality. Though his flesh was slowly coming away from his bones as God stripped him from his human skin, Satan had held on longer to it than all the other original generation. A disease resembling leprosy was cast among the first six hundred sixty-six a few years before, when the first curse was laid, and all of the Renegades had succumbed to it, except Satan.

As the first Renegade Angel to take the skin, Satan was the last of them to let it go, knowing only damnation and oblivion awaited him in spirit.

He had agreed to find the missing child for them; at a price.

Crying and desperate, Sara had agreed. She paid in blood. As her Angel blood infused Satan's failing body with a burst of blueish-white lights, he could hold off damnation a while longer.

Anna was found that very night, huddled in a swamp, with a terrible secret embedded deep into a ball of fire in her mind.

The angelic blood of Jerold that she had ingested fused into her, giving her all his strength. Through the blood of his father, Jerold's gift of fire touched Anna's mind in a soft distant place she had to grow into: a place that burned with Satan's blood.

As Anna fell into Hell, that ball of fire in her mind burst into flames that tinged her every thought and movement.

Anna strangled on her own screams on her descent into the clawing nothingness that was sucking her down.

In the flames of her brain, large chains of Jerold's and Satan's memory lay next to hers, as she found the pieces and snatched at them.

Anna saw Michael standing before her, glowing with the flickering shadow of fire . Instantly, she knew he had made a deal with the devil and paid in the same coin her mother had used. As the nothingness violated her, Anna embraced the fire left in her mind so long ago.

A scream erupted from Anna's soul, so deep and vast that she lost track of the ghastly sensation of the thousand needles that ripped at her and screeched to a stop in her flesh. The whispers quieted and a great horrifying shadow reached out for her.

The sensation of falling slowed, until Anna floated softly down.

In her mind, Anna was holding a baby; a boy.

The blackness around her was still nothingness, but smoking wisps of white silvery light infused it. Anna held the baby up to her face, startled by his appearance and the sudden silence of her flesh.

She was filled with wonder as she saw the face of her firstborn son. Unlike real life, she saw the baby in her hands wiggle once, then twice. Her ancient heart burst with joy.

As he kicked his tiny leg, Anna giggled rapturously, gripping him tightly. For a moment, she forgot that her child had never taken a breath.

Anna saw with a heartbreaking crunch that it was not her baby, but Morgan's. The subtle differences crushed her as she sobbed out in sorrow. The baby cried out, too, as she settled onto the black sand ground. She searched the nothingness around her, horrified at the trick.

Not seeing a place to cast him down, Anna held the baby to her chest, and they cried together. The tiny baby was inconsolable as she tried to calm herself.

Anna looked down on the infant , frustrated, and her tears fell onto his tiny face. In slow motion, she watched as her own tears merged with his, as they twisted and fell down his cheek.

Understanding dawned on Anna; at first slowly, then with a startling burst.

The baby was the son of God.

Born from the body of an Angel, the child was expelled as a perfectly formed human.

The boy was the next generation of human; a link, to balance the unnatural evolutionary leap between the Mortal's and the human race. Anna knew in an instant that this child was now the most evolved being on earth.

Through his blood, all humans would evolve.

As she fell under the weight of knowledge, Anna realized the boy's blood also carried the cure to the final curse. The terrible condition that had forced death upon their Mortal babies, could be reversed with a drop of the child's blood. .The final curse had robbed Mortal's of a future; now, through the boy, their own evolution could be restarted.

Satan's memories pressed at her, and she saw the terrible plans he had for the baby. That same drop of blood would seal Satan into perfect immortal flesh, and with the child dead, Satan would rule the earth and every creature on it.

It would give him the power to summon other Angels as his slaves.

Sitting up in the nothingness, Anna started to realize that the baby was no longer in her arms, or anywhere near.

Looking down, she saw herself wearing a white thin robe of some type. A single bullet hole pierced the fabric directly over her heart.

Anna's senses reeled as she was quickly pulled back from Hell and into her own wounded body with a quaking slam. She could feel the slight furrow that marked the path of the bullet going slightly into, and under her heart. She knew that she was dying.

Anna's eyes stuck together in a pasty twitch as strong hands pulled at her. She knew in an instant that they were Michael's hands.

Anna popped her eyes open as she felt the forbidden caress of him roughly grasping her arms.

The pain of the bullet-riddled body she was in hit her as she gasped again. Anna was shocked to realize that she had only been shot moments ago. The firecracker smell of gunfire still hung in the air above her. It wafted to her as her senses slammed awake.

The life of her leaked out slowly from one bullet hole as she struggled to come up from the ground with the unfolding sensations searing her fevered flesh.

Michael held her as his grief was battered into agony. He saw her heart was wounded.

They looked into each other's eyes for the first time in centuries. He saw Anna's soul was just as wounded as the cursed heart she bled from.

Her upward motion made her buck, then buckle backwards, as her mind registered the pain that made her flesh mortal . Michael held her, his hands shaking her, as he broke down completely and sobbed uncontrollably.

While Anna still lived, he collapsed onto her as he mourned her prematurely. He did not see her small hands moving. As he squinted in agonized sorrow, he gazed into her eyes, allowing her to pull at him.

Had Micheal used his advantage to slip into her mind, he may have seen fate coming. Had his grief not been so forgetful, he may have remembered for whom he grieved. .

Anna drew him into her pain as her wounded heart shattered. She whispered words into his mouth, their lips just inches apart.

She said softly to him, "I would do anything for my family …But not that."

Gripping the sword by the blade, Anna let it cut into her palm as she brought it up. Her right hand swung unimpeded as the tip expertly slipped between his ribs and pierced his cursed heart.

Michael's eyes widened, and then narrowed. Suspended above her, he gasped. Rivulets of his blood trickled down her arm.

Anna pulled him slightly into her thoughts and she watched as death came to him on the shadows of Hell that she had just escaped. He reflexively pushed up and away from her as she lay on the grass watching the only man she had ever loved die by her own hand.

The brother she had known only in love blinked at her heavily. Michael pitched his head, unbelieving, causing the rest of his body to twist slightly. Anna reached her hand up and caressed his left cheek with the back of her knuckles; she touched his lips with her fingertips that were covered in his own blood.

She whispered, "Shhh, I'm here. See? I saved you from me after all."

As they gazed at each other, Michael tossed his head again. This time, the sway of his body took him down and he landed hard, face first on the ground beside her.

The wound under his arm burst with fire and the blood on her hand and arm started smoking. The sting of it made Anna's eyes tear up, painfully. The blood started burning into her skin. The pain forced Anna to do something and she started rolling away from Michael's body. Wiping her hands on the dried grass, it spurted bursts of flames in some of the places that were touched earlier by the baby's thaw. The clumps closest to the ground were wet with a slick sheen of humidity.

As the blue flames overtook Michael, Anna watched through eyes that cried freely. She rubbed her hands on the wet grass, pulling it up in clumps, rubbing it on herself.

With a steel will, Anna turned to observe the place where she had fallen with Abby. The others in the group still remained shattered and in shock. Anna's mouth gaped open as she watched Doug loudly mourn the newborn baby he was shaking.

The child's limp nakedness was still so warm, little puffs of mist rolled off him as the coldness of winter kissed him tiny form.

Maria, also crying loudly, was trying to pry the baby from Doug's grasp.

The dead baby…Anna's gut twisted as she recognized the terrible stillness of it. Her memory stirred, buried deep under the loneliness of time.

Anna watched as Maria finally won the struggle and took the newborn. The trained doctor started hacking away on the still attached umbilical cord with the only tool she had, a shattered piece of sharp pine. Anna gasped at the awfulness, feeling one of the five useless bullets in her leak out. It came out of her on a fresh gush of blood that pulsated with bursts of white. The face of her own stillborn children haunted Anna her from a memory so faded it seemed to be an etching onto her translucent soul. She sobbed in the moonlight.

That Michael and his son had both died this night, did not seem real to her. She knew the boy's human mother could not have survived his birth, either.

Anna picked up the sword that Michael had cast out of his body when he sat back abruptly. She looked at the face of Michael as it began to char; she knew that the bond that had set so sweetly in her soul was betrayed forever.

Anna staggered to her feet using the sword to steady herself.

Now that she was dying, she almost didn't mind the sureness that she would forever be alone. The impact of it actually removed the pain of her still bleeding heart and shifted it to her now searing soul.

Swaying on her feet, tottering dangerously, Anna turned towards the slight movement to her rear right. Looking at the corner of the convent, Anna could not have known that her eyes followed the exact path of the devil that had killed her. Instead, a different devil appeared.

Adam stood up from the shattered tree line; Anna blinked hard, recognizing him instantly. She almost smirked as he popped up, staggered to his own right, and then turned to the corner of the building as well, running away from her.

So, the little bastard was here! Anna was not surprised in the least.

Before her smirk could settle, she thought of Jerold. Already following Adam, she watched him disappear around the corner of the building.

She couldn't wait to get that little bastard. Anna had watched Adam many times and knew he was as cruel as his father. She had always believed that Jerold had passed his arrogance on to all of his children. Anna actually never called Adam by his name; she just called him simply, 'the little bastard'.

Throughout centuries, everyone who knew them both knew Anna was talking about Jerold's oldest surviving son anytime she used the phrase.

Anna thought of Morgan's genetic arrogance and she smirked, then her heart broke. Only slightly more steady, she staggered up the slope in a slow awkward walk. The image of her beautiful cousin, lying serenely in the moonlight behind her, pierced her already dying heart. Anna allowed herself to slip into the pain that raked at her from every inch of her living corpse. The pain turned into an anger that gave Anna more strength as she struggled against the madness the pain descended into.

Anna slipped onto the edge of insanity, letting it make her stronger. She thought, 'What the hell!' and found comfort in madness, as it eased the tension of her shattered body. She let herself slip further into chaos, knowing she was too weak to pull away from it now.

Anna cursed Jerold. She knew that he had let himself be led by his father. He and Satan had made a frightful bargain and Anna moved to follow their pawn. She grinned like a rabid fox as she thought about the secrets of the two elders. She had just confirmed that the younger of the kinsman had no idea of the 'lie' that he was.

Without warning, Jerold suddenly staggered forth in front of her and he, too, ran after his son. Anna stopped cold.

As Jerold ran into her line of view, he tried to gather his will and focus. Her beauty made him shake as his body trembled. He had not even cooled yet from the fever that burned in him. Trying to maneuver past her and away, Jerold focused on her clothing and grinned in glee as the hem of her long smock coat caught fire at her frozen feet.

He pressed on after Adam, not looking back to watch her burn.

Anna gaped down in horror; she at first thought her wounded heart had finally expired. She looked down to face her own death. In an instant, she realized the seeping bullet wound had not thrown flame, but that flame had engulfed her coat. She dropped the sword as her hand instinctively reached down to swat at the flames.

As her hands passed into the heat of it, the flame died out in an instant.

Anna gulped in shock as the smoke from the charred spots made her eyes burn. She jerked up her hands and held them close to her face, blinking hard.

The pain had passed into just a slender sliver as the madness intoxicated her senses.

Anna blinked at her hands again, frowning… then smiling…Smiling a concerned frown. She twisted her hands in the moonlight. The light burns on her right hand had already shrunk to only debris on her skin.

Anna said, "Holy crap."

She stretched her arms away from her while examining them from arm's length.

Anna touched the spot of flame in her mind that had been left by the son of Satan. I It had always seemed distant and far from her. Now it seemed closer. The spot reached back for her as a sapling directly in front of her outstretched hands burst into a weak flame.

Anna's eyes widened as she snatched her hands back.

The outstretched flame of memory raced through her mind. If she could have felt the pain of her body through the madness, she would have felt the blue-green charge of fire that raced into her human heart.

With no pain, certain she was mortal, Anna was sure it was a quiver of her oncoming death.

Drunkenly, from a different mind than her own, Anna studied her hands, again.

She uttered, "Hell yeah!" and threw her hands forward once more.

The larger pine in her path burped, then popped, with a pathetic spark, then a small flame. The flame widened some as she again jerked back her hands, putting them under her armpits as she watched the small flame pop onto the tree.

Anna's mouth gaped as her jaw dropped. She inspected her hands closely once more.

Anna smiled as madness made her accept it.

She said, "Very cool!" to nobody.

Jerold had slipped away behind the corner to the front of the building.

She staggered forward again in the same direction.

The blue-white flame that flickered in her wounds glowed green, then yellow, as the colors combined. The yellow lights that flooded into her heart heated up until they glowed bright red.

Because Anna had gained the knowledge of Jerold's blood before the second curse, as an innocent, she carried it's instructions within her mind. In all the years she had shielded her heart from the horror of life, Anna was never aware that she was the only Mortal who retained the knowledge of how to heal a wounded heart.

Only she and Satan had ever dared taste the blood of another Angel before God had cursed any of them. It carried in it the instructions for immortality.

It had been there the entire time, and her body began responding to directions that her mind was barely aware of giving.

In madness, she played with the fire that she had refused to touch or acknowledge her entire life. She let the flames consume her.

Doug's mournful cry, from behind her, crept up on her like a hostile presence.

In the flames of memory, Anna saw the dead baby that Michael had fathered. Although Diana never knew who she was, Anna had always known whom Diana was. She had kept tabs on Michael; they had kept tabs on each other.

As Anna staggered after them, she cried out at the sorrow. Michael was dead. His son was dead. Everyone was dead. Her sons…Her mother…Her father… Her brother her human brother, Joseph…Abby…Morgan lay helpless… Gail unprotected, and the baby in the hands of his murderer.

Anna sobbed as she propelled herself faster. She knew she had failed, but she still refused to die unsatisfied.

She was dimly aware that the blind corner was suicidal. She couldn't summon the courage to care, as she was sure that she was dead anyway.

Anna could feel the damage. She pushed the feeling of it away as it throbbed and itched. She resigned herself to the thought that her death was inevitable. She pulled to the corner, still trembling with weakness. She had faith it would all be over soon.

Anna grinned in mad glee as she thought of the family reunion she was about to crash. She couldn't wait to see Adam's face when she told him what he truly was. The little bastard!

She could not wait to tell Adam that Jerold was so determined to rid himself of his own flesh, that he had sold his son to Satan, for the price of that singular mortal death.

As she stumbled, agonized by failure, Anna prayed she that she wouldn't burn down God's house. She smiled at the insanity of it; sounded cool, anyway. Picking up speed, she rushed the blind corner touched by leafy hands.

Chapter 32

Not knowing what else to do, Webster followed Gail into the narrow passage around the stairs. The federal agent barely kept up as Gail went along at a dead run.

In Gail's mind, Sara spoke to her.

"Make your offerings upon the altar of Thy Lord."

In an instant, Gail understood the priest's destination.

Webster crowded her from behind as they passed closed doors on either side of the hallway. He dimly realized that they could be ambushed from any one of them, but he raced along anyway. After three gulping, gasping eternities, Gail reached the end of the hall. The door to her left stood in a dim antechamber that was partitioned off from the rest of the hall.

Gail stopped in confusion; she saw the door had been chained and locked. The chain was wrapped around the door pull and locked firmly. She barely remembered that Katherine was going to lock in the nuns, as had been the plan; the lock and chain were both undisturbed. She was already turning to look back into the hall as Webster's feet hit a slick place on the floor and careened into her back, nearly knocking them both into a heap. The door that was immediately to the right on the same wall stood ajar just a sliver. Gail bolted back, past Webster, leaving him standing in confusion at the locked door.

She darted to the room that had been Frances' personal office and started looking around, desperately, gun and sword both held aloft. It was deserted, but a small door at the far end of the space to her right stood barely open. It led to a narrow staircase.

Gail felt the panic rising in her as she jumped through the door and onto the crowded staircase. There was another entrance to the sanctuary at the top of those stairs and another yet another bolted door beyond it.

Gail hit the first locked door with both weapons thudding harmlessly against the wood as she paused to listen. With almost an instant sigh of relief, she realized that the priest had also come to a chained door. Behind the door that closed off the stairs, Gail listened as Timothy rattled the chains of the other door. She heard him chuckling as he thumped and kicked something hard.

Gail knew the upper door that led out above the altar was not sturdy like the other doors of the structure. It was built small and plain, only meant to be hidden from the congregation and not as a serious impediment. The lower door was the clergy's main entrance.

Almost before Gail could blink, Webster had raised his gun to the locked door in front of them.

Gail grabbed the barrel, pushing it violently away.

She hissed, "No!"

As Webster looked at her, Gail ground her teeth and shook her head.

She hissed again, "He's in a stone chamber, you'll hit the baby!"

Webster started shaking, realizing what he'd almost done. The chain of the door of that chamber rattled violently as Timothy tried to stay ahead of them.

Gail bit her lip and suddenly brightened. She turned as she spoke hurriedly.

"You stay here! If he gets through that door before I get through the one below, then shoot the latch!"

Gail looked back up at Webster as her eyes lowered dangerously.

"Do NOT shoot that door unless he's broken free of the other one."

Webster stopped, frozen by the glint of violence in her eyes.

He swallowed hard, understanding. He promised solemnly.

"I won't."

Gail nodded and was gone in a downward rush. Webster put his ear to the door as the man with the baby started violently kicking something that Webster could hear cracking slightly.

Gail passed back through the office, coming back to the chained door she had already approached. Without thinking about it, she put the pistol to the padlock and pulled the trigger. A hole erupted through the padlock but it held firmly in place as the bullet passed through it and lodged in the door.

Gail looked at it in disbelief. She shot the padlock again, this time at the joint of the curved bolt; again, it jumped but held.

As the door above her was assaulted by violent kicks, she screamed out in frustration at the lock.

" Clever little humans!'

In a panic, she jumped up and kicked the lock into the door so hard it almost crushed her knee. The chain, lock, and door all held.

Now snarling, suddenly inspired, Gail shot the chain itself instead of the lock. As the door above her cracked loudly, the chain exploded into two parts as shards of the ruined metal sent shrapnel splinters sticking into her and leaving the door looking like a metal porcupine. As she pulled off the broken chain, Timothy was literally kicking the door above her into oblivion.

The chain free from the door, Gail started forward, acting on instinct and faith, trying not to think at all. She pulled out both weapons and kicked the double doors open with a sound *thunk*.

Gail froze in shock.

A strange human stood in the center of the sanctuary looking at her. Not human anymore; Gail's stomach fell as she saw the yellow fire dancing in his eyes.

She knew that Satan had arrived for the baby. The door above her burst and cracked as Timothy freed himself from the small chamber.

Looking into her eyes, Satan smiled in glee. The silent nuns all physically sank away from the figure as a pig squeal of laughter emanated from him.

His body was smoking heavily now as he burned from the inside.

In the instant that Gail recognized him, Satan too, knew whom she was; the anointed one who had been touched by the blood of Christ himself.

Before either of them could react to recognition, the front doors were shoved inward as Adam appeared through them. The entire population of the room turned to see his arrival.

Gail was momentarily stunned, again.

Satan truly squealed with delight upon seeing him.

Gail knew instantly that the body prepared for Satan had arrived as she blinked in confusion; she contemplated her young cousin as he stopped to recognize her.

The giant crack from the upper door was followed by a large 'thunk' sound as the door Father Timothy was attacking finally gave way above Gail.

The quick shuffling that followed made her aware that Timothy was zigzagging onto the outer staircase, coming down from the balcony, so Gail moved to intercept him a few steps to her left. Webster's gunshot never sounded. Her confusion brought her to a halt at the bottom step.

385

Gail watched Adam closely as Timothy came into view above her. He saw that she had moved to cut him off, so he paused on the landing above her.

The priest was on the high ground as Gail looked at him helplessly from below. Timothy smiled and she almost drew up the pistol to shoot him just out of anger and frustration, but she stopped herself. Father Timothy had the baby enfolded to his chest, as if the infant was his bullet-proof shield.

Satan watched the man run down and then stop as he held a tiny child to himself.. He squealed again, sending peals of mad laughter bouncing off the stone walls, contaminating the church by his presence.

The stillness was complete except for Satan's snickering, and the sniffling from the nuns who were crossing themselves and crying copious silent tears. Most still knelt in prayer with eyes closed to the horror around them, beseeching God for mercy. They didn't know any other way to combat something that had smoke coming from the pores of its body.

In an instant every sister in the vast cathedral understood they were in the presence of evil. It was not a matter of faith, but a reality none could deny.

The baby was here. Satan was here. The sanctified hands needed to kill the child held him even now. …And the anointed one alone was the last defense against Satan's all-consuming blood lust. The Anointed One shook from head to toe with fear. She had stopped breathing.

Gail looked at the men who mocked her with sneering grins, knowing they had her trapped. Her, and the baby, and Matthew, all trapped. To her horror , Jerold, himself, appeared behind Adam.

Within a heartbeat, Gail knew that she was dead. She could not overcome these odds.

With a sorrow so deep that it flooded her spirit with contempt and resolve to see this through, Gail turned her face upward to look once more at the baby before she was torn asunder. She nearly fell to her knees in surprise at what she saw.

Sister Elizabeth's tiny aged frame had pushed and pulled the much bigger Matthew into the void of the door that Timothy had shredded.

The mad priest smiled sweetly down on Gail, all the while making sure the baby was his shield in case she got any bright ideas.

This was his moment…the angel had promised.

The young priest and the tiny nun staggered to a stop above and behind Timothy . Matthew's knees were trying to lock so he could stand, but he was losing that battle to the morphine haze he was in. Sister Elizabeth was literally holding up the mountain of him, pausing as Satan's shrieks died instantly as the baby's Guardian came into view..

The smoking figure hung back, suspended on the uncertainty.

To everyone who had a family stake in the outcome, the sight of Matthew's presence rolled over the room as surely as the thunder had touched them all earlier.

The Guardian had arrived. Matthew stood twenty feet from the baby, with nothing between them but gravity.

In an instant, it was apparent that the Guardian himself saw nothing but pain and the wretchedness of his own body. Matthew's entire frame trembled as his eyes rolled blindly. His huge body twitched as fresh blood seeped into the giant bandage covering him from breast to throat on his right side.

Matthew stumbled; Sister Elizabeth was barely able to twist her old body around to correct the balance. Matthew moaned, a pathetic loud gasp of agony.

Satan laughed again and actually danced a quick jig of celebration.

Gail met Elizabeth's eye as her jaw dropped. The old woman smiled down at her sweetly. Gail knew that the woman had just broken her lifelong vows . It didn't matter, though, whatever consequences came tomorrow was a moot point , if you didn't live to see it.

Gail turned to look at the three men who were coming for her blood. She meant to face them and fight, but she crossed her gun laden hands and sobbed into her arms. Fighting didn't always mean winning. Gal knew she could not win this fight. Just as she lost all hope, the odds shifted again.

Through the door behind Jerold, still some six feet from him, Anna passed from the moonlight into the threshold of the sanctuary.

Jerold stood with his son between him and the body his father had stolen. They had all stopped in surprise when they saw the Guardian appear at the top layer of balconies. Jerold grinned as he saw that the man was not only already severely wounded, but kissed with the pall of death itself.

Jerold stepped forward as he sensed Anna behind him. The fever did not come, had not alerted him to her presence, but his awareness of her rippled through him like the beginnings of a tidal wave.

Satan bristled to a stop at the sight of the Guardian in such close proximity to the baby. He felt Napoliss' weakening, wasting heart actually stop for a few beats. Satan had most definitely over-stayed his time in this fragile human shell. He knew that he had to jump to new skin quickly before death took him with it.

Satan didn't have the time to deal with dying again when he was so close to immortal flesh.

The human body of Napoliss was melting. Satan was preparing himself to jump out of his skin even as he heard the woman's voice from behind him. Trying to gather his mighty will, he turned to his prepared body that stood behind him. Adam was distracted, looking behind himself, completely unaware his skin was not his own.

Anna looked at Adam as he, too, sensed and then turned to her.

Anna blurted out , "Hello, you little bastard! Did you know that you're a half-breed?"

Her sword hung limply in her left hand.

Jerold froze in mid-turn at Anna's words. Adam looked at her, startled, before his eyes snapped to Jerold. Jerold refused to make eye contact with his son .

Anna seemed highly amused as the truth settled over the entire room like an explosion of silence. Gail blinked hard, trying to understand why that even mattered at the moment.

Jerold's jaw gaped as he studied his son's slow sneer. He had told Adam that his gift would come; it could take millennia to manifest, his father assured him to be patient. .. When Adam's 's toe did not grow back, Jerold had taught him to mask it. To hide it from the others. Jerold swore to his Adam that he was no different than other full-blooded Mortal males. The other males of the family went along with it, finding it a perfect running gag.

Until that moment Adam could not have known if it were true, or not, but Jerold's look of surprised guilt confirmed it all. .Adam never registered his fear as his sneer became a snarl; he reached out his hand and soundly slapped his father as hard as he could directly across the face.

As Jerold's head snapped backwards, Anna used the first lesson she had ever learned in life; she aimed for his eyebrows as she threw out her empty hand.. A pathetic spark popped, then flared as Jerold's eye lashes and brows burst into flames. Jerold swatted at his face with hands full of pistols.

The flames died immediately but the burned tissues crackled with horrendous pain.

Jerold staggered, blinded, ad unable to focus past the pain. Anna did not pause as she crossed the distance before Adam could react from the explosion of flames.

In a move made slightly clumsy by her wounded body, she swooped and pivoted the slender sword and took Jerold's head in a smooth snap.

The room exploded as the nuns panicked. Fleeing away as a group, much like antelopes before the lions, the women hurled themselves to the far wall, screaming out to God in desperation.

When Anna had revealed Adam's secret, Gail put her arms down in shock to look at her startled cousin. In that instant, they all recognized the truth.

Gail gasped as it all made sense ; Jerold had betrayed his son. Half-Mortal, and Half-Human, Satan expected to rule both once Adam's skin became his own. With the dread of understanding, Gail knew her instincts had been right. Adam had made no deal with Satan. His father had offered him up like a lamb for sacrifice..

Gail instantly knew that Adam's blood, was not Adam's blood. He was not a creation, but an imitation, as she was. A clone. Jerold had betrayed his own son, all of his family, and his own race..

Jerold had betrayed every Angel in Heaven and sold them into ten thousand years of slavery on earth.

As Anna's pyrotechnics blinded Jerold, Gail moved forward to the smoldering dead man. When the room erupted, some of the panicked herd of nuns ran into Gail , throwing her back.

She looked up, just as Elizabeth's old body jerked in shock at the decapitation below her. Sister Elizabeth lost her grip on Matthew and he pitched forward down the staircase, almost in slow motion. His badly bleeding shoulder virtually gushed as he seemed to be suspended for a moment, then plunged downward in a limp heap.

In a heart-breaking moment, Gail, too, felt herself falling, as her mind registered the surety of his death. Even as she pushed towards Satan, Matthew fall was all se could see.

Needing to get to Napoliss, Gail pushed against the fleeing figures as she fought to get past the altar to face the smoking dead man that was stumbling towards it. . She allowed herself one lingering backward look as she saw Matthew land head-first in a crushing blow on the first roll of the long drop before him. Gail's screaming became a part of her battle cry as she pushed further into the church..

She ran straight at a now staggering Napoliss. Smoke virtually billowed from every pore of him as he sank slowly before her oncoming rush. He could no longer see her as the frail human eyes melted.

Just as she was in her final steps, he blindly stood straight up to meet her attack. As she thrust the sword, she saw the glow of fire leave his damaged eyes as a great shadow leapt from him and into the body of Adam who stood behind him. Just as the flame flickered and died, Gail's blade sank deep into his sternum, cracking it with a sickening thud.

Adam was slammed upright as the shadow enveloped him from above, sucking out his breath with it. Matthew's shattered body rolled down the stone stairs, breaking open his fresh wounds, creating even more, just as critical.

Matthew's massive limp frame slammed into the insane, kidnapping priest as he landed hard. With a sickening thud, their bodies met in the air above the elevated landing and all three bodies smacked soundly against the stone of the platform, stopping Matthew from falling the other half of the way down..

The baby was swept from its would-be murderer by Matthew's bleeding weight. As he literally flew across the floor, his tiny face was slammed against the cold stone.

In the middle of the room below them, Adam screamed as a great vastness opened through him. Gail was propelled downward, with her sword still lodged in the body of Napoliss.

Anna tried to step past Jerold's body as it pitched and exploded into flames that almost singed her. She stepped back as his headless body pitched forward and blocked her with a burst of rippled flame.

Gail started walking quickly towards a still distracted Adam. Now that Satan was in the flesh of a Mortal, even a half-bred one, all that was left was to add the child's blood. Until then though, Satan was still as mortal as they were.

As the stolen eyes started glowing with a yellow hue, Gail took her chances in the enclosed area and raised the gun. As she closed in on him, she fired the gun repeatedly as she clawed for the other weapon. If she missed, she'd hit her sister who was rushing to her assistance from directly behind her target.

Adam's body curled into himself, shielding his heart from her volley. All of the rounds caught him in the upper body and limbs, but none found their mark. The guns were empty; they only clicked now so Gail hurled the pieces at him from the distance and started ripping apart the Kevlar vest she wore, loudly popping the Velcro tabs along her ribs.

Gail screamed in frustration as Satan uncurled, grinning, his eyes yellowed with glowing flames. She was pulling her head out of the vest, intending to lash him with it, as Anna swooped in on Adam from behind like the avenging fury she was.

Adam never had time to turn as Anna's blade dug into him and straight through him. The ribs snapped under the crushing blow as Anna furiously cleaved into his heart like a crazed butcher in an abattoir.

Before Adam's body could explode into the fire Anna expected, a great gush of heavy shadow pulled both the sword and her outward and up as Satan panicked and tried to save himself from the death of his new skin and picked the easiest to enter.

The shadow leapt away from them, slower this time, going over Gail's head and seemed to land behind her.

Matthew had not moved after he had fallen. A shocked Sister Elizabeth, unable to catch his rapid pitch forward, stood in shock at the melee below them. Matthew's body stripped the baby from Timothy's arms and had pushed the lighter man into his own terrifying roll down the lower set of stairs. Though Timothy had smacked to the floor of the cathedral with a solid thump, he was already trying to come to his feet at the very foot of the staircase.

The agony of death dropped over Matthew like a welcome friend.

Before Matthew could open his eyes to face it, large tears of sorrow and hurt leaked from them. He knew he could no longer hold onto the life force inside of him. Gail would no longer be able to hold him together and keep him whole.

The sorrow of the knowledge that flooded Matthew's mind as death was imminent made his eyes pop open and he screamed at God, into the rafters above the altar that had been built by blessed hands.

"Father, why hast thou forsaken me?" Matthew asked in horror.

His face broke into agony as his useless body lay on the cold stone. He only wore the jogging pants that Gail had dressed him. He was so cold. .

Matthew sobbed to the speechless ceiling as he felt himself dying. He saw Gail's eyes looking at him with the greatest love he had ever known, as she prayed over him in memory.

Matthew cried, angry at the God who had cursed him to this! He thought about his fall from grace. The church had already stripped him of his robes because of Joseph's death. They believed what they wanted to believe.

Matthew cried for his family. He cried for her. He cried for his lost friend Joseph, and the confusion of the pain that withered his soul.

Matthew lay there crying , disgraced, dying on the unforgiving floor of the house dedicated to the God he'd finally turned to, to find peace. He cried out at the horror of it. He wanted to turn away from the beauty that stared back at him silently from a lit stained glass window above him.

Matthew turned his head to see a baby's face lying beside his own.

Matthew gasped in horror at the huge dent in the baby's head, right above his tiny eyebrow. The baby lay still, his eyes closed, as Matthew's wounded shoulder moved instinctively, trying to flop his arm towards the little form. He cried out, cursing at God as the cruelty of it sank in.

He had never seen this baby before. Seeing the blood on the baby's lips, clogging his tiny shattered nose, Matthew clumsily swiped, trying to get it off the baby. As his shoulder throbbed with a weakening heartbeat, he forgot it all in a primal urge to clean the child's face and wipe the blood from the infant.

From his wisps of memory, Gail's voice came to him.

She had told him of a baby. What was it she had said?

Matthew tried to grasp the thought as it refused to be caught while his fingers weakly swiped in an effort to clear the baby's nose. He cried out weakly as his mind accepted the baby's death, though his heart would not.

Gail's voice soothed him from memory. No, not Gail's...his angel's voice, the one from his dreams with eyes so like his beloved. She spoke to him, from the air above him.

The Angel asked, "Would you die for him?"

. He studied the infants's face. As the voice rolled away like retreating thunder, Matthew responded calmly through the pain and sadness. "

"Yes. I would die for him."

It never occurred to Matthew not to sacrifice himself for such an

392

innocent child. . He felt his heart slow down…once…then twice.

Even as his answer hung on the still air, the baby's wounds sparkled with a burst of green-blue fragments of light.

Matthew heard Gail screaming as the baby's blood that was on his hand burst with the sting of hellfire.

In his mind, he was talking to them both as he spoke his last words.

"It's ok, baby. I love you."

The sting was worse than a hundred scorpions and Matthew dragged his arm to his face and with a primal instinct gnawed at the stinging sensation as he bit into the baby's blood on his fingers .

Matthew watched the stained-glass images as his heart stopped. …Once…Then twice. Then a third time. His gaze clouded as he felt the stinging enter his mouth; it burned his tongue.

It was the last thing MMatthew felt, as he surrendered his soul to death and was greeted softly. The Angel of Death reached out for him with welcome arms.

She smiled at him with eyes so like Gail's, with tears on her cheeks like perfect drops of clear fire. The sensation of burning receded as she wrapped her arms around Matthew and pulled him away from his mortal core. . He smiled proudly at her, bringing pleasure to his death mask.

Sister Elizabeth reached his side a moment too late.

As Adam's body had pitched forward off Anna's sword, Sara's voice had boomed through the structure, coming from everywhere at once. Some of the nuns whom had huddled against the far wall, stopped crying and looked around in wonder as the voice shook through them.

"Would you die for him?" the voice asked.

Anna and Gail both stopped in shock and looked at each other in combined awe and fear.

Matthew's serene voice had immediately followed

"Yes. I would die for him."

Gail screamed as she flung herself around to stop Matthew from sacrificing himself.. Her shock at her hearing her mother's voice giving Matthew a choice, was dispelled completely by Matthew's answer. Uncaring of the danger that still lurked, Gail screamed louder as she reversed her course.

Anna lunged forward over Adam's burning body. Her sister outdistanced her as Gail almost reached the staircase. .

Anna watched as Timothy stood up at the bottom of the stairs. He stood up to meet Gail head-on as she rushed forward, straight at him, her sword left behind in Adam's burning carcass.

The great darkness that had slammed into Father Timothy as Adam fell, totally encompassed his being, helped by the flames of insanity that were already burning in the priest's mind. The yellowing eyes brightened with glee as Satan saw the Anointed One rushing at him.

Satan giggled as he suddenly remembered the long ago taste of Sara's blood. When she had struck a deal with him to find Ana in the desert.

Before Gail could stop her momentum, the blackness leapt again, going forward in a sweeping arch and hitting Gail full in the face.

Anna stopped dead in her tracks, not four feet behind her sister as she watched their mother's sin descended squarely into the middle of Gail's face. Anna's blood chilled instantly, knowing the terrible cost of it in her bones as Gail screamed. The shadow slammed into her with a massive weight.

Gail didn't have to invite Satan into her blood; their mother had already made that deal so long ago. Gail's blood as a half-breed was not her own, but her mother's, replicated.

The blood of Christ had kept Gail hidden and undetectable from other Mortals, and Satan , but here at the altar all sin is known. Sara's sin fell onto Gail with the burn of hellfire and the smell of sulpher.

Anna begged God for mercy as she started sobbing.

Sensing the danger, seeing the face of the enemy in one she loved, Anna extended the blade, and then lowered it, confused by her own istincts. She frowned as the sword started to tremble in her hands, unsure of what was happening. .

Gail's body was pulled upward, and she strained to breathe as the choking blackness violated her mouth, nose, and throat. Satan was weakened by the enormous energy drain of the repeated jumping, but he still string enough to overwhelm her completely. Gail resisted him once, then felt herself fold under his incredible strength.

She screamed, "God forgive me!" and propelled herself onto the point of Anna's outstretched sword.

Anna had seen Gail throw herself forward and had stiffened her arms, unsure what to do. As Gail pushed her body onto the sword Anna tried to pull back; but her sister's weight sent the sword to its intended destination, straight to the heart.

From the balcony came the cry of a confused, yet seemingly healthy baby.

Anna stared into Gail's eyes as a yellow glow first flared then dimmed just as quickly in their depths. Hot wet blood traveled down the blade.

Anna sobbed in disbelief, stricken to the core.

Gail was smiling, and in a gasp, she said, "I love you."

Anna blanched in horror, her elbows finally unlocking enough to drop the sword she still held. Gail sagged against the sword still impaling her and both women dropped to their knees as gravity made them face the inevitable. together.

Anna cried out like a wounded animal as she felt Gail's trembling through the steel. Her confusion creased her brow as Gail's blood used the sword as a conductor.

From the heavens, a great thunder shook the building as sheets of rain dropped from the clear night sky.

A shadow lifted from Gail, again leaping behind her, crossing the distance more slowly than ever as it took the Father Timothy to his knees again.

The rain pounded into a buffer of sheer white noise as it overtook the silence, replacing it.

Anna stared at her sister as she bawled. She shook her head in confusion. This simply could not be. She said mournfully,

"I don't understand!" Anna screamed helplessly.

Gail was trying to swallow. She lost the ability to control it; death was coming quickly.

Gail said in a croak, " Sacrifice, not suicide... Because I love you."

Her voice cracked as the smile widened. Gail's mouth filled with blood.

Father Timothy stumbled upward like a demented marionette, his body jerking with the pain of a million needles. His eyes glowed yellow then amber. He staggered, shaking his head violently.

Gail used her last breath to tell her sister, "Go beat his ass."

She grinned as she fell backwards and down; her eyes glazed and she was gone, no longer aware of any pain.

Anna reached for her face just as Gail fell backward, her sister's face... Their mother's face. Her own face. Anna felt her stomach twist as she reached for the void.

Satan's puppet watched them. With a hideous jerk, he twitched around, now desperate for the baby's blood.

From the landing above Timothy, Matthew refused to see Gail's sacrifice. He registered it but did not see it play out as he crossed back into this life.. It was as unreal to him as his newly formed vision...Perfect vision.

The new flesh of Matthew's skin had seamed his wounds together perfectly, leaving no scar. Even as he watched it, the torn flesh of his chest renewed itself as it throbbed and flushed, matching itslf to the color of the skin around it flawlessly with no discoloration at all, not even a bruise.

Matthew felt the old wounds deep in his bones as they also stitched and healed with fresh life.

The baby lay beside Matthew's leg, his tiny body perfectly warm on the cold of the floor. The child kicked uncomfortably as his tiny, busted nose burst with tiny bolts of blue green light. His little nose was no longer broken.

Matthew jerked around as he felt Sister Elizabeth put a dagger into his hands.

It was small and gold with a fat ruby in the perfectly balanced hilt. Atthew didn't trust his new eyes, certain that death was a bizarre place indeed. He shook his head as he admired the beautiful blade. The emblem of the Guardian glowed in the handle, sparkling mystically.

The possessed priest at the foot of the stairs turned upward toward them in a jerking unsteady parody of a step. The creature that was human no more turned eyes of sulphur to watch the only obstacle between it and the baby. Matthew couldn't suppress his trembling. Elizabeth was prodding him forward with her calm grey eyes.

She said to him evenly, "You killed, and died to save him...Now live for him."

Elizabeth smiled at Matthew warmly as she backed away. The Timothy creature rushed upwards, now desperate to take the baby.

Like Anna, Satan never gave up while there was still a chance. Elizabeth struggled to swallow as the burning priest came up at them in a lurching run. She watched Matthew as the weight of her words settled into him. Matthew had been discarded by the very church that had saved him. He could never go back; he knew it in his broken heart.

Gail lay facing upwards on the floor far below him. A savage hatred burst forth as Matthew saw the figure of the woman who had held the sword. He knew she was innocent, but hatred flared just the same.

Matthew looked at the upward rushing figure with all the calm that he could muster. The eyes flared with flickerin flames at him, and Matthew did exactly what Joseph had taught him to do: he threw the knife. The teaching had never been put in this context, but Matthew could see that his entire life had been preparation for this moment.

The blade firmly landed in the priest's smoking throat, neatly slicing off whatever breath Satan had left.

A shadow flared from out of the wound and flickered briefly before subsiding like a breaking wave goes back to the ocean. Inside the shattered human body, Satan heard the tick-tock of Timothy's heart stop and falter before he could escape the body. The sudden reversal of energy shocked Satan as he realized time had run out.

The rain beating loudly on the roof roared the news that he had failed. His time was up. Before Satan could summon the strength to slip into nothingness, he was caught like a thief by the hands of the Angel of Death.

From the ruined throat, Satan cried out in an agonized roar. The roar built in volume and rivaled the ferocity of the wind as it rushed out of Timothy in a final jerking thrust. A torrent of invisible energy blew forth into the room, enveloping it.

No one escaped the Angel of Death. Not even Satan.

Anna held onto Gail's body as the wind pushed itself into and around the room, whipping into a frenzy while picking up small pieces of debris and turning them into a veritable tornado of trash. The force of it continued to build for several seconds as Timothy's body pitched backward down the steps. In a cataclysmic whoosh, the volatile gust flew out into the night through the still open doors and rolled into the sheeting rain. In mere moments, it was gone.

The silent room was broken by Anna's grief. She sat splayed on the stone floor with Gail's body in her arms, rocking back and forth as if to soothe a tired child. She cried and she rocked and she cried.

The flames that normally consumed their kind did not touch Gail. Instead of her body heating up, it went cold in Anna's arms.

Matthew looked at his hands, suddenly realizing that not only was he very much alive, he was more alive than he had ever been. As the wind pushed itself from the immense chamber, he finally jumped in panic, trying to get to Gail as reality set in.

397

In all his heart Matthew knew that she was dead. He cried out from healthy lungs as the unbearable hurt touched his mind and his soul. He had gone to his knees without realizing where he was, but now he jumped up and started scrambling down the stairs.

Anna watched as Miguel came through the doorway, carrying Morgan in his arms as if she was an offering to the gods, which wasn't all that far off.

They were both soaked by the rain and rivulets of blood from Morgan's terrible wounds dripped a trail as he walked with her limp form. Anna's grief was beyond tears, a total desert of pain with no hope of sustenance. Her soul was as dead as these precious ones…her family. She tried to lay Gail gently to the floor as Anna came to her knees and finally stood. Morgan's total stillness was echoed in Anna's heart, but at least she was still able to function through the numbing calm.

Miguel walked forward slowly with the body of the woman he'd loved since he was a child. Anna knew the devastation he felt; she shared it.

Doug was next through the doorway with a man's body draped in his arms; Maria was at his side. They entered from the sheets of relentless rain into the protection of the vast room.

Miguel laid Morgan beside Gail, their bodies as close in death as they ever were in life. Matthew threw himself down next to them and huddled there in his misery, touching Gail's face.

On the balcony, Sister Elizabeth picked up the baby. His eyes were open wide as he tried to focus on her face. Mirroring her smile, his tiny face split into a huge grin and he wiggled with delight.

Anna was beyond numb; she felt like someone had filled her entire being with Novocain. Nothing was getting through, and it made the whole thing so bizarre. She knew it should be hurting but she didn't feel anything. Doug and Maria also brought Abby's body and laid him next to Morgan.

Anna looked at Miguel and then to Morgan's silent face.

She asked blankly, "What happened to her?"

Miguel tried to speak then faltered. Doug put his hands on Miguel's hunched shoulders and responded for him in a shaky voice,

"She killed herself." Doug whispered.

Anna turned her head sharply and looked at him, frowning, but Doug had lowered his eyes. Anna looked back to Morgan, not understanding. Neither Morgan, nor Gail burned, as their kind did.

Miguel held Morgan's slender limp hand in his as he looked down at his lost love. Matthew held Gail silently in a hug. Doug watched the young priest and spoke to Anna firmly.

"Morgan was trying to crawl when Maria put the... the baby... into her arms...The baby's mother is dead. All of a sudden, a few minutes later, this...this voice said...'Would you die for him?' and Morgan just smiled and said 'Yes'...Just like that.."

Miguel gulped as he finished it. ,

"Then she just reached out and...and... shot herself, with your pistol." He looked at Anna as she felt the impact of losing Morgan tear through her.

Miguel pressed on, now sobbing, his words nearly incoherent.

"Then...Then the baby just started crying and the rain hit us....It was so quick no one could stop her! " Miguel shook as his voice rose.

"The rain hit so fast that her body never sparked when she pierced her own heart!" he said miserably, explaining how she had not burned.

Miguel lowered himself to the floor as Anna looked away. Her mind was so weary she didn't have time to think of her own cheated date with death.

The bullet that had pierced her own heart had leaked out onto the floor during the fight, rejected and harmless as Anna's heart mended itself. Her soul, however, was shattered beyond repair.

For the first time, Anna realized that Maria carried a tiny baby who kicked at her rudely. She shook her head. She thought of Gail's body before her, with no scorch marks.

Anna numbly stared at Micheal and Diana's child, knowing it was a miracle that he had lived.

Matthew had stopped rocking as Miguel told the story of the voice. He blinked at the man rapidly. Matthew and Anna looked at each other. She looked away from death and saw his hands still covered in blood. Anna blinked hard, trying to understand. .

She asked him with a frown, "Whose blood is that?"

Anna could see that Matthew's body was completely healed, which should have been impossible. There should have been no blood on him.

Matthew released Gail only slightly as he looked at his own fingers. .

He said thoughtfully, "The baby that was up there... I think it is his blood."

Matthew pointed, and they looked up to see Elizabeth holding the child gently. He was no longer injured. The old nun smiled back at them warmly as she cuddled the boy.

From behind Anna, a strange rattling noise scraped gently at the silence. She turned her head completely around, expecting anything but what she saw.

She followed the noise to Abby and blinked dumbly at his ruined face. The blood and rain mixture bubbled from his nose as he tried to draw a breath inward, then out. Anna reached to him to caress her old friend's face as she found bittersweet knowledge that he still lived.

One inch from his face Anna stopped. Her brow rose sharply as the truth started to make sense in her shattered mind.

She said sharply, "Matthew, come here."

Matthew moved to do so, and then stopped.

Anna snapped her eyes upward to Doug's suspicious gaze.

Matthew mumbled, "Huh?" from behind her.

Doug looked past Anna towards his little brother and his face softened. The relief he felt was matched only by the confusion of seeing Matthew had not a scratch on him. Doug had prepared himself for weeks to see his brother dead, or dying, afraid Matthew would not make it. Doug thought of his uncle's dead body in the cold rain outside. He flinched and looked back to Anna.

She smiled at him beautifully, shyly. She asked Doug in all sincerity, "Do you trust your brother?"

Doug was stunned by the question. He looked back to Matthew who was looking at him now, also expecting an answer. Doug looked down at the floor. He saw his parents in his mind, as they had been when he was a child; before Matthew killed them. … Accidentally… Doug swallowed hard, as Miguel watched him now, as well .

Doug couldn't answer. There was no easy answer. Anna smiled at his downcast head.

She said, "Perhaps this will help."

Doug snapped his head up to look at her as she turned and said, "Come here, Matthew."

Not knowing what else to do, Matthew skirted Gail's body and came face to face with the brother who hated him. He flinched in the knowledge of his own guilt.

Anna took Matthew's bloody hand and winked at Douglas as she

400

guided the fingers to Abby's suffering lips. Anna gently swiped Matthew's already bloodied fingers gently onto the blood on Abby's lips, wiping a clean path.

Matthew felt a shock, then a sharp tingle and he jerked his hand away from Anna's grip. .

The wounds on Abby's face glinted then glittered as a blue green army of tiny lights attacked the wounded tissue.

Doug couldn't have been more shocked if God himself had stepped into the room and done a tap dance. As Anna laughed, the wind howled through the night to greet the sound.

Chapter 33

It had only been four days since they had left the convent and returned to Louisiana; Abby wandered the isolated property in the rain like one of the ghosts of the slaves who had built Anna's remote cabin.

Around the globe, the rains gushed from the sky for the entire four days, bringing life back to the driest places on Earth. It had flooded the lands, replenishing dry rivers and man-made reservoirs. In the wettest places, it formed soft mists as the water came down and gave the Earth a good scrubbing, like a mother washing the day's filth off her child.

Anna would often watch Abby as he passed the windows, silent and aimless in the rain as he searched for nothing at all hours. She watched as the old cleric disappeared into a direction that she refused to acknowledge. Anna knew where Abby was going. She sighed from behind the window as he passed her steely gaze and disappeared into the twilight.

Anna grieved for her old friend; she refused to grieve for anything else.

Morgan's baby cried softly in little hiccups from the bed behind her. Anna tried to shutter her mind as she watched the rain outside, now just fat drops loosely falling. In true Louisiana tradition, the cabin had been built on a flood plain so that four day rains were normal there, even when it wasn't a worldwide phenomenon.

The first night they'd been back was the second night after Morgan's death and her baby had cried incessantly. His hunger was apparent to even the most dim-witted of creatures. Both children had screamed in pain and anger as the nuns had tried to feed them milk dripped from rags. It had seemed to work for a time, but after a few feedings it was obvious the babies needed more.

Anna had resisted until the swelling in her breasts had turned them rock-hard and they throbbed painfully with every movement. She wanted to just scream. All the Mortal females could make milk with the awareness of a baby's cry. Anna resisted less than twenty-four hours as the duel cries of hunger tortured her.

Despite feeling put-upon, and after more than a few tears, Anna had relented and fed Morgan's baby first, then Michael's.

Morgan's boy would not latch on, and after taking some stranger's milk, he would not be forced into more. Michael's son had taken it greedily, never knowing any other source.

Anna knew that for better or worse, her brothers child belonged to her now. She was not sure how to fee about it.

There on the bed, Michael's son slept peacefully while his elder by three weeks kicked weakly. He had stopped crying long ago, and instead just stared quietly with droopy eyes when he wasn't sleeping, which was more and more of the time.

Anna knew the boy was fading quickly and she wasn't sure what she could do about it. Her own children had not lived long enough to ever nurse, so she felt zero natural maternal instincts.

After putting Morgan and Gail to rest, she and Matthew made the most logical plan they could think of. Abby had nodded absently, not really caring what the outcome might be. Even he possessed more maternal feelings than Anna. Abby cuddled with the baby for hours as he and Anna sat together, bound by silence.

Sometimes, Abby would absently start telling the boy about his mother. He would forget Anna's presence and become excited as he told his audience of one all about his grand adventures with his mama through ancient lands. Abby was aware that the baby was weakening but unable to think of a solution, he pushed it behind him.

The plan was simple. Anna would take Michael's son to raise in the mountains of Colorado with Miguel, so that their presence would not attract any other Mortal's to Morgan's son .

Abby and Matthew would remain at the cabin and raise Morgan's son there. It had always been Anna's safest place. The boy would be fully absorbed into the world of humans and allowed to live a normal life s much as possible. It was his destiny to be discovered among them, his blood carrying the cure to most of their diseases.

Anna was glad Morgan's son would remain here, It was right that he was here.

Anna went to pick up Morgan's son. He stared at her, his fuzzy blue eyes unnaturally calm. He was feverish, burning up.

Anna smiled at him sadly and he surprised her when he smiled back. After she had nursed him for the first time, he refused to latch on again.

Anna knew he'd had enough to live on for a time, but he went the next two days refusing anything offered. The new baby bottles sat around them, all filled with different offerings; they had tried everything.

In the corner of the room, Kia sat still as a statue, also watching the child. She stopped writing in her journal as Anna tried again to feed the boy, ad again was rejected by the one-month-old. After they both grew frustrated Anna laid him back down and shook her head at Kia.

Anna secretly thought the baby was dying of a broken heart. His screams of hunger were primal and inconsolable that second day, so she did the only thing she knew how to do. She slipped into his very unquiet mind and left him a soft soundless ball of silent memories...Her dreams...Her hopes. It had calmed the baby for a while, but he still refused to eat.

Anna had been shocked to find that she had started her menstrual cycle. She had not had a monthly period for over four millennia. The face of Nefertiti was outlined in the baby staring at her with a calm hunger. After all this time, Anna's memories of her favorite aunt were as crisp and clear as a fall morning.

Anna had to have a heart to heart with Abby. She loved him dearly, but he needed to wake up and add his resources. She knew that Abby had thousands of trusted followers. Anna shook her head at Michael's son who so unfairly slept like the innocent that he was.

Matthew had accepted their company because he didn't know where else to go. The black-haired woman that he knew was Gail's sister avoided his eyes. Sometimes it angered him, but he knew that what Gail had done was not her sister's sin. He even knew that Anna bore the brunt of the choice that had not been hers to make.

No one discussed Abby's apparent reversal of the clock as his grey hair darkened quickly and the effects of time rippled backwards across him.

Matthew missed his brother already. Their newfound faith in each other had been abruptly halted by the need to deal with the aftermath. Maria and Doug had taken Edwards' body back to his grieving wife for burial.

Diana was returned to her family; they were infuriated and insisting that the police investigate what happened to her baby's body. No one was offering any more explanations than were necessary. Next to them, the Sphinx looked like a chatterbox. Her death was actually attributed to the helicopter accident she had endured.

Webster escorted Doug and Maria to FBI headquarters, and in the custody of his own agency, they had allowed him to notify Napoliss' widowed father of his son's death. They had immediately taken Webster back into custody and that was a small comfort to him. There was no way on earth that he could tell that man the truth about why he couldn't, and never would be able to, claim the remains of his son.

Maria, Doug, and Agent Webster all were still in custody.

They all told an amazing story that the police didn't believe for a single moment, but they couldn't prove anything else. They had explanations for everything. They charged the coroner for illegally dumping a body. Her lawyer automatically exclaimed that she had left it at an emergency room, for God's sake.

Every time Webster's fellow agents hounded him about details, he told them the same thing: crack the code on Joseph's journal and their own evidence would prove him right. They all three knew that their careers were over. They told the truth as Anna had instructed, and they were all counting down their minutes as the charges went nowhere.

In a few years, when it was safe, Anna would make sure that Doug and Maria were relocated quietly, wherever they wanted to go. She had more than enough homes to house them. She was a veritable real estate conglomerate.

Anna looked at Morgan's child as she flinched. She only had one tomb. The baby's weight loss was already apparent in his tiny body. Anna was never one to shirk whatever nasty chores life had handed out, and there had been many, but watching this baby starve himself in grief was unbearable.

Leaving both infants with Kia, Anna walked out of the room, determined do something.

Matthew was sitting in one of the wonderful big rockers on the porch of the cabin as Anna stepped out quietly. He had just come from Anna's tomb. He looked at her, then away quickly, as Matthew willed himself to feel nothing. He dared not judge the woman whom had saved them all from certain death. .

Anna, too, looked to the trees as Matthew said, "Are you going to have a talk with him?"

They both knew he was talking about Abby. As she looked at him, he nodded his head in the direction where the man had disappeared.

Anna frowned upward as she gave a solid nod.

"Yes."

405

Matthew asked , "Can I walk with you?"

The young man looked at her thoughtfully from the rocking chair.

"He may need us both." Matt added.

Anna grinned at him from the corner of her mouth. Her old friend was a strong man. She had been Abby's friend for most of his life. Morgan had met him because of her proximity to Anna's life. Quietly, from behind the years, she had learned to love Abby too. Her respect for his gentle humility and quiet kindness knew no bounds.

Abby had been fine looking, too, and as the years receded from his flesh, he had taken back that beautiful image of a vibrant Arab male.

As Matthew rose to join her, Anna thought, 'Abby's eyes are still old though.'

They set out into the twilight to go to the tomb she had never intended to use. Like all the other hidden treasure troves Anna had accumulated, the huge chambers of the tomb were underground, accessible only to the wise.

Anna thought about her own elaborate grave. Though sure that her remains would burn, she had nonetheless had the two rooms carved out of the bedrock the cabin was built on. The children of the slaves who had built the cabin had used the hands she had set free to carve her tomb. The only other people now alive who knew of it's existence were Abby and Matthew.

Into a ravine they trudged, careful not to fall into the rushing water below. This channel begun as a run-off from the bayous that surrounded them. A huge stone sat against the natural wall of earth, as if it had naturally fallen vertically with smaller boulders into the crevice of the ravine."

Anna stood back sulking as Matthew grinned. He stared at the rock like a dumbfounded kid and then used only one finger, very deliberately, to push the spot he now knew to look for.

The huge panel of stone shifted down, then around, turning completely sideways into the earth behind it. Matthew marveled in wonder at the perfectly balanced rock. It was awesome.

It had taken fifty men to lower it into place.

The room within gleamed brightly from a million points of bold color. The entire room was covered with scrolls of ancient Egyptian hieroglyphs bordered with frescos of the painted figures of God's long forgotten. Anna's own hands had painted the space, with mathematically perfect symbols covering every inch of the space.

The large room that appeared was supported by two large columns that were also brightly, joyously painted as a snub at death. At the foot of each column was a heavily carved stone coffin.

Each of the rectangular artifacts was carved in slate of the darkest grey. The sight of them sobered both Matthew and Anna as the candlelight of the room trickled up to, and then jumped over them.

In the clear space between the flanking coffins, Abby sat facing them. The candles at his feet illuminated his miserable frame as he sat at Nefertiti's feet. The giant image of the female pharaoh sat in eternal silence on the decorated wall in a perfectly proportioned space between he columns. The cleric blocked the view of the offerings that were painted at her feet.

Anna couldn't help but admire her own handiwork as she read the words she, herself, had written. In the hieroglyphs, the story of her family was told in amazing artwork. She took comfort in the first written language she had ever known.

The cleric stared at them hatefully, drunkenly. Matthew paused, acknowledging the man's tension. He looked at the beautiful ancient coffins and admired the small scroll works carved into them as Abby glared at them.

Anna always knew that one day she would have to make a place to bury the ones whose remains could be salvaged. She had carved the words on the coffins so long ago. Since Anna never knew for sure whom would rest in them, she had written words of love and honor . She did not know who she would have to bury, but she had been sure even then that they would carry only her most beloved.

Anna knew her loves would rest here; otherwise, what's the point?

Anna looked at her last husband's coffin to the right. He had rested undisturbed for years. Of them all, Anna had loved him most. Her heart was still saddened at his loss.

His coffin was the first to be filled, almost seventy years before. Anna's heart hung heavy in her chest as a lump closed her throat. She swept her eyes to Morgan's eternal vessel to the left. All those years they had stood empty, now all three were filled.

Anna deliberately pulled her eyes back to the face of Nefertiti.

Abby glared at her hatefully; she tried to ignore it.

Abby kicked at a bowel of withered grapes. The copper bowl also held a few overripe tomatoes and a piece of sagging, sliced cheese. Two tomatoes rolled to the floor as Abby took a long swig of the vintage wine he'd found in a closet of the cabin.

Anna rolled her eyes as she looked at the scroll work that covered everything, even the ceiling. Abby was downing a fortune in fine wine. It was lucky for her wallet that Abby was still working on the first bottle .

It seemed he couldn't hold his liquor any more . He recovered from his 'two-sip' benders surprisingly quickly though.

Anna looked at Abby sternly , as he seemed intent on messing up the floor of her immaculate tomb; she could see he was probably on his fifth sip.

Both she and Matthew sighed heavily as Abby drank a deliberately long pull straight from the bottle. He lowered the bottle and narrowed his eyes at Anna.

In Aramaic, he said drunkenly, "What?"

He also rolled his eyes, at her.

Abby said loudly, "See...I brought YOUR gods offerings and that didn't work either!"

Matthew and Anna looked down at the greasy slice of yellow sandwich cheese on the rim of the copper plate.

Abby said proudly, "See! I even brought them wine!"

He looked at the bottle dumbly.

Without meaning to, both Anna and Matthew tried to suppress their laughter. Both choked it down, but Matthew had to clear his throat; he really didn't want to upset the man. Abby got upset anyway and started cursing in Aramaic; it lost nothing in the translation.

Anna allowed herself to smile openly.

Forcing some steel into her tone, she said, "Abby, Morgan's son will die soon if something is not done."

Abby instantly grew quiet as he sat down the bottle and rubbed both hands over his face. In some ways, his own face felt unfamiliar to his touch; he couldn't get used to the new and improved Abby. He could feel the baby's presence in inside him like a ghost. He and Matthew were unaware that they were both struggling with the same feelings. They could both feel the baby in their minds, they could hear his heartbeat.

Anna reminded Abby, "Drinking is not allowed in your religion, Abdullah."

Abby jerked his head up and sneered at her as he deliberately picked up the bottle again; he saw Morgan's coffin and put it back down.

Abby said softly, "Maybe the women in my family know of a woman with milk…"

He sighed as he looked at the copper plate that lay in disarray. Anna responded to Abby sharply.

"Milk is not the problem, I have milk. He is dying of a broken heart, Abby. I do not know how to unbreak it."

He finally met Anna's eyes and staggered upward, suddenly ashamed of himself for disgracing her tomb. Abby knew she used it as her church. Even though her gods would not listen to him, he knew she found comfort there. The faith that she never shared, coming from the soul of an angel, had sanctified this quiet, beautiful place.

Abby tried drunkenly to chase down one of the wayward tomatoes. He found himself once again at the side of the cold slate coffin that held the body of his beloved. Without meaning to, he started crying, as he forgot the tomato. His fingers splayed across the carvings on the surface, digging into their tiny grooves.

Matthew retrieved the tomatoes and slapped the wet cheese back fully onto the rim of copper. He let the cleric sag, then took him gently under his arms. Matthew brought the smaller man up by his armpits as Abby sobbed. He was finally able to get his legs steady under him and stood upright as Matthew put his arm around the man's shoulder.

Abby tore his eyes from Morgan's shrine and looked at the younger priest. They now looked almost the same age.

Matthew said, "Let's go pray over the baby…?"

Abby blinked at him drunkenly.

He asked dryly, "Pray?"

Matthew grinned and said, "Yes… Pray."

Abby turned his eyes away, considering it. Guiltily, he confessed. ,

"I think I'm having a crisis of faith." Abby sighed.

Matthew chuckled," I believe in you."

Abby blinked, and then nodded. In his fluid world, it made perfect sense. The younger man stood the cleric upright completely, making sure he was balanced before letting go of his shoulder.

Abby laid his hand on Morgan's coffin then walked past Anna. As he brushed by her, she softly tried to comfort him.

"Abby…nothing about our lives has changed. It's simply how we feel about it that has made us question our reasons."

Matthew paused as he heard Joseph's words above a bleeding Sara. He had said, "All that you know will seem to change, but it really only seems that way."

Anna and Abby looked at Matthew, startled, as he unthinkingly said Joseph's words aloud.

Anna smiled as Abby looked at the floor.

She said, "Exactly."

Abby pondered that thought as he went out into the night. Anna and Matthew lingered to look at the giant painted relief of Nefertiti sitting eternally on her throne. She bore the crook and flail in her eternally bent arms, and her very lovely face held the false beard of Pharaoh.

Matthew said absently, "If you don't mind, I'll walk back with you too…?" He glanced at her.

Anna still studied the wall that held one of her finest masterpieces.

She nodded as she said, "No…I don't mind at all."

Matthew looked at her uncomfortably and said, "I'll…I'll wait in here… while you… um… have a minute alone if you like. "

He bowed his head back to the wall before them.

He said softly, "I just left her not too long ago…"

Anna said, "Yes… Thank you… I'll only be a moment…"

Walking quickly into the chamber's far reaches, she walked up to the painting of her enthroned aunt. On the necklace that was painted onto the stone wall, Anna pressed at three slightly raised places. The entire wall shifted sideways with a soft tug as tons of weight moved smoothly inward at the touch.

Matthew watched her disappear into its reaches and be enveloped into an inky black void.

Anna stepped into her own burial chamber. Her black eyes adjusted quickly to the familiar shadows that she didn't bother to light. The light from behind her spilled into the space and she automatically went to the left. The sparse light hit the piled gold objects. Rich woods gleamed from a neatly arranged stack that loomed high over Anna in shadow lumps. A chest of ancient Lebanese cedar stood at the foot of the stacks of breathtaking artifacts.

From a pocket of her long loose coat, Anna pulled out a silver flask. It held the ashes of Adam and Jerold. A clear label had been carefully etched into the silver box that very evening. Anna put it into the cedar trunk. She pulled a second box from the other pocket, this one labeled 'Francis, and Katherine'. There were many of the silver flasks in the trunk , almost all identical. Anna closed the lid slowly as she thought about her father, uncle, and brother, all lost.

They had been horrible evil people, but they were, after all, her blood, the blood of angels. She laid the lost members of her family to rest with a solid *thunk*.

Anna went to the three tiny coffins that stood alone in the center of the large room. The entire ceiling of the chamber had been painted blue, with white gold-rimmed clouds rolling around them, their motion forever suspended.

The clouds seemed to pick up the dim candlelight showing through the door. The room glowed with a soft quality almost as translucent as the moonlight itself. Anna went to her sons' ancient coffins, suspended in the center of the glow on high thin pedestals.

As Anna stood over her forever silent children, she thought about the baby that sucked so greedily from her. She saw the baby she could not save. As savage failure clawed at her she wept over her sons, tracing her fingers over the tiny carvings that had encased them, undisturbed, since she had retrieved them from their long-forgotten graves.

Anna prayed. She begged God to listen. Her sorrow overwhelmed her as she tenderly caressed the tomb of her youngest.

Anna heard the echoes of her sniffles and was startled by their unfamiliarity. She pulled her will together and thought of Matthew listening in the outer chamber. She forced herself to look at her own tomb. It, too, seemed unfamiliar in the shadows of the room.

Against the far wall opposite her treasure, Anna's own solid coffin lay lengthwise against it. At the foot of each side were stone columns close to the wall, forming a large niche for the huge grave monument she would never lay in.

Anna had not put her husband in here because she somehow felt it was wrong for her to put him in a coffin she prepared for herself years before meeting him. Unable to bear the thought of Gail resting anywhere else, Anna had put her body in it.

Anna knew she would never know the pleasure of it.

411

Anna stared at it in the dark, realizing something was not right. As she approached through shadows, she could see the stone slab had been pushed aside and still sat atop it at an angle.

Anna froze as she saw the tomb had been violated. In her mind, she immediately suspected both Abby and Matthew. Anna rushed forward again, this time angry. She sobbed, thinking of Gail's disturbed spirit.

As she thought it, her eyes flew to the figure sitting in the deep shadows at the bottom of the column to her right.

Gail sat curled up, shivering, at the bottom step of the platform. Anna's knees buckled as her sister's head rose weakly, and their eyes met in the gloom.

The baby's blood had not healed Gail from death. After Abby had been cured, Matthew had desperately tried the same trick on the other still forms that had been laid around him, to no avail.

Anna blinked hard as her jaw dropped. Gail's body had been stripped and Anna had redressed her in the finest robe she had. She had personally wrapped her sister in the finest of Egyptian cotton. She had felt her cold flesh.

Anna choked on her tears as she moved forward, unbelieving, yet sure of what she saw. She fell to her knees in front of her sister.

Gail trembled, but not from the cold. She watched her sister go to her knees and she tried to smile at her. The robe was ruined, as bloodstains made it apparent that she had started a menstrual cycle.

Gail had never had her cycle, as she had been born after the last curse was laid.

Both women looked at each other, one with tears of joy, and the other with tears of discomfort.

Gail brought her hands to her breasts and said weakly, "A baby crying woke me up..."

Her smile twitched as she drew the cotton of her own death shroud around her.

Anna said, "Yes...I know... he's hungry."

Gail shook as a violent tremor passed into her, then through her.

As Matthew stepped through the chamber opening to investigate the confusing sounds, Gail told Anna, "Go get the boy, I'll feed him."

The two women burned with joy like glowing embers huddled in the darkness.

As Matthew's eyes adjusted to the dark, he cried out in confusion, then in sheer joy.

Anna sobbed as she stood up to go and get the boy. As she came outside, still crying freely, she stopped in sheer pleasure.

All over the world, the rain had stopped falling.

Matthew's cries of renewed faith and love followed Anna from her tomb and into the dark night.

THE END